Also by Chad Oliver

THE WOLF IS MY BROTHER
BROKEN EAGLE

THE CANNIBAL OWL

Chad Oliver

BANTAM BOOKS
New York • Toronto • London • Sydney • Auckland

THE CANNIBAL OWL
A Bantam Book / July 1994

9 1 0 4 0   ISBN 0-553-29656-6

Published simultaneously in the United States and Canada

Bantam Books are published by Bantam Books, a division of Bantam
Doubleday Dell Publishing Group, Inc. Its trademark, consisting of the
words "Bantam Books" and the portrayal of a rooster, is Registered in
U.S. Patent and Trademark Office and in other countries. Marca Reg-
istrada. Bantam Books, 1540 Broadway, New York, New York 10036.

PRINTED IN THE UNITED STATES OF AMERICA

RAD   0 9 8 7 6 5 4 3 2 1

Introduction

by Dale L. Walker

In 1950, a twenty-two-year-old student named Symmes Chadwick Oliver, working toward a master's degree at the University of Texas at Austin, sold his first short story to the science fiction pulp magazine *Super Science Stories*. Two years later, the year he was awarded the graduate degree, his first novel, a young adult novel titled *Mists of Dawn*, was published. The publications and degree marked the beginning of two unusual and productive careers: Chad Oliver, distinguished anthropologist, and Chad Oliver, acclaimed science fiction and western writer.

He earned his Ph.D. in 1961 at UCLA and taught at UT Austin for thirty-eight years (1955–93), serving twice as chairman of the Department of Anthropology. He taught such courses as Introduction to Cultural Anthropology, Man, Society, and Culture, and Indians of the Plains, his classes always filled to capacity. And he wrote such scholarly books as *Ecology and Cultural Continuity As Contributing Factors in the Social Organization of the Plains Indians* (1962) and *The Discovery of Humanity: An Introduction to Anthropology* (1981).

The popular writing pursuit that began in 1950 continued throughout Oliver's academic life. His science fiction novels and story collections—*Shadows in the Sun* (1954), *Another Kind* (1955), *The Winds of Time* (1957), *Unearthly Neighbors* (1960), *The Edge of Forever* (1971), *The Shores of Another Sea* (1971), *Giants in the Dust* (1976)—are marked by the author's application of anthropology, ecology, and the natural sciences to futuristic, speculative storytelling.

As well, these applications were made in Oliver's other novels—his westerns—and it is a hallmark of all Oliver's fiction that he fused his science to his writing; his books and stories are a synthesis of solid commercial fiction and scientific—especially anthropological—fact and theory.

Another special significance of his work is that while he wrote only three western novels (including *The Cannibal Owl*) and is best known as a writer of science fiction, all his work has decided western overtones. John Clute, in his essay on this author in *The Science Fiction Encyclopedia* (1979), says, "Most of Chad Oliver's science fiction could be thought of as western, eulogizing the land and the men who survive in it."

Oliver's first western novel, *The Wolf Is My Brother* (1967), was as felicitous a beginning in western fiction as Louis L'Amour's *Hondo* or Will Henry's *No Survivors*, and like those auspicious first novels, Oliver's debut book would be reprinted many times and would win significant awards (including the Golden Spur Award from Western Writers of America, Inc.). *The Wolf Is My Brother* is a story set in the Texas Panhandle of the 1870s. It involves Fox Claw, a Comanche chief driven to kill the white man to avenge the ravaging of his tribal lands, the slaughter of the buffalo that provided sustenance to his tribe, and the murder of a young brave he loved as a son. Fox Claw comes into direct conflict with Colonel William Foster Curtis of the 12th U.S. Cavalry, a veteran soldier who knows and respects the Comanche Nation and who is tormented by his skepticism of the army's policies against the tribe and his own duty to enforce those policies.

The novel, in addition to telling a memorable and instructional story, is a valuable and dependable source of Comanche lore and folkways, and established Oliver as a significant new voice in western literature for his sympathetic, meticulously researched depiction of the Native American.

Admirers of *The Wolf Is My Brother* had to wait twenty-two years before Oliver's second western novel, *Broken Eagle*, was published by Bantam Books. In this novel (which earned the Western Heritage Award from the National Cowboy Hall of Fame), the author, while adhering to his favorite western theme of the tragically fading way of life of the Indian, moved the locale northwestward from Texas to the Great Plains to tell his story. It is a powerful one: The Cheyenne warrior Broken Eagle, whose wife and child were killed at Sand Creek, reacts, as did the Comanche Fox Claw, in the only way he can: seeking revenge against those responsible for his personal tragedy, for the dwindling buffalo herds, and the relentless invasion of his tribal lands.

We come now to this book, Chad Oliver's third western and last novel, *The Cannibal Owl*, the best of all illustrations of the author's synthesis of anthropology and historical fiction.

Oliver returns to Texas and Comanchería in this story, set in 1855, a decade after statehood and a time when the Comanches are in a great state of restlessness: The People have earned their freedom, earned the right to their way of life; they have outmaneuvered and outfought the whites (specifically the Spaniards); have nearly driven the Lipan Apaches out of Texas; and have defeated the Tonkawas and all other rival tribes that stood in their path.

But, for all that, the end of the old Comanche days is approaching.

At the time *The Cannibal Owl* takes place, the Comanche were just beginning to recover from the small-pox and cholera epidemics (1848–49) that had reduced the tribe by almost half, and only a couple of years have passed since the tribe made a treaty with the United States government at Fort Atkinson, Kansas, that guaranteed the Comanche $18,000 in trade goods per year. (Whatever the intent of this treaty, it did not prevent the Comanche from continuing their raids in Texas and Mexico, those south of the border usually conducted under a full moon—the dreaded "Comanche moon.")

The events of *The Cannibal Owl* occur two decades before the Red River War, the pivotal battle of which took place in Palo Duro Canyon, a sanctuary for Indian and buffalo in the Texas Panhandle. There, in the fall of 1874, with the destruction by Colonel Ranald Mackenzie and his pony soldiers of a large camp of Cheyenne, Kiowa, and Kwahadi Comanche under Quanah Parker, resistance of the tribes in the Southern Plains effectively ended.

By then the buffalo were also gone. One estimate has it that 3,700,000 buffalo were killed in the years 1872–74, and of these, 150,000 were killed by Indians.

In *The Cannibal Owl*, the end of an era is personified by a man and a town: Owl, a Comanche hunter and scion of many generations of hunters; and the settlement of Stafford on the San Gabriel River, not far from the new Texas capital at Austin.

Owl is a Comanche traditionalist, a true son of the People and of the ways of the People. He is a great hunter: restless, "something of a prowler," his senses always attuned to the hunt, a man who likes "to touch things, see things, cover the ground," who values his horses (so much so that he kills a Mexican captive boy who is supposed to be minding Owl's mare but allows the horse to die in foaling), and who knows he is a special man. For in the deerskin medicine pouch he carries on a thong around his neck is a piece of flint, an ancient spear, or lance point, which he found embedded in the bleached bones of *piamempits*, that thing of transcendent terror to the People, the Cannibal Owl.

But even Owl, great hunter and mystic, has succumbed to some of the ways of the *Taibos*, the whites. He may be painted for war and carry the traditional sinew-backed horn bow, but his arrows are trade arrows with metal points, and his knife is a trade knife with a pearl handle. Also, the white man's town of Stafford looms over him like a specter, wagging a menacing finger, and it is in Stafford, through his own choice, that the rest of Owl's life, and his fate, is to be decided.

All Owl's children are females, and he desperately wants a son to carry on the hunter tradition of his forebears. In Stafford he has been furtively studying the family of Cole and Ruth Nesbitt. He knows all the details about the Nesbitt family and the Nesbitt house, and has determined to kidnap their ten-year-old son, Otis, and flee with the boy to the land of the Stone Walkers, along the Guadalupe River near the settlement of Kerrville. There Owl has determined that he will teach his new son the ways of the Comanche, the ways of the hunter, and will bequeath to his son the flint point that killed *piamempits*, the powerful Cannibal Owl.

Oliver's story is so striking and discussable, it is tempting to give away too much of it here; but *The Cannibal Owl* is to be read first, discussed later, and so it is best to leave it to the reader together with such questions as these: Why does Spirit Shadow, to whom Owl takes the wounded Otis Nesbitt, demand, besides such common medicine-woman currency as juniper berries and crow feathers, some bones of the Cannibal Owl as payment for healing the boy? Just what *was* Owl's mysterious flint, and what great beast had it killed? What, indeed, was the Cannibal Owl to begin with? And what were Stone Walkers?

In these questions and their answers (be sure to read the postnarrative epilogue), and in his deep knowledge of nineteenth-century Comanche history and customs, is epitomized the splendid synthesis of Chad Oliver's science of anthropology and his gift as a storyteller.

Part One

THE BOY

Some memories are very long.

The land always remembers. It goes back, when it wishes, to the beginning of forever. It can also reach back only to the edge of yesterday.

This piece of land, still feathered with the lace of mesquite and shimmered by a hammering sun, can pick and choose from an eternity of memories.

Some might call them dreams, but they are special dreams.

They are remembered things, and this particular memory does not go back very far.

The year is 1855.

The place had names by then. One of the names was Texas.

Dates do not stand alone. They are tiny islands in a river of time. Some say that dates are artificial things because they are invented by people.

But people are what it's all about. There is much

that can happen in a land without people, but there can be no history.

Here is a fragment of what this Texas land remembers.

After the fall of the Alamo in February of 1836 and Sam Houston's victory over Santa Anna at San Jacinto in April of that same year, Texas became a republic in 1839. Houston was elected President with more than three-fourths of the vote: a whopping total of 5,119 votes out of 6,640 votes cast. (Old Sam! Could there ever have been a Texas history without Sam Houston?)

In 1845, after President Anson Jones convened a Constitutional Convention in Austin, Texas joined the United States as the twenty-eighth state. The first state legislature met there in 1846.

Austin was founded in 1839. (Sam Houston never liked the place.) Despite being the capital city of the Republic of Texas, Austin might fairly be described as in the middle of nowhere. It was a frontier settlement that wore a false face and had big ideas. It was either on the edge of Comanchería, the home of the Comanches, or in it, depending on how the wind blew. Austin was seventy hard miles from the relative civilization of San Antonio to the south.

By 1855, the population of the capital city of the Lone Star state hovered at about 3,000 people.

Comanchería, Summer

The man called Owl neither knew nor cared that the year was 1855. What concerned him was the simple fact that too many summers had passed. Owl was not old, but he had enough years to feel some urgency in his blood.

Owl smelled trouble, the worst kind of trouble.

He literally smelled it, although he did not understand how this could be so. There was no wind to carry scent to him. The sultry summer air was usually motionless at this time of day. It seemed to hold its breath, too hot to move, unless a storm was coming. That didn't happen often, but when a storm broke, the wind could grow into a howling fury that made the hides roar on a four-pole-based tipi.

Owl could see the trouble as well as sniff it. It was just within range of his physical eyes, but he saw it clearly with the eyes of his mind.

What he saw would have been big trouble for any Comanche, but for Owl it was a very special kind of trouble.

The trouble would have been directly along his

3

backtrail if Owl had ridden Heart in a straight line. Of course, he had not done that. The truth was that Owl was something of a prowler, whatever his stated objective. Owl liked to touch things, see things, cover the ground. It was as though by contacting every part of his domain—every rock, every bush, every clump of green-brown grass—he could somehow keep it for himself and for The People.

When Owl rode a straight course, it was a good idea to get out of his way.

The trouble that he saw and smelled was a hard distance back, wavering a little in the moisture-sucking heat, but he could sense all that he needed to know.

How many times had he seen them like that? Those black, slanting shadows in a great sun-seared sky. There was nothing else quite like them. The big naked-headed buzzards were not soaring on the warm updrafts of the air, as they were so fond of doing. No, not at all. Look at them! They were swooping like swallows, close to the earth, rising just above the far cottonwoods that fringed the river, then sinking as if their straining black wings could not sustain their weight.

Those birds were working.

The anger in Owl was not slow to build. It was mixed with disappointment and sorrow, and that made it stronger. Owl was killing mad.

The boy, Haysoos, had sent no signal. Owl had depended on him for that. There could be no excuse for such a thing. Owl never had any interest in excuses. One did or one did not. That was all.

Owl touched the deerskin medicine bag that hung from his neck on a worn rawhide thong. He needed to be sure. He did not remove it from the medicine bag, but he felt the familiar unyielding outline of the grooved flint. His confidence surged within him. Sometimes his medicine allowed him to see things that other men could not see.

When he thought about himself at all, apart from the driving necessity for going on, Owl did not consider himself to be strange. Unusual, yes, but not really *strange*. Were not all men who mattered unusual?

He was sufficiently honest to recognize that there was no other Comanche in all the world named Owl. Owl was not a good name to have. Still, given the life he had lived, how could he be named anything else?

Think on the horse that had brought on this trouble. He had ridden her for many seasons. Wise One was a mare, and Comanche men did not ride mares unless conditions were unusual indeed. Well, so be it. Wise One was the best horse there was, and Owl had yet to meet the man who dared mock him for riding her.

He knew too that he was not a safe man to cross. However, there was nothing unusual about that, let alone strange. He was a man of The People. He was hard because he had to be. The Earth that he knew might be his Spirit Mother, but she was unforgiving.

He spoke to the horse he was now riding, just as he had spoken so many times to Wise One. His voice was neither soft nor loud. He was just making conversation, passing the time. "Heart," he said, "what has been done is finished."

The gelding snorted patiently through his flaring nostrils. He understood. In their own way, horses understood many things that fools missed. Heart sensed what was coming next too, but he waited for a nudge from the stiff-soled moccasins of his rider. Owl had been known to change his mind.

"It is finished," Owl said again. His words seemed suspended in the hot hush of the dead air. "It is finished, but we must go back to end it."

If Heart found that to be something of a riddle, he gave no sign.

Owl gave Heart a firm but gentle touch with his right moccasin. He would never kick a horse without a compelling reason.

Heart moved. He seemed pleased with himself, as though he knew that only great horses had names that were not just color names. He set a faster pace than was usual in the oppressive heat of early afternoon. He knew the way.

Owl felt the slight breeze caused by Heart's motion against his unpainted face. Even among The People, who were considered by other Indians to be perhaps the finest horsemen who had ever lived, Owl was exceptional. He rode so well, so easily, that he was totally unconscious of it. To him, riding took about as much effort as breathing. He was aware of it only when he was *not* riding.

Owl shook his beaver-tied braids. One flopped down his back and the other slapped his chest. He wished that he had styled his black hair some other way, as he often did, but Owl was not free of vanity and he figured that he looked good in braids. The problem with the braids was that they were wet-heavy, partly from grease and partly from sweat. It took a lot to make Owl sweat, but he had long hair and it was a nuisance when it got dense and slippery.

Owl did not have his rifle with him. He was a fair shot, but his opinion was that the rifle was clumsy and unreliable. He much preferred his sinew-backed horn bow and his bright-feathered arrows in their skin casing. Both the bow and the arrows were slung over his right shoulder. His left wrist was protected from the force of the bowstring by a buckskin band.

Owl had a pearl-handled trade knife in a sheath belted around his slick, hard waist.

It was the knife that he fingered as he rode. His anger flowed from his hand to his knife.

He knew exactly what he was going to do. That knife of his would soon taste blood again.

Why should he risk damaging a good arrow on one who had failed him so miserably? A dogwood arrow with a metal trade point took many days to make.

The anger in him continued to boil. It was not eased by the task he had turned away from. As always at this time of the year, most of the buffalo had shifted northward to escape the summer heat. They were difficult to locate. In truth, his chances were better with deer. They bunched up sometimes, and the deer seemed less alarmed by all the banging and sawing that came from the raw new town the *Taibos* called Stafford. Just the same, in the middle of the day, he needed to scout away from the San Gabriel River, not toward it. He already knew what could be found along that river, including the *Taibos*.

There was much bitterness in Owl. As he rode, the deep sounds that grumbled up from his chest sounded very much like the threat-growls made by a predator just before the attack.

The Sun Father was low in the sky when Owl rode out of the scorched brown grass of the prairie and into the cooling scrub oaks and cottonwoods that lined the San Gabriel. There were few well-marked shadows; there was simply a sudden transition from brightness and glare to shade and the old green smells of brush and leaves that had not yet been sucked dry.

Heart scented the river water. He flicked his ears forward. He wanted to run. In this country, man and beast drank whenever they could. There wasn't much of a flow in the San Gabriel at this season, but the deeper pools never dried up completely. There was water.

Owl held him back, dancing him along with short, quick steps. Owl could smell things too, and it was not water that he was scenting.

There was a rush of coarse feather-flapping wings ahead of him as the buzzards lifted from their feast. The heavy birds stank in the warm trapped air of the stream valley.

When he reached the remembered clearing, Owl saw precisely what he had known he would see. There were no surprises. The crude brush hut was still as it had been; there was no need for a real tipi on a summer scout. There was still only one other person in the camp, the Mexican boy. It was senseless to scout in large groups. The idea was to cover as much territory as possible.

The boy, Haysoos, was sobbing. Owl did not like that, but he ignored it. What did sobbing matter now?

Owl slipped out of the hide-covered, elm-framed saddle with a single effortless glide. He felt no stiffness from his long day on horseback. He did feel less sure of himself with his own feet on the ground.

He dropped the reins. Heart would stay, water or no water. When Owl trained a horse, that horse was not likely to forget what it was supposed to do.

Owl stared. He was half crouching, almost numb with outrage. His heart thudded as though a fast drum was being beaten in his chest. Anticipated or not, what he saw was like a club blow in the face. It carried that kind of shock. Owl could not speak. It was all he could do to snarl, and he was unable to stop that.

His mare, Wise One, was down on her side. When a horse is dead, rather than resting, you know it at once unless you have seen very few horses. For Wise One, at this place and in this time, there were other signs that burned Owl's eyeballs. Wise One had been ripped and torn and gashed like a hated enemy staked to the ground. She wasn't even decent meat.

The sight of her stabbed Owl with pain. It was the worst pain he had ever known, and Owl was no stranger to hurt. He loved that horse as he had loved few other things in his life. Yes, *still* loved that mare, what was left of her. If he had not loved her, he would have left Wise One behind with the rest of the herd. There would have been no need for Haysoos.

There would never be any need for Haysoos again.

Owl could see Wise One plainly as she had been when he had gone out on his scout. She had been so swollen with her foal that she had seemed close to bursting. That had not worried Owl very much. That was as it should be. Mares were often like that when they were heavy with a foal. They sometimes got huge, their belly skin taut as a drumhead, and nothing might happen from one full Mother Moon to another.

Something had happened this time. Something terrible.

The lacerated body of Wise One remained distended, even in death. The swelling was partly from gas and partly because it took time for a horse to regain her normal shape after a birthing, even if nothing went wrong. In this mockery of birth, everything had gone wrong. There would never be time enough for Wise One now.

Her foal, loosely connected to her by the short, ruptured, ropelike umbilical cord, was out. It was partially encased in what was left of its pale sac. The sac had been ripped some by the buzzards, but Owl could see that it had been torn before that. There had to be a rent for the sharp little hooves to push through. . . .

There was a large, irregular dark stain on the ground where the fluid had been. It was already dry. The foal had not lived.

Owl moved forward, cramped and hunched over. He continued to ignore the captive Mexican boy who stood shuddering between Wise One and her baby. The boy had been trying to keep the buzzards away, give him that. He had failed there too.

To Owl's experienced eye, what had happened was a plain as the print of a bobcat's big paw in wet sand. That foal had never drawn a breath. Whenever a foal did not come out properly, its long head and nose on top of its forelegs, there was trouble. Sometimes it was fixable trouble if you knew what to do. Sometimes it wasn't.

Owl figured that he would have had a good chance. He had been in that situation before. *If.* If he had been summoned in time.

This foal had gotten twisted around in the birth passage. It just happened once in a while. Its hind legs had been tucked up and there had been a rip in the sac. Even with a newborn's fatty pads, the foal's hooves were sharp. Sharp enough to cut Wise One's insides like lances driven through a hide bucket. Sharp enough to impede birth until it was too late. Sharp enough to steal the life from both animals.

Owl knelt down, getting even closer. Funny. Even with the stench of blood and dung and death, the distinctive odor of Wise One stabbed his nose with a rich cloud of memories. She had her own smell, different from her foal, different from all other horses. It was sweet, pungent, familiar. It brought up memories like smoke. That smell had always been reassuring to him, a constant in a life that had few fixed points. He could find her in a night-black horse herd, just by her smell. She would nicker when *she* sniffed *him*, of course. . . .

He shut off those thoughts. He could not bear them. He very carefully moved one long leg of the foal. The dead foal had been a colt.

Still on his knees, he studied the teats of Wise One. The tips were waxed. The coating came from the sticky liquid that appeared before the true milk was ready. It was a sign the boy should have seen unless he was blind or asleep.

Owl stood up. He was not a tall man but there was an aura about him that filled a lot of space. He did not look directly at the head of his dead mare. He and Wise One had taken too many journeys together. He hated the thought of her being alone. It was not right that he should live and she should die.

Haysoos had stopped his sobbing. He just stood where he was. Perhaps he knew that he was already dead.

Owl could speak some Spanish. The Comanche and the Mexicans had traded for over a century, when they weren't busy killing each other. He knew that the river San Gabriel was a Spanish name. A black-robed Mexican holy man had once explained to him the meaning of the name, Haysoos. He knew that Haysoos was the Spanish name for the Son of God. He had never seen the name written—Jesus—and could not have read it if he had, but it had seemed a good omen to him. He did not really comprehend why such an ordinary boy could be named after the Son of God, but it was the *son* part that had interested him. Owl would have laughed aloud at the idea of himself as any sort of god, but he needed a son desperately. There were some things a man could give only to his son or grandson. Owl's living children were all girls. By the time he had a grandson of the proper age, Owl would be riding Wise One again.

Haysoos did not yet have a name among The People. Here, a name had to be earned. It was not that there was any dishonor in beginning life as a captive. One of the greatest of all The People, Wolf Tongue, had started that way. But a Comanche name must be won or acquired naturally; it could not simply be given as a casual gift.

Owl was quite certain that Haysoos would never have a Comanche name. That bothered Owl. It was not because of what he must do with Haysoos. It was because he had to begin all over again.

Owl's instructions had been clear, simple, and positive. Haysoos was to *watch that mare*. Not sometimes. Not when he felt like it. *As closely as it took*. He was to check her many times during the day. He was to examine her carefully at night, using his fingers if he could not see. The instant there was pre-milk, he was to signal Owl with smoke and mirror. That would have given Owl time to get back, even if the waxing had begun at night and the signal had to be delayed until dawn.

It was a true responsibility for the boy. Owl was giving him a chance to be somebody. If he had passed this test, Owl might begin to be his father.

It was unusual for them to be out so far alone, away from Owl's relatives and his band's camp. That was what happened when *Taibo* villages like Stafford sprouted in the dust. Owl had reasoned that he could certainly not scout effectively with Wise One so heavy with foal, and he was afraid to leave her with the herd. It was not that he distrusted his own people, but only that where Wise One was concerned, he trusted himself more. He felt that he owed that to her. He would ride Heart—a fine gelding, a splendid horse if he lived long enough—and attend to the birthing himself when it was time.

Owl did not spare himself. He knew that his own pride was partly responsible for what had happened. That knowledge did not help him.

Still, he would not have failed if he had been called. That was the thing.

As Owl saw it, pride or no pride, he had only taken

two chances. One was that the interval between the waxing and the birth would be too short for him to return. It was not common for the foaling to be that fast, but it was possible.

The other risk had been Haysoos. Owl had trusted the boy. He had wanted to believe in him, needed to believe in him.

Haysoos had betrayed him. That was all there was to it. For whatever reason—sleepiness, distraction, carelessness, stupidity—there had been no signal. The only sign Owl had gotten had come from the buzzards.

Owl was hard, but he was not completely unreasonable. Not even where Wise Owl was involved. He could have accepted it if the boy had sent for him but he could not get there in time. He could have accepted the bad luck of a freak thunderstorm, rare in most summers, that blocked the signal.

Such things might happen.

But when Haysoos simply failed to carry out his assigned task, that was another matter entirely.

Owl said nothing. Without hurry or wasted motion, he slipped the pearl-handled trade knife from its sheath.

The Mexican boy had not been taken captive yesterday. He knew Owl. He had no hope.

Haysoos made no attempt to run. There was nowhere to go. The world was not big enough. Even dismounted, looking clumsy on foot. Owl was faster than he was. And his endurance was total.

The boy only had one fragment of an idea in his pounding head. He wanted to shrink. If possible, disappear. If not, make a tiny target.

Haysoos fell flat on his stomach, twisting like a snake, scrabbling with his knees and elbows against the thorns and the rock-hard earth. He was fairly quick, quick enough to leave a trail of slippery blood.

He wasn't quick enough.

Owl was on him with a smothering speed that came from battles beyond counting. His body was heavy and hot. There was no wild slashing. He was very deliberate. His knife glinted a little in the last crimson rays of the fading sun.

Owl did it cleanly. He twisted the boy on his back as easily as he might kick a beetle over with his moccasin. He sliced Haysoos open with a single practiced motion. It was much simpler to spill the guts from the belly up. Otherwise, you had to go around the backbone. That was sloppy work.

The boy was soon past screaming, but he did not die all at once. People seldom did. Life had a way of lingering.

Owl wiped his knife on dry grass. It turned the grass the color of the setting sun. He sheathed the knife. Soon, when he reached the river, he would wash it. Otherwise, both the blade and the handle would get sticky.

Owl looked directly at the pale and sweating face of Haysoos. He made sure the eyes were still tracking. Then, with his left hand, Owl made a wriggling motion in the hushed air. He wanted the final understanding for Haysoos to be the fact that he had tried to escape by crawling like a snake.

Snake was an old sign for Comanche. Owl knew that Haysoos understood the sign; Owl himself had taught it to the boy. There was no malice in what Owl was doing. He was telling the boy that crawling like a snake was as close to being a Comanche as Haysoos would ever get. To Owl, this was a simple statement of fact. He was not taunting. This boy might have become his son.

Haysoos was past caring. His eyes were clouding with death.

Owl turned away from the boy. He was through with him. It was over.

Owl did not look again at any of the dead things in the clearing. He did not try to speak. There were no words to say. There had been little room for sentiment in Owl's life, but now there were tears in his eyes. He was glad that only Heart could see them.

He cried mostly for Wise One, of course. If there were any tears left over, it might be that they were for

himself and the boy and the colt, and what could have
been.

Owl walked to where Heart was impatiently trailing
his reins. He was not graceful when he walked, and now
his back was bent more than usual. He felt a little better
when he swung into the saddle. A man should have a
horse under him.

Heart needed no urging. He tossed his head, shook
his mane, and trotted away from that place of death, toward the river.

Already Owl's senses had pushed beyond the river
San Gabriel. What was past was past.

He knew that he would have to go into the *Taibo*
town of Stafford.

He touched the deerskin medicine bag that was suspended from his neck. He felt again the hard outline of
the grooved flint. Owl would have need of all of his medicine now.

He did not want to go into Stafford. The danger was
great.

But he had tried everything else. Stafford was where
Owl's future waited, if he had a future.

2

Stafford, Texas, Summer

The town of Stafford was two years old. Like so
many frontier villages, there were no transition zones
around Stafford. It started suddenly in the midst of a
great rolling prairie and ended the same way. It was as
though some careless giant had simply tossed a random
collection of houses, saloons, a stagecoach stop, and a
post office out of the sky and then had gone off and forgotten them.

Lee walked out of the Nesbitt house and squinted
his eyes against the glare of the sun. He had nothing particular on his mind except the keg of beer at the Stafford
Cooperative Store. Ruth Nesbitt was as close to him as
his own mother—closer if you wanted to stick to the
truth. But Ruth Nesbitt did not allow spirits in her
house. And Cole Nesbitt, her husband, had a mind too
shattered to have opinions about anything.

Lee was proud of that house. It did not have a tin
roof like the Jenkins place, but it was a better house. It
was cool, and caught the breeze just right. When there
was a breeze. It was a house that had strength in it. Most

of that strength came from Ruth Nesbitt. There had been a time when Lee had been surprised that such strength could flow from such a tiny woman. Nowadays, nothing that Ruth Nesbitt did surprised him.

Lee's scuffed boots kicked up tiny puffs of dust in what passed for the street. Although he did not dwell on it, Lee was conscious as always about how unlikely it was for him to be coming out of that house. *His* house, in a way. It was a fact that his rooms were not in the main part of the house, but it was also a fact that they were *connected* to the big house, not set off in a separate structure. That was important.

Lee's dark-backed hand brushed against the butt of his Paterson Colt. It might have been an accident. Certainly he was not threatening anybody. However, it was not an accident that Lee was virtually the only man in town who habitually packed a revolver on his hip.

There were exceptions, of course. But it was unusual to encounter Lee without his gun. He was one of those men who looked half dressed without it.

Lee stepped around an ox-drawn wagon loaded with lumber destined for the railhead at Round Rock, tipped his wide-brimmed hat politely, and entered the Stafford Cooperative.

There was no real bar yet, just some planks set up on sawhorses. There was a keg of beer at the far end of the planks from the door. There was a tin cup hooked to the keg on a nail.

Lee filled the cup and drank it down with one long, slow, continuous swallow. The first cup was on the house. If there were any objections to Lee using that cup, they were not voiced.

Lee put down his money for a second round. Beer had gone up from a nickel to six cents. It was a point of honor with him never to stop with the free beer, whether he really wanted two beers or not.

"I'll have another," Lee said.

The words rattled around in the silence. They were the first words that had been spoken since Lee walked into the store.

Despite what he had done in the raid on Webster, Lee still made some folks uncomfortable. He was used to that. It was his practice to maintain his distance in public. He didn't crowd anyone.

He didn't back off either, if it came to that.

Lee sipped his second beer. There were three other men in the store along with the storekeeper. None of them was armed, although Lee knew there was a loaded Beecher's Bible Sharps carbine stashed behind the flour barrels at the back of the store.

Lee knew the men in the Stafford Cooperative very well indeed. They had been together a long time. There were few strangers in a place like Stafford.

And yet, there it was. Lee was not shunned. Neither was he entirely accepted, although any man in that store would have come to his defense if he had needed them. After all, two of those men would have been dead meat if it had not been for Lee.

Lee reflected that saving a man's hide created a kind of a tie, even if it didn't improve the conversation much.

The silence was getting a shade uncomfortable when Otis Nesbitt came running into the store and skidded to a stop a couple of precarious inches from Lee's beer. It sometimes seemed to Lee that the boy Otis only had two gaits—gallop and full stop.

The Cooperative was not a real-for-sure saloon, but Otis would never have come there on his own. Otis Nesbitt was ten years old; a sandy-haired gangly kid, big for his age, but not old enough to fit comfortably in the Stafford Cooperative. It was not difficult for Lee to figure out what was going on, but he did not step on Otis's play. These were important events for a boy of ten.

Obviously his mother had needed to get a message to Lee. It would have been unthinkable to send the only other capable person in the house. Otis had a sister, Lisa, at home. But Lisa was a pretty girl of eighteen years. Ruth Nesbitt may have been tougher than a keg of nails, but she would have died of shame before she sent her daughter into an establishment that sold beer.

"Mister Lee, Mister Lee!" Otis hollered. Nothing distant or awkward about *him*.

Lee grinned, almost in spite of himself. The boy made him feel good. Lee replaced his beer on the plank. "Well, son," he said. "Spit it on out."

"Mizruth says for you to come." Like many Texas boys, Otis often called his folks by their first names. However, Ruth Nesbitt was just too formidable a figure to make that sound right. So Otis compromised: "Mizruth."

"She say anything else?"

Otis turned beet red. "She said please, Mister Lee."

That was for the benefit of the others in the store. It made no difference between Lee and Otis.

"Cole?" asked Lee.

The boy nodded. "It's Pa."

Lee asked no more questions. Whatever had happened with Otis's father, it was not the business of anyone else in that store. Of course, they all knew anyway. There might be few strangers in a town like Stafford, but there were no secrets.

"Let's go," Lee said.

The two of them went back into the shock of sunlight, neither dawdling nor rushing. They were totally different—man and boy, experienced and green, dark-skinned and light—and they belonged together perfectly.

If Lee could have chosen a son, it might have been Otis.

If Otis could have picked his father, it would have been Lee.

That was the way of it.

Cole Nesbitt had fallen. It wasn't the first time it had happened.

Somehow Ruth Nesbitt had wrestled her husband onto the bed. She had gotten his boots and pants off and had covered him with a spotless sheet. The sheet barely came up to Cole's chest. Cole had some funny ways. He counted it as unlucky to remove his shirt. In bed, he did

not like to be uncovered above the waist. Probably it had
something to do with that unthinkable day in Webster.
When the shrieking fury of the Comanches had struck,
Cole Nesbitt had been shirtless.

But who could really know such a thing? What was
certain was that Ruth had to trick him periodically to get
that damned shirt off. There were times when that shirt
could walk all by itself. There were times when Cole
Nesbitt could be smelled from outside the house. Way
outside.

Cole had lost weight, but it remained a minor miracle to Lee how Ruth could pull him around and even
lift him. Ruth Nesbitt was anything but a big woman, but
she had a unique quality about her. She always seemed
to have exactly enough strength to do whatever needed
doing. The girl, Lisa, was at home. She was generally
willing to help, despite her delicate good looks. But
Otis's sister was basically just fluttering around in the
hallway, rather like a butterfly caught between flowers.
Ruth Nesbitt was very particular about who helped her
husband and when.

When this tiny woman absolutely did not trust herself to do the right thing, she sent for Lee. Ruth Nesbitt
had a faith in Lee that went far beyond affection and
trust. It was a mystical thing. Lee knew things that other
people did not and could not know. Ruth Nesbitt was
certain that this was so.

Lee knelt by the bed, getting as close to Cole as he
could. When Ruth's husband had these falls—and sometimes when there had been no fall, and no apparent reason for his fading away—it was crucial not to misread the
signs. Lee was fully aware that one mistake could kill the
man.

It was Cole's hair that first caught Lee's attention.
He could not have explained why.

The hair was shoulder length and it was splayed out
on the pillow like a halo. The hair was white, not gray,
and it was so fine that it stirred even from the slight air
pressure of Lee's breathing. The hair was not lank and
lifeless, the sort of hair often seen in a sickroom. The hair

seemed charged with some kind of radiant energy. It was not the hair of a normal, healthy human being. Nor was it the hair of a sick and dying animal.

That hair told you something about Cole Nesbitt, if you could understand the signs. It said that this was no ordinary man, even in a land where the unusual was commonplace.

Cole did not speak. Indeed, it had been so long since he had said anything that Lee was not sure whether or not he *could* still talk. But his eyes were open, and they were profoundly alive. The eyes were a pale watery blue in a face that was translucently pale all over. It was a face that had not seen the sun for many long months. It was also a face of strange power. It was a face so strongly and perfectly chiseled that it might have been hewn from Texas rock by some master sculptor.

Amazingly, one of those blue eyes winked at Lee. That eye was an older and wiser version of the blue eyes that marked Cole's son. It was an eye that had seen much, maybe too much.

Lee grinned. That old bastard! He had a second pulse in him somewhere. It kept him going when younger men would have been dead and buried.

"Well, Old-Timer," Lee said. The term came naturally to him even though Cole Nesbitt was only a decade older than Lee himself. Somehow, Cole seemed to belong to another age, one that was half forgotten but still intruded on the present. Lee reached out and touched Cole's bony shoulder. There was no sweat on it. "It appears that we're not rid of you yet."

Cole managed another wink. It used up whatever strength he had. He closed his eyes, let out a sigh that was much like a snore, and went to sleep. He began to do some serious snoring. Lee reflected that the old gent had a very raucous snore for such a frail man. That was nothing new. Cole's snoring around a camp fire had kept Lee awake many a long night.

Ruth Nesbitt had seen and heard everything. She missed very little, and nothing where her husband was concerned. She was a genuine matriarch, having co-founded the town of Stafford with the widow Goacher and Mrs. Goacher's sons. She had a head for figures, and she was wealthy by Stafford standards. Stafford was a town that kept raw materials moving, mostly hides and lumber. Nothing moved in Stafford without Ruth Nesbitt having a piece of it. She controlled the farrier, the wagons, and the storage sheds. With her husband helpless, Lee was her emissary. It was understood in Stafford that when Lee spoke, he spoke for the Nesbitt family. If some found that peculiar, they were not dumb enough to say it right up front.

Despite what she had just seen and heard, Ruth Nesbitt still had to ask. She had to be certain. She needed the words. Lee's answer would ease her burden some. Lee knew things.

"Should we call Doc Patterson?"

Lee shook his head. "No point in that."

Doc Patterson was the only doctor in Stafford. Nobody ever inquired too closely into his training; people in Stafford figured they were lucky to have a doctor at all. In fact, Doc Patterson was a damn good doctor in many ways. He was the best Ruth had ever seen when it came to children's illnesses that would not respond to home remedies. He could pull a bad tooth with the best of them. He was particularly good with stomach complaints; Charlie Conway had walked doubled up with pain for years, and Doc Patterson now had him back on steak and beans.

But you didn't ask Doc Patterson to set a broken bone. There were more than a few crooked arms and legs in Stafford that were due to Doc's inability to get things lined up properly. And the man was notorious for his incompetence in dealing with gunshot wounds. The joke in Stafford was, "Are you going to let Doc Patterson treat it, or just fire another round and end it for your own self?"

Doc had seen Cole many times, of course. It was obvious that he did not have the faintest idea about what to do to improve his condition.

"How about Austin?" Ruth asked. Small as Austin

was when compared to towns like Nacogdoches or San Antonio, it was fairly close and did have several doctors. One of them was quite good if you could catch him sober. It was understood that Lee himself could not venture into Austin. Slavery there was not the burning issue that it was in East Texas, but there was a lot of cotton grown near Austin.

Again Lee shook his head. "Mrs. Nesbitt," he said, "your man is the same as always. No worse, no better, to my way of thinking. He'll probably come out of this in a few days and be about like he was. I'd say, try to get some soup in him. I'll be here. Just you let him sleep, and don't you worry about nothing."

By "like he was," Lee meant after Webster, not before. He did not need to explain that.

As for "Mrs. Nesbitt," he always called her that. She had once told him that it was a form of address that made her less than comfortable, but Lee could not bring himself to call her Ruth. When it came to something like "ma'am," that was impossible for both of them.

Lee excused himself and left the room. There were times when Cole and his wife needed to be alone together. This was one of those times. Even if Cole had passed out. Even if Ruth Nesbitt let her guard down now and maybe cried a little. It might help some.

"Is everything going to be all right?" Otis asked. He too had to hear it for himself.

"I'm here, ain't I?" Lee responded. He wasn't trying to dodge the question. But what could he say to the boy that was at once reassuring and not a lie? "Now, get along with you and find something useful to do. Help your mama."

"Yes, sir, Mister Lee!" Otis ran off to be useful. He was like a very young horse, all legs and energy. He might not be entirely sure what was useful and what wasn't, but he was prepared to do _something_ at a high rate of speed.

Suddenly and without any warning at all, Lee felt a weariness that was beyond his years. He had a crushing awareness that this was the closest thing to a family he had on this earth.

He had told Ruth Nesbitt not to worry.

But Lee was worried. He was always worried. His fear did not center on himself. Lee could handle whatever life threw at him. He had demonstrated that a few times.

He was concerned about Lisa Nesbitt.

With her mother distracted and her father drifting in some world of his own, Lisa was vulnerable.

It wasn't Coffee's courting that bothered him, although he had scant use for Coffee and knew that the sentiment was mutual. Coffee's courting of Lisa was none of his business, really.

It was not just that there were Comanches in the area. There were always Comanches around. This was still their country, no matter what the Texans thought.

Lee didn't know everything, as Ruth Nesbitt believed. But he knew some things.

He knew Comanches. He had lived with them, hunted with them, slept with their women. He still visited Comanche camps now and then, when his need drove him. Lee was a man without a wife. He was also a man who had to steer clear of Texan women and Mexican women. There were no slaves in Stafford. That was one reason he could live here as he did.

There was a growing restlessness among the Comanches. Lee could sense it. It was more a feeling of resentment than anger. The People found it difficult to grasp how brazen the Texans had become. They acted as though *they* owned the world.

Only a few years ago the Comanches had sacked and burned Webster, a town that had been a lot like Stafford. They hadn't done it easily, but they had done it. Comanches were no more fond of losing warriors than any other people, but they seldom ducked a good scrap. They were fighters.

There had been other places since Webster. Some of them had not been lucky enough to have a gun like Lee's.

But Lee's worry took a different turn. A raid was not necessarily aimed at wiping out a town, or even killing a bunch of enemies. That was unusual, really, and growing less common all the time.

Horses were there to be stolen. Anywhere. Anytime. So were Texan girls.

It was no myth, no shudder story that folks used to keep the kids in line. It was a rare month that passed without a girl being taken captive by the Comanches.

Lee had seen them in the camps of The People many times. There was nothing especially secretive about the practice. Everybody knew that Comanches grabbed Texas girls whenever they could get them. Once in a while Lee was able to help bring them back home. More often he couldn't. A man had to be careful. Some of those women didn't *want* to be rescued. It wasn't a bad life, if you survived the first year or two.

Of course, Lisa Nesbitt at eighteen was on the old side to be taken and raised as a Comanche. And Stafford was hardly an isolated homestead. There were easier pickings.

But Lisa Nesbitt was a perfect target in another way. Many of the Comanche captives were held for ransom, pure and simple. It was a business. You couldn't call it a game, but everybody knew the rules.

From the Comanche point of view, Lisa was ideal. Her family was rich and prominent. Better still, she was being courted by Coffee.

Coffee was a Ranger. The Rangers would get Lisa Nesbitt back, no matter what the cost.

Comanches knew more about the Texans than the Texans knew about the Comanches. Comanches understood such things.

What might be left of Lisa Nesbitt if she were stolen and rescued or ransomed was anybody's guess. It all depended. There were Comanches and then there were Comanches. They were like most other people Lee had known. They weren't all the same. They were on the rough side, true enough, but there were good ones and bad ones and some in the middle.

What was for sure was that Ruth Nesbitt did not need another tragedy in her family. Ruth Nesbitt was a survivor if there ever was one. She was far tougher than her daughter. Ruth Nesbitt's husband was no weak man, but he had broken. She had not.

Not yet.

She had already lost a son at Webster. To have her daughter abducted might be too much. It was the classic horror story of the frontier.

If God could spare her that—

God?

Or Lee?

Lee summoned up a smile. He didn't confuse the two. But it was Lee who had told Ruth Nesbitt not to worry. As far as he knew, God hadn't said anything.

And Lee just had a hunch.

He hoped he was wrong, but he had learned from bitter times never to ignore his hunches. He had gotten that from the Indians, and some of it was in his blood.

Lee sat in his hard-backed rocker and smoked his pipe. He had taken off his boots, and his stockinged feet rested on a trunk that had seen better days. The trunk lid was fastened by a padlock the size of a Texas blue jay. On the wood floor there were three empty green bottles. They were not liquor bottles. There was a small wobbly table next to the rocker.

Lee knew how to read, but he was not much of a reader. Reading was a skill he had picked up late in his life, and it was too difficult for him to be enjoyable. It wasn't much fun when you had to puzzle out nearly every word.

He did value his Bible some. What he liked about it was that he at least recognized some of the folks in that book. He knew what slaves were, sure enough, and prophets, even if most he had run into personally had been windbags. But much of the Bible, like the few other books that came his way, seemed to have nothing whatever to do with him or anyone he knew.

He respected the Bible, partly because of how Ruth Nesbitt felt about it. He wished that he could respond to it more.

Mostly, when he was in his quarters, Lee seemed to be doing nothing and seeing nothing. That was deceptive. If you had asked him, and if he was of a mind to tell you, he would have said that he was imagining a trail that stretched out in front of him. He did not know what was at the end of that trail, and he thought about it a great deal. He did know what lay along his tangled backtrail. He seldom looked back that way. That trail was closed forever.

Lee was not a poor man anymore, even when it came to cash money. But his part of the Nesbitt house was so stark it almost seemed empty. It was his choice that it be so.

There was no mirror. Lee hated mirrors. He supposed that went back to his mother. She had carried a scrap of glass around with her and she would often sneak a look at herself. Invariably, she cried. She had no time to spend making herself pretty.

There were no pictures on the walls. There were no curtains on the windows, even though Ruth Nesbitt fussed at him some about that.

He had a wood-burning iron cookstove and a few pots and pans. Usually he ate in the big part of the house with the family, but not always. His unpainted table had one short leg. No matter what he stuck under it, the table was unsteady.

There was a bed. Lee didn't much care; he was content with a pallet on the floor. But the bed had a good mattress and it was neatly made. There were some square nails in the walls. The few clothes Lee owned hung on the nails.

Lee was not a man who surrounded himself with knickknacks and mementos. Still, the room's barren look was more than the product of a don't-give-a-damn attitude. There were no clues to Lee's past life here. It was as though he had built himself an empty box with no memories.

Whatever identity he had, whatever he really was, that person was buried way down deep. He didn't come out easily.

He had spells of loneliness, but he was basically a sociable man. When he had half a chance, Lee was good company.

Where he lived, there were just two things visible that were completely out of the ordinary.

One was his carbine. It was on the wall near his bed, supported by wooden pegs he had driven in himself. Lee wanted no nail scratches on his rifle. It was a Hall-North percussion model 1838. It was a .52 caliber breech-loader and it fired premade paper cartridges. It was a far cry from the muzzle-loaders that were still in general use. For that matter, it was more advanced in its ammunition than Lee's Colt. On that carbine, the wood glowed and the polished metal gleamed. It was one beautiful weapon.

Lee loved guns. He admired them, understood them, and cherished them. He knew when he could use them and when he could not. Guns were the keys to his freedom. He never forgot that.

The second unusual thing was his Paterson Colt. It rested in its holster—supple as a good glove—exactly sixteen inches from Lee's hand. All that was really showing was the polished walnut grip and the hammer. If you got close enough, you could tell from the contours of the holster that there was no trigger guard under the leather. If you knew Colts, you knew that there was no trigger either, not with the hammer down.

It was a good gun, a quality gun, and there were not all that many Paterson Colts around. There were those who said that the .36 caliber five-shooter was slow. They meant that you had to take the gun apart to reload it. Lee always carried an extra cylinder in his pocket, primed and ready to go. Nobody who had ever seen Lee use a Paterson Colt called it slow again.

There was another thing that was unusual about Lee. It was not entirely invisible, but you had to know him well to see it.

It was his feeling for the Nesbitt family. Lee did not put a name to it; he was not sure that it had a name. It had something to do with trust. It had something to do with belonging somewhere. It had something to do with a warmth that he could not deny. Whatever it was, it had made him cry for the Nesbitt boy lost to a Comanche lance at Webster. Lee did not cry easily.

Otis was growing up so like his brother . . .

Lee did not know his own father. He had never seen him. His mother, when she mentioned him at all, had said that his father was part Indian. She didn't say what the other part was.

Part Indian! Lee had thought about that often. Sometimes it even amused him. What kind of Indian? They were all different. When Lee had once ventured into East Texas, the Cherokees had tried to make him a slave again. The Paterson Colt had been busy that day. At this very moment the Seminole Wild Cat was trying to *free* the slaves of Texas.

There were times when things got a little complicated.

Lee had killed Comanches and they had tried to kill him. Just the same, it was not hatred he felt for The People. If anything, it was kinship. As a man who had lost much of his own past, Lee knew full well what the Comanches saw in the blue smoke of their camp fires. They were staring at the shadows of a fading life.

Lee's mother was more or less black. She was black enough to be a slave. She thought she had some white blood in her, and maybe she did. One of Lee's earliest memories—one of the hardest to erase—was in the cabin with his mother. She would take out her reflecting glass and trace the outline of her face. She would stare at the color of her eyes. She seemed to be searching for something she almost found, before the tears came.

"Balls," Lee said. He did not like to think about it. But when he did, he figured that he was about as much one kind of man as another. It was not important to him, except in terms of how he was accepted or not accepted by others.

To most Texans, of course, Lee was not white, and that was all that mattered.

Perhaps that was why the Nesbitts were so special.

Lee tapped out his pipe. He knew one thing with no ifs, ands, or buts. If the Comanches came for Lisa Nesbitt, they would have to come up against him again. He was ready. He intended to watch Lisa very closely.

The People could not get her unless they killed him first.

3

Owl, Summer

Owl was painted for war, and that served his purpose in more than one way. War paint was black. It made a man hard to see at night.

Owl owned one of the old war helmets, made from a buffalo scalp with the full sharp horns of a male buffalo sticking up from the head. He had left the helmet with one of his wives. The war helmets were fearsome things, but they were awkward to wear. They got in the way.

This was a task for stealth. He did not even carry his many-layered round hide shield, decorated as it was with the personal signs that told of his exploits. Shields were strong medicine, and a man did not go into danger without one unless he had a very good reason.

Owl had two reasons.

The shield, like the horned helmet, was cumbersome. This was not going to be a typical horse raid with all the usual yelling and commotion. Owl needed to move silently, invisibly, and alone. If he needed a shield, the game was already lost.

Aside from that, Owl had other medicine. He had

the most powerful medicine in the world. If he was not protected, then nobody was protected.

As the red sun dropped beneath the stand of pecans, oaks, and cottonwoods that fringed the San Gabriel, Owl did something that he reserved for the gravest of occasions. It was no casual matter. He did more than touch the shaped stone in the deerskin medicine pouch that hung from his neck. He actually removed the flint from the bag and held it in his hand.

He felt the power. It made his hand tingle and there was a flashing of firelights in his head.

There it was, touched by the shadows, consecrated by time and more than time.

Out of the corner of his eye he caught a glimpse of it. There in the thicket of cedar, swelling above it like a monstrous dark cloud dropped somehow to the earth. He could smell the Beast, heavy and strong. He saw the curving gleam of ivory. He heard the huffing and chuffing of those mighty lungs. He saw the snakelike trunk dancing in the air—

Would it speak to him, as the medicine beast had done before? Would it give him ancient words of wisdom?

No.

The giant creature of the shadows faded as quickly as it had come. It was gone.

Owl was left with the grooved flint point he held in his hand. It was medicine enough. Was not this the flint that had killed the Cannibal Owl?

He was not a man given to dark broodings about the supernatural. Indeed, Owl considered himself to be something of a skeptic about such matters. He had once said of men who dreamed their whole lives away, "They are all dances and no arrows."

But *this*!

It was beyond *puha*, power, as that word was ordinarily understood. Supernatural? The flint he had in his hand was as solid as any other rock. The beast he had glimpsed in the cedars was as real as a flyspecked horse turd picked up out of the living dirt. Its odor was just as distinctive.

Owl had seen a few Comanche stone arrowheads in his time. They were not common. Some of the old men carried them on arrow shafts that had aged to brittleness. The arrowheads were unimpressive and nondescript. Metal trade points were so much better that nobody made the stone points anymore.

The flint that Owl cradled in his hand was not Comanche and it was not an arrowhead.

He had no idea what man or being had made that point. He was certain, without knowing why, that it came from a faraway time, perhaps even before the Comanches rode south from the Shining Mountains. It was much too big to be an arrowhead: the flint was nearly as large as his hand. It was finely chipped, superior to any stone-work done by The People. Its most unusual feature was a fairly long groove or channel running up from the base on both sides of the point. Removing such long flakes was beyond the skill of any Comanche known to Owl. Creating indentations like these, which he could easily grip with his fingers while holding the base against the palm of his hand, would thin the point at the back end, of course. Even a slight miscalculation while working the flint would shatter the whole thing.

It had to be a spear or lance point. He was sure of that. Only a giant of incredible strength could shoot a shaft burdened with such a point from a bow. It would simply describe a short arc and thud into the ground.

Although Owl protected that point with deerskin resting on his own body, the finished point was anything but fragile.

After all, it had killed a Cannibal Owl!

He himself had found that point, still embedded in the huge bleached bones of *piamempits*, the Cannibal Owl. He had been young then, only a boy, but he understood at once what he was seeing. The Comanche doctors, the *puhakuts*, used such bones in their healing. The bones were particularly helpful in drawing out the poison from wounds or boils. Owl was familiar with them, even as a child. He had seen bones like these before when the doctors worked, and the doctors had no difficulty in confirming his identification of the bones. Indeed, the doctors were eager to add them to their collections.

Especially to a child, the Cannibal Owl was a thing of terror. The living creature, often discussed but never seen, was an ominous warning of misfortune and destruction. Parents threatened their children with it: "If you don't behave yourself, the Cannibal Owl will get you!"

That such a creature could be at the same time an omen of disaster and an aid to healing was one of those mysteries that a child had to live with. Unlike some other mysteries, as the children grew older they found that this puzzle did not get any clearer.

It was just the way the Comanche world was.

Whatever the truth of the matter, it was a fact that a weapon that could actually *kill* a Cannibal Owl in the long-ago time was powerful almost beyond belief. Owl was a hunter who sprang from generations of hunters. He knew what he was looking at when he saw a spear point encased in a skeletal rib cage, no matter how peculiar the animal and no matter how unusual the point.

When the Spirit Beast had spoken to him in the quest that had transformed Owl from a boy into a man, that had settled things with a finality that could not be questioned.

The grooved point was all the protection that Owl needed. All he had to do was to keep it safe from harm, cherish it, use its power wisely.

And when the time came, pass it on to one who understood.

The medicine flint would take care of the rest.

It was not that Owl considered the task before him to be so dangerous that only the flint could save him. It was just that he was more than willing to take all the help he could get. What he had to do was risky, yes. But Owl knew what he was doing. He had lived all his life with risk.

Comanche boys played at this game from the day they learned how to ride, which came early. Of all exploits, stealing a tethered horse from the middle of an enemy camp was perhaps the greatest. Boys dreamed about it, talked about it, carried out mock raids until they knew all the tricks.

Indeed, that was how Owl had gotten Wise One, many seasons ago, from the Utes. It was almost always better to steal a good horse than to breed one. For one thing, you knew exactly what you were getting.

Sooner or later Comanche boys pulled off the raids for real. Either that, or they did not live to become Comanche men.

This was not going to be so very different.

Taking a boy involved pretty much the same tactics as taking a horse.

Owl just had to keep his head on straight, remember what he knew, and hold fast to his medicine.

Then he simply had to go into Stafford and do it.

Owl waited through the night. He could see the silvery orange of Mother Moon reflected in the San Gabriel. As the night wore on, the air turned a little cooler, but not much. There was no breeze. The air seemed heavy and damp and waiting. The moon dwindled in size and became pure silver.

He was close enough so that he could hear an occasional dog barking in Stafford. That was both good and bad. Good because the dogs were barking at nothing in particular and nobody would pay much attention to them. Bad for the obvious reason that the dogs were in the town at all. Owl had considerable respect for dogs. He was more concerned about the dogs than the people.

Although the old men liked to make it seem complicated and mysterious, there were no deep secrets about a successful raid. Any fool knew what was needed. A man had to know the exact configuration of his target—where everyone was, and every horse, whether he was after horses or not. And he had to have every move planned in advance. He had to know precisely what he was doing and why. Sometimes plans did not work. Sometimes a man had to improvise. But he could not improvise from nothing.

Young warriors often got too excited. They forgot the basic rules. Unless they were very lucky, they did not survive to become old warriors.

Owl was almost within shouting distance of a fort, which he knew was called Goacher's Fort. He was in fact between the fort and Stafford. This was neither bravado on his part nor stupidity. Despite its name, Goacher's Fort was not a manned post. There was no garrison there.

Goacher's Fort was nothing but a stone-walled enclosure with a springhouse, a storage room, and an old cracked church bell in a wooden tower. There was some ammunition there but no soldiers, unless you counted Old Man Goacher. The fort was for protection in case of an Indian attack. It was a place where people could run if the church bell sounded. It was a place to make a stand. It was exactly the type of structure the settlers had needed at Webster.

Owl smiled. The *Taibos* had a way of building their forts a shade late and in the wrong place.

Fort or no fort, Owl was actually more troubled by his proximity to the Stafford cemetery. He did not like graves. There had been few burials at Stafford yet, but there were some raw, fresh scars in the earth. The spirits of the dead did not bother Owl unduly. He just preferred a tree or scaffold burial. It seemed wrong to put dead bodies in living earth.

Owl not only knew Stafford, he knew the layout of the Nesbitt house in some detail. He had watched for many days and nights. There were no real hills around Stafford, but this was also not true plains country. It was not flat and treeless. It was gently rolling country with a good deal of vegetation. There were rises where a man could lie in the brush and see without being seen. The main problem was that he had to approach and leave on foot. Owl never walked if he could ride.

He had Heart waiting for him now. The gelding was on the other side of the San Gabriel and he was well-hidden. Owl had even tethered him lightly, although he trusted Heart to stay when he dropped the reins. It was best to take no chances.

Owl knew all about Lee. He had encountered him at Webster, but more importantly, he had seen him on rare occasions in the camps of The People. He knew Lee's name. It seemed short and funny to him, like part of a Comanche word that had been chopped off from the rest.

The man Lee was not funny. That one was a warrior. Owl had built his whole plan around where Lee would be and what he would be doing.

There were no sentries posted at Stafford, of course. It might have been said that the *Taibos* were slow to learn, but the fact was that Comanche villages were also usually left unprotected at night. It was for each tipi to watch out for itself.

Owl waited until he saw the first faint pink fingers of Father Sun pointing up out of the eastern sky. He could still see many of the stars. It was not yet dawn.

But it was close.

Owl did not hesitate. He moved—and he moved fast.

Every morning, at almost exactly the same time, just before daybreak, Lee went to the privy in back of the house. Owl figured that he liked to be through there before the rest of the family needed to come out. His bowels were on the slow side. Owl had counted the time. What Lee did, he sat in there and smoked his pipe. It was usually the only time of the day or night that he did not have the Paterson Colt on him or within easy reach. Lee's quarters were at the back of the house, near the privy, but there was a space. It was a big enough space, to Owl's way of thinking.

No matter what Lee may have thought, he was too far from his Colt.

Owl was aware that the girl-woman and the boy-child slept on opposite sides of the house. Owl approved of that. That was as it should be. The girl-woman was old enough to be married, and she would have been if she had lived in a Comanche camp. The boy was at an age when he should not sleep near his sister. Very soon, if the boy had been Comanche, he would have to move to his own small tipi erected behind the lodge of his parents.

That boy *was* going to be a Comanche.

Owl cared nothing about the girl-woman. His wives had given him so many girl-children, he sometimes had trouble remembering all their names.

It was a son he needed.

The boy's window was open. It had to be. It was too hot to close it. There were heavy shutters to protect the window against the freezing winds of winter, but this was not winter.

Owl came in at an angle where he could not possibly be seen from the privy. His black paint in the uncertain light made him hard to see, even if you knew where he was.

There was one dog near the house. The dog was big and Owl had been expecting him. He got the dog with a single arrow driven all the way through the throat. The dog went rigid, then dropped like a stone. He didn't even get off a good whine.

Owl did not take the time to retrieve the arrow. Speed was what counted now. In any case, Lee would not need an arrow shaft to know that a Comanche had visited the house.

Comanche moccasin tracks could not be readily disguised. They were like hard-soled boots with trailing buffalo tail fringes. It had been very dry, but there would be trace marks in the dirt. Lee could read them when the time came.

Owl wasted no time on such speculations.

He took a deep breath, ran five steps, and hurled his body through the open window of the boy's room.

It was difficult for Owl to see in the darkness of the sleeping room. It was darker inside than out.

He managed. Again he did not take time that would slow him down. He moved before his eyes had fully adjusted to the gloom. He thought to himself that The People had many jokes about how Owl could see in the dark.

The boy-child was in the bed, or at least on it, dressed in the sacklike garment they called a nightshirt. There was a musket on the floor by the bed. Owl could barely make it out. The musket was as long as the boy was tall.

The boy sat up with a start. His sandy hair was tousled. His eyes looked bigger than Owl's.

The boy may or may not have been terror-stricken. He must have been shocked with surprise. Just the same, he knew what to do. He did not holler for help that would come too late. He flipped his body off the bed in a movement that would have made a snake proud. He went for the musket.

Owl liked that. He liked that a lot.

"*Toquet*," he whispered. It is good.

There were few men who were a match for Owl, even on foot. There were no boys.

Owl was on him before the musket left the floor. He did not fool around. He dealt the boy one tremendous blow to the head with his stubby, rock-hard fist. For a moment he feared that he had killed him.

No. The boy yet breathed. He would not wake up for a good long time, but he was not dead. He would have a hurt in his skull that he would never forget.

That would be the first of many hurts.

In one fluid movement Owl slung the boy's body over his shoulder, took one long step, and jumped through the window. He hit the ground running.

It was still not full dawn, but there was much more light now. Owl felt as though he were a dark buffalo caught on a flat slab of stone.

There was no alarm. The only noises were the sounds of morning.

Owl ran silently along a course he had chosen long before, a pathway that kept him shielded from most eyes.

He could have been seen if someone was looking for him, but nobody was.

Not yet.

The boy made no sounds at all. Owl could not even hear him breathing; his own puffing prevented that. The boy was a clumsy burden. He flopped. He was like a half-empty sack of maize meal.

Owl reached Heart just as Father Sun emerged as a red ball on the horizon. Owl was amazed at his good fortune. It had been much easier than he had anticipated. His medicine was very strong.

Heart was smart enough not to whinny a greeting.

Owl untethered his horse and, with the same rawhide thong, he tied the boy's legs under Heart. The boy was still completely unconscious. Owl had to throw him up on the horse. He was not gentle.

"Go," he said.

Heart went.

It was very good to be on a horse again, particularly a fine animal like Heart. That was mainly what Owl felt. He had a sense of being home. He did not like to walk long distances on foot. He hated to run.

He grabbed the boy's soft and curly hair in one hand. It felt strange. It was not Indian hair. It needed a good application of bear grease.

Owl permitted himself a small sense of satisfaction.

Now they would see what they would see.

He had no way of knowing exactly when Otis was first missed.

(He did know that it was full morning and Father Sun was burning in the sky before he heard the distant pealing of the old church bell at Goacher's Fort.)

4

Coffee, Summer

Coffee rode alone through the cedar brakes and the feathery mesquite. He was an observant man, and he noticed that the stubby deep-rooted mesquite was more common than it had been a few years before. It was taking over with the clearing of other vegetation.

Coffee had left Austin early that morning, riding right by the domed Capitol building and the massive spired stone St. Patrick's Church at the corner of Brazos and Ash streets. He still found it difficult to adjust to the sudden change between the growing city and the countryside. If civilization was on the way, a man couldn't tell it five miles beyond Austin. That did not displease Coffee. He had nothing in particular against civilization, but he was not about to build a fire under it to hurry it along.

Coffee knew that, whatever he was, he would not mix very well with an excess of civilization. Let it come, by all means. But there was no great rush.

Coffee was on a yellowed dirt and caliche road rather than a trail, but the distinction was simply that a wagon could be hauled along a road with a fifty-fifty chance of not losing a wheel.

Despite the heat, Coffee wore a stained leather vest over his long-sleeved blue cotton shirt. His red bandanna was knotted with a certain jauntiness around his neck. His precisely cocked gray felt hat had a rim big enough to throw some shade. The hat was not free of sweat stains, but it was a very good hat and Coffee was proud of it. Coffee had given twenty-five dollars for that hat at a time when his pay had been $1.25 a day.

Coffee had no visible badge. The badge thing came and went. He figured that if it took a badge to convince someone that he was a Ranger, maybe he should get into some other line of work.

The closest thing to an official uniform he had was the heavy .44 caliber Walker Colt six-shooter he packed on his right hip. Walker Colts were not restricted to Rangers, but they were not exactly raining down out of the sky either. He no longer carried the traditional long rifle. It was not the gun for a mounted fighter. Coffee's rifle, the worn stock of which protruded from his saddle scabbard, was a solid but unspectacular Sharps .52 percussion carbine.

He had a coiled lariat fastened to his saddle. The rope was in good shape and had no fray marks. Coffee was not planning on roping anything, but he would no more ride off without his lariat than he would forget to put on his pants in the morning.

There was a saying that a Ranger was only as good as his horse. Coffee would not go quite that far. There had been times when he had gotten the job done with a borrowed horse that was less than first-class. Nevertheless, it was a plain fact that the great Ranger captain, Jack Hays, would not accept a volunteer who had a horse worth less than a hundred dollars. That was a lot of money when you could buy a perfectly decent horse for twenty-five. Coffee did not really bother his mind with such figures. What he knew for sure was that he could outride any man he was likely to come up against, and to do that he had to trust his horse.

Absolutely.

Coffee depended on his big bay gelding, Prickly Pear, so thoroughly that he didn't have to think about it. He took Pear for granted, just as he took his ability to shoot. Pear had spent some time in South Texas, and he had developed a fondness for prickly pear. Coffee had picked many a fine cactus spine out of his velvety nostrils.

Coffee had just passed through Seward Junction when he saw the rider coming his way hell-for-leather. The man almost certainly was a messenger of some sort. There was nobody behind him trying to ride him down, and no man rode a horse at that pace without a very strong reason.

Coffee was not pleased. In his experience, messages usually meant trouble. Coffee had intended to bed down for the night on the south side of a thicket somewhere and ride on into Stafford the next day.

He was not thinking about Comanches.

He was thinking about Lisa Nesbitt.

The closer the rider got, the more Coffee's heart sank. He could recognize that the messenger was coming from Stafford. It was his business to take in such information at a glance.

Coffee pulled up on Pear, took off his hat and waved.

Then he waited.

He had no idea what the trouble was. He had no way to know whether it involved Lisa or not.

But he was certainly sure that he would be riding into Stafford this night, not tomorrow.

When the rider came up beside him, Coffee placed him at once. His name was David Walters and he was indeed from Stafford. David Walters was kin to John Walters of Hornsby's Bend, on the east bank of the Colorado about nine miles below Austin. He was a man of some substance.

If you were going to get information, it was very

helpful to know what the source of that information was. Much might depend on how solid a citizen David Walters was.

Coffee had him sized up with approval.

That man was killing that horse of his, though.

"Howdy, Dave," Coffee said. He had replaced his hat and now he touched its brim. "You appear to have been moving along at a right rapid pace."

Dave Walters was so full of his story he could hardly get it out. If he caught the slight criticism in Coffee's words, he ignored it.

"Cap'n!" he said, trying to control his snorting mount. Many people addressed all Rangers as Captain, whether that was their actual rank or not. If you used a title at all, it seldom did any harm to aim too high. "Just the man! Injuns. They got the Nesbitt kid."

Coffee felt his stomach turn to stone. His expression did not change. His voice stayed exactly the same. It was slow, precise, and deliberate. "What Nesbitt kid?"

"The boy. Otis. They got his brother at Webster—"

"I know the family." Coffee did not show the relief that surged within him. He was, in fact, ashamed of it. The loss of Otis would just about finish off old Cole Nesbitt. But Lisa was safe! He rejoiced, God help him.

"How many Indians? Who else was taken? How many hurt?"

"One Injun, Cap'n. Comanche. He got a dog with an arrow. Just come through a window and plumb took off with Otis, that's all. Nobody else hurt, far as I know. But Mrs. Ruth, she's in a bad way. And Cole—"

"I know Cole." Coffee tugged at his earlobe. He needed to sort this out as he talked. There were times when getting all riled up didn't do much good. "You were coming to Austin to get me?"

"Get *somebody*. No offense, Cap'n. We don't have a real lawman in Stafford. You know that. We need some Rangers, and we need 'em sudden."

Coffee nodded. There was an old story about a riot in Eagle Pass, across from Piedras Negras. An urgent summons went out to the Rangers. The Rangers dispatched one man. "Only one Ranger?" the people asked. The Ranger, so the story went, nodded calmly. "Only one riot," he replied.

"I'm going to ask a favor of you, Dave," Coffee said.

"Anything I can do." Coffee knew the man meant it, from taking on a rattler with a twig to riding straight through to San Antone without stopping.

Coffee took out a pad and pencil from his saddlebag. He wrote a short, accurate note and addressed it to Captain Rip Ford. Rip's real name was John S. Ford, but nobody called him that. The note was not scribbled. It was as neat as a piece of schoolwork. He handed the note to Dave Walters.

"Please continue on to Austin. Find Captain Rip Ford and give him this note."

He didn't have to explain who Rip Ford was. It would have been like asking Dave if he had ever heard of the Alamo. John Ford had gone into the Mexican War as a doctor, and one of his jobs had been to sign death certificates. He had gotten into the habit of adding "Rest In Peace" to each document. There had been enough deaths so that he shortened his postscript to R.I.P. to save time. The initials stuck, and he had been Rip Ford ever since.

"What the note says is that I'll be in Stafford before you get to Austin. No offense. I'll take charge unless I'm replaced. When I know what I need to know, I'll contact Austin or San Antone for help."

Sensing some doubt in Dave's eyes, Coffee added gently: "We need to find the boy first, Dave. God knows where he is or where they might be taking him. It's better to have the Ranger net in place than for everybody to go riding off in all directions for no purpose. I can track a Comanche as well as the next man, but I can't track him far—not with the head start he's got. We've got to find Otis some other way, whether we try the tracking or not. It's our heads and our eyes we've got to use, and maybe our ears. This isn't the time for a pile of shooting and hollering. I'll tell you one thing. I'll find that boy, friend. You count on that."

David Walters nodded. Clearly, there was still more he wanted to say, but he couldn't bring himself to spit it out.

Coffee saved him the embarrassment of asking. "If you can't find Captain Ford, just give the note to any Ranger. They will take it from there. And Dave—" He paused, searching for some words of reassurance. "There are plenty of guns in Stafford. You know that. If the Comanches had planned an all-out raid, they wouldn't have sent one warrior in ahead of the game to take Otis and warn everybody. We can man the fort, just in case. I will see to it that sentries are posted. Your family is as safe as it can ever be in a settlement like that. I have already told you that I will get assistance if I require it."

Coffee's tone was matter-of-fact, not boastful, but it strongly suggested that he was unlikely to require assistance from anybody in the foreseeable future.

David Walters relaxed somewhat. There was something about Coffee's quiet assurance that inspired confidence, even in a nervous man.

And Dave Walters was plenty nervous.

"I'll carry your note, Cap'n," he said. "I will consider it an honor and a trust."

Coffee reached out and shook his hand. The hand was hard, the hand of a workingman. Coffee was fairly particular about whose hand he took, but he liked David Walters. Besides, he figured that in the situation he was going into he might need all the friends he could get.

"One other little thing, Dave."

"Sir?"

"Name's Coffee, not sir. Dave, I'd slow down some on that horse of yours. It won't help Otis a lick to kill your horse on the way to Austin."

Dave took it with a smile, although it was not easy to be told how to ride his own horse. He set off again toward Austin, this time at a more sensible pace. Coffee knew that he'd get there. Dave was a good man. He knew also that Dave was doing more or less what he had left Stafford to do in the first place. The difference was that now he was convinced that all this was somehow Coffee's idea.

"Come on, Pear," Coffee said, nudging his horse. "We'll rest some and drink in a while, but we've got a good spell to go yet."

Pear responded with a walk that was a little faster than necessary. He wasn't tired and meant to show it.

As Coffee rode, he pulled the Walker Colt from its holster. He just slipped it out; he wasn't practicing any fast draws, and in any case the heavy Colt was poorly designed for that kind of work.

He simply enjoyed the feel of the gun in his hand. He pulled the hammer back to half-cock so he could spin the cylinder with his thumb. The Walker Colt was as solid and sturdy as a crowbar. The joke was that you could always use it as a club against a man who wasn't worth shooting. It was not always a joke either, and that was invariably the next line.

There was a load in the chamber under the hammer, and that meant that Coffee did not have to concern himself about where the cylinder stopped. It was not impossible to fire a Walker Colt by accident, but it took some doing. The gun was made to take rough handling.

He continued spinning the cylinder for a minute or two before lowering the hammer and returning the Colt to its holster.

It didn't mean anything. It was just a mannerism he had while riding, like pulling on his earlobe when he needed to stall a little.

Right on schedule, an hour after sunset, the chuck-will's-widows called out from their insect-seeking flights. Of all the night birds, Coffee liked their songs the best.

Then the moon rose. It was gigantic as it lifted above the horizon.

Despite his mission, Coffee felt a certain peace.

It was bright enough so that Pear did not have to pick his way once the moon was high. It was a full moon, fat and butter-yellow. Some called it a Comanche Moon.

Certainly it was ideally suited to night riding. Except for the absence of color, Coffee could see as clearly as though it were daylight.

He caught the mournful hooting of an owl on the still air. It was not close. There were coyotes yipping and crying, at least four of them. He paid them no special mind. Usually when you heard an owl or some coyotes, that was precisely what they were: an owl and some coyotes. In his experience, Indians who communicated by using bird or animal noises were on the rare side.

Coffee tried to keep his mind off Lisa Nesbitt. She disturbed him some, and that was a fact. It wasn't just her honey-blond hair or those shockingly direct blue eyes. Lisa gave him the feeling that she was looking right inside him. Coffee was sure she knew what was on his mind every minute. That bothered him, because Coffee was not a man who was ignorant of women. What he was thinking was apt to be almost painfully specific.

Of course, Ruth would be considerably agitated now. Courting Lisa was not easy at the best of times, and this was not going to be one of the good times. Ruth would have little patience with playing games.

Although hardly one to feel sorry for himself, Coffee did reflect that it was no accident that most Rangers stayed unmarried until after they had left the service. A Ranger had to be free to range. That was what the word meant.

He did not like the idea of either Ruth or Lisa living in the same house as a black man. He did not like it one little bit. There were times when it made him sick to his stomach.

Still, give the devil his due. Pear snorted as though signifying his agreement. Lee—he didn't even know whether that was his first name or his last, not that it mattered—was no stranger to a gun, especially a handgun. He knew something about Indians and their ways, maybe too much. He seemed to be genuinely fond of Otis. So how could he have allowed this thing to happen?

What it came down to was that you just couldn't

trust a black man. That was what Coffee figured. Even one that seemed to have some good qualities. Even one that nobody would mistake for a slave.

That man just flat out made him uncomfortable. He should not have been in that house.

Coffee could catch just a hint of the San Gabriel smell now on the slight night breeze. The air was always damper at night, even in dry weather, but the river scent was different. He did not have very far to go.

This whole business did strike Coffee as strange. He did not hold with the notion that Comanches were just crazy savages who did things without rhyme or reason. When you found out what they were really up to, it usually made a kind of sense. Why, then, would a single Comanche come for Otis Nesbitt? Right in the middle of Stafford?

What made Otis so special?

It wasn't the fact that the Indian had taken a male. After all, as everybody knew, the first white Comanche captive in Texas had been Stephen F. Austin, the self-styled Father of Texas. They had named the capital city of Texas after him, although Austin's original colony had been saddled with the high-flown designation of Washington-on-the-Brazos. It hadn't even been on the right river!

It wasn't even the fact that a lone Comanche had done the job, although that was unusual.

There was just something about this situation that did not point clear, and that was all there was to it.

Well, he thought, there were lots of things these days that weren't as clear as they once were. Sometimes it was hard to even tell what side Sam Houston was on, and that gave a man pause. Now that Texas was a state, the role of the Texas Rangers was more than a little uncertain. Supposedly, the United States Army had taken over the job of protecting citizens against Indian attacks. That was a laugh. The army, what there was of it in Texas, wasn't worth a wad of spit in a norther.

Coffee supposed that Dave Walters had reacted the same as most Texans would. When trouble came, you went for the Rangers. They were the ones who got the job done, regardless of who was *supposed* to do it. Coffee reckoned it would stay like that until the majority of Texans believed different.

Still, things weren't quite the same.

Certainly the Indian Agents had no power when it came down to fish or cut bait. Robert Neighbors wasn't a bad sort, the way Coffee saw it, but he could no more get Otis back than he could pull a star out of the sky.

Coffee was quite capable of riding all night, and often had, but he could have used a cup of coffee. The wordplay with his name did not escape him. He had heard it perhaps a thousand times.

Coffee's full name was Noah Coffee. He was related to the most famous Ranger of them all, Jack Hays. Nobody had ever suggested to his face that the kinship had advanced his career. Anyone who knew Jack Hays realized that it would work the other way. Jack Hays was a man who bent over backwards to be fair.

Jack Hays, the first of the great Ranger captains, carried the formal name of John Coffee Hays. He had come to Texas in 1837, at the ripe old age of twenty-one years. He had come from Wilson County in Tennessee. That was where the kin connection was, back in Tennessee. Most everyone in Texas had "gone to Texas" from somewhere. The Spanish-Mexicans, the Texans, the Cherokees, even the Comanches—all had moved in from elsewhere. Maybe the Tonks and the Karankawas were real natives; Coffee wasn't sure.

Around God only knew how many campfires, those men who were close enough to him to get away with it had tried every possible twist on the joke conjured up by his name.

"Well, gents," they would say, "I do believe it's time for some coffee. Hold it! Not him! No coffee for that horse thief. Why, dang me if his own *name* ain't Noah Coffee!"

That was the main reason why Coffee went by his last name. Only total strangers and friends of long standing ever called him Noah. Lisa Nesbitt did it sometimes as a tease.

It was somewhere around midnight when Coffee sighted Stafford. Normally, at this time of night, there would be no lights showing at all. Tonight, though, there were lamps burning in the windows. Even if he hadn't known where it was, he could have spotted the Nesbitt house by the number of lights.

He was challenged long before he actually rode into Stafford. That was good. They had sentries out. They weren't all huddled at Goacher's Fort, leaving the town abandoned.

The old adage about locking the barn door after the horse was stolen danced through his mind.

No matter.

There was another old saying: Better late than never.

His heart speeded up just a little bit at the prospect of seeing Lisa. That was his heart.

His head was fixed on Otis. Coffee would not truly rest again until he had Otis back or found him dead.

5

Lee, Summer

Lee could make no peace with himself. In his own eyes, there was no excuse for what had happened. None.

It probably did not make a vast difference, but the disappearance of Otis had not been noticed for several hours. It was assumed that the boy was just sleeping late. He did that sometimes. He was a boy, after all. There was no urgent need to call him.

Incredibly, Lee had not at first seen the dead dog, much less the Comanche arrow. The dog was screened by Ruth Nesbitt's little garden, but a man could have seen it if he had looked carefully. There had been no reason to look. There was no stink even now, but there were blowflies and a few circling buzzards.

Lee had rigged a trip wire from Lisa Nesbitt's window to his quarters. The wire was set to jerk the rickety table if it was so much as touched. He had put a tripod of empty green bottles on the table. There was *no way* he could have slept through the commotion if anything had struck that wire. No way. He had complete confidence that Lisa was safe. When he went to the privy, he had removed the trip wire from the table and fastened it to his left knee.

That morning, once he made certain that Lisa Nesbitt had not been harmed, Lee put the matter out of his mind. The Indians, he knew, would never come in broad daylight. Not unless they came in overwhelming force, in which case he would need no trip wires.

He had not been negligent. He had been stupid. A kinder judge might have said that he had been so obsessed with one idea that there had been no room for another. To Lee, he had just been plain stupid.

Otis!

Good God, why Otis?

The possibility had simply never occurred to him. Even now he found it hard to believe. It was like a bad dream.

He knew, of course, that the Comanches sometimes took boys, as well as girls. It had been nearly twenty years since the most famous Comanche raid of them all, but no Texan would ever forget it. Cynthia Ann Parker, nine years old, had been seized within sight of a walled stockade. Cynthia Ann's grandfather, Elder John Parker, was scalped and mutilated. John's wife, known as Granny, was pinned to the earth with a lance and raped by a series of warriors. Cynthia Ann's father, Silas, was shot so full of arrows trying to protect his children that he looked like a porcupine. Her mother, Lucy, was grabbed and carried off, but dropped when the pursuit got hot.

The Comanches escaped with Cynthia Ann. It was rumored that she had given birth to a Comanche son, Quanah. Quanah was said to be about eight years old now.

The Comanches also got young John Parker, Cynthia Ann's brother. He had been six years old.

That didn't end it. The same raiders captured two young married women, Elizabeth Kellogg and Rachel Plummer. They also stole Rachel's infant son, James.

Lee was as familiar with that story as any man in Texas. He had heard it from both sides. He knew full well that two of the three children seized had been boys.

He had seen a few Texan boys in Comanche camps, although they were hard to tell from the Indians by the time he saw them.

So how could he have ignored the threat to Otis? He worried the idea like a cat with an injured bird. Perhaps it had something to do with the fact that the Parker raid had been a large-scale attack. He hadn't been expecting anything like that, even after Webster.

More likely it was due to all the whispered stories he had heard on the frontier. They were terrible stories, fearful stories, and they were *always* about Indians who abducted girls. Lee was far from brainless. He knew that there was an element of the race-sex horror in such stories. How could he not have known, being who he was?

But knowing was one thing. What you felt in your bones was another. Had he been so infected by the myth—the Indians were only interested in females—that he had forgotten the evidence of his own eyes and brain?

Lee shook his head. He hated what he had done.

Fool! Stupid fool!

Otis . . .

Why, he loved that boy. He loved him as much as anything on this earth.

And he had failed him . . .

When Ruth Nesbitt discovered that she had lost her only surviving son, she had gone more than a little crazy.

She had grabbed the first thing she could find, which happened to be an iron poker, and charged into Lee's quarters. She had never in her life gone in there without knocking. This time, she blew through the door like the mother of all dust devils.

She had struck Lee with the poker. She had hit him as hard as she possibly could. She was a short woman, and so it was a glancing blow on the front of his left shoulder. Just the same, it hurt, and not just emotionally. Ruth Nesbitt was very strong for her size.

"Don't worry!" she screamed. Her voice was like a shrill cackle, totally unlike her normal voice. "Don't worry! That's what you said. Don't worry about anything. You'll be here. You! That's what you said."

Lee had never heard her scream before, not even at Webster. He was so shocked that at first he was unable to speak.

It wasn't just the screaming, bad as that was. She had struck him. Actually struck him!

"Mrs. Nesbitt," he whispered. He was close to tears. "For God's sake, Mrs. Nesbitt!"

She shuddered, that tiny woman, and something like a mask of madness slipped from her face. She let herself go, just for a moment, and stood before him nakedly, as what she was: a whipcord-tough old lady who had taken one fearsome blow too many.

She sagged against him, dropping the poker from a hand that was suddenly powerless to hold it.

"Oh, Lee!" she gasped, horrified. "Lee! What have I done? Oh, God! I'm going out of my mind. Lee! You, of all people. I'm so sorry, so deeply sorry—"

He could not, even overcome with emotion, bring himself to embrace her fully. It went against the traditions of a lifetime. He carefully put his left arm around her, his hurting arm, and let her cry herself out. She sobbed against his chest and he did not draw back. That was the best he could do.

"It's all right, Mrs. Nesbitt," he said softly. "It's all right."

He said it over and over again, almost in a singsong, calming her as though with a lullaby.

Gradually the sobbing subsided. Her body stilled.

"It's all right," he said again. "I'll get your boy back. Nothing has changed."

But something had changed, and they both knew it. Something had happened that could not be undone. It could be forgiven, and was, but it could never be forgotten.

It would stand between them, for the rest of their lives.

Lee knew in that moment that he would have to leave this house. It could not be his home forever. That was over. It might take a long time, it might take years, but he could not stay.

There was grief in him, grief for Otis and Ruth Nesbitt and for himself. It is a hard thing when a dream dies.

And Lee knew that they had sent for the Rangers. That meant Coffee was coming, and that was bad news.

Coffee tended to his own horse when he got to the Nesbitt house shortly after midnight. As was his custom, he said not a word directly to Lee.

Coffee slept a few hours in Otis's bed, and in the morning he studied the same signs Lee had read earlier. They weren't quite as fresh now, but Lee did not doubt that Coffee could get as much out of the signs as he had. Like him or hate him, the man knew what he was doing.

The Ranger offered no opinions and shared no ideas. He was not discourteous to Lee. He simply ignored him.

Lee knew that for a number of reasons it would have been wise for him to leave his Paterson Colt in his quarters. Some of the reasons made sense, even to him. This was no time to prod Coffee, and an incident between them could not help Otis any. Just the same, Lee wore his Colt. He was not about to be faced down by Coffee's mere *presence* in the house.

Perhaps, if it had not been for the poker, his better judgment would have prevailed.

But the poker was real. The impossible blow had been struck.

Wearing the Colt was a small gesture, but it was one he had to make.

Lee knew as well as any man that this was no time for mindless action, no matter how deeply he ached for the boy. It also was not helpful just to go on kicking himself in the butt.

There was an obvious problem, however.

Lee went to Cole Nesbitt. He could not help thinking of him as an old geezer. Cole was not all that old in years, but his manner marked him.

Cole Nesbitt was still the man of the house. He had a right to be consulted.

Cole had been told. He knew exactly what had happened. His emaciated body twitched beneath the sheet. His shirt was stained and stinking with sweat. He made constant vocal noises. The sounds had the rhythm of human speech, rising and falling and pausing and changing pitch, but the noises did not connect into words. If Cole Nesbitt was saying anything, it was in a language totally beyond Lee's understanding.

Lee reached out and gripped Cole's damp, bony shoulder. He didn't know what else to do. It seemed important to him to make a contact that could be recognized.

Inadvertently, his hand touched Cole's strange, weightless hair. It was like brushing against a cloud.

"Cole Nesbitt," Lee said. "Old friend."

The noises continued. There was no other response.

Lee groped for words. He felt as though he was having no better luck than Cole. He did the best he could. "Old-Timer, I know you think you've gone and lost your last son. I'm not the man to lie to you. Maybe you have. But then again, maybe you haven't. I want you to pull yourself together long enough so we can talk a spell."

Cole Nesbitt became very still. He was rigid, like a corpse.

"It's Otis we have to talk about," Lee said. "Do it for him."

Cole Nesbitt thrashed, literally thrashed, in the bed. His chest heaved. The sheet got twisted and tangled. Lee watched him in both sorrow and amazement.

That old man was trying to get up. He wanted his boy back more than anything in this world. It was killing him to lie there helpless, no use to anybody.

By God, Cole Nesbitt was going to get out of that bed by a sheer effort of will.

Lee steadied him with his hand. As gently as he could, he pressed him back down on the mattress. The body seemed to have no flesh on it. It was all rope and bone. "Not that way, Mr. Nesbitt," Lee said with the respect he had always felt for this man. "Maybe someday. Not now. For now, you need to calm yourself down some. Just listen. Can you do that?"

Gradually Cole Nesbitt's contortions slowed and then stopped altogether. He lay there panting. His watery blue eyes were wide open. There was a spark in them that might have been intelligence. The eyes seemed not to blink.

"Well, now," Lee said with a heartiness that was only a tiny bit genuine. "That's more like it. I'll tell you what. You got some sand in you, Cole Nesbitt."

The old man grunted. It was as close to true speech as he had come.

Lee moved his hand away. He hitched a footstool up to the bed and perched on it. "Fact is," he said, "the problem we got to face, you and me together, is what to do about your wife and Miss Lisa. I need to have your thinking on this."

Cole Nesbitt made a swallowing noise. His eyes were not vacant. He was listening.

Lee took a deep breath. "I can go after Otis, and that is my intention. It is my fault that this thing happened."

It was possible that Cole Nesbitt shook his head. Hard to tell.

"I don't have to explain to you that I may be gone a long time. I don't know where Otis is. I don't know who has him. I can't make no promises to you if I'm not sure I can keep them. The only one I can give you is the one you already know. I'll give it all I have in me."

Cole Nesbitt blinked his eyes. Lee could only guess at the effort it cost him.

Lee went on. "That leaves Mrs. Nesbitt and Miss Lisa alone in the house with you, Old-Timer. You know Coffee will ride out of here, same as me. We can't get no Ranger to sit the house. No offense to you, my friend, but you're in no kind of shape to protect anybody."

That made Cole Nesbitt mad. Beads of sweat dotted his pale brow. It took a massive strain on what energy he had, but he spoke. His voice was dry and raspy, but his words were clear.

"I can," he said distinctly. "I will."

Lee pretended not to hear him. It wasn't going to be that easy, not for either one of them.

"We could send Miss Lisa away," Lee said. "Have her stay with kin somewhere. Maybe even in Austin. Your wife is a pretty fair shot—there's some mighty dead Indians out there who could testify to that. Maybe she's not as good as you were once, but she's no helpless lady, and if she's afraid of anything, I ain't seen it yet. The neighbors won't let this house be alone. Stafford folks been through enough. They won't let one of their own down."

"Lisa stays," Cole Nesbitt croaked.

Lee went right on going. "The proposition I'm putting to you is this, my friend." Lee felt like the worst kind of hypocrite. He knew the old coot. He knew the man who still lived down in that shell somewhere. He wasn't giving him a fair choice. That was not his intention. "I'll stay if you tell me to, fair enough? I'll watch Miss Lisa like a prairie dog watches a rattler. Or I'll got out after your boy and try to bring him back. You decide."

Cole Nesbitt's eyes flashed. He was fully engaged now. He was indignant. He was downright angry. He reached out with one of his claws and grabbed hold of a bedpost. Somehow, he dragged himself into a posture that was close to a sitting position. He shook like a man with a raging fever.

"Go and be damned to you," he husked in his rusty voice. "I'll find a way to take care of what's left of my family."

Cole Nesbitt tried to say more, but he wasn't capable of it. He understood the position Lee had put him in. The two of them went back a good way. He made some meaningless sounds and then just sat there, sweating. He could not get all the way up and he was unable to lie back down.

Lee didn't help him any. A man had his pride.

Sometimes, the most you could do for a friend was nothing at all.

Lee eased himself up from the footstool. "They won't come back here, you know," he said. "I been wrong before, but not this time. They got what they came after. Things like Webster are over and done with. You'll never see 'em again, Old-Timer. Not here."

Cole Nesbitt somehow found the strength for one more word. It was "Bullshit!"

Lee was feeling the pressure of time now. A day or two probably wouldn't matter. But a man never knew. And he needed a release. He wanted to get out of this house and put it behind him.

But he could not leave without saying something. There was a very real chance that he would never see this good man again.

He stared at Cole Nesbitt, suspended between the bed and his boots, caught somewhere between life and death. He remembered a lot of things.

What Lee could not remember was the magic word he had never heard.

The word that would take away all the hurting. The word that would bridge the gap between one heart and another.

Lee finally said, "Don't drink no alkali water,"

Then he left Cole Nesbitt's room.

Lee had devoted a great deal of thought to the problem of a pack mule. He didn't even consider a packhorse, although he knew that Coffee intended to outfit himself that way. As Lee figured it, keeping an eye on one horse in Comanche country was trouble enough. Watching two horses was the next thing to impossible.

A mule was sort of in between. It was a target, no question about that. Comanches liked mules. But it was not as tempting a target as a good horse. A warrior would be laughed at if he offered a mule as a gift to his bride's parents.

A mule could carry many things that might prove

useful. But Lee did not trust mules. He had known skinners who handled them just fine, but he didn't have that knack. His mules had a way of making the wrong moves at critical times. Worse, they often would not move at all.

Lee decided to take just his own horse and what he could carry. He actually opened the big padlock on his trunk—he almost never did that—and took out a few items he might be able to use if it got down to bargaining. He also took a slicker and a fur robe and all the ammunition he had.

He had scouted the Comanche trail just far enough to prove what he had already guessed. There was only one Indian horse, and it was carrying double. Well, one and a half, anyway.

That really told him very little. He could not even rely on the direction the hoofprints indicated. Unless the Comanche was stupid beyond belief—and Lee doubted that very much indeed—he would not leave a plainly marked trail for long, and he would not hold his horse back much. Otis was not heavy enough to make much difference. If he did, he could simply be dragged at the end of a rope. That had a way of making a person trot right along.

There were tricks, many of them as old as raiding itself. Comanches could lose an entire herd of horses if they wanted to play games. If Lee just stuck to the trail, he could be certain that it would vanish at some point and he would be up a box canyon in the middle of nowhere. The thought amused him a little. There were few box canyons in this country. He could just head for one of them, on the Frio maybe, and spare himself some time.

No. All he had learned from his brief scout was what the unshod horse trail looked like. He would recognize that print if he ever saw it again.

Itching as he was for some action to make him feel better, he knew that was not the way to go. The trick was to find Otis—where he was, or at least where he was being taken. Almost the only way to do that was to nose around some Comanche camps, keep his eyes and his ears open, and ask questions when and if he could.

He might get lucky. He might not. But barring a miracle, it was the only chance Otis had.

Lee was not good at farewells. He had already proved that with Cole Nesbitt.

This was one of the worst. It was not just the shame that had come between him and Ruth Nesbitt. It was Lisa, who he might be putting in terrible danger.

And it was Coffee.

Coffee stood by Lisa as though the two of them were growing out of the same stalk. The damned Ranger was right there in the sitting room with Lee, and he still acted as though Lee did not exist. Lee felt invisible.

He did not make the mistake of underestimating Coffee. Sooner or later they would have to sort it out between them. Lee had learned the hard way not to take a man like Coffee lightly. It would not be easy, when they had it out. Lee was not at all certain who would win.

It wasn't that Coffee was a particularly big man. Sam Houston would have dwarfed him. So would Big Foot Wallace. Coffee was neither tall nor short, neither fat nor thin. His mustache was very ordinary, with the ends neatly clipped. There really wasn't much there to make a man—or a woman—take a second look at him.

There were his eyes, of course. They were a cool and metallic gray. If you needed someone to stare a dangerous man down, Coffee would fill the bill. There was a quick intelligence behind those gray eyes. It was a hidebound intelligence, and it had some holes in it, but it was there.

And there was his manner. No matter what you thought of him, it was undeniable that Coffee had a way about him. He was not quite himself here, because of Lee and because of Lisa, but Coffee normally had a nononsense air about him that inspired trust in most people. "I'll ride to hell if I have to," he seemed to be saying.

And he would. Lee did not doubt either his determination or his ability.

It was a damned shame, in some ways, that Coffee's blindness cut him off from Lee. The two of them might have made a pretty good team.

Well, that could never happen.

Not in this world.

And the devil take Coffee now.

They would be riding the same trail. They would not be together. They would meet when they met.

That was all.

Right now, this instant, Lee had to deal with that tiny tough hurt lady, Ruth Nesbitt.

Ruth was so appalled at her own behavior that she was uncertain how to act. She was a woman who was not easily thrown off stride. She had taken the worst that life could throw at her and had not lost her brass.

But she had failed her only living son. And she had used a poker against one of the few men she truly admired. She had beaten Lee as though . . .

She could not even think the words.

Lee!

Somehow, she had to make the move. It was putting too great a burden on Lee to make him start a good-bye that might well be final.

Lee was ready to do just that when Ruth Nesbitt took it out of his hands.

She stepped forward and hugged him. That made Lee nervous as all hell, but he endured it. He respected what she was trying to do.

She felt his strength. She allowed him to see her tears. This was a woman who did not cry from one year to the next, at least not where anyone could see her.

"Oh Lee," she said. "Please come back. Promise you'll come back. Come back with or without the boy. Come and stay with us again, just for as long as you've a mind to."

She understood. Lee realized that Ruth Nesbitt might believe that he was the one who knew things, but she could see a far piece down the road herself.

Clumsily, Lee patted Ruth Nesbitt on top of her head. Her blue-gray hair was surprisingly thin. She seemed so short, almost like a child. Lee did not know what to do. He certainly could not embrace her, even if that was what he wished to do. Not with Coffee standing in the room.

"I won't go up in smoke," Lee said. He kept his tone lighter than he felt. "After all, I'm leaving my trunk behind! Most of it, anyway." He stopped. This was leading nowhere. "Mrs. Nesbitt, I will try to bring your son back to you. When the time comes, I will say a proper goodbye."

Ruth Nesbitt backed off. She too was finding the words hard to come by.

"I have one favor to ask," Lee said.

"Just ask." Her voice was weaker than usual.

"You take Miss Lisa now," Lee said. "It makes no difference whether we think there is danger or not. You move her into the room with you and Mr. Cole, you hear?"

He thought of asking Coffee to side with him on this. It was clearly the right thing to do. But he could not bring himself to ask Coffee for anything.

Besides, Lisa Nesbitt was Coffee's girl. Leastways, that was what Coffee thought. That made things complicated. Coffee wouldn't accept any advice concerning Lisa Nesbitt from Lee. He'd shoot himself first.

Or Lee.

Or all of them.

That man's contempt and resentment could be sniffed from across the room.

Ruth Nesbitt solved that problem, as she had solved so many others. "Yes, Lee," she said. "Cole and I were going to keep her with us anyway, but thank you."

That seemed to be that.

Lee jammed his hat on his head, tipped the hat to Miss Lisa, and turned to go.

Lisa Nesbitt wasn't having any, Coffee or no Coffee. She was a Nesbitt too.

She ran to Lee, literally ran to him, and gave him a

quick butterfly kiss on his cheek. She smelled like flowers.

"Y'all come back now, you hear?" she said. "I'll pray for you, Lee. For you and Otis both."

Lee was startled. This had been a day of surprises. He had not known that Lisa Nesbitt felt that close to him. He was touched.

"Why, thank you, Miss Lisa," he said.

He was acutely aware that Coffee was about to foam at the mouth and throw a fit on the floor. His girl had actually kissed Lee. On the face!

The tension was so thick Lee was afraid it might bring the whole house crumbling down in ruins.

It was time to go. There had been enough talking. Too much, maybe.

He took care to get no closer to Coffee than he absolutely had to. Using a side door that was seldom opened, Lee left the Nesbitt house.

He had no idea whether he would ever see it again.

6

Owl, Summer

The boy was conscious.

He did not twist his head around to look back at Owl. He seemed to know very well what was riding behind him on that horse. He was not eager for his eyes to confirm what he knew.

He did not moan or cry out. All he did was shift his position a little, which was not easy to do with his ankles tied. He reached out one hand to steady himself by gripping Heart's mane.

Owl was satisfied with that. He was even pleased. He was fully prepared to deal with the boy sharply no matter what he did, but it was much simpler for him if the boy did not try something stupid.

It was more than convenience that Owl was thinking about. He did not want a stupid boy. He had all the experience he needed with stupid boys.

He also did not want a broken boy. However, it would be good for the boy to understand exactly how things were from the very beginning. Uncertainty could lead to fatal mistakes.

True understanding, as opposed to knowing what he could and could not do, might come later. It might not. In any case, that was not the problem now.

The boy was still in his nightshirt. He was barefoot. Owl knew that it was hurting his crotch to straddle the horse as he was. It was going to hurt a lot more as time went on. With the thongs binding his ankles, the boy had little choice about his position.

Good. Let him hurt. Owl had other matters that required his attention.

He had no plan of riding to one of his own camps. Later, perhaps, much later. Not for many suns and moons. Those camps were the first places they would look. The man called Lee would soon learn Owl's name. He would know where the camps were.

The truth was that Owl was not entirely certain where he was heading. That was fine. If he did not know, his pursuers could not know.

The thought came to him that he might ride north, even as far as the Shining Mountains. Maybe only to the Llano Estacado, where the Kwahadi band of The People lived. He had relatives there.

Then again, perhaps not north at all.

The important thing was that he had to keep moving. Moving on a horse was as natural to a Comanche as sitting in a house was to a *Taibo*. He would need some sort of a shelter when the north winds came, but a tipi was not rooted to one spot. It could be shifted around. There were ways of sending messages.

At this moment his job was to avoid close pursuit. It would not be good to be tracked and overtaken. He did not fear for himself, but he would certainly lose the boy, and what was the sense of that?

Virtually without thinking, Owl employed all the usual tricks. He rode in the river water, which was mostly very shallow. He came out on limestone ledges where there would be no clear prints. Without metal horseshoes, scratches would be few and far between. He switched directions, doubling back and going off at an angle. He turned up side streams if there was any water in them. He took care to leave no obvious sign. Once, when Heart dropped a couple of turds, Owl went back and scooped them up. He later hid them in a thick brush no horse could ride through.

When he finally got serious about choosing a direction and opening up distance, Owl halted Heart and dismounted. He seemed to ignore the boy, still tied to the horse. Out of the corner of his eye he could see that the boy was squirming some.

Owl smiled. Let him get really miserable.

Owl knew all about horseshoes, of course. He had stolen shod horses before. But he had no iron shoes. He had no way of nailing them to a hoof, even if he had them.

And they were the opposite of what he wanted.

He hoped that even Lee would not know about *his* horseshoes.

Owl had his own hoof boots. He had brought them along for precisely this situation. Ordinarily the hoof boots were for lame or tenderfooted horses. They were simply roughly shaped rawhide pouches that were soaked in water and tied over a hoof. He had four of them, and Heart was very patient.

The horse, he observed, was a good deal more patient than the silent swaying boy.

When Owl got the hoof boots on, the best tracker in the world could not have recognized Heart's print. A good tracker might guess what happened, but he could not be sure. And it would have to be a very lucky guess.

The boy reached a point where he could not contain himself. He was sore and chafed. The bruises on his face where Owl had hit him were swelling and showing an angry red.

None of that mattered.

What counted was that the boy had not urinated since Owl had grabbed him from his bed.

Owl was impressed. He was also amused.

The boy knew no Comanche. That did not keep him silent any longer. He was desperate.

The boy used English, and he used it fast. "Hey!" he

hollered. His voice had not yet deepened into that of a man, but it was not the bleat of a terrified child either. "Hey, mister! I gotta pee. Right now!"

Owl did not know the words. The meaning was abundantly clear, however.

Owl thought it over. He took his time. He was not ready for the boy to believe that he had any say whatsoever in what was going to happen to him. It suited Owl's purpose to let him hurt a little.

But there was a problem. If he did not untie him and allow him to dismount, the boy would piss on his horse.

Owl did not care for that idea.

Owl grunted. Deftly, he removed the short thong that looped under the horse and tied the boy's ankles.

Otis moved about as fast as a person could move. He was off the horse and into the bushes with the speed of a lightning strike. Owl did not try to stop him. He just listened to the splashing of the liquid, which was considerable. If the boy were foolish enough to run now, hurt and hungry and barefooted, he was too stupid to be of any use to Owl.

Owl could kill him and be done with it.

The boy emerged from the bushes without prompting. He stood there in the still Texas air, a skinny but defiant figure in his torn nightshirt. There was some blood running down the insides of his thighs. He did not cry. He did not shake with fear at the sight of the black-painted Owl. He looked like what he was: relieved.

Owl considered giving him a sip of water, maybe with some pemmican to chew.

No. That could wait.

Owl gestured toward Heart. The boy did not hesitate. He had some difficulty climbing on, and Owl could see clearly how raw his pale skin was. The bleeding was understandable. Owl deliberately delayed his own mounting of Heart.

Let the boy make a break now if he was fool enough to try it. He had the horse, and Owl was not in the saddle. Heart would not leave Owl in that situation, but the boy could not know that.

The boy tried nothing.

Owl grunted again. He needed to teach the boy to speak the tongue of The People, but that would take much time. It was best done when the captive was with the other boys of a camp, and that was impossible now.

Still, he could show him that cooperation was rewarded. That simplified matters. He could also show him that resistance brought swift retribution, just in case the boy did not understand that yet.

Owl did not retie the ankles. That allowed the boy to shift around some on Heart's back. If it didn't heal the crotch and thigh bruises, it would at least give him some new places to hurt.

Owl swung into the saddle behind the boy and touched Heart with his stiff-soled moccasin. The booted horse moved at a good pace. The rawhide on the hooves made a soft squishing sound. It was very different from the slight plopping and clicking noises that usually came from unshod horses.

Owl looked back. He was leaving almost no trail. The marks that did show were faint and irregular.

Owl was satisfied.

This was good.

This was very good.

This time, finally, he might win the greatest game of them all.

Owl's world was changing. There was a new urgency in his life. He understood some of it. He knew that time was no longer forever.

There was also a new uncertainty. For the first time in his life, Owl was unsure of the world around him. It seemed to be wavering beneath his feet.

He still felt and believed that this world was his. He was free to go wherever he wished, and The People had earned that freedom. They had outmaneuvered the French. They had driven lances of fear deep into Mexico.

They had nearly driven the Lipan Apache out of this place they called Texas. They had fought the Tonkawas and anybody else who got in their way.

The People were not to be taken lightly.

Treaties meant nothing to Owl. Lines marked on map papers were the same as lines scratched with a stick in the dirt. He was not connected to such things. It seemed to him that as long as he could find a horse to ride, the world was his. He could float across it like a cloud crossing the sky.

But there were facts he could not ignore.

It had not been yesterday, but it had also not been in the faraway time when The People had roamed San Antonio at will. Then, late one winter when the winds were blowing cold, twelve of the strongest Comanche leaders had met in conference with the *Taibo* Texans. This had been in San Antonio, which The People regarded as their town. The Comanches wanted to talk of peace. It was a hard thing when *everybody* was your enemy.

The People did not fear those Texans. They did not fear any men in this world, and few in the next. Nevertheless, they recognized that these *Taibo* Texans were different. They had come to stay.

The Texans had little interest in peace talk. They wanted to talk about white captives The People had. The Texans were crazy with the idea. They would not let go of it.

Owl had not been there, but he knew the story. It had been burned into him. The Texans had called in the Army, and all twelve of the Comanche leaders had been killed right there in the council room. Shot at a peace talk! In San Antonio, where they had feasted and plundered whenever they wished

A few seasons after that, when the Texans had left Austin for a time, the Comanches had moved some villages there. They had pitched their tipis right in the streets of an abandoned Austin. Owl remembered *that* vividly. He had been there.

In this day, such a thing would be unthinkable. A

tipi in Austin would not last as long as gunpowder in a fire. Things had changed that much.

And now, this very summer, there was something called a reservation for Indians on a part of the Brazos River near Camp Cooper. Who could imagine such a thing? He had heard that there were some Comanches there. They were *Penahneh*, from the Wasp band. Were they all sick in the head?

There were *Taibo* roads cutting through Comanchería. Owl crossed them frequently.

The uncertainty that he felt was not born of timidity or intimidation. It was simply that there were new ideas in Owl's world, ideas he had not encountered before. New ideas were always troublesome.

With all of his freedom, he was not sure where he could go with the boy. In his whole lifetime he had never had to think of such matters beyond the level of caution that his cousin, the coyote, might show.

On this day, at this time, where could he ride? What was left?

There was a small measure of safety in shifting villages of The People, of course. He had many relatives, to say nothing of wives who wanted him around occasionally. There were his girl-children, who could not understand his disappointment with them. Females were not the same as males, everyone knew that much, but they were *something*.

Just plain numbers would help somewhat. It was tougher to attack an entire village than a single warrior, no matter who the warrior was. It would also be easier to hide the boy if there were many tipis and many children.

But the one thing he dared not do was to ride into one of his own camps. His lodges were known. His name would become known to those who were certain to come after him. It might already be known.

In time, yes. He could return to his own lodges. But not yet. Not until there was some forgetting.

To have any hope of keeping the boy for what had to be done, Owl had to avoid the places where they might expect to find him. *All* of the places. In itself, that was no big thing. Owl came from a social world that moved all the time. A Comanche warrior could be at home wherever he was.

That did not solve the problem.

He could not sit in one spot, like some of the Pueblo Indians he had seen. He had to move. He had to keep moving.

Where?

The Kwahadis were far to the north, between Owl and the Shining Mountains. The Nokonis, the Wanderers, might be almost anywhere between the Pecos and the Canadian rivers. It was said of them that they always turned back before they got where they were going. They had turned camp-moving into a wild game. The advantage there was that Owl never associated with the Nokonis; he considered them to be careless and sloppy in their habits. But if he found them, what impression would they make on the boy? Were these The People Owl wanted him to know?

There were so many places that had once been his. It was not that he *owned* them; one could not own the earth. They had been his because he was free to go to them, and they were places where he felt a rightness. Now, he had to take care.

It was the same with other groups: Whether bands of The People, or camps of his friends the Kiowas, or settlements like old San Antonio where he could not be challenged. It was all different now. He could not be *sure*.

Comanches on a reservation! That might make sense for a Caddo or a Waco—who could say what such people might feel—but it was a sickness for a Comanche. A sickness and a death.

Owl remembered a place. It was the land of the Stone Walkers. It took him many days to think of it, during which he wandered as aimlessly as any Nokoni. The wandering was fine. If he himself did not know his direction, what could his pursuers know?

The Stone Walkers!

Owl felt a surge of hope.

Texas was a land marked by rivers, most of them flowing southeastward to the faraway sea. Owl knew this, as he knew many surprising things. His good horses (ah, Wise One, remember, remember!) had given him the ability to travel great distances.

There was a river called the Guadalupe, which rose from cold limestone springs in Comanchería. It was closer than the Nueces and it was in the high country out of the smothering heat. He would have much to show the boy there.

He knew a place quite near the headwaters of the Guadalupe. He had been there as a boy, and it was the kind of place a man never forgot. There were great tracks in the limestone of the riverbed. Beneath the clear, running water, when the light was right and there was just enough underwater vegetation but not too much, a man could see those tracks.

So could a boy.

Some of the tracks were round holes, like the butt end of a lodge pole might make if it could be driven into solid rock. Others were three-toed depressions, such as a leaf-scurrying lizard might make—if the lizard were bigger than a buffalo! If the lizard were bigger even than the dream-beast he sometimes saw when he touched the flint point in his medicine pouch!

Long ago he had played with the idea that the tracks had been left by a giant bird. Perhaps a Thunderbird. Perhaps even a Cannibal Owl . . .

With the tracks there were grooved lines in the stone, not quite straight, lines such as a huge snake might make if it did not have to twist its body to move.

Owl had no real understanding of those stone tracks. But he had paced them off and he had thought much about them. He knew tracks when he saw them, even if they were prodigious medicine tracks that printed in stone. He knew too what kind of sign a dragging tail would make, even if that tail was so big and heavy that he could hardly comprehend it.

A tail, yes, not a giant snake. Snakes did not move that way. Not in Owl's world.

The sweetwater springs from which the Guadalupe flowed were not a great distance from the settlement of Kerrville. Owl knew that there were Rangers in Kerrville.

Not a great distance, no.

But far enough.

"Come," he said to the boy. *"Keemah."* The boy knew few Comanche words as yet, but Owl talked to him constantly. Sometimes, rarely, he got a few words back. He knew now that the name of the boy was O-tis.

A new name might come, in time.

"Come, O-tis," he said again, as though the boy had some choice in the matter. "I will show you some things that most men see only in dreams."

The summer earth was more than hot. It was parched and beaten. Even the powerful rivers were sluggish and shrunken. As Owl crossed the south San Gabriel—no wider than his arm in some places—and then the Colorado and the Pedernales, the air grew less heavy. White puffs of clouds drifted through a pale blue sky. There was not a hint of moisture in those clouds.

The grasses, what were left of them, were straw-colored and lifeless. The flowers that were everywhere in spring had vanished many suns ago. Not even the husks remained. Owl could remember times in late summer when other flowers grew, small delicate flowers of white and purple. There were none of them here. There had not been enough rain to bring them up.

The broken country was not treeless, but even the stunted cedars with their blue juniper berries looked dry enough to splinter.

It was like riding through a desert. If Owl had not seen it so many times, he would not have believed that anything but rattlesnakes and prairie dogs could survive here. Owl knew better. The rains would come, and the cold, and then the rebirth of this world. But it would take half a year or more. He did not know whether or not he had that much time.

His years of experience helped him. There was food,

if a man knew where it was and how to get it. White-tailed deer were plentiful if you could spot them early in the morning or just after sunset. There were rabbits so big that they could be mistaken for long-eared deer. There were roots and berries and fat birds that roasted nicely on a pointed stick. Owl had shown O-tis how to get the feathers off by stone-boiling in a rawhide pouch. The boy was really getting quite good at it. Owl saved some of the turkey feathers.

They were not hungry. When there was no time to make a fire, warm salty blood from the veins of a deer or rabbit was sustaining. Owl sometimes took the trouble to make a sauce for the meat when he cooked it. He made the sauce of water, honey, and the tallow from around an animal's kidneys. The kidneys themselves, of course, were eaten raw.

Owl could not show it, but he desperately wanted O-tis to enjoy himself. Owl knew something about boys. Feed them enough and they might forgive a lot of things.

He could have used an iron cookpot, but the trade pots were too heavy to carry on one overloaded horse. He had to use the old ways. Perhaps that was best.

Owl's greatest fear was that his horse would fail or go lame and leave him on foot. He hated to walk, and it would be very dangerous with O-tis. He had removed the hide pouches over the hooves long ago, and Heart seemed as strong as his name.

Still, you could never tell about horses. It was a worry.

Owl's other great fear was for the boy. O-tis had skin that blistered and burned and peeled easily. No matter how much grease Owl smeared on it, the skin was blotched and there were tiny smears of blood where the skin cracked. The boy's hair attracted vermin. Owl braided it and dressed it with buffalo dung he had moistened in a spring. He showed O-tis his porcupine quill brush and instructed him in its use. Still, the bugs would not leave the boy alone.

It was not simple pity that gnawed at Owl. His fear was that if the boy sickened or died, it would mean that

O-tis was not fit to be a Comanche. A boy of The People could not be weak. If it was all not meant to be, that would be a terrible blow. Owl would not endure forever, and in the manner of his people, he did not wish to do so. It was not a good thing to be old. Old age was misery and uselessness. Who would desire such a thing? How much better it was to die in battle with your senses fresh and vigorous!

That did not mean that Owl was in a hurry to die. There was a rhythm to such things. The time was not now. The place was not here.

Owl had a mission to complete before he could meet death.

That was what the boy was all about.

Owl had many skills, but one of them was not making clothing. That was woman's work. It was with great reluctance that he tried to outfit O-tis. The boy could not know the pain it cost him.

He fashioned some crude moccasins out of chewed deerskin. He could not make a proper hard sole—he had no convenient buffalo hide, and not much inclination even if he had the difficult material—but he did manage to shape a moccasin that at least looked Comanche. It was a kind of boot, really, that reached to the boy's knobby knees. Owl wondered if all *Taibos* had soft feet that did not toughen up with use. Given his hatred for walking, Owl had some sympathy for that.

A plain breechclout was no problem, but Owl had very little experience with shirts. The boy's nightshirt was in tatters. Still, using it as a rough model and remembering what he could of buckskin shirts he had seen on Cheyenne friends, he concocted something that at least protected the skin. It was a shapeless garment tied together with thongs—Owl could not sew—but he was not ashamed of it.

For a man, the shirt was not too bad.

What the *tuinep*, boy, thought of all this was impossible to say. Looking at him with his bruised face and cracked bleeding skin, all dressed up in clothing any of Owl's wives would have laughed at, it was hard to imagine O-tis as a *tuivitsi,* a handsome young man with proper clothing, on a beautiful horse of his own.

But that was what had to be. In time, in time.

Owl had taught the boy just enough Comanche so they could communicate little, simple things.

Even had he wished to do so, the boy was still unable to ask the big question: Why? What was the reason for his strange captivity?

Would he ever see his home again? He must wonder about such things.

Perhaps, thought Owl, it was just as well that he could not ask.

Not yet.

By the time they reached the sparkling headwaters of the Guadalupe, the country had changed dramatically. The boy was a long way from the home he had known in Stafford.

For Owl, too, this was an alien if familiar land. This was not buffalo country at any season of the year.

There was no level ground here, and even the rolling terrain of the San Gabriel was gone. This was a broken land of cliffs and dry washes and sudden drop-offs. It was all made out of rock. The cliffs were not towering and the drop-offs were not deep; this was not the country of the Shining Mountains, where distances turned blue and hills touched the sky.

But it was different. The air was cooler, fresher. The air smelled pungently of cedar. The mesquites were few and far between, and the scrub oaks somehow thrived by thrusting their deep, tangled root systems through cracks in the rocks. The oaks were dropping green acorns. Whole handfuls of acorns fell whenever the breeze stirred. They made a pattering noise like hail when they struck the rocks.

There were many cat tracks. The big cats liked the high places. Owl avoided them when he could. The cats seldom attacked a man unless they had no alternative, but stranger things had happened.

Besides, cats were not good eating.

There were some dull, plodding armadillos dragging their pointed heads and makeshift armor on courses that generally led north. The animals, Owl knew, were much more common south of the Rio Bravo. Like the mesquite, for reasons Owl could not fathom, the armadillos were spreading northward. Things changed.

The deer were plentiful. They crunched up the acorns until their bellies bulged. Owl could eat acorns too, but they had to be shelled and boiled to get the bitterness out. It wasn't worth the effort, in his opinion, unless a man was starving.

The bucks had velvet on their horns. It seemed that every female had a fawn, frequently two of them. Owl had watched deer births; he knew that twins were not unusual. The fawns were not newborn, but they still had their spots. They were very easy to find. Owl only had to watch closely as Father Sun dipped below the horizon. That was when the does always nursed their fawns. Owl simply had to wait until the females left the fawns to forage for themselves, and that was it. The fawns would not move. They were very beautiful, he thought. A man could walk right up on one and kill it with his bare hands. The meat was sweet and tender.

Owl saw no real connection between the does raising their fawns and what he was trying to do with O-tis. Meat was meat. People were people. That was about all there was to it.

There were exceptions, of course. Coyotes were common here. They yipped back and forth in the rocks nearly all night. They seemed always to be laughing at something, particularly when Mother Moon was fat and yellow-orange and low in the sky. Coyotes were not like other animals. Everybody knew that. You could not trust a coyote. They were great ones for playing tricks on you. Some of the earliest stories Owl had heard had been about trickster coyotes. They were true stories. Nothing so delighted a coyote as helping a man make a fool of himself.

There were buzzards soaring on the updrafts. There

were eagles too. Owl thought it a strange thing that it
was hard to tell them apart when they were far enough
away.

The clouds that scudded through the pale blue sky
had billows of darkness running through them like swollen veins. There was moisture in those clouds. The air
was no longer completely still.

It was not a true wind that was blowing, but there
was a stirring around, a getting-ready. It was like a great
cat that had gone into a crouch.

The world did not turn over quickly, but it turned.

Owl was disappointed that the tracks in the limestone riverbed were not clear. He wanted to astonish
Otis with a sudden and dramatic gesture.

It was not going to be that way.

Owl had to wade out into the sparkling water and
try to scoop out the mossy vegetation with his hands.
The water was just deep enough so that he felt a current
around his knees. It was not hard work, but it was a nuisance.

He did not know why it was important for the boy
to see these things. It just was.

The boy watched him without seeming to look.
Quite possibly, he figured that all Indians were crazy.

Or maybe just this one.

Owl saw some fish darting as he tore at the water
plants. He gave little attention to them. Fish were of no
use unless a man was starving. Owl would catch and eat
them only in desperation. He would plaster mud or clay
all over them, encasing them, and then pile red-hot coals
on top of them. The meat was soft and full of tricky little
bones. It was not good food for a warrior.

The boy had healed some. He seemed stronger. After a while he began to amuse himself by wading the
shoreline, turning over flat rocks and catching crawdads.
The crawdads would wave their pincers frantically and
try to scuttle backward. Owl didn't rate them very highly
either. The boy was interested, though, and he caught a
lot of them. He did not try to borrow Owl's knife. He
knew better than that. He found himself a sharp-edged

flake of glistening gray flint and neatly chopped off the segmented tails of the crawdads. He did not bother to kill the wounded crawdads. He just pitched them back in the stream.

It seemed wasteful to Owl, but he gave no sign. If you were going to catch crawdads, why not cook them whole? Or eat them raw?

However, Owl was pleased to see the boy making a cutting tool out of flint. That was very good. That was a very old Comanche way.

Owl said nothing to O-tis. The boy said nothing to Owl. The boy was unlike a boy in some ways. He never smiled. He was not sullen. Just solemn. He needed a scorpion up his butt.

Man and boy, they were living in two separate universes. They did not touch. Owl pulled soggy weeds out of depressions in the river bottom. The boy caught crawdads and chopped off their tails.

High overhead, above the buzzards and the eagles, Father Sun climbed up one side of the sky and then down the other.

The cat-tensed air chilled just a little, and the dark shadows came.

A hunter always knows when he is being hunted. It is an awareness that is simply a part of him, like his blood or his eyes.

Owl did not have a feeling of the closeness of enemies. He realized that they were looking for the boy, of course, but that was nothing to him. Every other man's gun was itching to get a Comanche in its sights. He was used to that.

For now, he could forget it.

When he had done all he could do to clarify the track outlines in the bottom of the river, Owl turned to the intent, unsmiling boy.

"Come," he said.

It was possible that O-tis was enjoying his crawdad catching. Certainly he was doing it with more energy and enthusiasm than he had shown in many days. However, he obediently came at Owl's command.

Owl could not tell whether the boy was interested, afraid, or just trying to make the best of a bad situation.

Owl pointed to the tracks.

"Stone Walker," he said. He knew that O-tis would not understand the words. They had not made that much progress. Still, it seemed necessary to say the name.

It was plain that the boy did not comprehend. He looked obligingly at the cuts in the river bottom, but they had no effect on him. They were just big scratches in the rock.

Owl could not let it stop there. It was vital to him that the boy grasp the meaning of the stone tracks. He could not have explained why this was so, even to himself. It simply *was*.

In the web of the world, it was all bound up with the immensity of time and Owl's place within it. It had something to do with change and a lot to do with tradition. It was involved with what the boy might one day become.

Look at me! Owl was trying to say. *Open your eyes! See me! I am not just a savage. There are wonders in my world!*

Owl needed help. He touched the grooved flint medicine in his deerskin pouch. He did not remove it and hold it in his hand.

He only felt the hard outline. That was enough.

Owl sensed it instantly in the cooling shadows. He saw it. He smelled it.

The Spirit Creature was immensely strong here. It belonged. It was right *there*, against the rock wall, in the brush on the far side of the river. Owl could hear it breathing.

The great curving ivory tusks caught the rays of the westering sun. The sharp points of the tusks twisted inward, so that the points almost came together. Owl wondered about that. However the beast used its tusks, it could not impale with them.

The snakelike trunk was segmented like a caterpillar. It was a gray-brown color and it had bristle hairs in it. Perhaps it used that to destroy its enemies. Or maybe it was the teeth. They were in the great jaws under the trunk. There were rows of them and they were ridged with cusps. Crushing teeth, not piercing teeth.

There was no hair on the ears. They were big ears, but small for the size of the animal. It was the same with the eyes above the trunk. They were old eyes, sad eyes. They had seen much. There was a distinct bulge, a dome, on the top of the skull. That was odd, thought Owl. It was as though a gigantic mosquito had bitten the animal and the head had swollen.

The patches of reddish-brown hair on that huge gray hide were swarming with insects of some kind. They looked almost like maggots. Swallows swarmed on the hide, feeding. The Spirit Creature made no effort to dislodge the birds. Welcomed them, probably.

Quite suddenly the trunk lifted. Saliva dripped out of the mouth like a small river. The beast trumpeted. It was a scream as loud as the world. It shook the rock hills. Even the echoes were deafening. Owl feared that there might be a rock slide. . . .

If the boy heard or saw anything, he gave no sign of it. He just stood where he was, not impatiently, waiting for Owl to do something.

Owl was disappointed but he was not surprised. There had been many other times when the Spirit Creature had come and only he could see him.

Still, it hurt. If O-tis could only see what he saw . . .

Well, he couldn't. That was the way it was.

Owl removed his hand from the deerskin medicine bag.

The Dream Beast disappeared. Instantly. Just like that.

Owl could still smell him. He knew that he could cross the river and find the pools of saliva.

The swallows were still darting. They seemed confused. They dispersed, looking for new insects.

Owl was shaken. He had lived with this *puha*, power, for a very long time. He had even listened to that

Beast of Dreams on his spirit quest when he had become a man. Oh, it could talk when the mood was upon it. Just the same, he was not used to it. It was not the kind of thing you *ever* grew accustomed to. It touched his world but was not in it. When it was gone, wherever it went, it left a hole in the universe as big as the biggest cave there ever was.

One day something would come to fill that hole. Owl could not imagine what that thing might be.

Owl pulled himself together. There was still much to be done. If the boy could not see or grasp all of it, then he must be shown the part of it that could get through to him.

Owl dropped to all fours, like an animal. The boy was visibly startled. *That* got his attention. Owl's face was actually in the cold spring-fed water of the river. He bent back his thumb and little finger.

Extending his other three fingers as far as he could, Owl crawled down the bed of the river. He tried to place his fingers in the three-toed tracks. It was very hard. He kept swallowing water and could not cover the distance between tracks with a single forward movement of his arms. He had to lurch and waddle from one depression to the next, like a sick turtle. When he was able to get his fingers into the grooves, the tracks dwarfed his fingers.

He felt more than a little foolish. He was pleased that his wives could not see him now.

The boy watched in utter astonishment. At least, Owl thought, he had *some* expression on his face. That was an improvement over blankness.

As Father Sun drifted down and the light became uncertain, Owl forced himself to go through the rest of it. He stood up, spat river water out of his mouth, and grabbed a thick cypress limb that had a fairly round end. Daring the boy to laugh, he hopped and splashed from one postlike depression to another. As he reached each hole, he rammed the cypress end into it.

Determined to get the whole thing over with, he dropped the cypress limb and broke off a long and reasonably straight willow branch. He clamped it to the back of his breechclout with one hand. Keeping a perfectly straight face, he proceeded to splash again through the river, this time dragging the willow pole. It went right through the narrow tail cut dredged out of the limestone bottom of the river.

It was quite a performance. Owl was breathing hard. He was soaking wet. He stared at the boy. Had he understood anything? "Stone Walker," Owl panted. "Stone Walker!"

The boy was not laughing. That was good. This was one occasion where Owl was not seeking amusement. The boy's expression was serious. He realized that Owl was trying to tell him something that was important. He was doing his best to grasp it. His blue eyes reflected a struggle with ideas never before encountered.

Owl waited. He did not know what kind of reaction he expected. He did not know what kind of response there could be.

Something.

Anything.

The Dream Beast was a private thing for Owl. He realized that it was connected in some way to the medicine flint that had killed the Cannibal Owl in the long-ago time. It was not surprising that others could not see it.

The Stone Walker was different. There it all was, right in front of their eyes. There was the river. There was the rock over which the river flowed. There were the tracks.

Of course, anyone with half a mind could see that the Stone Walker was not a part of *this* world. It did not belong to the world in which Owl and the boy lived. Animals that were not of the Spirit World, no matter how heavy they were, did not leave trails in solid rock. And anyone should be able to see that there were two kinds of Stone Walkers. Two different racks, two different animals. That was the way of it, even in the Spirit World.

Stone Walkers were not private things. O-tis ought to be able to see something. If he saw nothing at all, just some holes in the rock, he would never be capable of learning all that he had to learn. He would forever be what he now was: a *Taibo*, caught in a half-world where dreams meant only that you were asleep.

That was not the way to become a Comanche.

The boy surprised Owl.

O-tis did not attempt to tell him what he had figured out. He did not have the words. Instead he acted.

The boy scooped water out of the river with his cupped hands. He kept at it until the sand and gravel of the riverbank was thoroughly wet. Father Sun was gone now, below the horizon in the land of the dead. The sand and gravel would not dry quickly.

The boy did what Owl had done, except that he made his own tracks. He dropped down and crawled in the soaked sand-gravel of the shore. He made a three-toed track with three fingers. He made an indistinct postlike print with his fist. He drew a moist line with one finger and pointed to the back of his crude breechclout.

Then he gestured toward the Guadalupe River, where Owl had cleared the underwater tracks.

"Stone Walker," O-tis said carefully. He did not get all the sounds right, but Owl understood him.

Owl whooped with joy. He had never made such a sound in the presence of O-tis. He was immensely pleased with himself, and pleased with the boy.

O-tis had gotten the significance of the tracks! He was quick, this one. He could learn. It was all going to work out! This time the quest would not end in failure.

The boy reacted to Owl's hopping and yelling with a look that was unfathomable. It might possibly have been satisfaction. He was certainly aware that he had done something correctly. At the very least he had avoided a beating.

O-tis did not smile.

The boy turned and went to gather his crayfish tails. He was washing them off in the river when the abrupt awareness of a storm came over the man and the boy at the same instant.

The clouds had been thickening all day. A part of Owl had been aware of it, but he had been too distracted to pay close attention. The air had alternately been very still and stirring in swirls. It was not cold, far from it, but some of the heat was gone.

When the rain does not come for many days, or even for an entire season, a man is never ready for it. It sneaks up on him. It is a trick that Old Man Coyote plays when he is feeling particularly clever.

Owl did not like rain. He was no farmer. There was no rain in the Comanche afterlife. The weather was always fair and clear. Raiding weather.

But rain was not the bad thing. What Owl hated was the thunder and lightning that often came with the rain. Thunder and lightning came from the Thunderbird, of course, but that did not ease Owl's mind. One of the strongest of all Comanche oaths dealt with storms: "May the first lightning and thunder of the spring take my life if what I say is not the truth!" A storm blocked out Father Sun. It was bad medicine, day or night.

Just the same, a storm was coming.

With the awareness, the first fat drops of rain began to fall. They were widely spaced. Surprisingly, they were colder than the river water.

Not far away, too close, the sullen, dark sky flashed with lightning. The thunder growled and grumbled. The lightning did not hiss down in flaming arrow shafts yet. The thunder did not crack and split as it did when the shock of it was enough to knock a warrior from his horse.

But it was coming toward them.

Owl ceased his prancing around. This was serious. He shouted to the boy and ran for his horse. He could still see; it was not full dark, and he was grateful for that.

Heart was snorting nervously. He too did not like storms.

Owl threw on his saddle and tightened it up. He stepped into the willow wood stirrup, swung into the saddle, and grabbed the hair bridle. He reached down his hand to assist O-tis. The boy mounted gracefully, still clutching his wad of crayfish tails.

Again Owl felt a surge of definite satisfaction. The two of them were working together fairly well at last.

Owl got Heart out of there. Only a fool would taunt
the lightning by sticking up on a horse near water.

With a smack like a beaver's tail, the storm struck.

The wind came slamming in with the slanting walls
of rain. This was no maybe-it-is-and-maybe-it-isn't
breeze. This was a wind that cracked twisted old cypress
limbs like twigs. This was a wind that roared. This was
a wind that ripped at Owl, almost knocking him from
the saddle.

He needed shelter. He needed it fast.

Owl clutched the boy, seated in front of him on
Heart. He was not using the boy as a shield. He was trying to hold him on the horse.

The rain pelted him. It was as though the Creator
Giant had upended the river and sent it shouting down
the sky through an icy tunnel.

Lightning bolts sizzled the rocks, and the sharp
cracks of thunder all ran together into a single blasting
drumbeat.

The storm was so bad that it was almost comical.
There seemed to be no way through it. Owl felt like an
infant released from its cradleboard and thrust into
quicksand.

He was dazed. He had to make an effort to remember where he was going. Or where he was trying to go.

There was a rock shelter in the cliffs. He had played
in it as a boy. It was big enough for the two of them. It
faced south, away from the wind. There wasn't much of
an overhang, but there was enough to give Heart some
protection.

The problem was locating the rock shelter.

Owl just held on and yelled encouragement to his
horse. He could give little guidance. He had no real control in this chaos of wind and driving rain and flashing
lightning. There were times when a man just had to trust
to his horse.

If they got there, it would be Heart's doing.

If they could just hold on . . .

They never made it.

With a suddenness that took his breath away, the

storm passed on over them and was gone. It just stopped. It had been thick and intense, but it was narrow. It was not a storm of fall or winter that howled for days on end.

Already Owl could see silver stars camping in the sky. They looked fresh and clear. It was almost as though he could reach up and touch them. The wind died to a cool whisper of air that began to dry his wetness. It seemed to Owl that he had spent much time in the water this day.

The storm turned into a distant rumble, fading away toward the south. Owl could hear the frogs starting to call. They were beyond number. It was always that way after a heavy rain. It was as if they had fallen from the sky.

"Ai-eee!" Owl shouted in sheer exuberance. "We are through it! We were meant to be!"

The boy was hunched down in front of him, wet and cold and probably miserable.

Owl could not help himself. He was overcome with happiness, with joy. Good feelings poured through him like honey. There could be no two ways about it. He had been given a sign! Success was in his grasp!

He desperately wanted O-tis to share his pleasure. That was what it was all about. He understood that it took time for a boy to get over losing his home and family. But there were other homes, other families! Could not the boy realize how young he was, how many wondrous things were ahead of him?

Were they not good together, father and son?

Could not the boy respond, just a little?

Owl was proud of the boy. He had done well. He had promise.

Half as a joke, half as a tribute, Owl slipped out one of the fine turkey feathers he had saved. It was dry and sleek to touch. A good feather, an honorable feather.

Comanches did not value feathers in their hair, even eagle feathers, the way some Indians did. But they liked them, and sometimes they used them as a fancy decoration.

Owl could remember a time or two in his own life when feathers had done the trick for him.

Tuivitsi, a handsome young man all dressed up on a good horse.

Yes, that was the thing!

Carefully but firmly, Owl reached forward and fastened the turkey feather in the back of the boy's hair. That sandy hair was wet now, but the grease held it in place. It had grown. It was plenty long enough to tie in a feather.

For what seemed a very long time, O-tis did not move. He sat absolutely still. It was as though he were frozen.

Then he reached slowly back with one hand and touched the feather. He could not see it. He had to feel it to be certain of what it was.

Owl smiled expectantly.

The boy took his hand away. His body was completely rigid. He did nothing at all for an eternity. He seemed not even to breathe.

Mother Moon cast a silver glow through the thinning clouds. She might have been watching.

There was no warning. There was not so much as a hint, not even a tightening of muscles.

Suddenly the boy twisted around on Heart. Abruptly he was face-to-face with Owl. His expression was beyond loathing. With a violent wrench he reached up and tore the turkey feather from his hair.

The boy said nothing. He simply spat in Owl's face.

O-tis had not been entirely idle. He had been chewing the raw crayfish tails.

Owl was struck by a considerable wad of spit, mucous, and slimy fish-smelling shreds.

Owl reacted instantaneously. He did not think. There was no need to think. His action was as instinctive as if he had looked down and spotted a scorpion crawling into his breechclout.

Owl seized the boy from behind. He lifted him up as though O-tis weighed nothing at all. He hurled him from his horse to the ground.

Owl was a powerful man. He threw the boy as hard as he could. There was no anger, no rage, no disappointment.

Nothing.

Emptiness.

He just threw him. Hard. Too hard.

He heard the liquid plopping noise when the boy's head struck rock. It was exactly the same sound a squash made if you slammed it down on a boulder.

Owl sat trembling on Heart, stunned.

He was certain that he had killed the boy.

Owl was shocked to the depths of his being. The enormity and the madness of what had happened overwhelmed him.

It all had to be some kind of deception, he thought. Some feverish dream that had been brought on by the violence of the storm.

A son did not spit on his father!

A father did not kill his son!

The two acts of insanity were about equal in Owl's eyes.

He did not know what to do. He did not even know whether he could stop shaking long enough to do anything. A part of him had stopped. A part of him had ended.

He could see the crumpled body in the moonlight. He could see blood on the deerskin shirt he had made for the boy. In the light of Mother Moon, the blood was black.

O-tis was curled up on his side. His neck was twisted so that the face was looking up. If he had opened his eyes, he would have stared straight at Owl.

He could not open those eyes, of course.

O-tis lay there in a motionless heap. He was very small. He was very thin.

And still, so still.

Heart snorted and blew. A death one way or another was not a big thing in his world. *Get on with it,* he seemed to be saying. *Do whatever it is you are going to do, and let's go!*

The silver-splashed, rain-washed night closed in around Owl. He was dazed. It was difficult for him to catch his breath.

He sat there until he had his body under control. It was wrong for a warrior to shake like a leaf in the wind.

He thought that there was nothing to prevent him from just riding on as though nothing had happened. He could sense some of Heart's feelings. What was one more abandoned body in this land of harshness and death?

Owl found that he could not do it. He did not reason it all out. He did not ask questions that had no answers.

One conviction filled him. One thought put something back in the emptiness. He did not want that boy to be dead.

Owl swung out of the saddle. He knelt down before the boy. A terrible sadness burned within him. He recognized that sadness, knew it of old. It had been exactly the same with the death of Wise One.

There was a hole in the world. It was as deep as forever.

Very slowly, as though touching a red-hot coal, Owl reached out for the boy's head. He felt a sticky yielding, a mushiness where hard bone should have been.

He was careful not to roll the body over. That was sometimes a big mistake. Instead he slipped his tough square hand inside the damp buckskin shirt. He thought he felt something moving in the ooze. Owl maneuvered himself around until he got his ear directly against the boy's skinny chest.

Yes. There was a heartbeat. It was weak and irregular, but it was there.

That was enough.

Whatever Owl's plans had been, they were useless to him now. His world had turned over.

All the possibilities were reduced to one. He had to get the boy to Spirit Shadow, the medicine woman. The

Grandmother, *Kaku,* would know what to do. She was the only one.

That meant going back the way they had come, back toward Stafford and the San Gabriel. That meant riding into certain discovery.

That meant keeping the boy alive until he reached Spirit Shadow. How could he do that?

That meant going as fast as he possibly could without jarring the boy. And that meant leaving a fat and easy trail as plain as the prints of a Stone Walker.

Well, so be it. It was only failure that Owl feared. He could handle anything else.

Very gently, Owl lifted the boy from the ground. With the boy in his arms, he eased himself back into the saddle. That was nothing. As a boy, he had played the game of mounting a horse without using his hands. Owl cradled O-tis against his chest, trying to give him some warmth from his own body.

The whisper of the wind was cold. The world was pure silver.

Owl nudged Heart with his still-wet moccasin. The gelding responded with an air somewhere between resignation and enthusiasm. Heart understood what he was supposed to do. He headed north, back along his own trail. He picked his way with care, but he set a rapid pace.

Up in the rock cliffs that gleamed in the moon glow, Owl heard the yelping barks that danced from one ridge to another.

Owl could not smile. He did not have it in him. But he was grateful for that familiar yipping that assured him that this place had some connection with the world he had known.

Yes, yes. He welcomed the company.

He recognized what could only be the mocking laughter of Old Man Coyote.

For once in his life he was glad to hear it.

Part Two

THE MEN

7

Coffee, Late Summer

Coffee was both very good and very lucky. He knew all the tricks. He had seen them before, one place or another.

As far as he was concerned, it was basically just a matter of figuring out which tricks the Comanche would try, and when. It never crossed his mind that he was doing anything out of the ordinary.

Determining where the Indian's horse had entered and left the river water of the San Gabriel was not child's play. It was also not impossible. What it took mainly was experience, patience, and time. If he missed one faint set of tracks, he could always cast about until he found others. He understood what the Comanche was trying to do.

Where he got lucky was in the fact that it did not rain. Rain would have washed out the trail. Then again, rain in Texas at this time of the year was hardly an everyday occurrence.

Coffee located the place where Owl had dismounted and shod his horse's hooves with rawhide boots. He could read that sign like a book—better, in fact. He even found several of Otis's bare footprints. Coffee did not jump up and down and crow with triumph. He wasn't that kind of man.

He did permit himself a slight satisfied smile. He tugged on his earlobe just a little.

He did not make the mistake of thinking the game was over. He knew it was only beginning. But it was a start.

Coffee picked up the trail of the booted horse. It was difficult, and it was slow. What made it ultimately hopeless was that the Indian himself apparently did not know where he was going. The tracks wandered this way and that, heading nowhere in particular.

Coffee stuck it out until it was obvious that he had reached the hind end of a box canyon. He might indeed follow those smudged tracks to the end of the trail, if there was one, but it would serve no purpose. This kind of reading sign was slow, slow work. He could never catch up with Otis. Unless he could guess where the Comanche was going, he had no chance at all. The only way he could make such a guess was to have some sense of the trend of the tracks, no matter how disguised that trend was.

There was absolutely no way of telling how long the Comanche might wander without a clear direction. It might go on all winter, for all Coffee knew.

That would not get the job done, no matter how expertly Coffee did his tracking.

There had to be another way.

And he had to find it.

Soon.

It was said of some men that they did not give up easily. There were even those who said that about Coffee. They did not know him very well.

The truth was that Noah Coffee did not give up, period.

He might seem to abandon a task he had set for

himself. He might appear to forget what he had promised to do.

But Coffee always came back.

If you were on the run, and you had to have a man on your tail, you would not choose Coffee.

This did not mean that Noah Coffee was perfect at what he did. It did not mean that he never got tired or discouraged or confused. Right here and now, he was all three. It took all the determination he had to keep on going.

It was his own image of himself that sustained him in difficult times, and he was perfectly well aware that by no means did everybody everywhere love and admire the Texas Rangers. That was a stall crammed with horseshit. The United States regulars, if you could ever find them, regarded the Rangers as a bunch of undisciplined frontier ruffians. The Indians might not hate the quiet warriors who took so many lives so efficiently, but they certainly did not worship them as gods on earth. The Mexican people, in particular, reserved an especially venomous section of Hell for the Texas Rangers. Partly, Coffee knew, this was an accident of history. Texas and Mexico had been fighting each other forever, it sometimes seemed, and the fighting had often been ugly. Mexicans figured Texas belonged to them—even now, when the Republic was finished and Texas was a part of the United States. Even Coffee had trouble thinking of Texas that way. The Mexicans did not like the fact that, where Mexicans were concerned, the Rangers were fond of shooting first and asking questions later.

Much later.

Mostly, maybe, it was that the Mexicans were a proud people. In the Rangers, they had collided with a group of men so arrogant that they could pretend to be modest. Rangers were not loud, boastful blowhards. They just knew they were better than anybody else and were prepared to prove it with very little prompting. They did what they had to do quietly, and then they rode on without a backward glance.

That was hard to take if you were a Mexican. Mexicans set a high value on honor, and it was not a small thing to see that honor stained.

Coffee knew all this as surely as he knew his horse or his Walker Colt. He was not an educated man in any conventional sense, and he had more than his share of blind spots, but Coffee had not been absent when the brains were passed around.

He was not given to speaking of such things. But the way Coffee saw it, he judged every man on his own merits. He would never shoot a man in the back, given any choice at all. He would not shoot an unarmed man unless the circumstances absolutely forced him to do so.

No woman ever had a reason to fear Coffee.

No child need ever run from him.

Was that not worth something? To Coffee, the question was not even worth asking.

He did not have the kind of skeptical intelligence that caused him to doubt that his people had God on their side.

Coffee knew that their detractors—even in Texas— referred to the Rangers as spies on horseback. That suited him fine. He was well aware that the best chance he had of getting Otis back alive was information. He needed exactly the kind of information that mounted spies might bring to him.

Somewhere, sometime, someone would spot Otis and his captor. They would not vanish from the earth.

But he could not afford to just sit back and wait. He had to force the issue. He had to make the play.

Give the Comanches enough time with Otis, and there would be no Otis to rescue. A boy, maybe. Perhaps even a physically healthy boy.

But not Otis.

Bone weary as he was, Coffee kept going.

At night, his head resting on his saddle, he never once dreamed of the object of his search. He dreamed only of Lisa. Sometimes she was with her father, a skeleton of a man with pale silver hair and empty blue eyes.

Coffee was the first to admit that he could use a little luck.

Wilbarger luck.

It was not just the Indians who learned from dreams.

As Coffee pushed Pear and his increasingly skittish packhorse from one miserable Indian encampment to another, he reflected on the fact that he had it a lot easier than the men who had preceded him. Compared to what they had been through, Coffee had it soft.

The story of Josiah Wilbarger had happened nearly a quarter of a century ago—1833—and it was as alive as though it had occurred yesterday. It was as familiar to Texans as the fall of the Alamo, which happened four years later.

Coffee found it fitting that Wilbarger had met his fate at just about this time of the year, the month of August.

Dreams?

Josiah Wilbarger could tell you about dreams.

Coffee had no reason to question the story. He himself knew both friends and kin of Josiah Wilbarger. He had ridden Pear under the limbs of the very tree that had sheltered Wilbarger.

After all, the whole thing had taken place within ten miles of where the town of Austin now stood.

In those rough days there were few settlers outside of Stephen F. Austin's original colony. One of them, of course, was Reuben Hornsby, down the Colorado from Austin. Another was Josiah Wilbarger, who had come to Texas from Missouri in 1828. He built himself a place where the village of Bastrop is situated today. Until Hornsby arrived, Wilbarger's closest neighbor was twenty-five miles away. Even to Coffee's way of thinking, that was bordering on lonesome.

Back then it was not unusual for established families to take in young unmarried men for protection. They still did, as a matter of fact. There was some safety in numbers.

In August of 1833, Wilbarger was visiting Hornsby in that famous Hornsby house that dominated a startling three-mile-wide valley, stirrup-deep in wild rye. Staying with Hornsby were two young men, Standifer and Haynie, and one married couple named Christian.

Standifer and Haynie were looking for a place to settle. All the men except Reuben Hornsby rode out on a scout.

When they reached Walnut Creek, just a few miles from where Austin was now, they spotted a single Comanche warrior. The Texans called out to the Indian, intending to have a peaceful little talk. Or so the story went. Coffee had to grin a broad grin at that one.

The Comanche, not being a total idiot, took off like a bolt of lightning had struck his horse. The Texans could not catch him. Eventually they stopped for lunch. Wilbarger actually unsaddled his horse and turned him loose to graze. The idea made Coffee frown. Folks certainly took long chances in those days.

With the abruptness that was common to Indian attacks, the country erupted with Comanches before the men had finished their lunch. Somehow, one Comanche had turned into fifty. Coffee nodded. He had seen that happen too.

The Texans had made a large, fatal mistake. Its name was carelessness.

Christian was hit by a musket ball that broke his hip. Another shot smashed Christian's powder horn. Wilbarger got his gun primed, but before he could fire, he took an arrow in one leg. Almost before he realized what was happening, Wilbarger felt a second arrow ripping through his other leg.

Standifer and Haynie jumped on their saddled horses. Wilbarger tried to run after them, but it was hopeless. His legs wouldn't work and a musket ball caught him in the back of his neck and came out under his chin. Wilbarger went down. He looked dead and, for a fact, he could not move or speak. But he remained fully conscious, to his immense regret.

Christian got his throat cut. One more widow for Texas.

Haynie and Standifer hightailed it for Hornsby's Bend. They later said that they believed that both Christian and Wilbarger were dead. Quite possibly they did think so.

But Wilbarger was not dead. He just wished he was.

Paralyzed, he knew precisely what was going on when the Indians stripped him buck naked except for one sock. Figuring his neck was broken, they scalped him while he was still alive. They took their time about it. Then they left him for dead.

Wilbarger thought about a few things and then, mercifully, passed out. He was unconscious throughout the night. When he came to, he was naked, alone, and bleeding crimson soup from a jagged hole in the top of his head. Wilbarger took the one sock—all he had—and stuck it on his exposed skull. He was trying to stop the flow of thick blood.

He barely knew his own name. He was one sick man. He was hot and he was thirsty. Desperately thirsty. Fever burned through him.

Wilbarger commenced dragging himself on his elbows. He did not have the use of either leg, even when he broke off the arrow shafts.

Coffee shook his head in wonderment. By God, they made men tougher in those days!

Wilbarger snaked along about six hundred yards—Coffee had paced off the distance, as had many others—when he collapsed in the shade of a friendly oak tree. The maggots were working now. Wilbarger did not think his chances looked bright.

That was when the first of two dream miracles occurred.

Wilbarger told the story many times, and always with absolute conviction. As he stared an ugly death straight in the eye, beneath the oak branches with the green acorns starting to fall, he saw his sister standing before him.

Her name was Margaret Clifton.

Wilbarger knew that he could not be seeing his sister in the flesh. Margaret Clifton lived far away, in Florisant, Missouri. Half dead as he was, he nevertheless realized that he was looking at an apparition, a spirit of some sort.

What he did not know, and had no way of knowing, was that Margaret Clifton had died yesterday in Missouri.

Margaret Clifton spoke. Her voice was clear and steady. She said to him, "My brother, hear my words. Do not try to move farther. You are too weak. Stay where you are and I will get help. Friends will come here to assist you before sunset."

Although he begged her to stay with him, his sister-spirit said nothing else. She silently turned and walked away in the direction of Reuben Hornsby's house.

The night of the Indian attack, after Haynie and Standifer had made it to Hornsby's Bend with the tale of the deaths of their two companions, Mrs. Hornsby suddenly sat bolt upright in bed. She awakened her husband. She told Reuben that she had just had the strangest dream of her life. In her dream, Wilbarger was alive. He was naked, wounded, and scalped. He was lying under an oak tree.

Mrs. Hornsby was a strong no-nonsense lady. She was hardly the type who swooned and saw phantoms down in the old corral. She took no guff from her husband or anybody else. If she had seen Wilbarger, dream or no dream, then Wilbarger was there.

She woke everybody up, even the distraught Mrs. Christian. She went to work doing the sensible thing: she fixed breakfast. By daylight she had the coffee boiling and stacks of griddle cakes and sausages ready.

Reuben Hornsby was not stupid enough to argue with his wife. He got a relief party together to go to Wilbarger's aid. There was a total of six men close enough to be reached. Not a one of them believed that

Wilbarger could be alive. They all figured that they would have an Indian fight on their hands.

Late that afternoon they found Josiah Wilbarger. He was sprawled among the partially exposed roots of a live oak tree. At first they mistook the bloody, naked figure for an Indian. They were set to open fire.

God knew how he did it—Wilbarger certainly could never explain it—but he managed to sit up. He waved a torn and stained arm.

"Boys," he said in the firmest voice he could muster, "it is Wilbarger. Don't shoot."

Then he passed out.

The men wrapped Josiah Wilbarger in a sheet. They got him up on Hornsby's horse, and Hornsby rode behind him, holding him in the saddle.

When they got to Hornsby's Bend, Mrs. Hornsby dressed his shredded skull in bear's oil. After Wilbarger had rested up a few weeks, he was taken by sled back to his own cabin. The jolting of a wagon was too much for him. The sled was smoother, even without snow.

Josiah Wilbarger lived for eleven years. His scalp never grew back to cover the naked bone of his skull. He always wore a black wool patch over the hole, exactly where he had originally plastered his one remaining sock.

In time the bone in the skull degenerated, exposing the brain. Josiah Wilbarger finally died. In the opinion of his doctor, a sawbones named Anderson, death came to Wilbarger when he bumped the top of his head against the low door of his cotton gin building.

Nobody ever explained the vision of Mrs. Hornsby.

Nobody even tried to explain how Josiah Wilbarger's sister, who had died seven hundred miles away on the previous day, had appeared before him.

It was just one of those things that happened.

After all the years, Noah Coffee still marveled at the story. It was his considered opinion that Josiah Wilbarger had been one lucky son of a bitch.

To find Otis in this hard land of shifting Comanche villages and long, long memories, Coffee needed the same brand of luck. He could have used a hand from Wilbarger.

But the dreams that Coffee dreamed under the blaze of Texas stars did not help him with Otis.

He dreamed of Lisa, often.

The father of Lisa and Otis came to him with unusual frequency in dreams. Sometimes he saw him as a rotting corpse. Sometimes he saw him stinking in his bed. Sometimes he saw him actually moving through the night, his pale hair glowing like the moon.

Once, in a dream that came straight from his loins, he dreamed of a particular widow woman in Austin.

But no matter how he set his mind to it, Coffee could not dream of Otis.

Wherever Otis was, he could not reach him.

To Coffee, it was just another miserable Comanche camp, different from all the others in only one respect.

He hit the village in a driving rain. That cut down on the smells. The storm had taken him by surprise. It had come up out of nowhere, slamming across the rolling hills with a blast of wind and hissing cracks of lightning and thunder. The rain was so heavy it poured off the creased front of Coffee's felt hat like a greasy waterfall. It was hard to see through it.

You couldn't quite call the storm a norther. That was Coffee's judgment. It wasn't entirely a question of the direction of the wind. It was simply too early in the year for a true norther. This wind was cool enough to offer some relief from the incessant sun heat that would come later in the day, but it did not carry the icy bite that froze your tail to your saddle.

It was a wet, gray dawn in the Comanche village. The drying racks were mostly empty. There was no smoke, not even from tipi cook fires, at this early hour. It had been too damned hot to keep fires going. Skinny, canvas-colored dogs, all ribs and jaws, barked at his arrival without much interest or conviction. Mostly, the hide flaps of the tipi walls were rolled partway up to let some air in. Where they had been hastily dropped by the women as a screen against the storm, they flapped and snapped insecurely in the wind. The women had not had time to weight them down.

Coffee welcomed the storm in that it covered up some of the odors. The Indians might have been used to them, but he wasn't. Apart from that, he could have done just fine without the storm.

He didn't especially mind getting wet, although no slicker really worked in this kind of rain. He wasn't worried about his ammunition. He would not have lasted this long if he had not had ways of keeping his powder and loads dry.

The problem was that the storm complicated his entry into the camp. Coffee could not expect warm and loving greetings from Comanches. He had no uniform that might protect him. He had no badge to hide behind.

He had no friends here.

What he needed was enough respect to keep him alive. If he couldn't have respect, fear would do. He needed to make an impression.

It was hellishly hard to make an impression when you were being pelted by sky-rivers of rain. He didn't feel awe-inspiring, and he knew he didn't look it either.

Besides, who was watching? This was no morning to be out for a stroll.

He could not simply duck into a lodge and start firing off questions. That was too absurd to think about. At best he would receive stony silence. At worst he could expect an arrow right in the gut.

There were times when a man had to wait it out. This was one of them.

Coffee stayed where he was, sitting bedraggled on Pear and keeping a slight tension on the lead rope to his packhorse. He had a healthy respect for Comanches. He knew they were quite capable of stealing a horse from directly under his mustache.

The sky was brightening some above the leaden rain. As he squinted past the sheets of dull silver that streamed down from his increasingly heavy hat, he told himself that the storm would pass in due time. It was not one of those all-day-and-all-night toad stranglers that marked the real end of summer.

It was nothing but a freak thunderstorm. It would stop as suddenly as it had started.

It did.

Almost without a perceptible beat of time, the air was wet, but no more raindrops were falling. The lightning became a flicker in the distance. The thunder was a soft muttering that turned into an eerie hush.

The tipis dripped. There were great puddles around them. It was as though the hide cones were rising out of miniature lakes.

The children appeared first. They seemed to come out of nowhere. They were ragged and solemn and big-eyed, and when they saw Coffee, they disappeared as quickly as they had arrived. It was generally like that when he rode into a camp. He had to look fast to see any children at all.

The Comanche village stirred. It was almost as if the first rain-glistened rays of the sun had brought it magically to life.

Coffee wiped his eyes with the crinkled sleeve of his slicker. It didn't help much. The slicker was the wrong kind of material and couldn't absorb the water.

But Coffee had to make some sort of move soon. He didn't want to do it blind.

Camp smells seemed to ooze out of the mud of the village. Wet hides, urine, black food kettles that had gone cold and sour with greasy chunks of nameless meats and soggy roots and wild onions and God knew what—

That was when, exactly when, just out of the corner of his smudged eye, Coffee saw the nigger.

Lee was sauntering out of a Comanche lodge, bold as brass. He acted like he owned the damned place.

Coffee felt a sudden hard throb of satisfaction. His distrust and loathing of this man had been justified. He, by God, *knew* what Lee was doing in this village.

Lee was here to shield Otis from him. Maybe he wanted the boy for himself, to be a big hero. That would be just like him. Maybe he was in cahoots with the Indians. Maybe they were going to split the ransom money.

It didn't matter.

What mattered was that Otis Nesbitt was in this stinking village, and so was Lee.

Coffee figured he had the black man right where he wanted him. No doubts here who was right and who was wrong.

Anger surged through him like liquid fire. His hate was bitter spit in his mouth. There were many scores to settle here. Many!

Coffee loosened his slicker. The fingers of his right hand tensed, but he did not draw his heavy Colt.

Coffee played no games with himself. He knew that Lee was good. And he could see that Lee had his Paterson Colt strapped on exactly where it should have been.

Lee was ready. And when you got right down to it, a Paterson was probably faster than a Walker in a gunfight.

That didn't matter.

The way Coffee saw it, if he couldn't beat a black man, then it was time for him to hang up the hardware and go to herding goats.

"Lee!" he called, loud and clear.

8

Lee, Late Summer

Within a week of riding out of Stafford, Lee knew Owl's name. He knew what the Comanche had done, even though he did not completely understand why he had done it.

There were ways of getting the information a man had to have. There were also lots of ways that would not work.

You couldn't do it with bluster. You couldn't do it with threats. Unless you had miracles on your side, you could not do it by shadowing a trick-filled trail that might lead to the other side of nowhere.

Call it guile, if it had to have a name. Lee thought of it like horse trading or poker. Not crooked, really. He demanded no answers. He told no flat-out lies.

It was not for nothing that Lee had named his horse Doc. Doc was a sorrel gelding that most men could not or would not ride. The thing about it was that Doc was good, he was very good, but you had to watch him. Doc was slippery in the old frontier sense: "Never play cards with a man called Doc."

Lee could trade presents for information. He spoke of them always as gifts. They were only effective when they carried no hint of a bribe.

Just a little exchange between friends.

There were more pleasant ways of digging down after Otis. Lee used them.

Lee heard it said that women were treated like trash by the Comanches. Mostly, the people who said that had never been close enough to a Comanche to have one in their rifle sights. But there were some who said it who knew what they were talking about, up to a point.

It was said that Comanche women were treated like slaves.

Lee hated that word. But whether he wanted to or not, he knew more about slavery than most.

For openers, slaves always had more information than they were supposed to have. *Always.*

Beyond that, when you got in close, it was not always a simple matter to tell who was the slave and who was the master.

There was more. In a loose and shifting society like that of The People, without a head chief or a tribal council, everybody still had kin. That was a plain fact of life. The women always knew where their relatives were, even when they had not seen them for years.

Some relative, somewhere, knew where Owl was. That was the trail that had Otis at the end of it.

It was a trail that Lee knew very well.

He rode it.

Feather Fringe was not as soft as her name. She had gotten the name from her skill in working feathers into the sleeves of her buckskin dresses.

Her dress was off this warm night in the tipi, and the body of Feather Fringe was taut and urgent against Lee's. She was no longer a slim girl with long plaited hair. She was not yet heavy with age, her hair cropped short and red paint outlining the part.

Feather Fringe was in-between. She was solid, she

was giving, and she was good enough to make Lee forget why he was in this village.

For a time. The time that was forever by one measure and a few short minutes by another.

Lee was drained and he was grateful. In Lee's life, there were often many months without a woman.

"Is my man content?" Feather Fringe asked.

Lee did not know Feather Fringe well enough to risk clumsy jokes with her. He took care with her feelings. He did not say, "Does a bear live in the woods?"

He said, "You have given me rest."

Feather Fringe was feeling playful. That was not like her. Perhaps it was due to the heat. "Rest?" she said. "Is that all?"

Lee was too much a gentleman to yawn. He *was* tired. There had been rough riding and little comfort since he had left Stafford. "That is all for now," he said. "Later, we shall see."

Feather Fringe gave an audible snort before she slipped off to sleep. Lee did not have to use his knowledge of Comanche to understand her. She was saying: "Men! Their words always last longer than their bodies."

Lee did not care. He was too weary even to whisper words that might yield more information.

He slept.

Somewhere toward morning, long before the sun spilled the first pale light up from the rim of the sky, the storm struck the Comanche camp. Lee was instantly awake. It was a wonder to him that Feather Fringe kept right on sleeping, a slight, bubbly snore coming from her lips.

The storm was not just something he heard. The wind slammed through the open tipi. The rain blew in with the wind, splattering over the sleeping-robe. The temperature dropped as though it had tumbled over a waterfall. It was not really cold. But it was cooler, and the contrast made Lee grope for his shirt.

He managed to get some of the tent flaps down, enough to stop the free flow of wind, and he attended to his Paterson Colt. If he got wet, that was not a matter of great importance. If his Colt got water logged, that could be serious. There was a space beneath the rawhide slats that held the sleeping-robe. However, there was no drainage trench around the tipi. The village had not been expecting rain; summer dry spells could go on for many moons. Lee was concerned that if water flowed into the tipi, it could get under the bed. He decided the risk was too great. He took the Colt, holster and all, and stuck it into his pillow, which was a deerskin casing stuffed with grass.

With his head on his gun, Lee felt more secure. He considered waking up Feather Fringe but decided against it. If she could sleep through *this*, maybe she needed some rest.

He lay there, wakeful but still, admiring the tilt of the tipi smoke hole. It was set at an angle that prevented any water from pouring in through the top of the tipi. With a four-pole foundation and an additional eighteen poles to support the hide cover, there were many tricks a woman could play in erecting a tipi. It was not a simple thing. Lee had tried it and failed miserably.

He liked the heavy drumming of the raindrops on the hide cone of the tent. He enjoyed the crashing of the thunder as it wrestled through the night. He even took pleasure in the lightning flashes, which were sometimes so bright he could see the livid forks right through the sides of the tipi.

Not for the first time, Lee asked himself some difficult questions. If he found contentment here, why not stay? If The People accepted him as an equal, was he not betraying them by his quest for Otis? If a village takes you in, do you repay the hospitality by asking questions that might cause harm?

To Lee, these thoughts had nothing to do with loyalty to the Nesbitts. In the end he would do what he had to do. He would rescue Otis, even at the cost of his life.

Just the same, Lee saw the Comanches through eyes that were not clouded by hate. He felt an attraction there that he could not conceal from himself.

Oh, if he had to, he would shoot a Comanche as fast

as he would shoot a rattlesnake. But it all depended on what that Comanche was doing at the moment. Lee was not bent on extermination.

The People understood that. Raiding was a way of life to them. They did not loathe a man who fought back. As a matter of fact, the way Lee saw it, their vision was clearer than that of the Texans.

The conflict between them had little to do with hatreds, tribal or otherwise. It was about horses. It was about plunder. It was about strange dreams and goals that were only half understood. It was about manhood, and it was about freedom.

To the Comanches, these things were important. Lee shared that conviction. It was not a matter of personal vindictiveness.

Just before dawn, Lee dropped off into a troubled sleep.

It was the barking of the dogs that woke him up again.

Lulled by the pelting of the rain, Lee was not really alarmed. Dogs barked. That was a fact of life. Usually the barking meant nothing at all.

He dozed until the storm stopped with an abruptness that was eerie. The cessation of a strong storm can be as startling as its onslaught.

The world dripped. The sky held its breath. Lee was seized by a sense of waiting, of expectancy.

Something was wrong. He had no idea what it was.

The eyes of Feather Fringe were open. They were no longer playful. "What is it?" she asked.

Lee reached into his grass-stuffed pillow and eased out his holstered revolver. There was something different about his movements now. They were not sudden, but they flowed decisively. "I do not know," he said. "Stay here, please. Keep your head down."

Lee got up. He was a shadow figure in the light of morning. He dressed.

That meant buckling on his Colt.

He stepped outside the tipi.

* * *

Lee saw him at once. Sitting on that Pear horse of his, the raindrops still glistening on his yellow slicker.

Coffee. The last man on earth he wanted to see.

Lee didn't have to do any hard thinking to read Coffee loud and clear. Under the dripping, grooved brim of his hat, Coffee's expression said it all.

Opportunity.

Resentment.

Hatred. This *was* personal.

Lee saw him loosen his slicker. He saw where Coffee's right hand was. Lee had not lived this long by failing to anticipate the obvious.

His heart died a little. It was not from fear. It was from knowing what was about to happen and being powerless to prevent it.

"Lee!" Coffee called.

That was it. There was no way out. The challenge had come.

Quietly, just loud enough for Coffee to hear, Lee said: "I am moving away from the tipi. There are people in there."

Coffee said nothing.

Lee moved to his left, just far enough to put him in front of a fat-trunked oak tree. The tree had only survived in the village because its limbs were too thick to cut for firewood. There was a squirrel's nest high in the tree, but the squirrel had been eaten long ago. Incredibly, there was a morning blue jay perched just above Lee's head. It had come in looking for food scraps. It seemed to know there was trouble in the damp air. It made not a squawk. That was not like a blue jay.

"Lee!" Coffee called again.

Lee crouched but he did not draw.

"You are making a mistake, Mr. Coffee," Lee said. He still did not raise his voice. He knew the attempt to settle this with words was futile, but he had to try. "We are on the same side."

That seemed to infuriate Coffee more. "You've been called, boy," he said. "I won't call again."

Lee ignored the *boy* thing. Those were the words of a fool, and Coffee was not a fool. He was just blind where Lee was concerned.

It was far more than the sting of an insult that bothered Lee. It was the whole damned situation.

Lee figured he could beat Coffee. Maybe he was right, maybe he wasn't. But if he had to bet, he would have bet on himself.

Forget about crazy trick-shot stuff. Coffee was way too good to mess with that. If and when Lee fired, he would have to shoot to kill.

A black man shooting a Texas Ranger? It was unthinkable. And it would be known. There were some stories that could not be hidden.

If he killed Coffee, even the Nesbitts could not save him. They might not *want* to save him.

Lee had two choices, not three. He could let himself be plugged, probably in the gut. Or he could somehow duck out and run. He didn't much care for the alternatives.

He could not shoot Coffee. That would really put him on the run, a fugitive forever.

No more flirting with the idea of becoming a Comanche. He would *be* a Comanche. He had no other option.

"Shit," Lee said.

Coffee drew. He was very fast. The Walker Colt looked like a cannon. His horse was as motionless as a statue.

Carefully, making no quick moves, Lee eased his right hand away from his Paterson Colt. He did not draw.

Coffee's Colt exploded in a burst of smoke and flame. The crack of the shot was louder than any thunder had been.

Lee waited for the shock of the slug. He wondered why he could not feel it. Maybe he was already dead.

The answer splattered down upon him. Coffee's .44 had blown the blue jay apart. The spray of feathers, blood, and guts wouldn't make a decent meal for an Indian dog.

"God damn you, boy," Coffee said, holstering his Colt beneath his slicker. "I can't shoot a man who won't fight." There might or might not have been a suggestion of respect in his speech.

Again, Lee ignored the *boy*. A time would come to deal with that. He was surprised to find that he was still alive. "I see that you are not a murdering man, Mr. Coffee," he said.

"I'll have no judgments from you." This time Coffee left off the *boy*.

"No judgments, then. I just want you to remember one thing. I do not threaten you. But you want to think long and hard before you draw on me again. I don't know where and I don't know when, but I will fight when I decide I must. It would not be a good idea to misunderstand that."

Coffee spat at nothing in particular.

Lee had one more thing to say. He did not know whether or not it would make any difference, but it was his duty to say it.

Like it or not—and neither man liked it at all—they were both riding the same trail.

"Otis ain't here, Mr. Coffee. I don't know where he is. I hear tell that he is with a man called Owl."

Coffee digested that. His expression did not change. He offered no thanks for the information.

But he shrugged off his dripping slicker, folded it once, and cinched it to his saddle horn. He was too trail wise to pack it into a saddlebag wet. He lifted his sodden hat, brushed back his hair with his hand, and nudged and whistled Pear to turn around.

Still leading his packhorse, Coffee rode out of the village. He said no farewells. He did not look back.

Lee understood that there were things Coffee could not say. He was what he was, and he would not change in a hurry.

If ever.

But he had accepted Lee's word about Otis. He hadn't even bothered to look around.

Maybe that was something.

Lee turned and went back into the lodge. He was trembling violently. He was sick to his stomach. It took all he had left to keep the vomit down.

What he had done that morning had not been easy. It wasn't how close he had come to death that brought on this reaction. He had been close to death before.

It wasn't fear, and it wasn't hate.

It was his iron resolve that Coffee should not see any tremor in his hand, hear any quaver in his voice.

That mattered.

And, by God, he had pulled it off.

Now he could shake and shiver until he brought the tipi down, if necessary. His voice could be the strangled babbling of a choking baby.

He was alone except for a bewildered Feather Fringe.

She could not possibly understand what had happened or why her man was acting so strangely.

But she did not mock him. She took Lee in her arms and soothed him.

She hummed and whispered little baby songs to him.

She did this until the trembling ceased and Lee was a man again.

9

Owl, Fall

Owl halted Heart before an exceptionally large and handsome lodge. There was a slight chill in the air but the entry flap was open. As always, the doorway faced the east, the land of the rising sun. The flap was covered with an additional pelt. It was stiff and had a weight on the bottom.

The tipi was painted. There were vermilion circles and squares. Owl knew that they represented the stars in the sky. Around the top of the lodge there was a circle of yellow, sharp-angled lines. They were the signs of the beaks of eagles.

Smells poured out of the tipi. They were good smells. Owl recognized sweet grass, sage, and river onion. He could smell a special smell that took him back to his youth. Spirit Shadow cooked her soups and pastes by stone-boiling them in hide pouches, the old way.

He could not simply dismount and carry the boy into the lodge. That was not the polite thing to do, and Owl knew better than to neglect courtesy around Spirit

Shadow. She could be prickly. She was quite capable of refusing her services if she was offended.

He did not call out. He just slumped in his saddle, cradling the body of O-tis in his arms. That body was even thinner now. It barely had breath in it. The blue eyes were open but they were not seeing anything.

Owl was bone weary. There were aches and pains in his legs and his shoulders. It had been a long tough ride.

He was not too tired to call Spirit Shadow. It was all a matter of approaching her correctly. Spirit Shadow did not care to be summoned like an ordinary woman.

Besides, what kind of a doctor would she be if she did not even know who was waiting outside of her tipi? What quality of vision was that?

Spirit Shadow emerged after a suitable interval. More exactly, she cascaded. Owl thought that there was at least one obvious reason for the size of her lodge. It took a big tipi to hold her.

She was an enormous woman, a huge woman, even larger than Owl remembered her. The ropes of medallions that laced her poncho-style blouse were ample enough to construct a corral. Those shirts, Owl knew, were made from the skin of a single animal. It had to have been a buffalo or a bear. Her beaded moccasins were the size of snowshoes he had seen in the Shining Mountains. Her hair was wild and loose, and her eyes were outlined with red paint. Her ears were smeared with red, and she had a jade Pueblo bracelet on her left wrist that could have been used to hobble a horse.

She was called *Kaku*, Grandmother, for that is what she was. A Comanche medicine woman had to be beyond her child-bearing years. It was necessary that she be one of the wives of a man who was himself a *puhakut*, a doctor. The best possible situation was for such a woman to be the right age, with a dead husband who had passed his power on to her.

That was how it was with Spirit Shadow.

Owl did not underestimate her for a moment. If he had not had a high respect for her skills, he would never have brought O-tis to her. She was more than blubber.

There was an ancient wisdom in her dark, slitted eyes. There was also a quick intelligence that a man neglected at his peril.

Spirit Shadow had once made it happen that one of Owl's wives gave birth to a male. The boy had later sickened and died, but that had not been a part of the agreement he had made with Spirit Shadow. He was not likely to repeat that mistake.

The lodge impressed him. Doctors did not work for nothing. It was clear that Spirit Shadow had received many payments. That would not happen to a doctor who obtained no cures.

She knew who he was, of course. Few people ever forgot Owl.

"So," she said. "It is the Mighty Father who can have no sons." Even her voice was fat. It layered words that sank like stones in the still air.

Despite his tiredness, Owl was stung. Spirit Shadow had a trick of reaching the hidden places, the places that hurt.

"I have a son," he said. Heart was almost motionless under him. He understood that this would be a bad time to act up.

"Him?" she asked, gesturing toward the boy.

"He is my son."

"Is he Comanche?" She had to know that in order to treat him. There were many medicines that had power only for The People.

Owl considered. It was the exact truth that was needed here. The life of the boy might depend on it. "He was not born Comanche. It may be that he is not yet Comanche. He will be a Comanche, mostly."

"Hnhh." It was not a word. It was a sound that Spirit Shadow often made. It might mean anything.

"He is my son," Owl repeated.

"Hnhh," she said.

She moved in close. She displaced much air. She smelled of stone-boiling grease and crushed peyote. She reached out the arm with the jade bracelet. She touched the boy's left shoulder. Her touch was not gentle. Owl thought he could hear the bones grind.

"It is his head," he started to explain. "When he fell, he struck a—"

She did not permit him to finish. This was her territory, after all. Even if she had not been a *puhakut*, there was nothing wrong with her eyes. "I know what it is," she said. Her tone was short and sheathed with tallow. She did not appreciate someone making a diagnosis on her patient.

Owl gave a weary smile. If she thought of the boy as her patient, then half the battle was won. She would doctor him.

"Hnhh," she said. "I will tell you of some things that are of interest to me."

Owl understood this game. A doctor must accept any gifts that were given for her work. That was the way. Still, it would break no rules if she mentioned a few items. She was not discussing a fee.

Just talking.

"Meat for my lodge gives me much pleasure. There are those who help me in my work. A lodge this size requires assistance."

"Meat is good," Owl agreed. He was really too tired for all this, but he had no choice. The boy was so light he almost seemed to be built out of feathers, but he was becoming a burden. Owl needed to shift the weight around. His shoulders throbbed.

"It is cooler now," she said. Her voice was casual. Just a little conversation between old friends. "The buffalo should be returning." She knew very well that with the scorching heat gone, the buffalo would be drifting back from the northern pastures.

"I will find them."

"Bulls are big, but they are very tough."

"Cows and calves," he said.

"Juniper berries are very useful to me." She eyed him keenly. "They are good for head injuries."

"It is too early for juniper berries," Owl said.

"A man can trade, if he wishes."

"That is truth."

"Crow feathers are good." Spirit Shadow laughed a liquid laugh. "The crow and the owl, they are enemies. The feathers of the crow keep owls away. Even the big Owl." She enjoyed the play on words. In speaking of the big Owl, she was not referring to Owl himself, except in a joking way. She meant *piamempits*, the Cannibal Owl.

"It would not be good to put the feathers in the hair of the boy," Owl said.

"Hnhh. Do not tell me what I already know."

Owl let that one pass. He was in no mood to argue. He could feel the life draining out of O-tis even as they spoke. *Get on with it*, he thought. *Get on with it, old woman. There is medicine that must be made here.*

He did not let himself think that *he* was the cause of what had happened to O-tis. He was moving the blame around to Spirit Shadow.

She understood that clearly. It might have been that she really could see what was in his head. "The last thing that is of interest to me is a thing of great importance," she said. "I think of it often."

Owl's arms felt like tipi poles that had supported hide covers for too many seasons. Now it was his turn to see into her mind. He knew what was coming.

"The bones of the Cannibal Owl," Spirit Shadow said. She opened her dark, shining eyes wider than he would have thought possible. "Spirit Shadow knows the origin of your name. Spirit Shadow knows what you carry in your medicine pouch. Spirit Shadow knows your vision. And Spirit Shadow knows you remember where it was that the Cannibal Owl was killed, so long ago."

"It may be that Spirit Shadow knows too much."

"Hnhh. That is for you to decide. Would you prefer one who knew too little?"

Owl had no reply for that. It was his thought that this coup counting with talk had gone on long enough. The boy could die while they haggled. He was close to death now.

"I will get you all that you desire," he said.

"Your words are big. Spirit Shadow desires many things."

Owl felt anger beginning to stir in his veins. *"Will you take the boy?"*

She relented. Enough was enough. "I will take him."

Anger was replaced by relief. Owl started to dismount, keeping O-tis as steady as he could. Owl's legs were so stiff that he was not certain he could move correctly, but he kept his face impassive. He would not show a lack of strength to Spirit Shadow. After all, she was a woman.

"No." She reached out her hand and stopped him. The jade bracelet seemed to have a cool fire in it. Her hand was thick and fat, but it had much power in it. Owl was not certain that he could have shoved her aside, even had he wished to do so. "The boy must be mine for a time. I will take him."

She stretched out her arms. Owl had no choice. As carefully as possible, he transferred the body of O-tis to her.

The boy vanished. He was swallowed in medallions and animal skins and flesh. Out of a jumbled mass of long hair and red paint, Spirit Shadow began to croon a medicine song that was like a lullaby.

"How long must I stay away from my son?"

She ceased her crooning reluctantly. "You have much to do. So do I. You will know when it is time to return."

Owl understood that to mean: "Don't come back until you get what I have told you to get. And don't come in a hurry."

She resumed her crooning.

She turned, a Shining Mountain of fat, and padded on her snowshoe moccasins back into her painted lodge. She left a hole in the air behind her.

Owl felt very strange. His arms were empty. He did not know if he had done the right thing or not.

Heart snorted. He too was weary of this game. He was overdue for some attention himself.

Owl heard him. He knew horses.

"You have done well, Heart," he said. "When I reach my camp, we will both rest a little."

Somewhat mollified, Heart cocked his ears.

"Let's go," Owl said.

They went.

The splendid lodge of Spirit Shadow smoked into the chill of the sky.

Owl's visit with his wives and unmarried daughters was satisfactory but anxious. They knew that something was wrong. He knew that he should not have been with them. It was true that he no longer had the boy, but his pursuers did not know that.

Wherever he was, as long as the boy lived and had not been returned to Stafford, Owl was a target.

He had no wish to bring disaster upon his family. The best course of action for him was to get away and stay away.

Before a week had passed, Owl mounted Heart and rode out. Heart was not high-stepping with eagerness but he was sufficiently rested.

Owl knew exactly where he was going.

Crow feathers were no problem. He already had the juniper berries. They were hard and dry, saved from last season, but they would work for Spirit Shadow. They could be boiled.

The buffalo merely required a certain amount of planning. He was certain that they had returned to this southern fringe of their range, but they would not be in large herds at this time of the year. A few big bulls here and there. Small groups of cows and calves. With Heart to cover the ground, he could pick them up whenever he chose. The trick was in getting the animals skinned and transporting the meat. Spirit Shadow would be less than pleased if he just tossed a dead carcass next to her lodge. She wanted the buffalo properly butchered. Owl did not doubt that she got hungry frequently and was not in the habit of wasting her time preparing cuts of meat.

The skinning and cutting up and transporting might require the assistance of his wives. That was all woman's work, and they were good at it. He did not wish to expose them to danger again, but there were times when it must be so. A man did not always have the luxury of choosing his own trail.

But the buffalo could wait. They would not just disappear. They were as much a part of this world as he was. It would not be tomorrow that he hunted them, or the next tomorrow.

The bones of the Cannibal Owl came first. That was as it should be.

Owl knew precisely what he had to do, and he knew how to do it. He was riding a familiar trail. But this time there was a sense of dread in him that was alien to his nature.

Wonder, yes. Awe, yes. Respect, yes. All that he had felt before. It was to be expected.

But this cold clay in his gut was new. It did not belong. It was an intruder.

Even when he touched the grooved point that hung in the pouch suspended from his neck, he was not reassured. The fear remained. It was very strong.

Spirit Shadow could see as far as anyone into the other world. It was, after all, the land of spirits and shadows. She had not won her name by accident.

But there were some things she could not see.

It was not his feeling that she had deliberately sent him into a trap. Rather, his sense was that the focus of her medicine eyes had not been sharp enough. She had missed something.

Something big.

Owl did not know exactly where the danger lay, or what it was, but he did know that it was ahead of him.

He rode like a man riding into a certain ambush. All that he knew and all that he felt screamed at him to turn back.

Every sign was wrong.

But there was the boy. The boy who might have been, or might yet be, his son.

O-tis. The sightless blue eyes staring into nowhere. The head pulped by the man who would be his father . . .

He could not turn back.

He could only ride onward, to the place where first he had heard the name of Owl.

It was a place like no other on earth. It was not sacred to The People—too many others had passed that way, and left their marks—but it was sacred to Owl.

Whatever he was, it had come from there.

It was not a great distance from the San Gabriel and the *Taibo* town of Stafford. He could have made it in the hard ride of a single day and night. But he dared not ride a straight trail. There were small settlements to avoid and roads that it was unwise to travel.

His purpose was not to fight. Not this time.

It took him all of three days and part of a fourth.

As he drew near, he began to feel the old excitement, the old thrill. He opened himself up, wanting the essence of the place to flow into him before he actually saw it. He wanted to touch his roots. As with any greatly pleasurable thing, the expectation was part of the joy.

But the thrill died before it was truly born. There was something that was not right. Something was gone, and something else had come.

Owl closed himself up again. He slowed Heart's pace. He was not a child. It was a time to use his head.

And his eyes.

There was a way to reach this special place by riding up a deepening canyon from the Pedernales. Owl had chosen the other trail, the trail he had first followed when he was hardly older than O-tis.

That second trail took him across a perfectly ordinary grass prairie. It was flat country for this part of Texas. It was marked with the usual clumps of oaks and thickets of cedar. There were many agarita bushes with sharp-edged leaves.

If you did not already know better, you would think that there was nothing unusual here. It was the last place a man would look: a very gently rolling grassland beneath a great gray sky that was leaden with the advancing fall.

Owl knew better.

When he hit the drop, invisible until he was almost upon the steep slope, it was like coming home. The only thing was that when he came home he did not expect to see tracks. They were tracks made by horses with iron shoes. Perhaps five horses; it was hard to tell from scratches in the rocks.

And he smelled wood smoke. It was mixed with the fragrance of cedar and the faint tang of drying cypress needles, but it was there.

Wood smoke.

If there was a fire, Owl knew where it would be. There was a way he could get close enough to see and not be seen.

He only had to be careful. And they had to be careless.

Owl touched his medicine pouch. He felt nothing, saw nothing. He unslung his bow and nocked a feathered arrow. That felt better.

"Easy, Heart," he said. He did not whisper and he did not shout. "We will need to approach them quietly."

Heart blew with disgust. He did not blow hard, though. He was just letting Owl know that he did not need instructions in an obvious situation.

Then they started down, horse and rider.

The trail was narrow, dropping between weathered limestone ledges. It was steep enough to cause some slippage, even for a surefooted horse like Heart. It was always damp here.

When they reached the bottom, the canyon was fairly shallow. It got a lot deeper and more precipitous, Owl knew, as you moved closer to the waterfall.

There was a stream flowing down the canyon. It was a beautiful stream, Owl knew, but he was not much interested in that. What *did* concern him was the noise the stream made. The stream was not large—Heart could have jumped across it—but its current was broken by a series of whitewater rapids where the water tumbled over exposed cypress roots and limestone shelf rocks. The splash and gurgle were enough to make a covering sound. Owl could move up the canyon in relative safety. The only danger was in meeting someone going the other way.

That was what the arrow was for. Owl had other arrows in his quiver, and he had his knife.

He did not want to use them.

If there was a fight, or even other eyes to see, it would not be easy for him to go to the bones of the Cannibal Owl.

Owl nudged Heart and proceeded along the narrow trail that wound up the canyon. It might have been wiser to dismount, but Owl was not fond of walking.

Out of the corner of his eye, he spotted fish finning in the stream pools. They were surprisingly large for such a small stream. Owl knew that they were bass.

The limestone bluffs that formed the canyon walls reared higher and higher. Father Sun could not reach this trail unless he was straight up in the sky. There were cracks and crevices in the stone walls. Some of them were cave openings, Owl knew. Almost all of them held bats. They would not come whirring out until nightfall, but Owl did not like bats. The grease in his hair attracted them. They stank.

Owl went as far as he dared before dismounting. There was a very large, deep rock shelter on his left, between the trail and the creek. It had a fire-blackened roof and it sloped back into total darkness. It was plenty big enough to conceal both a horse and a rider. Owl knew all about it. He had camped there before. So had countless generations that had come here before him.

He looped Heart's reins around a pillar of limestone and whispered words of reassurance. There was no food for the horse here, and no water. His tether was slack enough so that Heart could work himself free if Owl did not return.

Owl ducked out of the rock shelter and wormed his way through openings in the rocks and trees that lined the trail. There was enough moss to make the footing uncertain. There was a fine mist in the air. He could not tell whether it had started to drizzle.

The smell of wood smoke was not stronger, but he could hear voices. He knew exactly where the voices were coming from, and for that reason it was easy to position himself where he could see and remain concealed.

Yes, there they were.

Five of them.

In *his* place.

They had built a small fire on the gravel beach that lined the great pool at the end of the trail. The water was green and clear, just as he remembered it. The waterfall that slipped over the edge of the world stitched a broken line of white bubbles. There was no roaring from the falls. The sound that it made was more like an undulating hiss at this time of the year when the flow was not great. Nevertheless, the waterfall was more than ten times taller than Owl himself. He had been up there, where the water dropped from the edge of the limestone. He knew that it was the same stream that wound down the canyon. It was as though the earth had cracked and created a vast hole into another world.

Again Owl touched the grooved point he carried in his medicine pouch. Again nothing happened. That was both puzzling and alarming. Here, of all places, the Spirit Creature should have revealed itself. Why, it was right *here*, on the side of the pool under the rock overhang, that Owl had first seen it. That huge creature with the great snake between its curving tusks had *spoken* to him in this place. Here, where there were swarms of cliff swallows to pick the bugs out of its patches of red-brown hair on its gray hide, *here* was where it belonged. . . .

It would not abandon Owl, not after the lifetime they had shared.

Could it be the *Taibos*, getting in the way as usual?

Or was the Spirit Beast trying to tell him something about this place?

Owl tried to dismiss it from his mind. That was impossible. If his medicine had lost its power, or if there was something about it he did not understand . . .

Why, he was defenseless, that was all.

That was no situation for a warrior to be in, and Owl despised the feeling. Something had changed. Was he on his own? Or was it worse than that?

Owl moved his hand from the medicine point to the nocked arrow he had strung in his bow. That was better. At least, it felt as it should have felt. To settle himself a little more, he touched the pearl handle of his sheathed trade knife.

He studied the situation. There was nothing else he could do. He would have to make this decision without any help.

The five *Taibos* formed a semicircle around the fire. There were two youngish women in long dresses and bonnets. There was one older woman, severely dressed in too much black.

Owl smiled a little. He understood *that* situation. The old one was there to keep an eye on things.

There were two young men. They had boots and big hats. They had six-guns on their hips. Owl's dark eyes flickered. There. The rifles were still in their scabbards, on the saddled horses staked out on the right side of the pool by the leaning sycamore tree. The sycamore still had some leaves on it. They were greenish-red.

There was much talk. It was harsh to Owl's ears. He had no idea what they were saying, but his eyes could interpret the scene without difficulty.

He even knew the *Taibo* word: *picnic*. It was very strange, stranger than most of the weird things the white people did. They would take food in baskets and go out to some lonely place to eat it. Then they would go back home where they had their tables and chairs and enough eating utensils for a tribe. They seemed to particularly enjoy going on these picnics when there were clouds in the sky and a good chance of rain.

He understood the horses too. The women would ride them sidesaddle. It was a stupid way to ride. But there was no way to get a coach or a buggy down the steep rock trail to this place.

Owl did not know where the *Taibos* were from. They did not move their villages, and so to return home they would have a long ride. It might take them more than a day and a night.

He could smell the food. The smell reminded him that much time had passed since he had eaten. He was not sure what all of it was. It had been cooked before they had come here. The fire was for coffee. In any case, they always made fires, whether they needed one or not.

Owl ran his tongue over his cracked lips. Some coffee would be good.

The *Taibos* talked and talked and talked. The young women laughed a lot. The woman in black was as silent as the rock she sat on.

Owl thought it over. He could kill all of them, of course. Unless he had lost his skills totally, he could drop the two men with arrows before they got off a shot. He was within range. The women might or might not be able to shoot. He suspected the old woman in black would be the most dangerous.

But one warrior against three women?

Owl had been a gambler in his time. He liked those odds.

He had not come here to kill, but that would not stop him. A man could change his mind. Scalps were always a prize, and there was much food.

The problem was the boy. It seemed to Owl that O-tis had brought many problems. When a man had a son, he had to think too much.

If he killed the *Taibos*, then what? He might indeed get the bones that Spirit Shadow wanted. But the white people would have told others where they were going. If they did not return, there would be search parties. Owl suspected that five scalped bodies might cause a fair amount of commotion. It would be even worse than stealing O-tis. He would draw so much attention to this place that he could never come here again. And it was *his* special place.

They might even find the bones of the Cannibal Owl.

He could not imagine anything worse than that. Anything might happen then.

They might also track him down, and that would mean the end of O-tis. Put enough *Taibos* together and a man had a gutfull of trouble.

No, that question was easily answered. He could not kill the fools who brought a picnic to this place. He knew that and it did not overly trouble him. Owl had killed before and he would kill again. He could wait.

The horses were another matter.

Five horses! Good ones too. That was a prize worth taking. His wives would be pleased.

Medicine or no medicine, a Comanche did not leave horses in peace unless he had absolutely no alternative. A man was judged by the horses he could steal.

Owl pondered that one for a considerable time. He felt that he was somehow betraying his own best instincts. But try as he might, he could not figure a way to get those horses without alerting their owners. It was a puzzle that had no solution. If he made off with the horses and left the *Taibos* alive, that was even worse than killing the *Taibos*. They would talk, and talk plenty. The men would have friends. They would all come back to this place and Owl would have his hands full with more than horses.

Reluctantly, he decided that he had to leave all of them alone. He had come here for a specific purpose. He could not abandon it. There was too much at stake.

Owl concluded that it was highly unlikely the men and women would spend the night in the canyon by the pool. If he knew Texans, they would at least climb back up the trail and start home before nightfall.

Then the rain began to come down. It was not heavy, but it might hurry them up some. Picnics were not good in the rain. There was always much laughter and scurrying about to leave wherever the picnic was.

Owl would just have to wait it out.

He worked his way back to the depths of the rock

shelter where Heart stood as silently as the stones themselves. Owl could smell his familiar scent and hear the soft snuffle of his breathing. That was all. There was not even a nicker of welcome.

Owl gave Heart's flank an affectionate pat. He was much pleased. A horse that knew what to do and when to do it was beyond price.

Together, hidden from anything except a search with torches, they waited. There was a patter of rain on the brown cypress needles outside. Shut off from them by the rock wall, the stream made no sound that they could hear.

Owl was good at waiting. A warrior who was trained in ambush knew how to remain still for long periods.

Just the same, he had grown restless when he heard the horses clicking along the trail. Although it was difficult to tell from where he was, it seemed to him that the darkness was coming. He listened to the chattering voices of the riders. Talking. Always talking.

The party of five passed directly in front of the rock shelter. Owl could see them clearly. One of the young men spat a wad of tobacco juice right into the shelter. Owl saw the brown stuff strike a limestone shelf and drip down.

The spitting reminded him of things he preferred not to remember. He did not move.

It seemed to take them forever to pass by, shadows never to be seen again, but Owl knew that he actually had them in view only for a very brief time.

When they were gone, there was more waiting. He had to be sure they were all completely up the trail and away from the cliff overhang. If he and Heart had to remain in the rock shelter throughout the night, that was no big thing. It was usually when a man hurried that he got into trouble.

He waited until he was certain.

Then he led Heart out of the shelter and mounted him. It was very good to feel a saddle under him again.

Somewhat to his surprise, there was still enough light to enable him to see.

After all, he knew precisely where he was going.

"Come, Heart," he said softly. "It is time to visit the death place of the Cannibal Owl."

It had been another horse, another time.

Heart had not been here before and he did not much care for the experience. He kept rolling his eyes, searching for something that was not there.

Or was it?

Owl felt the dread again. It was all wrong for this special place. He had known only wonder here.

They came to the blackened chunks and ashes of the camp fire on the gravel beach. The fire pit glistened. It was partly from the heavy drizzle of the rain, but Owl could see that they had thrown water on it from their tin cups. Except for the darkened coals, not much had been left behind.

There were some scattered small bones. The raccoons and the scavenger birds would take care of them in short order. Some of the bones had not been stripped of meat. Owl swung down from Heart and crouched. He picked up some of the bones. They were bird bones, light and easily cracked. There was a kind of batter stuck on the meat. Owl ate some of the meat. It tasted a little like turkey, but had a weaker flavor. He ate what he could find. He crunched the bones in his teeth.

He found white eggshells and bits of yellow-and-white eggs. They had been boiled. Owl guessed that the eggs came from the turkeylike birds. He ate that too, including some shell fragments. They were good for cleaning out the gut.

That was all, except for some dark brown crumbs. He was familiar with bread, but realized that this was not exactly the same. It was very sweet. He liked it. He scraped up the crumbs and wolfed them down. The crumbs were hard to separate from the gravel.

It did not occur to him to cover the dead camp fire. It was not burning, and one good rain would wash it away.

He walked to the edge of the green-water pool. He cupped his hands and drank. He knew quite well that he was stalling. He saw the deep dark shadow of a fish under the curving trunk of the sycamore. It was a catfish. He could see the whiskers clearly. The fish was as long as his leg. He was still hungry, but the big fish was down too far for an arrow. He was not concerned about that. It was tough to eat a catfish raw. A man had to skin it, and that was awkward work.

He let his eyes wander up to the layered edges of the cliff overhang to the left of the waterfall. There was still enough light for him to see, but it was going fast. The bats were beginning to smoke out into the drizzled air.

If he had not known his way, he might have hesitated.

But he did know the way.

"You wait," he said to Heart. He simply trailed the reins. Where he was going, no horse could follow.

He took a parfleche skin bag from his saddle. It was a big one.

Owl tried to empty his mind and just do what he had to do. What was he, a woman? How could he fear this place? What was he afraid of, ghosts? Ghosts could be troublesome, of course. At this time, with night falling, they were changing from dust devils and whirlwinds to humanlike form. That was when they were most dangerous. . . .

He shook his head. This was nonsense. It was not ghosts that he had to worry about.

There was a trail that went behind the pool and in back of the waterfall. It was very narrow and very slippery. There were places where Owl had to crawl on his belly. There were other places where he had to climb limestone columns to move from one ledge level to another. He knew where the footholds were, but it was not easy going.

If he had been *piamempits*, the Cannibal Owl, this would have been a simple flight. But he was only a man called Owl, and he had no wings.

He looked back and down. He saw Heart waiting, and that gave him some reassurance. He also saw something that he had noticed before. From here, behind the falls, there was absolutely no way any enemy could get to him. They would have to drop off the edge of the rock overhang—which would put them right in front of him with broken legs—or swim across the pool. He could hold out here forever, if he just had food. It was a perfect defensive position.

He kept going. The stinking bats were in his face. He moved as fast as he could. It was getting very dark.

There were several crevices he could choose. The bones of *piamempits* were not all in one place. He knew where the great skull was, but it was too heavy to carry. He knew where there were bones still embedded in the rock. Many of them were broken, as though they had dropped from above.

The best place was the closest. The bones were on the surface. It was the ledge where he had found the grooved point, lodged between the giant weathered ribs.

So long ago, it seemed. Another lifetime.

He found the ledge. The bones were still there.

He just needed fragments, although he could trace the outlines of entire bones in the crusted limestone. Big bones were too heavy to carry. Even smaller bones, such as sections of the spine, would not fit in his parfleche.

Don't stare. Don't think. Just do it.

Above all, don't remember.

He reached out and touched some broken pieces of the bones of the Cannibal Owl. The bones burned his hand. He stifled a cry. He touched them again. They were cold, of course, cold as death. He examined his hand. He could see no burn, but the light was so poor . . .

"Are you a man," he said aloud, "or a child?"

He hoped that it was the former.

A string of warm, furry bats brushed the back of his neck. He thought he felt blood there. It was probably his imagination.

Do it, do it, do it!

He did it. He swept up enough bone fragments to fill his skin bag. It seemed to him that there was an orange glow coming from the parfleche.

It was as though it had a fire in it.

How could that be?

Owl staggered. He wanted to run, but there was no way he could run in this cramped space. He started to retreat as fast as he could, but something stopped him.

He could not go back. There was one more thing he had to do. The thing had been hidden in his mind, but it was there. He could no more ignore it than he could turn himself into an Apache.

Whether he could carry it or not, he had to look again at that *piamempits* skull. He did not know how he could see it in this fading light, but he knew that it would happen. Some things were meant to be.

What lurked in his head was the short memory of the bones he had eaten on the gravel beach below. He thought also of turkeys and crows and swallows.

His mind was all around the edges of an idea that could not be.

The crevice he needed was slightly above him and only a short distance farther on. It was a miserable climb. He remembered it well.

He looked at the parfleche. There was no more orange glow. He could not get light from that source.

He clawed and wriggled his way up to the deep, chambered ledge. Only the edge was wet. Inside, it was as dry as summer dust. Somehow, what light there was hit it at an angle that enabled him to see. He had expected that.

The huge and terrible skull looked right out at him. It was stained and dull white. Its power struck him like a war axe in the chest.

It had not changed but it was different.

It had been waiting for him.

It might speak to him, if only he could hear.

Owl's heart thudded in his chest. His breath came in short gasps. This was the last place in the world he wanted to be at this moment, and he did not understand what had called him here.

He forced himself to look carefully. If he did not do that, why had he come to the head of the Cannibal Owl?

Enormous as it was, eerily luminous in the uncertain light, the skull was not intact. The lower jaw was missing. There were what appeared to be sockets on either side of the rather flat face. There was nothing in the sockets.

The skull rested upright, balanced by its sloping upper jaw. The top of the skull had a definite bulge in it, like a swelling of bone. Where the eye holes should be, there was a single slitlike depression. It was deep but narrow.

The skull was bigger than any real-world skull known to Owl. It was also more massive. The thing looked like it was almost solid bone—or what once had been bone.

There was no question of lifting that skull. Owl did not want even to touch it. He was not sure how close he could get. The aura of power was immensely strong. It was like a medicine circle that sealed in that mightiest of all skulls.

Owl wanted only one thing. He wanted to get out of there. He wanted to fly like a bat, slither like a snake, fall like a stone.

Anything.

But there was something he had to see. If he failed, it would haunt him for whatever was left of his life.

Owl dropped to his belly. It was badly scratched now. When he crawled forward, he left a crimson trail on the tobacco-dry limestone. He felt as though he were being shoved back. He kept on crawling. He got close enough to look.

He did not have to move the upper jaw. It was propped up in such a way that he could see under it. Poor as the light was, he could see enough. He forced himself to stay until he was certain.

There were teeth in that jaw. Far back, but they

were there. Prodigious teeth. They had rows of ridges on them. They were not pointed.

Grinding teeth.

Owl borrowed a sound from Spirit Shadow. "Hnhh," he said. Nothing else seemed to fit.

Now that he had done this thing, his terror overcame him. He knew that those awful eyes would open. He knew that the Cannibal Owl would somehow come together again. It would crush him like trade corn was smashed under a hammer stone.

He wanted to touch the grooved point in his medicine bag. It had killed the Cannibal Owl once. It would protect him if it still retained its power.

But what if it failed him here? Then what chance would he have?

He did not touch it. He could not run, but he could move. He did not know how he did it. The light was gone. He slithered and scrambled and waddled, but he moved. The rock walls ripped at his body. Wherever he crawled, he left a sticky trail of blood.

He did not want to leave a trail of any sort.

A trail could be followed.

But the choice was not his. Incredible as it was, all he wanted was to leave this place. *His* place. The hidden canyon pool where he had received the vision that made him a man . . .

Get out.

Now.

Take your bag of bones and go!

When he jolted out from the trail that went behind the pool and in back of the waterfall, he must have seemed like a ghost who had lost all control of himself. His behavior was so wild that Heart at first did not recognize him. The gelding reared and snorted.

It was full dark now and the rain clouds blocked the starlight. Still, Heart should have caught his scent.

Owl spoke to his horse. He did his best to keep his voice normal and controlled. "Heart," he said. "It is only me. I am the same man who left you here not long ago."

Owl hoped that what he said was true. The sound of his voice did have a calming effect on Heart.

Owl had no wish to linger. He retied the parfleche full of *piamempits* bones to his saddle. Heart jerked to the other side. Owl had to snatch up the reins and give a sharp pull. It might have been that he saw the orange glow again, coming through the hide of the parfleche.

Owl mounted. He could feel Heart trembling beneath him. He could summon no anger against his horse. Owl felt more than a little strange himself.

His world was slipping away from him.

He desperately needed to reclaim it.

That was why he did not give Heart the signal to move out. He could not do it quite yet.

After all, this *was* the place. Or it had been.

Sitting astride Heart, with the great darkness shrouding him, Owl reached into his deerskin medicine pouch and grasped the flaked stone of the grooved flint. He held it in his naked hand. He lifted it up toward Mother Moon, who was hidden by the clouds. He offered it to the four directions.

He waited.

Nothing happened. There was no Spirit Beast shuffling in the shadowed trail below the ledges. There was no Voice. There were no words. There were no weary, gleaming eyes.

Nothing.

His medicine was dead, or it was speaking to him in a language he could not understand.

He looked around, searching for a sign in the night. Any sign. There was no sign. The only sound was the steady patter of the waterfall.

Owl replaced the flint point in his pouch, retied the drawstring, and adjusted it around his neck. It sometimes happened that a medicine went away and then came back. It sometimes happened that a medicine was sending a message that was not recognized.

Still, Owl felt a terrible emptiness within him. It was not just the loss of the *puha* of the lance point that had killed the Cannibal Owl.

It was the Cannibal Owl itself, sleeping up there in the cliffs of the long dead.

Again the question that could not be asked forced itself into his mind. Owl touched the parfleche without opening it. He might or might not have felt some heat. He knew what those bone fragments were like. He had seen bones like them ever since he had been a boy.

He thought of the crusted bird bones he had eaten at the place where the picnic had been. He thought of other birds that he had killed and eaten.

He remembered that massive skull up there above him in the rock chamber that was the last resting place of the Cannibal Owl. It was almost solid bone. He remembered the rows of crested grinding teeth.

Those were not the bones of a bird. They were not the bones of any creature that flew, no matter how vast the wings.

Owl was sickened with facts he could not comprehend. It was as if his world had turned over and all the rules had suddenly been changed.

He was colder than he had ever been in any white blizzard in the Shining Mountains.

He told himself that a spirit bird like the Cannibal Owl could take any form it wished. If a thing had enough power, it could assume any shape. The weight of its bones meant nothing.

The explanation did not satisfy him. It was like a story told to a child, and he was not a child. The world had to make sense, hang together. There were some things that simply could not be.

He could not remain longer in this place of betrayal. He had gotten more than he had come here for. Much more.

Too much more.

He gave Heart the signal. Heart moved.

Owl just hung on, his stunned mind refusing to function.

More alone than he had ever been in his adult life, Owl rode out of the black canyon with his parfleche and the cold fire of ancient medicine bones.

10

Coffee, Late Fall

There may be no end to wandering, but a time comes when a man must have a break from it. Coffee had never quit a trail in his life, and he would not quit the search for Otis Nesbitt.

The plain fact was that he had no trail, hot or cold. He had found the black man. He had learned that he was looking for a man called Owl. That was all. Like his namesake, Owl seemed to glide in the night from camp to camp and then disappear. It was little to show for months of hard riding.

Coffee was not insane. He could not return to Stafford empty-handed, but Stafford was not the world and Lisa Nesbitt was not the only woman in it. He would be no help to Otis if he killed his horse and himself in the bargain. Besides, he figured that Otis was past the point where a few days one way or the other would make much difference.

Coffee slipped out his heavy Walker Colt, put it on half-cock, and spun the cylinder.

"Pear," he said, "let's you and me head back to Austin."

Pear did not actually click his hooves together with applause, but he picked up the pace some. Even the packhorse on the lead rope seemed to come back from the dead.

They were all tired and sore and hungry. They had all seen enough threadbare and stinking Indian camps to last them a lifetime.

Coffee was not a man who yearned for civilization. He had very mixed feelings about it. But he was damn sure ready for a taste of it now. Men who sang happy songs about long lonely trails had never ridden one or were full drunk.

The way you got through it was to ride with your head down. You sensed what was going on through the corners of your eyes. You looked straight ahead of you as seldom as possible. That way, you were always surprised by how much distance you had covered. You did not discourage yourself by constantly staring at empty space and wondering how long it would take to cross.

You did your best to ignore the weather. This was a time of the year in Texas when anything might happen. It was the kind of season that had given rise to the old saying, "If you don't like the weather in Texas, wait a minute." Usually the weather required no special precautions. When it got too cold or too wet or too something, it had a way of reminding a man to pay attention.

Coffee realized that he was weary enough so that it affected his thinking. Nevertheless, he was surprised at how little progress he had made. Texas was big, true. Indians were not notorious for pouring their guts out to Texas Rangers, true. Just the same, how long should it take to get a line on a Comanche named Owl who was riding with a white boy called Otis Nesbitt? Even if they had holed up somewhere, Coffee should have heard *something*.

Well, the hell with it.

Not forever. Just for now.

Coffee released the hammer on his Colt and returned it to his holster.

It was deep into November when he rode into Austin.

It was almost impossible for a Ranger to put down roots while he was on active service. A home and a family had to wait.

Coffee got himself a room at the Bullock Hotel on the northwest corner of Congress and Pecan streets. It was one of Austin's older hotels, but Coffee liked it and was known there. In front, the Bullock was a two-story log building with a balcony jutting out over the six heavy hitching posts that rose out of the Congress mud. Out back, the hotel was not so fancy. It dropped off to one story that was a warren of cramped little rooms. That was where Coffee stayed.

His room actually had a window, an honest-to-God bed, a wooden chair that would hold his weight, and a chamber pot that was not too fragrant. More importantly, it was a stone's throw from the bath room. The bath room was not a privy. It had a huge tub in it that was coated with white enamel. There was a stove right in the bath room, and a black man named Josh who kept the wood burning and the water boiling in the kettles.

That hot tub was important. It was more valuable even than a sit-down dinner and clean, dry clothes. Coffee soaked in the steaming water until he was slick with sweat. He smoked a cigar that Josh lit for him. He luxuriated.

Josh was a big jowly man who hummed and chuckled and fussed all the time. He washed Coffee's back with genuine soap. He seemed to be enjoying himself, and Coffee wondered why all black men couldn't be that way. He gave Josh a tip that was larger than he could really afford. That made him feel still better. He knew that Lee remained out there somewhere, doing what he himself was supposed to do, and the big tip was kind of a peace offering. After all, they were all more or less alike, weren't they?

Coffee sent word to Faith. She might need some time to get things squared away. It was a thoughtless man who just showed up at the door. Then he took an entire day doing what he needed to do.

While Pear was being groomed and spoiled, Coffee walked around Austin looking for Rip Ford. That ruined his newly polished boots, of course, but the idea wasn't to *keep* them shined. He marveled at the changes that seemed to occur daily in Austin. The town was growing up. The old log cabins and slapdash offices were being replaced by impressive colonial-style houses with pillars. There were some brick structures that looked like they were made to last. The Governor's Mansion on Colorado Street wasn't quite finished, and Governor Pease hadn't moved in yet. Just the same, it was *some* kind of house. The Greek columns were so white they nearly blinded the eye. All of Austin was talking about Abner Cook, the architect. Coffee had never met him. He didn't move in those circles.

He couldn't locate Rip Ford. It wasn't as though the Ranger had an office somewhere. Coffee bought a copy of the *Texas State Gazette* and glanced through it. There was the usual blather about the extension of slavery in the West. He strolled past the new City Hotel. He wasn't much impressed, even though the City Hotel was constructed of brick. He went to the end of Congress, to Sam Stone's Ferry. It was just about the only way to cross the Colorado River, unless you wanted to swim your horse or yourself. Sam Stone always knew who was in town and who wasn't.

From Sam he learned that the ranking Ranger in Austin was Captain Owen Shaw. Shaw was based in San Antonio, but Coffee knew him well. He was a famous Indian fighter from the time he had operated out of Laredo.

Captain Shaw was easy to find. He was sitting astride a bar stool at the Long Rifle Tavern on Pecan Street, not far from Coffee's hotel. Captain Shaw was drinking coffee. That made the usual horseplay about Noah Coffee's name inevitable. There was little or no formality between Ranger captains and their men. Coffee indicated his respect by ordering coffee himself. The two men retired to a table where their conversation was less public.

Shaw made no comment about Coffee's absence from the field. If Coffee needed a break, that was good enough for Shaw.

"Still think you can find that Nesbitt boy alone?" Captain Shaw asked. His tone was not accusatory.

"I'll get him."

"I figure you're not real close, being in Austin and all." Again there was no hint of a reprimand in Shaw's voice.

Coffee told him what he knew. "Any of the men hear anything?"

Shaw shrugged. "They say Old Man Nesbitt is acting mighty strange. Nothing about the boy. I've heard tell of Owl. Just the name, that's all. Crazy name for a Comanche."

"You want to change my instructions? Think we should go about this thing different?"

Captain Shaw looked him dead in the eye. "I can't change your orders, Coffee. Not even if I wanted to, which I don't."

"I don't understand," Coffee said. Actually, he understood it all too well.

Shaw seemed to change the subject. "I hear that Sam Houston will run for governor in 'fifty-seven," he said. "That's coming on close."

"Won't General Houston still be in the Senate then?"

Shaw snorted. "You think that'll stop Old Sam?"

"I hope not," Coffee said. "I surely do hope not."

There was a silence between the two men. They both knew that there were some things best left unsaid.

What it came down to was simple. With the Republic of Texas gone and statehood rampant, the Texas Rangers had lost much of their legal power. Everything depended on what the governor wanted to do with them, and what kinds of funds he controlled. There were Rangers who had seen no pay for months.

Sam Houston understood who the Rangers were and what they could do. Old Sam might drink more than was good for him—or for any other four men—but he would not sit on his butt and allow inexperienced U.S. troops to do the job that Rangers were born doing.

"Plain fact is," Shaw said, "we haven't got any other plan for that Nesbitt boy. I ain't got no army to throw into the field, even if I thought it would do any good. We can send you some men if you get into a tight, but you're going to have to find Otis Nesbitt your own self."

"That suits me fine, Captain."

Shaw smiled. "It goes down good with me, too. You'll get him, Coffee. You'll get him if anyone can."

The two men shook hands.

That was all there was to it.

It was understood that the senior officer would pay for the coffee, and it was understood that the joke about Coffee's name would not be repeated twice in the same day.

Coffee had done what he had to do. It was time to do what he wanted to do.

He took his supper at the Bullock and then walked through the crisp twilight to Faith's house.

The widow Guyler lived fairly close to Shoal Creek, but not on it. Shoal Creek was the western edge of Austin. The creek was prone to flooding, but it was also exposed to the occasional Indian raid. For a woman living alone with a half-grown son, it was best to maintain a corridor of settlement between her home and the stream.

Even before Coffee knocked on the door, he knew that this visit was not going to be exactly what he had in mind. Faith Guyler lived in what was essentially a modified dogtrot log cabin. It was divided into two square rooms, each with a stone fireplace and a chimney. One room was used for sleeping, and the other was a sitting room with a dining table in it. The old open passage of the dogtrot had been walled in. She utilized it for storage, cooking, and washing.

The front door opened into the sitting room. What Coffee heard before he entered the room was the sound of someone throwing up. More exactly, it was a boy with the dry heaves.

Faith Guyler greeted him, and, to her credit, she was not flustered. She wore a long cotton dress with puffed sleeves, and her auburn hair was neatly curled. She had splashed on as much perfume as she could without being unduly bold, but it was a fact that Coffee could smell the boy's sickness on her.

"Evening, ma'am," Coffee said. He held his hat in his hands and fiddled with it.

"Hello, Coffee!" She seemed genuinely glad to see him, and she had a wonderful smile. Her teeth were almost unblemished, and she liked to show them off, even the crooked one in front.

Coffee shuffled his boots. It was an awkward situation. "Your boy is sick," he said, stating the obvious.

Faith threw up her hands. They were hands that had seen their share of difficult work, but they were surprisingly soft and pretty. Coffee knew those hands well. "It's *la grippe*," she said. It was always called that. Coffee thought of the handsome French Legation. That building was a holdover from when the state had been the Republic of Texas, and he had walked by it that very day. "I'm doing just what the doctor tells me to do, but Thomas is not well."

Coffee nodded. He was familiar with Doc Worsham. Worsham was in many ways the direct opposite of Stafford's Doc Patterson. Worsham was a wizard on gunshot wounds, but he had some funny ideas about treating children. His remedy tended to be the same, no matter what the disease. Pour down the laxatives, wrap the kids tightly in blankets, feed them bean soup and corn bread, and once a day walk them around outside "to give them some fresh air." It was a wonder that any of them survived.

Coffee was not entirely sure how he should behave. Was he a lover or a sickbed visitor? "If this is not a good time," he said, "I can leave. Or I can stay and help."

Faith laughed. There was nothing artificial about it. "When you call on a lady, *she* tells you when to leave. I don't recall mentioning the subject. As for the boy, I want you to look in on him and say hello. He likes you, you know. Then we will see what we will see."

Faith was flirting a bit. It would have been more effective without the sickroom smell. There was nothing like bean soup and laxatives, Coffee thought, to stop a romance dead in its tracks.

But then again, this was not a romance and this was hardly the first time the two of them had been together. Faith Guyler was the widow of a Ranger Coffee had known well, Seth Guyler. When Seth had taken a Comanche arrow in the throat and left Faith alone with a young child, it had become an accepted thing for other Rangers to come to call from time to time. There were plenty of bachelor Rangers, and Faith was very big on what she referred to as "keeping up appearances." She would not accept just any man. She would accept money, though. She had to live. It was very important to her that the money came in the form of gifts rather than payments.

The problem was simple. Faith would never dream of going to a hotel with a man, and there was a sick kid in the bedroom. Coffee couldn't figure that one out. He left it to Faith Guyler.

"I'll see the boy now," he said.

He clumped through the dogtrot area. It was cooler than the rest of the house. He entered the bedroom. It was so hot it was stifling.

Thomas was propped up in the bed Coffee knew so well. Usually the boy slept on a pallet on the floor. Thomas clutched a small bucket in his hands, fighting back more stomach convulsions. He looked like hell. His face was flushed with fire, then white with pain.

"Howdy, pardner," Coffee said. His voice was not as hearty as he had intended.

"Hello, Mr. Coffee." The boy tried to smile. "Get any Injuns lately?"

"Been chasing a lot of 'em. Not catching the ones I want, I'm afraid."

"Keep after 'em," the boy said weakly. He had not forgotten the death of his father. To him, any Ranger was sort of like one of the family.

"Can I bring you anything?" Coffee asked. He knew what the boy needed: another doctor. But changing doctors in a town like Austin was a tricky business. It wasn't a matter of money, but of loyalty. Doc Worsham had been Seth's doctor at the end. He cared for his widow. He would work for free, if necessary. That was how it was.

"Nothing to eat, please," Thomas managed to joke. He looked more like Faith than Seth, Coffee thought. Coffee was instantly reminded of Otis, although the boys did not resemble each other except in age.

Thinking of Otis made Coffee uncomfortable. He fell silent, and the silence went on too long.

"You'll come back and see me?" Thomas asked.

"Count on it, son. I'll be back. I know you're a fighter. You just keep fighting, you hear?"

"I hear, Mr. Coffee." The boy did not say that it was hard to fight what he had. He made no complaint at all. Coffee liked that. He thought that Seth would have been pleased.

Coffee returned to the sitting room. Making love was not in his heart. He had been on the trail for a long time, but this was neither the time nor the place.

Faith understood. She was not a stupid woman.

She had saved a bottle of red wine, and they drank some of that. They talked a great deal. Faith spoke of her worry about Thomas and the coming of Christmas. She discreetly let Coffee know that she would be engaged at Christmas. That suited Coffee. The season was a wild brawl from Christmas all the way into New Year's. Roman candles whooshed at each other in the streets. Every drunk in town would want to play fast-draw with a Ranger. Coffee had no intention of getting involved in that. He talked about many things, including Lisa Nesbitt. Faith was a tolerant woman. Mostly he talked about Owl and why he could not seem to find him.

It was getting late. Most of the lamps in this end of town had been snuffed out. Thomas had gone to sleep, or at least had grown silent.

Faith's cheeks were glowing from the wine. "Tomorrow night," she said, "Mrs. Crawford will be visiting

Thomas. She is very good with him. I will be at her house most of the evening. Mr. Crawford is in San Antone, I believe."

Coffee felt some interest stirring.

He took his leave politely, saving his gift for another day. He sensed that she would not want his money now. If he was mistaken, she was entirely capable of asking for it. Discreetly, of course.

He walked back alone through darkened streets to the Bullock Hotel.

As it turned out, Mr. Crawford stayed in San Antonio for quite a long time. Mrs. Crawford visited Thomas frequently. Coffee suspected that Faith was dividing some of her gifts with the kindly Mrs. Crawford.

Coffee and Faith had enough hours together to turn urgency into pleasure and then into routine.

It was while they were in bed together at the Crawford place that Faith said something that nearly rattled Coffee's nearby boots.

"You know," she said, blowing in his ear, "I'd just love to take a trip somewhere. Even a buggy ride out to Mount Bonnell. Naturally, I know that can't be, what with Thomas so sick and all. There's just no way he can travel. Why, sometimes I even think taking him out in the open air is a mistake, no matter what Doc Worsham says—"

Coffee sat straight up in bed, as though a coiled spring had popped loose in his back. That wasn't quite the reaction Faith had expected.

"What in the world?" she asked.

Coffee was up, pacing around the room in his long johns like a caged bobcat. "That's it," he said. "That's it!"

"That's what?" Faith was not petulant, just confused.

"That's what I've been doing wrong. I've been asking the wrong questions and following a false trail. Me!"

"You want to let the widow woman in on the secret?"

"Yes, yes!" He grabbed her and planted a big enthusiastic kiss on her mouth before he reached for his boots. "I've been looking for an Indian buck and a boy like

Thomas, traveling together. What if the boy is sick like Thomas? Or hurt some way?"

"Or dead," Faith said. She had scant love for Indians.

"I can't think about Otis being dead. I *won't* think about it. But even if he is, it's the same situation, don't you see? Owl's alone. The boy is alone. They ain't together. So I've been looking for something that isn't there."

She tried to be helpful. "After what he's been through, it'd be a miracle if he *wasn't* sick. It'd be a miracle if he's alive."

"He's alive." Coffee added irrationally: "Thomas is alive, isn't he? Getting better, even?"

Faith shook her head. Her auburn hair was loose and silky in the pale light. Men! "You won't leave town without seeing Thomas, will you? That boy thinks a lot of you, Coffee."

Excited as he was, that hurt Coffee. "Faith, I'd no more pull out of here without visiting Thomas than I would cut my own throat."

"I know that, Coffee. I shouldn't have asked." She began searching for her clothes.

Coffee waited impatiently, then walked Faith home. Thomas was asleep. Coffee walked Mrs. Crawford back to her house and returned to the Bullock Hotel.

The next morning was raw and cold. Coffee saddled a less than enthusiastic Pear and loaded his packhorse.

On his way out of town, he stopped to pay a gentlemanly call on Faith Guyler. He had a long talk with Thomas. He wanted to hug the sick boy and tell him he loved him. A man couldn't do that. He settled for a firm handshake and a wink. It *did* seem to him that Thomas was almost out of the woods. Score one for Doc Worsham—or in spite of Doc Worsham.

Like a hound on a fresh trail, Coffee left Austin.

He had been in Austin one day longer than a week.

Coffee rode toward winter, and he was ready to pitch into anything.

This time, he knew that he would not be denied.

Lee, Late Fall

Lee was riding from nowhere to nowhere, and he knew it. His pride kept him from Stafford. It was unthinkable for him to venture to a place like Austin.

It was not bitterly cold. There had been years, Lee remembered, with scarcely a freeze from one January to another. There had been other years when ice crusted the small water, and the winds howled down from skies of ice. So far, it was only raw and unpleasant. But it was not yet December.

Lee rode with his head down and his creased hat jammed over part of his ears. He knew perfectly well that it was not the trail or the time away from his room that was bothering him. Hell, there had been years when he had ridden longer and tougher trails with Cole Nesbitt.

He missed the old codger, and he felt oddly close to him. That was part of the problem. Even though the Comanches usually took him in readily enough, Lee was alone. Lonely trails are always longer.

The rest of it was the sense that something was being held back from him. Knowing about Owl and finding Owl were two different things. Word about Otis simply had not come. That seemed peculiar to Lee. It should not have taken this much time.

It was true that the Comanches were scattered in little fragmented bands over a huge area from the Arkansas River south to the Nueces, and from far west of the Rio Grande to within a sea breeze of the Gulf of Mexico. Of course, the occupation was not unbroken and probably never had been. There weren't that many Comanches. It only seemed that way.

Still, the territory was vast. The links between one Comanche group and another were often weak and unreliable. It was possible for a man like Owl to vanish. It wouldn't be the first time.

Lee was in that unaware state that sometimes sneaks up on you when you have been in the saddle too long. He was awake but he was not alert. His horse, Doc, was no better. He was just plodding along, dreaming of some good hay and a rubdown. Then the inevitable happened.

The first Lee realized that something was wrong was when he heard a voice. The voice was close. The voice said: "Looks like we found ourselves a runaway nigger."

Lee had not lived as long as he had by being slow to react. He was instantly on guard, every muscle tense. But being a man of considerable experience, Lee did not show a thing. He remained slumped in the saddle, head down. If these folks thought they had a sleepy, black foot shuffler on their hands, that suited him fine.

He bought time with his eyes, narrowed beneath his hat brim.

There were three of the mothers. Lee knew one of them by reputation. He was called Monte Montero. He could be recognized instantly by his thin face, cratered by the pox, his high sombrero, which had a coonskin—head, tail, and all—wrapped around it, and a knife in his belt that was big and fancy enough to be a sheathed ceremonial sword.

What Lee felt when he realized he was up against Monte Montero was relief. He cared nothing for Montero's reputation as a gunman. Monte Montero was one of those men who lived on the loose edge of the law. Texas was full of them, men who had been driven out of every other hellhole in the country. He was a bounty hunter, he was a stagecoach thief, and he was careless with livestock that belonged to other people. He was based down Gillman way, but the only reason he had not been hung from the tallest tree in the county was that he managed to stay one jump ahead of the posse.

In short, Monte Montero was not the sort who would be missed. Just in case something should happen to him.

Montero's two companions did not much concern Lee. One was a big Lipan on a fine bay horse. He was the one who had spoken. Lee figured that he would do plenty more talking before a play was made. He had a Navy Dragoon Colt, but Lee was experienced in sizing up would-be gunmen. The Lipan did not count. The third man was a Navajo, or had been, judging by the silver conchos on his belt. Lee did not recognize his gun, except that it was old. He had no idea what a Navajo was doing with Monte Montero. He might be dangerous, but Lee doubted it. He would just have to be careful.

Monte Montero himself was the problem. He had a Billinghurst showing under the skirts of his long coat. The Billinghurst was a wicked weapon. It was an over-and-under rifle-shotgun. The rifle was .44 caliber and could fire seven times without reloading. The shotgun was a 12-gauge. The barrel was fairly short. Montero could bring it up in a hurry, and Lee did not doubt that his finger was on one of the triggers.

"Well, damn my eyes," said Big Talk, the Lipan. He did an adequate imitation of a Texas drawl. "I do believe we have come across a big fat re-ward."

Montero said nothing. He just smiled, showing his bad teeth.

The Navajo said nothing. Lee suddenly caught on to the fact that the Navajo was dead drunk in his saddle. He mentally downgraded the threat from that direction. Not a bad-looking horse either, although he seemed slightly lame in his right rear leg. Nothing serious, probably.

"Well, nigger," said Big Talk. "I reckon you better just drop that gun belt of yours and climb down off that horse."

Lee looked up for the first time. He tried to look scared to death. He even rolled his eyes a little.

"Can't you talk, nigger?"

Lee kept his voice down to a shaken whisper. He had to be sure.

"What is you going to do with me?"

Big Talk laughed. "Oh, maybe run you around a little. Have some fun, you know? Or if you give us any trouble before we take you in, kill you dead as a crowbar."

Nobody made any vocal response to that. Monte Montero grinned. The Navajo—if that's what he was—sat his horse in a stupor. Lee said nothing.

"You understand me, boy?" Big Talk said.

"I understand," Lee said. It was his normal voice, as though he were carrying on a casual conversation with some friends he had happened to meet. "Thank you."

Lee was so fast, and the three men had underestimated him so badly, that there was no contest at all.

The only thing Lee worried about was whether Doc would shy or not. He did that sometimes when there was gunplay.

Lee's Paterson Colt was in his right hand with the hammer back before any of the three realized that he was not about to drop his gun belt.

Lee took Monte Montero first. He did not like that Billinghurst over-and-under gun. A head shot was too dangerous. The target was small enough so that it was possible to miss. Lee gave Montero a .36 slug in the middle of the chest. He had heard it said that a .36 was not heavy enough to do the job. It was good enough to knock Monte Montero out of his saddle. The Billinghurst clattered away where he could not reach it.

The flame flash and the plume of smoke and the crashing concussion were twice as deafening because they were totally unexpected. Lee's second shot took Big Talk right in his open mouth. Lee was not worried about the Navy Colt. Big Talk never even got his hand close to the butt.

That left the Navajo. The loner actually gave a hint of beginning to sober up. His dark eyes registered something. Lee felt a little bad about it, but he had no choice. He hit the Navajo exactly between the eyes. That was painless. Lee was pleased with the shot.

The crashing echoes died away. Lee dismounted, giving Doc an approving slap. Doc had stood rock still. Lee checked out the great Monte Montero. He was alive, barely. Lee hated to waste the load, but he put the barrel of his Colt against Montero's temple, cocked it deliberately to free the trigger, and fired. Montero jerked some.

Lee wasted no time questioning his own course of action. He had killed men before, and better men than these. He knew precisely what he had to do.

First, he took a spare cylinder out of his coat pocket and broke down the Paterson to reload. The Paterson Colt was a five-shot revolver, but one loaded chamber was not enough to bet your life on.

Next, he chased down the three horses and got them under control. He had to rope one of them and tie the knots for a lead line. Where he was going, those three horses were priceless.

He then carefully collected all the guns and ammunition. He wrapped them in a bundle that Doc could carry. He was not taking them for himself, although he did have a sneaking admiration for Montero's Billinghurst. They were the greatest presents in the world. If he could not buy information with those horses and guns, he didn't know a norther from an arroyo. They were far, far better than the trinkets he had taken from his trunk.

Lee thought it over briefly, and decided to leave the saddles on the horses. They were already there, and they would make no difference in the speed with which he moved. Sometimes the Comanches liked saddles, sometimes they didn't. He could worry about that later.

Lee felt urgency now. If he was caught on the trail with three stolen horses and a pile of guns, neither fast talking nor fast shooting could save him. It would not matter much that one of the dead men he had left behind was Monte Montero. Lee might be swinging from a tree before that fact was even known.

What he had to do was simple. He had to get the hell out of there. He had to find the closest Comanche camp, and find it fast. Damn those camps for moving around like they did!

Lee was hardly filled with remorse for what he had done. Neither was he much impressed with the sanctity of human life. The fact was, life was dirt cheap on the frontier. People came and went, lived and died, and that was the way it was.

Just the same, Lee felt a trace of guilt.

It did not seem right to just leave the three bloody bodies in the uncaring dirt. He stared at them, knowing that he was wasting precious time. A small white worm of some sort crawled out of the coonskin fastened around Montero's tall-coned hat.

There was probably money on Montero's corpse. Lee considered taking it and giving it to Otis if he ever found him. He decided against it.

No matter how steady he had been, no matter how confident he was of the outcome, Lee could not kill three more or less human beings and feel absolutely nothing at all. There was a reaction beginning to set in.

For God's sake, man, don't start shaking now.

Get your tail up and ride.

Burying the men was out of the question, of course. Lee did not have that kind of time. Besides, digging holes was hard work. Even shallow holes.

Overhead, buzzards stained the cheerless gray sky. It didn't take them long.

Lee removed his hat. "Dust to dust," he said. "Ashes to ashes."

He added: *"Vaya con Dios."* Go with God.

That would have to do it. Lee swung into Doc's saddle, launched the procession as well as he could, and made tracks.

Too many tracks.

The nearest Comanche camp known to Lee was that of Wolf Eye. He had no way to tell whether or not Wolf Eye's camp was actually where it should be at this time of the year, but a reasonable guess was better than riding blind.

Lee and Wolf Eye knew one another. They had fought in the Webster raid. There was a kinship between old warriors, even if they had been on different sides.

Lee was not worried about Wolf Eye. The headman might have information or he might not. In either case, Wolf Eye would not ambush him or banish him from his camp. Lee and Wolf Eye had shared meals together. There was some conduct that was unthinkable between honorable men.

Lee was worried about what was behind him. He had the distinct sensation that he was being followed. As the leaden afternoon gave way to the darker evening, he had no trouble at all seeing ghosts. He had a feeling that they were all around him.

He could not move fast enough. Riding one horse and controlling three others took some doing. Doc was loaded down with hardware.

It seemed to take him forever, but Lee did find Wolf Eye's well-hidden camp. Wolf Eye even had fires burning. He must be very sure of himself or very stupid. Lee knew that he was not stupid.

Lee made plenty of noise, not that he had much choice in the matter. He wanted to be certain that the Comanches knew he was not sneaking up on them. It would be a terrible irony to lose everything now.

As he rode, Lee could not help wondering what sustained a man like Wolf Eye. How could he go on living, building fires and cooking meat and making babies? Did he not know what he was up against?

Wolf Eye had ten tipis in the camp. That meant

maybe fifty or sixty of The People, most of them women and children. Lee saw a decent pony herd pastured on the fringe of a cedar stand. The tipi hides seemed to be in good repair. The ones that had fires burning inside glowed orange in the gathering darkness. There were mouth-watering food smells in the still air.

It was like a secure haven that existed somewhere out of time. It had always been there and would always be there. Nothing of this world could touch it.

Except that the secure haven was a total illusion. The camp of Wolf Eye was surround by enemies. Not a few enemies. Thousands of enemies, and more on the way. It was true that the enemies were not actively trying to seek him out and destroy him. Not yet they weren't. It was pretty much a situation of staying out of each other's way.

But a handful of Indians camped on the edge of eternity? Did they not understand they had no chance at all in the long run?

Well, the Comanches had always won, hadn't they?

Were they not in charge here until someone proved otherwise?

Indians did not post sentries. Just the same, when Lee rode into the little camp, they were waiting for him.

Lee was all smiles and expansive gestures. He let it be known quickly that he had come bearing gifts. Might as well, he figured. Wolf Eye's people were not so friendly that he had a chance in hell of riding out of that village with three extra horses.

Wolf Eye came out of his tipi to greet him. That was a rare honor. Wolf Eye stood bare-chested with his hands on his hips. He had a fairly fresh scalp braided in his hair. He carried no weapons but had a look about him that suggested he might not need any.

"Has my old enemy come for food or daughters?" asked Wolf Eye.

Lee dismounted. He did not offer to surrender his Colt. Several young warriors took the horses away, all four of them. Lee was wise enough in Indian ways not to ask if he would ever see Doc again. The trick was, if you could not fully trust, at least act as though you could.

"Smoke first," Lee said. "My pipe or yours. We have many things that a man might want to talk about."

Wolf Eye laughed. He was a burly man, even for a Comanche. His legs might have been bowed, but his chest was like the trunk of a century-old oak tree. Muscles rippled in the firelight. Lee was impressed.

"You laugh," Lee said.

"My enemy-friend has visited me before," Wolf Eye pointed out reasonably. "Always, he has shown some interest in food and daughters."

"He has never come before with so many gifts."

"Ah." Wolf Eye did not have to think long on that one. "We will smoke, then. It may be that there will be much talk."

"Some of it can be about food and daughters," Lee offered. He felt comfortable with Wolf Eye. It seemed strange that they were on different sides. That did not mean that his Colt would become detached from him.

The two men entered Wolf Eye's tipi. It was so tall that Wolf Eye's women would have to stand on one another's shoulders to fasten the top flap. The sides were staked down in the cool weather. A dew cloth lining of buffalo skin hung from the lodge poles about six feet up. It made the tipi cozy with only a small fire in the exact center of the lodge. Wolf Eye seated himself in front of his elevated bed, behind the fire pit and facing the entrance. He placed Lee on his left, which was the position of honor.

There were no women or children visible. The two men were alone in the tipi.

They smoked Lee's pipe, which was a blessing. Comanche pipes were harsh and dry. A man felt foolish when he choked on the searing smoke.

The talk began. They were actually bargaining, but it was not phrased that way. It was all very oblique. There was much talk of Webster and old battles and the worth of children.

It was Lee's considered opinion that it was the

Billinghurst over-and-under rifle-shotgun that tipped the scales. Wolf Eye actually summoned a warrior and had the gift brought to him for examination.

Lee knew and Wolf Eye knew that the Comanches could simply take the weapon if they wanted it. Lee was good, but he could not prevail against the entire camp. That was not the way things were done between men of honor.

Wolf Eye finally nodded.

It was not a simple matter to understand exactly what he knew and what he didn't. Wolf Eye's talk remained oblique.

Nevertheless, by the time the stone-boiled venison stew had been ladled out and the proper daughter selected for the night, Lee had learned one of the vital facts that had eluded him.

For the first time, he heard the name of Spirit Shadow.

12

Owl, Winter

It was strangely dry, but the winter wind that whipped through the flaps of the great lodge of Spirit Shadow was very cold. The painted vermilion circles and squares seemed indeed as icy as the stars. The yellow beaks of eagles were frozen in their flight.

The *Kaku*, Grandmother, kept Owl waiting outside in the wind for a very long time. She had much courage. She was afraid of nothing. Owl was impatient and eager to see the boy. On top of that, he had fears about the loss of his medicine.

Owl was not in a playful mood.

He had handed her the parfleche containing the bones of the Cannibal Owl. She had accepted the hide bag without comment. There was no visible glow around it now. Had the fire died? Was the power weakened?

He had given her enough crow feathers and juniper berries to stuff an ordinary tipi. He had even found a few of the blueberries that were fresh. A man could never be certain of this world. Sometimes a tree produced berries when it should not.

The buffalo meat was a larger problem. Finding and killing the cows and calves was nothing; Heart could almost have done it by himself. But Owl was a much-married man. It counted for little that in the law of The People it was the husband who was the master. Owl knew better than to ride into his village and order his wives to skin and butcher buffalo for another woman. She might be Spirit Shadow, but she was female. There were some problems that had to be approached with great care.

First, he had to construct more than one travois. They were not complicated, consisting simply of dragging poles with crosspieces attached to them. They were narrow at the harness that went over the horse and wide at the dragging ends. Simple as they were, it took time to find the proper poles without dismantling a tipi. Lashing a travois to a horse could rub horseflesh raw if it was not properly done.

Heart hated pulling a travois, no matter how well it was made. It was an insult to a war-horse.

However, Owl needed a lot of meat. It was obvious to him that he must supply his own family first. The additional butchering, involving an entire calf and most of a cow, with the head and long bones removed, must appear to his wives to be an afterthought.

That meant several horses, and more than one travois. Owl could not carry the meat to Spirit Shadow on his back. He was just grateful that the weather was cool and pemmican had not been requested. If all of the meat had to be pounded up with fat and berries, he might never see his son again.

Owl pulled it off. His wives did the heavy cutting and fleshing and stayed in good temper. Owl just got bloody enough to show that he was not too big a man to help.

Owl made no secret of what he was doing. That would have been impossible in any case. The women knew everything, sooner or later. If they considered him crazy, they were discreet enough not to mention it.

That was well. In Owl's view, they had failed to provide him with living sons. He considered himself a tolerant man, but he could be pushed too far. There were some jokes he did not find amusing. A man who was unsure of his medicine was more dangerous than usual. Little things might set him afire.

In fact, Owl was close to anger while he was forced to wait outside the magnificent lodge of Spirit Shadow. The entry flap was closed, but there was smoke pouring out of the vent in the top of the tipi. The smoke was blue. It fairly bubbled with the juicy smells of green onions, sage, sweet grass, and hump meat steaming in a broth of crushed mesquite beans and pecan nuts.

Owl imagined that he could smell O-tis through the hides of that great tipi. The boy had much grease on him and some kind of pungent mush mixed into his hair. But it was O-tis. Owl was certain of it.

Spirit Shadow had not even told him if the boy was alive or dead. But she would not have accepted his gifts if O-tis had died. Not all of them, anyway. That would have been a very dangerous thing to do. That was how doctors themselves came to know death.

It was the thought of the boy that stayed Owl's hand. If the Grandmother believed that he must wait out in the wind, then he must wait.

Not forever, no.

But long enough for the *puhakut* to finish whatever she had to do. Owl set his jaw and narrowed his eyes against the wind.

She had better be doing more than stuffing that enormous body of hers. That was the trouble with doctors, Owl reflected. When you needed them, you were at their mercy. You did not dare interfere because of the harm that might be caused to the one who was sick.

You waited.

And waited.

And you too came to a boil, just as though a red-hot stone had been dropped into your blood.

Then she came out, that jiggling, hibernating bear of a woman. She balanced her bulk on her giant beaded moccasins. She was wrapped in a beautiful white fur robe against the wind. Her red ears flamed and her jade

Pueblo bracelet flapped on her wrist. Her streaming hair was as wild as a thundercloud.

"Hnhh," she said. Her red-lined eyes were wise and deep.

"I wish to see my son," Owl said.

"You shall see him," said Spirit Shadow.

She gave what might have been a huge fat-jointed bow, and held open the entry flap for him.

Moist heat gushed out of the lodge.

Owl smelled the boy. He was sure of it.

He brushed past that mountain of a woman, trying not to touch her, and almost ran into the lodge.

The boy who had been Otis Nesbitt was almost lost in the cavernous interior of the lodge of Spirit Shadow. The tipi was so big that it actually contained a sweat lodge. When the steam was released from the stone boiling, it rose through the slanted fire-smoke vent in the top of the tipi. The air in Spirit Shadow's lodge was heavy with moisture and the scent of herbs. Owl remembered the texture very well. When he had last escaped from it, at the time when Spirit Shadow had worked on one of his wives to bear him a son, the outside air had seemed so light and clean that he had gulped all that he could hold into his lungs.

Owl's first reaction was an audible groan of relief that the boy had survived. This son was not dead. It was one thing to know it in your gut. It was another to see it.

His second impression was that O-tis looked strange. The boy was propped up against an elevated bed. There was a buffalo robe thrown over him, but he was naked from the waist up. His blue eyes had been ringed with a darker blue paint, and streaks of the blue paint ran from his eyes to the back of his head. His sandy hair, thickened with grease, had channels cut through it to allow the paint to stick. On the back of his head, fastened with braided cords of sweet grass, there was a soiled skin cap smeared with a strong-smelling paste.

Nothing strange about *that*. When a doctor worked

on one who was very sick, the doctor had to do what was necessary.

No, the strangeness came from Otis Nesbitt himself. The boy who had been all bones and awkward muscles was flabby with fat. He was soft, very soft. Whatever else Spirit Shadow had done to him, she had certainly kept the food coming.

There was a focus back in the blue eyes. There was a mind. But it was a mind in turmoil. This was not the same boy who had caught crawdads in the Guadalupe sunlight and chopped off their tails with a flint knife he had made himself.

Much had happened to O-tis, inside and out.

Owl approached the boy but he could not bring himself to speak. Having endured so much, he had no supply of ready words. Wanting desperately to tell this boy what he believed and wanted and needed, he found himself mute.

Was it always to be this way with his son?

Was it his destiny to fail as a father?

It might have been that the loss of his medicine had something to do with it. Owl was unsure of himself. He felt somehow that things had gotten twisted. *He* was the boy, awaiting judgment.

Owl stood there. He was a warrior who had never faltered in battle. Yet this was a world he could not entirely comprehend.

He was very conscious of his surroundings. The lodge of Spirit Shadow was not like other lodges. Apart from its size and the sweat house in the middle of it, it had containers hanging from tripods and cross poles. Many of them were skin bags. They were Comanche-style, but very ornate. Spirit Shadow also had brass and iron trade kettles. There were even standing pottery vessels with curious black and white designs on them. Like her jade bracelet, those pots were Pueblo. There was a link between Spirit Shadow and the Pueblo peoples that had never been explained.

Every bag, every kettle, every pot was stuffed with dried plants and ground-up bones and bright gourds containing seeds and pebbles that rattled when they stirred. There were so many feathers in the tipi that they seemed to float in the heavy air.

Such a lodge was almost impossible in a real Comanche camp. It would take an army of women to strike it and set it up again in a hurry. It would take a herd of horses to carry all the paraphernalia that belonged to Spirit Shadow. Just to supply such a dwelling was no small task. If Spirit Shadow lived in her tipi alone, she had to be surrounded by responsible helpers.

In fact, this was not a true tipi, despite its shape. This was close to being a permanent structure, like a Pueblo cliff dwelling. This was not a part of the Comanche life that Owl knew.

It could only have existed in one of those villages that was a part of two worlds. These Comanches did not raid, and avoided the warpath. Imagine a Comanche who did not raid! They were peaceful and interested in trade. It was rumored that *Taibos* sometimes came to see Spirit Shadow when their own doctors failed them. The Texans might let this village alone until the reservation fever really caught on. It was a matter of great interest to Owl that all of The People were not alike and were not treated alike. The time might come when such in-between villages could not be, but for now, here they were.

It came to Owl that Spirit Shadow was taking a terrible chance to keep Otis Nesbitt here.

Things would not go well for her if someone found the boy.

As he had done before, Owl had to remind himself not to underestimate this woman's power or her will. Sheathed in blubber she might be, but she held the answers to many riddles.

Not all of the riddles were about O-tis.

As he stood there in a cone of silence, rocking back and forth on his high-topped moccasins, Owl heard a strangling, choking sound from his son.

Spirit Shadow seized Owl's rough scarred elbow. Her grip was surprisingly firm.

"He wishes to speak," she said. "There is something that he has wanted to tell you."

Owl did not hesitate. He dropped to his knees to bring his face to the same level as that of the boy. Owl would not have knelt before any other man or woman in the world.

His sharp old eyes drilled into the weakened blue eyes of O-tis. The boy was not strong, but he did not look away.

"Speak," said Owl. His voice was harsher than he had intended.

The boy swallowed, to clear his throat, and uttered noises that Owl did not understand. There were some Comanche words here and there, but it was not all Comanche. Owl was not even sure that all of it was language. He realized that they had been much apart. The communication they once had between them would have to be established all over again.

Spirit Shadow saved the situation. She knew Comanche, she knew some English, and she knew much about boys and sickness and fear.

She crooned some medicine words.

"Ask him again," she said to Owl.

"Speak," said Owl. He managed to soften his tone a little, but he was not pleased to be on his knees in front of a boy. And with a woman watching!

Otis Nesbitt said more words. This time they were clearer. His voice was weak but firm.

Spirit Shadow translated in a singsong. "Mr. Owl, my heart has been much troubled. I want you to know why I did what I did."

Owl was not eager to relive the spitting incident. He could still taste the mucous and the shreds of raw crayfish tails that had struck him so unexpectedly in the face. He did not want Spirit Shadow to know about that. Stupid! Of course, the boy had been with Spirit Shadow for many days and nights. They would have talked. She would know everything. That required no medicine knowledge.

"Speak," Owl said again. His knees were bothering him. He was not used to this position.

"Mr. Owl," O-tis said, speaking through Spirit Shadow, "it was when you fastened the turkey feather in the back of my hair."

"I remember," Owl said. He wanted to say much more. He wanted to tell the boy how proud he had been, how eager he was to have a son. He could not say any of that. Not yet.

"Mr. Owl," the boy said. "I thought that you were mocking me. You know, taunting me? I thought you were saying I was not good enough to be one of The People. I thought the feather was a joke. I had been trying very hard to be what you wanted me to be. The storm was confusing. I did not know what I was supposed to think."

The boy's voice was getting a little shaky now. That had been a long talk for one who had been much silent.

Owl did not move. He had not forgotten the storm, and now he had one raging within him. The truth was that the turkey feather *had* been partly a joke. But only partly. It had also been a tribute. More than that, it had been a gift born of exuberance. He had been proud of O-tis.

How could he tell him that? How could he tell him that it took amazing courage for a boy to have gone through what O-tis had and still have enough pride to spit in the face of his captor? How could he tell him that he was displeased with himself for hurling O-tis down against a rock?

There were some things that simply could not be said, man to man or father to son.

There was some moisture in the boy's eyes. It smudged the dark blue paint rings. But O-tis did not cry. That was good.

"I want to tell you that I am sorry for what I did," the boy said. "I was brought up better than that."

Owl stood up. This kneeling thing was too much. There was confusion surging within him. He was not comfortable with all this talk. It was not Comanche.

But there was another part to Owl. He was Comanche, yes, to the very fiber of his being. It had never even occurred to him that he might be anything else. He was also human. It was the human side that was getting him into trouble.

If a son could explain to a father, could not the father reach out to the son? Why was that wrong?

Owl wanted to say something like: "I should not have lost my temper. I should have taken time to understand."

He could no more say that than he could turn into a bat and fly out of a cave.

He said, "Hnhh."

Sensing that the grunt was inadequate, he managed: "That is over between us."

O-tis nodded. He was satisfied with that. But he was not through. "Mr. Owl," he said, "I want to go home."

Owl said nothing. He was determined to control himself no matter what the boy said.

"It ain't that I hate you, Mr. Owl. I don't care what you did. I suspect you got your reasons. But, you see, I already got a pa."

That hit Owl like an arrow in the stomach. The boy had learned nothing!

Owl folded his arms across his weathered chest. There was no softness in him now, and no uncertainty.

"You are home, O-tis," he said with quiet finality. "I am your father."

The boy did not even blink. There was a stricken look on his face. It was not hate, as he had said. It was not fear.

It was sheer, empty hopelessness.

"You have talked enough," said Spirit Shadow. There may or may not have been disapproval in her voice. "The boy is not strong enough to travel. For that reason, the Great Father must leave." Spirit Shadow was not above sarcasm.

One day, Owl thought, she might go too far.

"I must talk more," Owl said.

"Not this day."

"I must have words with you that are not about the boy."

"Hnhh. You speak of the loss of your medicine."

Involuntarily, Owl touched the pouch that hung from his neck. He did not trace the outline of the grooved point. "How do you know about that?"

"Hnhh. I know all of your questions."

Owl must have looked skeptical at that one.

"For instance," Spirit Shadow said, "you are troubled by the true shape of *piamempits,* the Cannibal Owl."

Owl was thunderstruck. How could she know this thing?

"So you see," the medicine woman said in what was almost a teasing manner, "you have much need of Spirit Shadow. It is still to be discovered who has a son and who does not. It is still to be discovered what was the true meaning of the message you received in the death canyon of the Cannibal Owl. And I will tell you another thing."

"What is that?" asked Owl. He felt like an infant who continually wormed out of its cradle board and got burned in the tipi fire.

"They are coming for you. I see not many, but enough. Two or perhaps three. They will find you before the flowers show the color of spring. When they come, they will take the boy."

Owl stared at that enormous woman. He sucked the too-warm moist air into his lungs. He wanted to scoop O-tis up and run for it. He wanted to stand and fight. He wanted an end to mysteries.

He was a warrior! This was not a place for warriors.

"We will talk now," he said.

"No. Not this day."

"Your own words!" Owl was more than frustrated. *"They are coming."*

"They have always been coming. Did you believe that they would just forget you? But there is yet time. We will speak. You and the boy will speak. There is much healing that must happen in this lodge."

The wind whipped around the medicine tipi. There was the moan of winter in that wind. The flowers were far away.

Owl glanced at O-tis. The boy was asleep.

"Spirit Shadow, I want your promise that when I return there will be enough time for talk."

"Hnhh. I make no promises."

There was anger growing in Owl. This meeting was not going as he wished. It seemed to him that his life was increasingly determined by others.

Spirit Shadow knew his anger. Spirit Shadow knew too much.

"Do not threaten me, Great Father," she said. "I have said that much healing must happen in this lodge. There are actions for which there can be no healing. That is one of them."

The anger in Owl was close to boiling over. To think that he had to hear such talk from a woman!

There was only one thing he could do. He spun on his heel and lurched out of the medicine tipi.

He said nothing until the hiss of the chill wind carried his words away.

The village of Spirit Shadow was not the village of Owl. He had neither kin nor friends there. If he could not stay with the medicine woman, he had to construct his own shelter. The distances were too great for him to ride back and forth between his camp and hers.

A tipi was out of the question. That would require four good poles as a foundation, and perhaps twenty more poles as stringers. It would take at least ten buffalo hides. In any case, that was woman's work.

He could have slept on the ground if necessary and built a cook fire in a hole. The weather was dry. It was not bitterly cold. It had been Owl's experience that winds usually blew something in ahead of them or behind them, but the wind calmed and nothing happened.

He built a crude brush dome of hooped saplings. It was barely big enough to hold him, and pitiful when compared to the huge painted lodge of Spirit Shadow. No matter. Owl was not interested in impressing anyone with a house. That was stupid. He did find a stand of shielding cedars for Heart. There was not enough grass there for a sheep, but there was bark and some winter shrubbery that would do for browsing. All Owl had to do was construct a skin container for water, and it was cool enough so that a horse drank but little. Heart was not pleased with his situation, but he was undergoing no real hardship. Geldings could put up with a lot.

That was more than could be said for Owl. He was very impatient and very worried. He knew perfectly well that every day he delayed increased his risk of discovery. More critically, it exposed O-tis to whatever was coming after him.

Owl took to walking O-tis the way he would exercise a horse that had not been ridden for many moons. He extended the walks each day. He wanted to get the flab off. A son of his must be lean and hard. He had no chance of survival otherwise.

The real question, of course, was whether Owl had a son or not. A captive was one thing. A son was another.

The speaking of kinship took place in the great tipi of Spirit Shadow. Owl understood that the boy was not yet healed. He saved his own questions to Spirit Shadow for a later time. The boy came first. The boy was everything. Owl believed that if he could just make O-tis *see*, then everything else would fall into place.

The relationship that they had once almost developed crept back by stages. Owl and O-tis could communicate if it was not too complicated. When their words and gestures failed them, Spirit Shadow moved between their worlds.

Owl found the medicine woman hard to figure, as always. She was very busy and she worked hard at what she did. The boy was not the only one she was doctoring. She ran her huge lodge with a kind of invisible efficiency. Somehow, things got done. And they were done right.

Owl sensed that she was very fond of O-tis. He did not know why that should be, but it was a fact. After all, Spirit Shadow had seen the sick and the hurt by the hundreds. She had doctored men and women and children. Not all of her patients had been Indian. What was different about Otis Nesbitt?

Owl also knew that Spirit Shadow had unusual feelings toward himself. They were not sexual. She did not love him. She did not hate him. It was just that he was special in some way that he could not discern. Sometimes it was joking special, sometimes playful, and sometimes deadly serious.

Owl started off by trying to explain what a son was. That was a large mistake. By the time he was well into it, he knew that he should be backing out.

Owl knew what a priest was. He had some knowledge of Mexican supernatural ideas, gained mostly from trading contacts. He understood that the Mexican religion was Christian. He assumed that *Taibos* shared the same general notions.

"You know," he explained to O-tis, "that your people call more than one person *father*."

O-tis looked at him blankly.

Owl was patient. "There is the man in the black robes who carries a cross. He is *Father*. Is that not true?"

The boy nodded. He did not see where this was going.

"But then," Owl said, proud of his own knowledge, "there is also the man who is married to your mother. He lives in your house. He too is *father*."

O-tis wanted to shrug, but sensed that that would be the wrong reaction.

"These two men," Owl prodded, "they are not the same."

The boy felt that he must say something. He said: "Yes."

"They are called by the same name but they are not the same person. You do not feel about them the same way."

"Yes."

Owl hunched forward. It seemed to him that he was making progress. It was critically important to him that O-tis understand this thing.

"With us," Owl said, "it is that way with our *tua*, our son."

O-tis went back to blankness.

"'I call the sons of my brothers *tua*, son, just as I would call my own son *tua*. That is because, you see, if one of my brothers died, I would replace him with his wife or wives. I would become the father of his sons.'"

O-tis grasped just enough of this to be shocked.

Owl hurried on, wishing that he had chosen some other method of getting through to O-tis. He noticed that Spirit Shadow seemed amused.

"What I am telling you," Owl said, "is that it might be that I would call many men or boys *tua*, son. But that does not mean that they would *be* my sons. I would know the difference, and they would know the difference. It is of very great importance that a man have a real son. Among The People, there are some things that can only pass from father to son. If that does not happen, when a man dies, his shade may be forgotten. It may become lost forever and unable to ride to the land beyond the sun."

Otis Nesbitt did not have the faintest idea how to respond to that. He said nothing.

"You must be my *tua*, my real son," Owl insisted. "You *are* my real son. It is not a matter for you to decide. We do not decide which woman gives birth to us, isn't that right? We do not choose our fathers when we come into this world. That is why you will not be just the name *tua*. You will be my *tua*. There. That is finished."

Otis Nesbitt decided that there were some things about the Comanche mind that he could never understand. He was getting a severe headache, and it was not just from his injury. But he could sense that Owl was trying his best to reach out to him. He could not just reject the effort. That was plain bad manners.

Owl realized that he had ridden into a swamp that had no end. This was the wrong way to communicate to O-tis the meaning of the link between a father and his son.

"There has been too much talk," Owl said. He felt more than a little foolish explaining himself to a boy. But he *had* to. Without understanding, he could not force O-tis to be the son he needed.

"You sleep now," Owl said. "When we speak again, it will be of visions and dreams and the Cannibal Owl."

He shot a look at Spirit Shadow. Her round, painted face was impassive.

Owl left the medicine tipi and returned to his brush hut.

He was not a happy man, and he knew full well that his time was running out.

As the sweat lodge dripped on heated rocks and the cook fire bubbled a fragrant kettle stew, Owl did his best to impress upon the boy what mattered in life and what did not. Spirit Shadow flowed back and forth in the great medicine tipi, supplying words when they were necessary. Despite her bulk, there was nothing clumsy about Spirit Shadow. She drifted from place to place like smoke.

Owl told his story with a careful attention to details. In large part, of course, this was because he had to make O-tis understand what was happening here.

But Owl had another reason.

He was talking to himself and he was talking to Spirit Shadow. There were troublesome questions that had entered his life. Owl needed answers, and he needed them badly.

"I was a boy not much older than you are," Owl said to O-tis. "I had no name. I was just *tuinep*, a boy who was not yet a man. I could not ever become a man without finding a name. I would be a boy forever."

That idea struck a responsive nerve in O-tis. The plain truth was that Owl could be tiresome, like most grown-ups when they insisted on telling stories. This time, though, it was not going to be like that. Owl felt the eyes of the boy fastened on him.

When she spoke, Spirit Shadow used a monotonous kind of singsong. The effect was very much like a trance.

Unconsciously, Owl lifted his right hand in the firelight and touched his skin medicine bag. There was a reassuring hardness there.

"There is a way to find a name," Owl said. He stared at O-tis. "When a changing boy is ready."

Owl described to him the enchanted canyon with

the grotto waterfall and the ancient cypress trees. He told how he had found the bones of *piamempits* there. He explained what the Cannibal Owl was and the horror it could bring. Using his outstretched arms and the firelight and the shadows on the tipi wall, Owl showed how the terrible bird of night could swoop down upon a village and carry children away.

O-tis was impressed.

Owl made no mention of the strange flint point that he had found when still a boy. There was a proper time to show such a marvelous thing, and that time was not yet. He told O-tis how he had brought some of the *piamempits* bones to Comanche doctors, shamans, and how the doctors used them in their curing. He glanced at Spirit Shadow. He knew that she had used bones of the Cannibal Owl in her healing of O-tis. The boy knew it too, and looked at Spirit Shadow expectantly.

Spirit Shadow showed no bones. This was not the time.

"When I was ready," Owl droned, "I returned to that canyon. I stopped four times on the way. I wore only a breechclout and moccasins. I carried a stone pipe and tobacco and a fire drill. I ate nothing."

Again O-tis was impressed. He had seen Owl eat.

Owl did not tell him that he had taken a buffalo robe with him for warmth. He did not tell him, as he had not told anyone, that he had already discovered the medicine flint that had killed the Cannibal Owl. He held back the fact that he had carried that flint on his vision quest. He suspected that Spirit Shadow already knew. Well, even *puhakuts*, doctors, cheated a little sometimes. It helped the medicine along.

"Four nights and three days I fasted behind the canyon waterfall. Four nights and three days I smoked where I could see that white sightless giant of a skull. Then on the fourth day it happened."

The hush in the lodge of Spirit Shadow was total. Not a spider moved.

"When the light from Father Sun struck it just *so,* I saw a very old flint lance point between the great curving ribs of the Cannibal Owl. It was not stuck there; the meat had long since disappeared. The point was just lying there. It was where the heart would be, if *piamempits* had a heart. I was a boy, but I was a boy from The People, who were mighty hunters. I had seen many kills. I knew at once that the lance point had killed the Cannibal Owl. It had happened long ago, before The People had even left the Shining Mountains, but it had happened."

Oh, he had them now! If it had not happened quite that way, that changed nothing. All the rest was precisely and exactly true.

"I had never seen a stone point of that kind. It was much too big to be the point of an arrow. The point had no ears, and it had a shallow channel or groove on the base of the point on both sides."

Owl gestured at O-tis. "The ears of a point are projections that extend down from the base," he explained. "They make it easier to fit the base into the shaft of a spear or an arrow."

O-tis had no wish to break the spell. He said nothing.

"I picked up the point. It was so hot that it seared my hand. It glowed like an orange coal."

The silence in the medicine lodge was thick enough to cut.

"It was at that very moment," Owl said, "that I heard breathing so heavy that it dampened the dust and fogged the air between me and the waterfall. I smelled an enormous animal smell that lifted the hairs on the back of my neck. I turned my head slowly and for the first time I saw the Spirit Creature."

Even the medicine woman, who had heard many similar stories, was transfixed.

"It was so gigantic that I could not understand how it had wedged itself between the rock ledges. It did not look like any other animal I had ever seen. It was not like any other vision I had ever heard about. It was not just the size of it. It had old man's ears, huge but hairless. It had long, curving ivory tusks. They were so twisted that the Spirit Creature could not have impaled anything. There was a tremendous trunk, segmented like the body of a caterpillar. The trunk had bristle hairs on it. When it lifted the trunk, like a snake standing on its tail, you could see into its mouth. The tongue was red. The white ridged teeth were like grinding stones. There was a bulging hump on top of the skull. The legs were bigger around than my body, and the feet had toes and flat pads. The eyes were small and they were very, very old. They were the saddest eyes I had ever seen."

Owl waited. Nobody said anything. It may have been that all breathing stopped in the lodge of Spirit Shadow.

"I smelled more than the animal," Owl offered. "I smelled dung. It was fresh and hot and steamy. It was like the dung of a buffalo, but the dung itself was as big as a buffalo calf. It was not the dung of a meat eater. It was plant dung. The Spirit Creature did not have a heavy coat on its gray hide, but there were patches of red-brown hair. There were bugs in that hair. The cliff swallows swarmed on that beast."

Owl paused for effect. He let the silence lengthen.

"Then in my vision-dream the Spirit Creature spoke to me. Or it may have been in this other world, the one in which we sit. Who is to know?"

If either the medicine woman or Otis Nesbitt knew, they kept their opinions to themselves.

"*I am your Guardian Spirit,*" the creature said. Its voice was huge and hollow and wet. "*I will be with you always. On this day in this place you become a man. In your medicine pouch, which you must always carry with you, there will be only one charm of power. It will be the flint point that is burning your hand. It was the grooved lance point that killed the Cannibal Owl. It has mighty power. Your name shall be Owl.*"

Owl looked at the boy and the woman to make sure they truly understood. It was not just the name of Owl that was so strange. It was unheard of to carry only a single medicine object in a medicine pouch. Usually, there were many things: oddly shaped stones, feathers, snake fangs, sweet grass. Usually there were songs to learn: chants that could summon the Guardian Spirit or get you

out of trouble. Usually there were tabus to be observed
and tasks to be undertaken.

To have only one source of power in your medicine
pouch was to take a frightful chance. The medicine might
indeed be potent, yes, but what if it failed?

A man could find himself utterly alone, unprotected
in any way.

"*You will always see me when you need me most,*"
intoned the Spirit Creature. "*There will always be a message. It is for you to comprehend the meaning of the message, but it will be truth. In return, I ask but one thing.
When you have a son and before you die, pass the medicine pouch to him in exactly the proper place. In that
way, the Spirit Creature will not fade into nothing. In that
way, the shade of Owl will know the trail.*"

It was at that moment, Owl said, that the shape of the
Spirit Creature began to flicker. The smell grew weaker
and there was a faint sickness in it. It was as though deliv-
ering the Guardian Spirit medicine words had exhausted
the Creature. The old, tired eyes went out.

There was only the cooling dung and the bewildered
cliff swallows that swooped and darted at nothing at all.

Now was the time, here in the great painted lodge
of Spirit Shadow.

If they could not understand it now, his cause was
hopeless.

Slowly, cautiously, Owl reached up and slipped the
worn rawhide thong from his neck. He held the soft
deerskin medicine pouch in his cupped hands.

He unfastened the knot. He opened the pouch.

He removed the point. He held it in his left hand. His
left wrist was the one protected by the buckskin band.

The great tipi of Spirit Shadow suddenly grew smaller.
It was as though the lodge was shrinking. There was only
the firelight and the hard man and the bulging woman.

And the blue-eyed boy.

And the grooved flint point that had struck down
the Cannibal Owl.

Did it glow, that ancient point?

Was it warm, just a little?

Owl could not tell. He did not know whether they could feel its power. He did not even know whether there was any power left in it.

Owl shut his eyes. It was not a prayer that he offered. It was a summons, a call.

"You will always see me when you need me most." Was that not what the Spirit Creature had said?

Was this not the occasion?

Owl saw nothing. He heard nothing. He smelled nothing.

Almost with embarrassment, he replaced the point in the medicine pouch and hung the pouch back around his neck.

"You see," Owl said lamely, "there is magic here. I must have a son or the magic will die. Already it is weaker than it was."

There was a long, uncomfortable silence. The tipi seemed to expand, resuming its former size.

There was a waiting.

Without any warning, O-tis threw off the buffalo robe and leaped to his feet. He was naked except for his breech-clout. The painted rings around his eyes were blurred. The corded skin cap on the back of his head fell off. Some pasty stuff dripped off and dribbled down his legs.

Owl was amazed that the boy could move that fast. He was not yet strong. There was still some flabbiness on him. But he had the strength to do what he had to do.

"Keemah!" the boy shouted. His voice was not weak. Come!

The boy ran out of the tipi. Owl lumbered after him, and Spirit Shadow glided in that oily fat way she had.

O-tis did not seem to notice the cold. There was nothing uncertain about his movements. He knew exactly where he was going, and why.

The boy darted to an old oak tree close to the lodge of Spirit Shadow. In the summer she sometimes hung hides on those gnarled limbs to dry. There were still some brown acorns on the ground that had escaped the birds and the squirrels.

O-tis studied the ground intently. He pushed some

old leaves around with his bare feet. He did not find what he was seeking.

He looked up. He searched with his eyes and his hands. The oak still had leaves on it. The leaves had little life in them, but some would remain until the fresh green leaves of spring pushed them off.

O-tis found what he sought among the leaves.

One patch, then another, then a third.

Long, thin clumps of reddish-brown hair. They were high up. O-tis had to scramble up the ridged bark of the tree to get at them. He handed them to Owl. Owl stared at them. No doubt about it: they were the sparse hairs from the gray hide of the Spirit Creature. There were even a few bugs tangled in the strands of hair. The bugs were white. They were shriveling in the cold air.

O-tis pointed up, higher than the leaves that had caught the hair. There were branches that had been stripped, bark and all. There was a hole in that tree. There was a gleaming wetness that shivered in the wind.

The Beast had fed.

Owl was shocked, confused, and grateful. How had the Spirit Creature shown itself to O-tis, outside the tipi? Why had it remained invisible to him?

But O-tis had seen it! And he had kept no secrets. He had shown the spoor to Owl at once.

Owl herded the boy back into the warm moist lodge of Spirit Shadow. O-tis collapsed on the buffalo robe. He might or might not have been smiling.

Spirit Shadow muttered and fussed, moving with uncanny grace among the bags and pots and kettles of her world. She replaced the poultice on the back of the boy's head. She repainted the dark blue circles, taking special care with the tiny ditches cut through the greased hair of O-tis.

Only then did she speak.

"He it was who needed to see the Beast," she said. "Not you. Not me."

Owl was still shocked. He felt both rescued and deserted.

"There are so many questions," he said.

"Yes," Spirit Shadow replied. "And so very little time. They are coming for you, even as we speak."

A moment hung suspended in time, and they both knew that it was the last day for them.

It had grown colder outside the painted tipi of Spirit Shadow. There had been no rain, and the earth was dry. It still had not frozen, but the wind stirred nervously. There was no peace in that wind. It was a searching wind.

On Spirit Shadow's mountain of skin-draped chest, ropes of medallions sparkled and glittered as if they were alive. Although they were inside the well-insulated lodge, the long, loose hair of Spirit Shadow seemed touched by a breeze that others could not feel. Her vermilion-circled eyes projected from the folds of her face. The eyes themselves were somber. Spirit Shadow had a playful side to her, but that was nowhere to be seen this day.

O-tis was huddled against the elevated bed. He had drawn the buffalo robe partly over him, but he was dressed. He wore moccasins and a breechclout and blue leggings that ran all the way up his hips. The leggings had wide fringes of buckskin. He had a beautiful shirt made out of two pieces of antelope skin sewn together. Owl did not know whether Spirit Shadow had made the clothing herself. He suspected that she had. He did know that it was a vast improvement over the slipshod clothing he had made for O-tis on the trail to the Stone Walker.

He also knew why O-tis was dressed. The boy understood. He might or might not be ready, but this was his final day in the lodge and in the world of Spirit Shadow.

"I speak now because time is short," she said to Owl. "I do not speak because I wish it to be so, but because they are very close. It would not be a good thing for any of us if they found you here."

"I understand," said Owl.

"Hnhh." This time the sound had meaning. It meant: "I doubt it."

He waited. It seemed to him that the silence was very long. If they were in such a rush, why did she not speak?

Spirit Shadow was not one who could be hurried. When she was ready, she spoke.

"There is a worm burrowing in your mind," she said. "It is the worry about the shape and the nature of the Cannibal Owl."

Owl was eager to explain. He began to tell her of how he had found the bones of *piamempits* and what kind of bones they were. In particular, he wanted to talk about the weight of those bones and the crested rows of grinding teeth.

"Do not interrupt," Spirit Shadow said. "Do not tell me things I already know. If you wish to speak, speak of how it took you a lifetime to notice such a simple thing."

Owl did not like to be spoken to in such a fashion, particularly in front of the boy. A part of him was angered because Spirit Shadow was only a woman. Another part of him realized that the answers to his questions were here, and only here.

Owl held his tongue.

"There is one question that you must not ask, even in your mind," she said. "You will know it when you next look upon the skull of *piamempits*. Until then, it is something you must not think about. It is very dangerous."

Owl let that one go too. It was like telling a man, "Do not think of a buffalo." Herds of buffalo crowded his dreams, snorting and bellowing and kicking up the dust.

But he would try.

"The shape of *piamempits*," she droned. She was almost chanting again, talking to herself. "I can tell you that the Cannibal Owl has more than one shape. It is a shape-changer. Sometimes it is indeed a great Owl. I have not seen it so, but I have heard it described by those who know as something like a man. A very big, tall man with hair all over its body. The hair is red-brown. It has huge feet, bigger than they have to be to carry a body that size. It is said that such a one wanders out in lonely places and just sits down and dies. It will lie there until the dirt blows in and covers it up. Then it is under the ground, and that is where you find it. That is what is said."

Owl was impressed. This was a story that was completely new to him. However, it failed to answer the question he desperately wanted to ask.

Spirit Shadow gave him no opportunity. "The Cannibal Owl can take many forms. For now, that is all you need to know concerning the shape of *piamempits*."

Owl understood when he could push Spirit Shadow and when he could not. There were times when he had to wait for her. This was such a time.

"You have much worry," she said when she was ready. "You worry that perhaps you have lost your power. Hnhh! Men always have such worries."

Owl was not pleased by the remark. She knew quite well what the nature of his worry was. Her comment was not necessary.

"It did not come," Owl said, without attempting to retell the story. "There in the canyon of the waterfall, I touched my medicine and asked for help. The Spirit Creature did not show itself. It did not speak. What kind of Guardian Spirit is that? It is in my mind that it either lied to me about always having a message or it is gone. What else is possible?"

"The boy heard the Beast. He found the hair in the tree. You still have it. It is real. So how can the Spirit Creature be gone?"

"It did not come to *me*. It is not the Guardian Spirit of the boy, not yet. Owl still lives!"

"Hnhh. If it is not gone, if it still lingers in this world, if it is still *your* medicine animal, then what does this say to you?"

Owl was in no mood for riddles. "It says nothing to me, and that is what the Spirit Creature said. Nothing!"

"Messages are not always in words."

Owl could have brained the woman. At this time, in this place, why was she playing games with him?

"I am speaking only the truth," she said. "You asked me a question. I am answering it."

Owl waited. Had he been a stone and been placed in a hide water bucket, the water would have boiled. He could have been a one-man sweat lodge.

"Your Guardian Spirit is not gone. Your Guardian

Spirit did not lie. The matter is simple. You did not understand the message."

"There *was* no message!"

"There was no *spoken* message. There was no visible message. That does not mean no message was sent."

Owl was tempted to say that a message that could be neither seen nor heard was not much of a message. Wisely, he did not say it. It was not just Spirit Shadow he had to think about. A man who belittled his Guardian Spirit was playing with fire.

Spirit Shadow had given the problem much thought. She chose her words with care. "The message concerns the death canyon, the place of the waterfall. The message is about silence and it is about power."

Owl waited. There had to be more than that!

"I am only human," Spirit Shadow said with a rare humility that had no mockery in it. "I cannot be certain. It is my belief that the Spirit Creature is giving you warning that there is much danger in that place. Danger for *you*. After all, it is a canyon that has witnessed a mighty death. It is a canyon where intruders are upsetting the balance. The message, you see, involves a paradox, a contradiction. That is why it is so difficult to comprehend."

Owl thought: *Riddles!*

"In that place of the waterfall, the Beast is still very strong. Remember that this is where the bones are, and the great skull of *piamempits*. This is where the ancient flint point was found, the point that you carry in that deerskin pouch that is hung around your neck. If the Spirit Creature comes to you there, it will be a powerful encounter. It will change things forever. It is not a meeting that you should seek lightly."

Owl digested that as well as he could. "Then," he asked, "is the meaning of the message that I should not return to the canyon of the Cannibal Owl?"

Spirit Shadow smiled. It was a smile that actually had some sympathy in it. "If your Guardian Spirit will not come to *you* anywhere else, if it is saving its strength for one final burst of power, then where else can you go?

Would you risk being alone forever, without a Guardian Spirit to guide your shade?"

Owl did not like what he was hearing. Was he not a grown man, a warrior of The People? Was he not a man who had shown that he could care for himself? Was he not a raider, a fighter, a man who had dared much?

Was he a fearful child, cowering in the dark shadows of the tipi?

With his left hand he reached up and touched the hard, unyielding point that was covered in his medicine pouch. There was no reaction at all. It was as though he had felt the outline of an ordinary stone.

"I am only human," Spirit Shadow said again. "I do not know everything. It is possible that I am wrong."

Owl had a hollow conviction that she was not wrong.

She said: "On the last matter of which we must speak, there is no mistake. I am certain. They are coming for the boy and they are getting close. There are two of them, and they have followed your trail from the beginning. There may be another. For the two, I am certain. For the third, there is an unsureness."

Owl did not even mention the possibility that he might stay and face his trackers where he was. Such an idea was unthinkable. It would expose Spirit Shadow to a danger she had done nothing to deserve. It would be as cowardly as leading his pursuers to one of his own wives. Besides, once they found the boy, it was all over. That was true no matter how well he fought. If he killed them, others would come. They would never stop coming. There would be no way to hide a death-fight in the exposed medicine tipi of Spirit Shadow.

Spirit Shadow did not offer him the opportunity. She was through with talking. She lifted the boy from where he huddled beneath the buffalo robe. She took care to lift the robe with him, wrapping the weakened body in its warmth. She embraced O-tis with her fat arms. She smothered him against her.

It was farewell.

It was possible that there were tears squeezing out. from the red-ringed eyes of Spirit Shadow.

O-tis squirmed against the strings of medallions that crisscrossed the undulating layers of her chest.

Owl stood with folded arms.

It was inevitable for Otis Nesbitt to be reminded of his parents, even though Stafford sometimes seemed like a distant dream. These people were their opposites, were they not? Mizruth, his mother, tiny and tough as a handful of nails. Cole Nesbitt, his father, as frail and vague as Owl was hard and sure at his core. He had not always been that way, but Cole was as unsubstantial as a vapor, with his fine white cloud of hair and blue eyes as empty as a summer sky. The dark eyes of Owl could drill through solid rock.

Yes. All that was true. And yet was it not also true that Spirit Shadow had nursed him through sickness like a mother? Was it not also true that Owl wanted to be a father to him, even at the risk of his life?

Otis Nesbitt had been through much and he had few illusions. He knew that the peril to him was great.

These people, who smothered and surrounded him regardless of his will. How powerful they were, how strange! They did not wish him any harm. O-tis believed that they even felt a kind of affection for him.

But they would kill him in a second if it suited their mood or medicine or dream. He was utterly at their mercy.

O-tis tried to pull back from the enfolding slabs of Spirit Shadow. He attempted to do it in a way that showed no disrespect to her. He thought briefly of the home he would probably never see again. How different it was from this great sweating lodge of animal skins and greasy bubbling smells!

Otis Nesbitt made no attempt to speak. What could he say? In the days and nights he had been with her, he had tried to thank Spirit Shadow many times. Always, she had brushed his words aside.

The boy showed no tears.

"He may not be strong enough to travel," Spirit

Shadow said to Owl. "I have done my best, but the boy was badly hurt when he came here."

There was no accusation in her voice.

Outside the painted tipi, the wind moaned and there was no rain.

"Not strong enough to ride?" Owl asked.

"It may be that this is so."

Owl's seamed leather face froze into an expressionless mask. "Then the boy will die," he said simply.

It was difficult for Spirit Shadow to turn the boy loose. He had touched her life in some way that she could not name. She could not resist a final offering. "The blue medicine paint," she said. "It goes around his eyes and back through the runnels of his hair. It is very important. I have prepared a pouch of it that is tied around his waist. Do not allow it to freeze. It may save him. It may not."

Owl had visibly hardened. "If he lives, he lives. If he dies, he dies."

"Do not forget the blue medicine paint," Spirit Shadow said. She knew that her words were inadequate. They were all she had.

Owl gestured, and O-tis clutched his robe and silently followed him out into the cold and the wind.

Heart was already saddled and waiting. Owl had decided against a second horse. The boy had some flabbiness on him, but little weight.

Owl mounted, and O-tis swung up in front of him. It was like old times.

Spirit Shadow stood by the entry hole of the great painted tipi and watched them go. In spite of her tremendous bulk, which the whipping wind could not touch, she seemed oddly frail and lost. Her jade Pueblo bracelet gleamed dully beneath a gray winter sky.

Otis Nesbitt, twisting on Heart to look back at her one last time, felt her eyes strike him with what was almost a tangible blow. Half buried in fat though they might be, they were nevertheless burning eyes that could see all the way to the other side of forever.

13

Coffee, Late Winter

Coffee's gloved hand was too cold for him to play his little game of spinning the cylinder on his Colt. His eyes were red-veined against the dry, draining wind. His mustache was not frozen, but it might as well have been. It was so long and dirty and straggly that it felt like a lump of animal fat that was pressing against his mouth.

Coffee was not a man who let his emotions run away with him. He figured that he usually had things pretty much under control. He was not even close to despair, but he could and did express his feelings with a single word.

"Shit," he growled into the wind.

Coffee knew he was getting close. He also knew that there was no way he could speed up the showdown. He just had to take it minute by minute, and hour by hour, and day by day.

Coffee kept his eyes fixed on the cold, dry earth. He was not in the least worried that someone might jump him. He did not waste his energy scanning the horizon or searching out possible places of ambush. His confidence was based on an exact estimate of his own abilities.

If they came at him, singly or together, they would meet precisely the same fate that had overtaken Monte Montero and his companions. Coffee knew all about that little incident, of course. He was not a Ranger for nothing. He also knew who had drawn on Montero, and with what kind of gun.

He could not prove it, but he did not have to prove it. He knew. It was not that he was after Lee to bring him in. Coffee cared nothing about Monte Montero. If you backed him into a corner, Coffee would have admitted that Lee had done about what he had to do. Saved the Rangers some trouble, probably.

That wasn't the point. The point was that Lee was ahead of him. The point was that Lee had been good, very good, and that meant that Coffee had to believe that he was even better.

If Lee could handle three men, Coffee could handle four. It was necessary for him to believe that.

Besides, he had to keep his eyes down. He was not following a trail in the sense that he was tracking Owl hoofprint by hoofprint. But he needed to see that mark occasionally to be certain that Owl did not veer off in some new direction.

Once Coffee had seen Heart's footprints, before Owl had tried the trick with the hide shoes, he would never forget them. The Comanche had not changed horses.

Coffee saw other things as well. There was more than one way to mark a trail.

He was thankful for the eerie lack of rain. It was the season for rain, but there was no rain. It was going to be hell on the farmers if it stayed this dry, but for a tracker it was ideal.

He had located Spirit Shadow. He knew her name. It had been his relationship with Faith Guyler and her son that had given him his lead. Once he knew that Otis was either sick or injured, the rest was just a matter of persistence. The healing powers of Spirit Shadow were well known, and that great painted tipi of hers did not move much.

He knew the name of Owl. He knew that Otis Nesbitt was alive. He knew that the black man had beaten him to the medicine lodge.

He did not know much else. That fat woman with the red-ringed eyes had answered many questions and volunteered nothing. She had to provide some information in order to survive, but there was no way to tell what she was holding back. Coffee had repeatedly asked her where Owl was taking the boy. She kept saying something about the death canyon of what Coffee thought was the Cannibal Owl. That might or might not have been the literal truth. It made little difference to Coffee. She might as well have told him to ride to the other side of the stars. Or it was possible that he had not understood her correctly. There were entirely too many owls in her story.

He rode through the winter wind, his head down and his wide-brimmed hat jammed tightly on his head. Coffee had reached the stage where small things annoyed him. Losing his hat in the wind was enough to make him lose his temper.

Pear never wavered. Pear was steady. He might not like it, but he would keep going to the end of the world if Coffee did not stop him. Coffee took this for granted, but he was grateful too. His packhorse just plodded along, and would have headed for rest and shelter in a hurry if it had not been for Pear.

Coffee was haunted by the fear that Otis might die before he caught up with him. If that happened, killing Owl would matter little. Coffee could not even imagine riding into Stafford with the body of Otis Nesbitt. That would be rough.

What could he say to old Cole Nesbitt? What could he say to Ruth? Most important, how could he face Lisa?

It also did not help that he was behind Lee. He could not close the gap without taking chances that he could not afford. If he lost the trail, nothing else mattered.

Damn that black man! Coffee was certain that Lee

would make some terrible mistake that would end any hope they had of getting Otis back alive. He should have shot to kill when he had the opportunity. He was well aware that he might not get another.

He thought plenty about the death canyon of the Cannibal Owl. Crazy Indian medicine talk, yes. But there was one kernel of fact that held Coffee's interest.

The country surrounding Austin was tolerably close to the center of the state of Texas. This was not flat plains grassland, but neither was it a land of thrusting mountains and roaring whitewater streams.

This was not canyon country.

If you figured on canyons that a man might reach in a reasonable time riding double with a sick boy, Coffee had a definite advantage.

He knew those canyons.

Every single one of them.

Texas weather was not unduly respectful of what month it was or which day of the week it happened to be. It had a way of shifting around according to its own whims.

It changed. It might be deep winter, but it suddenly warmed up. It did not pour down buckets of rain, thank God, but it heated up enough to make Coffee sweat. The wind that had plagued him when it was cold dropped to nothing. The air was dry and still.

Coffee shrugged out of his greatcoat and kept following the trail, his head down, his hat now making shade. He knew where the canyons were, but he could not yet be certain of which one Owl was trying to reach. It could cost him valuable time to pick a likely canyon and ride for it hell-for-leather. If he guessed wrong, he would lose whatever hope he had. He changed his trailing only to the extent that he did not stray too far from water. It was not summer heat that he was riding through, and it was far too early for rivers to go dry, but it was warm enough so that Pear could not go for long distances without water. Coffee did not care for the idea of being stuck out here on a drawn and thirsty horse.

It was after he had watered Pear and nooned a spell that he saw the last thing he expected to see.

He had picked up the trail again. It was not continuous, of course, and a man had to pay attention to pick up the tracks and rock scratches when they occurred. Coffee had kept his head down so long that he had a crick in his neck.

And then, quite suddenly, there they were.

More tracks. Different tracks. Another trail that seemed to come out of nowhere.

Coffee could not have been more surprised if a dust devil had ridden up in the midst of winter and called his name. He knew all about the prints of Lee's horse, Doc. He discounted those. He knew roughly where Lee was and what he was doing.

But he had never anticipated another rider on this trail. It was more than that. The way the trail simply appeared in the earth meant that Coffee had been missing some things. Horses did not drift down out of the sky. If he had not spotted this trail before, what else had he missed?

Coffee halted Pear and dismounted. He found a place where there were clear traces of hoofprints visible for twenty yards or more. He sorted them out.

Owl's tracks, as familiar to him as the heels on his own boots. Lee's, with the one slightly cracked and uneven shoe that needed the attention of a farrier. And the new prints, as distinctive as the sound of a man's voice.

The most obvious thing was that the horse was shod. And the shoes were clean and fresh.

That meant a white man's horse. It also meant a horse that had been recently outfitted for the trail.

"Well, God damn," Coffee said. He didn't need any more complications.

Coffee was a believer in information. He had learned the hard way not to rush into things with an empty head. If there was a third rider on Owl's trail, Coffee wanted to know who it was.

If a horse did not really come out of nowhere, where had it come from? Until he knew that, Coffee couldn't offer a decent guess as to who the rider might be.

The question was simple. Should he backtrack or not?

The answer was not so simple.

If he backtracked, he might have to go a long way. Even now that he knew what he was looking for, there was no way to tell how far back the trails had crossed. He could waste a lot of time. Enough time so that Otis might not survive.

If he did not backtrack, he didn't know what he was riding into. That was not a situation that Coffee relished.

He decided that he had no real choice. The welfare of Otis came first. He had to go forward and hope that the picture clarified.

He remounted Pear and pushed on through the still, warm air. He had been paying attention before, but now his eyes were glued to the drooping brown grass and the dry, caked soil.

Coffee wasn't about to miss anything.

The trails wandered on with almost an aimless just-out-for-a-ride character. Owl. Lee. The stranger. In that order.

Coffee needed no gloves now. He tugged thoughtfully on his earlobe, then slipped his big Walker Colt out of its holster. He half-cocked the hammer and spun the cylinder. The familiar action gave him some comfort. He figured that the puzzle would not go on forever.

It didn't.

Only a few hours beyond where he had nooned, Coffee saw the new tracks angle off to the left. They were headed directly toward a small clump of cedar. There were a few scrub oaks there too, and that meant water. A man might have to dig for it after the dry spell, but it would be there.

It was obvious where the rider had gone. This hunt would not involve a long and complicated trail.

He might still be there. Coffee didn't think so, judg-

ing by the condition of the tracks, but it was no trouble
to keep the Colt in his hand.

No matter how fast your draw, a gun that already
filled your fist won every time.

Coffee eased Pear around the stand of cedar. That
was the lee side, protected from the wind if there had
been any. He poked through the brush, every sense alert.

There it was.

A small clearing with a circle of stones that could
not have been more than a foot wide. Some white ashes
and black coals in the fire pit. Coffee could tell at a
glance that the contents of the fire pit were as cold as a
snake's belly on ice. That fire was *out*. It had been out
for a spell.

Coffee dismounted again. At first he touched nothing. He just looked.

There. An indentation in the dirt. An outline that
was as plain as a bear's smell. A saddle. He could even
see stirrup marks.

No mystery about the saddle. The stranger had
pulled it from his horse and used it as a pillow. Coffee
could see the faint scuffing marks of a body. It seemed to
have turned and twisted some.

He saw where the horse had been tethered. There
was dung there. It was not crumbly-dry, but it was not
moist-fresh either. Make it a day or two old under this
sun. The camp had certainly been made at night. That
meant that the rider might be many hours ahead of him.

Coffee holstered his Colt. There would be no gunplay here.

He got down on his hands and knees and crawled.
He was determined to learn what there was to learn
here.

He found two things, both of them surprising.

Where the saddle had rested, there was a single
white hair about three inches long. It was too fine to
have come from a horse. It was a human hair. A human
hair might have been expected. After all, it had not been
a catfish using the saddle as a pillow. But a *white* hair?

Back in the brush, where it must have been tossed,

he found a bottle made of dark blue glass. It was not a big bottle. It might have held a cupful of something.

Coffee picked the bottle up. The glass was thick. There was no stopper. The bottle was empty, but there was a sticky residue. It was brown in color with a slight touch of yellow.

He sniffed it. He got a trace of alcohol; not whiskey, but alcohol was not the main ingredient. Coffee knew that smell.

He licked the top of the blue bottle to be sure. Yes. There was that unmistakable bitter taste under the alcohol.

Opium.

The bottle had been full of laudanum.

Nobody had to spell it all out for Coffee. This had been a man in some pain. God only knew where he had come from or why he was on Owl's trail.

Coffee climbed back on Pear and circled until he found the tracks leading out of the stand of cedar. The rider had not rejoined the twin trails of Owl and Lee. He had angled off to his left, making his own trail.

That trail might lead almost anywhere.

Austin, possibly.

Maybe Stafford.

Possibly, one of the few real canyons in the area.

There was no point to speculation. Wherever the man was headed, Coffee had to follow the other trail.

He had a gut certainty that the trails would cross again. There was no way that this was good news.

With a terrible worry growing in his mind, Coffee picked up Owl's tracks and rode through the eerily warm afternoon toward the night.

14

Lee, Late Winter

It seemed to Lee that the damned trail would never end.

The weather had gone from windy and cold to still and warm and now back to the frigid winds that numbed his face and hands. The rains did not come. Owl remained ahead of him.

The lead had narrowed. Lee figured that he was no more than a day and a half behind the Comanche. It was a terrific temptation to cut Doc loose and just grab Otis while the boy yet lived.

It was because of Otis that Lee rejected that particular stunt. He could not gamble with the boy's life. If he guessed wrong and missed the trail, that was that. He could not be sure that Otis was alive even now. Give the boy another week or two in this bitter wind and the child was dead meat.

Lee could make Owl pay, maybe, but that would be a weak gruel to guzzle down. Lee had little interest in revenge. Even if he had been put together differently, his talk with Spirit Shadow messed everything up. What did revenge *mean* if a man chose a boy for his son?

He just wished that Owl had picked another town, another family, another boy.

As it was, they were all caught up now in a flint-hard story that could end only in death. The only question about the final outcome was who was going to die when. That, Lee reflected sourly, was a pretty fair reflection of what life on this earth was all about.

No sooner had he given birth to that somber thought than Lee broke into a loud self-mocking laugh. He was thinking crazy stuff.

"Man," he said aloud, "you been out in this confounded wind too blamed long."

There was something else. Lee sensed that he was not alone on Owl's trail.

Coffee, sure. He would not quit even if his brains were blown out. That Ranger was back there somewhere, and you could bet the farm on that.

Well, Lee had always known that the two of them would meet at the end. That was the way it had to be.

He did not worry about Coffee. When the time came, he could either deal with Coffee or he couldn't. In a strange sort of way, he was used to Coffee.

The thing of it was, Lee was virtually certain that Coffee was not the only one behind him. What made it worse was the nagging thought that he knew who that third person was. *That* worried Lee. It worried him a lot.

There is a special closeness between two men who have lived and worked and fought together. One can detect the other's presence even if there is no sighting of him. It is like walking into a dark room and knowing at once whether or not it is empty.

"Old man," Lee whispered into the wind, "you're going to get that boy killed."

Lee tried to tell himself that what he was thinking could not be. If it had been anyone else, he could have wished the ghost away. After all, some things were possible and some things weren't.

This was impossible.

Just the same, Lee knew.

He forced himself to focus on the trail. A man could fret so much about what was behind him that he would ride right smack into a buzzing hive of yellow jackets. There was trouble enough ahead of him.

The trail was as plain to Lee as the direction that water flowed in a river. He was lucky there was no rain, yes, but he could have followed that trail regardless. Lee and Otis had played some games together in their time, and one of them had been a kind of a treasure hunt with a small prize at the end of a marked trail. Lee knew exactly how Otis went about indicating a trail. On the ground, he would draw a little open-sided circle with his finger or a stick. The opening in the circle showed the direction to go. On trees that were barren of leaves at this time of the year, like hackberries or elms, he would break off a small branch but not detach it. It hung by its bark. Wintergreens such as cedars were more difficult. Usually Otis would try to strip some of the needles off a branch in the line of travel. That would leave a bare patch, but it was hard to spot.

Of course, doing all this in a game outside of Stafford was one thing. If you were a Comanche captive, you just had to do the best you could whenever you got the chance. Even Comanches dismounted once in a while, and apparently Otis did not have his hands tied. But he had to be very careful.

That was even more true of the blue paint. Lee did not know exactly what it was or why Otis had it with him, but he had detected it early on. When Otis was able to manage it, he was leaving a tiny smear of the blue paint on rocks and occasionally on dead grass.

That took plain raw courage. If Owl even suspected that Otis was leaving a marked backtrail, that would be the end of Otis.

Lee took a lot of pride in what Otis was doing. It was not just the spunk of the boy, but his certainty that his trail would be followed. Maybe he knew about Coffee and maybe he didn't, but he trusted Lee. His tricks with the elms and hackberries were aimed at Lee.

"You just hang on, boy," Lee said. "That's all you got to do. Just hang on."

Just at twilight the wind died as suddenly as it had started. There was a stillness through which shadows crawled.

Sometimes, just for a few moments, sounds can travel a long way through such hushed air.

There was a low rocky ridge behind Lee and to his left. With a shocking clarity, Lee caught the fragments of a song.

> *"Oh, it takes a medicine man*
> *To ride a medicine horse*
> *Way in the middle of the world.*
> *And it takes a medicine wind*
> *To move a medicine heart*
> *Way in the middle of the world ..."*

That was all he heard, though Lee knew the rest of the song. He could have finished it easily. He had heard it a thousand times.

There was only one man he knew who sang that song.

Lee stared at the growing darkness and the frosty fires of the stars. He felt a sickness within him. He also felt a kind of crazy admiration.

One thing he knew for sure.

If it was that man, Lee could take off and ride full gallop across a thousand rocky ridges.

Lee tipped his hat and said nothing.

He could never catch that man if he did not want to be caught.

This was one trail they had to ride apart.

No matter how good you are, you cannot track a single horse at night. Lee did not want to rest and he needed little sleep, but he had to hole up when it got too dark to see. His horse was grateful, and it did give Lee a chance to build a small cook fire and get some warm food in his gut.

He did not worry about being seen. He considered it profoundly unlikely that Owl would double back for any reason. If Coffee caught up with him, that would make little difference. He didn't want the company, but he already knew that regardless of what Coffee said, he would not shoot a sleeping man.

As for the singer beyond the ridge, Lee heard nothing more from him. He had no control over that one. That was a man who would do what he damned well pleased, and even under the best of circumstances, Lee was not fool enough to interfere with him.

These were emphatically not the best of circumstances.

What did bother Lee was a trivial thing. He had known rough times before, and he had ridden hard trails. But he was by nature a fastidious man. It had been a long time between decent baths and comfortable shaves. His clothes were stained and dirty. His whiskers had erupted like spikes in a salt and pepper pattern. He had a raw spot on his nose that dripped a little blood when the scab came off.

Lee looked like a wild man. He knew it. He didn't like it.

He was up with the dawn and back on the trail. He was headed southwest and the morning sun was behind him. He saw an occasional mesquite. Some of them were just beginning to leaf out. They did not have the bright green feathery look of summer. Indeed, a man had to look closely to see the leaf buds at all. But they were there on a few of the trees.

It had been Lee's experience that when the mesquite leafed out, that was the end to winter. There would be no more hard freezes.

It was very early for spring. There had been little rain recently, but mesquite roots went down a long way. Lee had tried to dig up some mesquite once. He wouldn't try again.

It was well into the afternoon and the sun was streaking in under Lee's hat brim when he saw the structure. There had been no attempt to conceal it. It was smack in the middle of the trail.

Lee reined Doc in. "If that don't beat all," he said. He was stunned.

Lee dismounted. He knew what the structure was without examining it closely, but a man never knew what he might find if he poked around a little.

It was the last thing Lee had ever expected to see out here in the middle of nowhere.

A sweat lodge.

It was very small, hardly more than a couple of deerskins stretched over a domed brush frame. It had been a hasty job. The hides were not properly fleshed, and if it had not been for the hardening effect of dense smoke, there would have been bugs and buzzards all over the place. They didn't have the scent yet because of the strong winter wind. Lee could smell it, though. The tiny lodge stank of bloody meat and grease and sickness.

There was a blackened fire pit in the lodge and a tripod of poles to hold skin bags of water. The stones that had done the boiling had been tossed carelessly aside. They looked very white and clean.

There was a small cold spring in a clump of oaks nearby. The moccasin tracks going to and from the spring were clear and deep. Owl had made a lot of trips. He had done it on foot too, and that was extraordinary.

Lee looked very carefully, but he saw no smaller footprints on that trail. Apparently Otis had stayed put and Owl had built the sweat lodge around him.

That was not reassuring. Owl was not a man who would pamper the boy unless Otis was very weak.

Lee did not have the slightest doubt that it was Otis who had sat in that lodge and endured the stifling, greasy heat. There were those who said that a person could sweat sickness away, but Lee's reaction was close to horror. Mesquite buds or no mesquite buds, it was still winter. Otis would have come out of that lodge shimmering with sweat, his hair dripping.

It had not been long ago either. The smells were fresh.

Lee studied the area with care, both inside the sweat lodge and out. He was looking for fecal piles or traces of vomit or blood. Man or boy, you could tell a lot by what somebody left behind.

He did not find what he was after. Perhaps that was good.

He did find something else, though. He could hardly have missed it. Again it was right in the middle of the trail. This time it was on the trail leading away from the crude sweat lodge.

It was nothing but a flat rock propped up with two sticks. The rock faced back on the trail.

It had a picture on it. The picture was outlined with blue paint.

It was a lousy picture. Owl was not a good artist. But he had left something else.

There was an arrow in the grass in front of the rock painting. It was a perfectly ordinary arrow. The shaft was hackberry, which had been worked on considerably to get it straight. The feathers were wild turkey feathers, and they were neat and trim. There were three of them. The arrowhead was a metal trade point. The point was barbed. It was a war point, not one used for game animals.

The arrow was broken into two pieces, right in the middle. Lee did not know the precise significance of that. It may have been a kind of personal sign that belonged to Owl. Whatever it was, Lee was sure that it did not represent a friendly gesture.

He turned his attention to the awkward blue painting. He suspected that the blue paint had come from Otis. Owl would have used vermilion if he had it. If Otis had no more blue paint, the trail would be more difficult.

Well, the trail was short now anyway. Lee was reasonably certain that he knew where Owl was heading.

Even allowing for the fact that Owl had no talent as an artist, the painting was peculiar.

It was just an outline with very little shading or detail. Obviously it was supposed to be an animal of some sort. But what kind of an animal? It didn't look like any kind of critter that Lee had ever seen.

Four legs. Great heavy legs, like stumps. A little tufted tail that was hardly long enough to brush off flies. A big head, a huge head, with a kind of bulge or dome on top. Tusks. Long sharp curving things that looked so heavy they must have given the beast a perpetual sore neck.

And a trunk. Lee had seen engravings of elephants. He knew what a trunk was.

But this did not look like any picture of an elephant that Lee had ever seen. Maybe that was because Owl could not draw accurately. Maybe not.

It made no sense, either way.

There were times when Lee figured he understood the Comanches fairly well. This was not one of those times.

He stared at the blue rock painting until the lowering sun began to hurt his eyes. It seemed to him that somehow the painting should tell him something.

Whatever message the painting held, it kept its secret. All Lee knew was that Owl had paused in a desperate flight to scrawl an outline of an elephant on a slab of rock. That was strange enough for anyone, certainly, but what did it mean?

Owl would not have done it just for the hell of it. Did it have something to do with his medicine? Was it about the boy?

Lee considered knocking down the support sticks and pitching the painted stone into the brush. He decided against it. It was not that he feared disturbing some mystic shrine. Lee didn't care much about that.

No. He just got a kick out of imagining what Coffee would think when he rode up on the painting. Coffee would understand the hasty sweat lodge readily enough. He hadn't been born yesterday. But a blue elephant?

Lee laughed, despite the terrible circumstances. He would have given a lot to have seen Coffee's face.

The laughter died away in the cold, calming wind.

Night was returning to the land. Lee listened closely, hoping against hope that he might hear the song again.

> *Oh, it takes a medicine man*
> *To ride a medicine horse . . .*

He heard nothing beyond the ordinary murmurs and stirrings of the coming darkness. There was no voice. There was no song.

Lee shook his head.

That old devil! How had he gotten here, if here he was? If he had moved on, how had he done that?

"Old-Timer," Lee said, "you are somebody special."

He might also be the fly in the ointment, the one element that Lee could not predict. He might do anything. Lee had seen him pull some surprises more than once.

Everything that was in Lee urged him to push on at once. It had taken Owl some time to build that sweat lodge, small as it was. It would have taken more time to cut up those two deer, and Owl could ill afford to leave all that venison to rot.

Lee knew that he was very close. There could not be much territory between them. He was almost certain that he knew where Owl was taking Otis.

Almost.

That was the plain hell of it. Almost was not quite good enough. A mistake now would be the end of everything.

Lee forced himself to rest. He did not sleep. He got up to check his horse over and over again. His worn saddle hurt the back of his head. He stared at the cold silver moon and he thought about everything there was to think about.

He was up before dawn.

He was in the saddle at first light.

It was very cold. The sun was not high enough yet to provide any warming.

Lee could just see Otis, naked and sweating, stumbling out of that lodge. He could feel the shock of the numbing wind.

It did not have to freeze in order to be cold.

Oh my God, Lee thought. *Oh my God.*

Aloud, he said: "Let's go, Doc. Let's see what you can do."

Doc responded and picked up the pace. He seemed to understand that the trail was short now.

Lee slipped his .52 caliber Hall-North carbine from its scabbard and held it ready across his saddle.

15

Owl, Late Winter

Owl knew that he had one chance, and one chance only.

He did not think that it was a very good chance, but the only alternative was to abandon the boy. He would not do that.

O-tis could not ride without slipping from Heart's steady back. Owl had to wrap both arms around the boy to hold him on. This was no simple matter. The buffalo robe in which Spirit Shadow had wrapped O-tis was bulky. Owl had an ache in his arms that he was sure would never go away.

The boy was so thin that he was almost weightless. It was like riding with your arms wrapped around a cloud. The boy's hair was right up against Owl's face. It was not sandy, matted as it was with grease, but the skin cap fastened to the back of his head had stiffened. The sweet grass that held the cap in place was not so sweet now.

Owl could not help seeing that the channels through the hair had grown out with fuzz. The blue paint was not sticking well, and it was almost all gone. When O-tis turned his head around, the blue rings around his eyes had no more color than charcoal smudges. The boy's own eyes were bluer than the paint, but they were not clear. They were dull and had red streaks snaking through them.

He did not regret the blue paint he had used to draw an outline of the Spirit Creature on the rock. It was medicine paint, wasn't it? If ever Owl needed help from the medicine world, the time was now.

Still, it would be difficult to doctor the boy when the blue paint was gone. He just had to hope that the canyon was strong enough to do the necessary curing.

Owl could not reach up and touch the pouched point that hung around his neck. He was afraid to remove the support from O-tis, even for a moment. But Owl could feel it. It felt as cold as the stone it was.

That was not a good sign.

It came to Owl that there had been few good signs lately. It was almost as though he had inadvertently stepped through the nest of a Thunderbird. There was no medicine that could fix *that* kind of trouble.

Owl was not a man given to self-pity. He despised weakness. He did not once allow himself to think that perhaps he had made a mistake in his quest for a son. What must be, must be. It was just that simple.

But the thought was swimming there, down in the shadows. Owl sensed it. He kept it down, almost as though he had weighted it with a rock.

"Hnhh," Owl said. He might have been speaking to O-tis. He might not. "Our journey is coming to an end."

The boy said nothing. He had not spoken for several days.

"Hnhh," Owl said again.

He was very proud of Heart. He was no Wise One, perhaps, but he had not faltered and he had not complained. He was carrying not only Owl and O-tis, but a good deal of meat and other gear. It had been a very long ride.

Owl did not need the words of Spirit Shadow to tell

him that there were hunters on his trail. He could feel them, smell them, hear them. They were getting closer. They would never quit.

Well, so be it. It was not escape that Owl had on his mind.

It might be that those hunters had forgotten what it took to make a Comanche die. Owl would remind them. He was not going to come out meekly and hand O-tis over to them.

O-tis was what it was all about.

Owl was very tired. There was some confusion in his mind. Was it the canyon of the Cannibal Owl? Or was it the canyon of the Spirit Creature? There were times, when his being floated off in the chill and the wind, that the two of them seemed to merge.

In a way, perhaps, it did not matter. Guardian Spirit or bones of *piamempits,* the pooled canyon was the center of his being. It was there that he had received the name of Owl. It was there that O-tis either would or would not become his son.

Owl did know one thing. It was true regardless of the riddles of Spirit Shadow or the silence conferred on him by his own Guardian Spirit. When he moved away from the canyon, he weakened. When he drew closer, he found strength.

That was good enough for now.

When he reached the windswept flatland that was at the head of the trail into the canyon, Owl did not hesitate. He barely glanced at the dull green of the prickly pear or the skeletal elms. He pushed Heart through the rippling brown sea of dry, winter-dead grass. He did not bother to check for tracks.

If anyone was ahead of him on the cypress-lined trail that cut through to the waterfall, that was unfortunate. Owl was not going to stop, could not stop. If he had to kill his way to the stone cavern that held the great white skull of the Cannibal Owl, then he would kill.

Owl was far beyond calculation. He was following his destiny, however uncertain it may have been. It would take death itself to move him from his path.

Even that might not be enough.

He wrapped his arms more tightly around the robed skin-and-bones boy, nudged Heart with his hard-heeled moccasin, and dropped down into the canyon that had given him birth.

The Ancient One was watching him as he turned up past the fire-blackened rock shelter beneath the upthrust limestone bluffs. Owl was as certain of it as he was certain that this was the rock shelter where he had waited out the *Taibos* while they intruded on this place with their picnic. How long ago had that been?

The Ancient One was somewhere on the other side of the clear, gurgling stream. There was less water now than when Owl had last seen it. The whitewater noise was less.

There was no wind here. There was no rain as there had been before, although it was always moist in this place. There was moss all year round.

It was quiet enough so that Owl felt he could hear the waterfall splashing over the ledge at the end of the trail. If the Spirit Creature, the Ancient One, was watching, why could Owl not hear it? Smell it?

The Spirit Creature was not silent. It breathed and snorted and crashed around through the brush. It was not odorless, like a raindrop. It had a heavy animal smell. There were bugs in its reddish-brown hide patches. It dropped dung.

But Owl could neither see it nor smell it. His conviction that the Ancient One was watching had no tangible roots. It was just there.

O-tis stirred in his buffalo cocoon. Did he sense it too? Or was he responding to something else?

There were too many questions. Owl could not wait for answers. If he did not find warmth and food and protection for the boy soon, there would be no purpose to anything. O-tis would be gone. Owl smiled a little. *Then* they would see some fighting to remember. But what for?

The smile vanished. Owl did not flank the slippery

path. He rode it straight down the middle, pushing Heart as much as he dared. The bluffs on either side of him soared toward the winter sky. There were so many hiding places in those cliffs, an army could have been concealed there. Owl felt other eyes besides those of the Ancient One. The eyes were either watching or they were coming.

Owl was past caring. If they would let him alone, he would do what he had to do. If they tried to stop him, he would kill them. Simple. No more riddles.

The dead cypress needles muffled Heart's hoofbeats. Owl did not slow down until he reached the cold green pool. The water still flowed over the cliffs' edge and made a row of white bubbles in the pool. The leaning sycamore had lost its leaves.

Now he had a decision to make.

He wanted to ask O-tis about it. It was true that a grown man should not take advice from a boy, but was it not different with a father and son? There were times when it was unwise to make decisions on your own. When you were tired, it was easy to make mistakes.

It hardly mattered. O-tis was barely conscious, if at all. Owl could get no advice from him.

The problem was that the gravel beach where the picnic had occurred was a good place for Heart, and a good place to build a fire. He could not take Heart through the narrow passages into the cliff caverns where the bones of *piamempits* waited. No man of The People wanted to leave his horse behind and walk. A man without a horse risked suicide.

But a good place for Heart was not necessarily a good place for the boy, fire or no fire. The beach was too open. It was vulnerable from the top, whether from rain or rescuers. Even out of the wind, it was not a good choice to give O-tis the secure shelter he needed.

It got dark very quickly in the canyon of the Spirit Creature. The rock walls were so high that they pushed the horizons in. When Father Sun was no longer visible, the long shadows came.

Already the bats were streaming out like black smoke from the holes and crevices in the cliffs.

"Hnhh," Owl said. He was beginning to talk like Spirit Shadow. He did not know what Spirit Shadow would suggest in this situation, but to Owl his course of action was plain.

He dismounted. With the boy in his arms this was no simple matter, but he was as careful as possible. He put O-tis down on the gravel, still wrapped in his buffalo robe. He filled a hide bag with water from the pool and forced some of the water into the boy's mouth. Most of it spilled out from the cracked lips, but Owl kept at it until he saw convulsive swallowing motions in the boy's throat. Not much, but some of it got down. Later he could make a warm broth.

The boy said nothing. The smudged blue eyes were open, but Owl could not tell whether they saw anything or not. He would have given a lot to know.

Owl pulled the saddle from Heart. There was a pad under it made of worn buffalo hide. Owl stashed the saddle under an overhanging ledge to the left of the beach. It was close to a buckeye tree, so that he could find it again if he needed it. He did not think he would need it. He tossed the pad on a pile with his meat, his weapons, and his parfleches. It might come in handy.

He removed the buffalo-hair bridle. There was no bit. Heart was free, and Owl had no inclination to tether him. His gelding had plenty of water and enough vegetation to browse successfully for a time.

It came to Owl that he was saying good-bye to Heart. It seemed to him that he was forever saying good-bye to horses that had served him well. He never could find the right words. Horses were tougher than people. They gave much and asked for little.

"Heart," he said, "it was a ride to remember. Eat well and grow fat."

Owl turned away. The look in Heart's eyes was worse than what he saw in the eyes of the boy.

Owl forced himself to scan the backtrail and the cliffs that surrounded him. He still felt that he was not alone in this haunted place. He saw nothing suspicious. The riders would come. He was certain of that. But he had no targets yet.

His thoughts wrapped around the grooved point in his medicine pouch. He could touch it now if he wished. He could even take it out and hold it in his hands.

He decided against it. Power, *puha*, had its own laws. There were times when it was best to save it. He could not risk failure now.

But he spoke to the Spirit Creature. "Beast," he said in a conversational tone of voice, "I know that you are here. You have made promises to me. You have given to me my name. I expect you to come when you are called."

The canyon world seemed to hold its breath. There was a complete hush except for the hissing bubbles of the waterfall. No man spoke to his Guardian Spirit in that manner. It simply was not done. It may have been that it had never been done before in all the history of the world.

Owl did it, and he was pleased that he had.

It could be that there were times when a man had to take back some measure of control, even from the spirits. Owl was weary enough to simply follow his impulse.

He knelt down and got his face close to that of the boy. He asked him a direct question. "Can you walk?"

There was a flicker of intelligence in the boy's eyes. He heard the words. He understood them. "Try," he said. His voice was shaky from disuse.

O-tis managed to stand up. He clutched the buffalo robe to his skinny frame. He swayed like a sapling in the wind.

"Where?" asked the boy.

Owl pointed to the trail that wound behind the pool and in back of the waterfall. The boy could not see much of it from where he stood, but it was clear even in the gathering darkness that this was not an easy trail. It would take some crawling. It would take some climbing.

Owl felt that he had to explain. He had no wish to be cruel simply for his own amusement. "There is a safe place back there," he said. "I can build a fire and cook something that will bring you strength. If you can walk, I can carry in the wood and get us started faster."

It was not likely that the boy understood too much of that. But he was game. If Owl wanted him to walk, he would walk. He took a deep breath and began.

He staggered, but he walked. He made it all the way to where the rocky trail narrowed and got slippery from the waterfall spray. Then he fell. He got up once. He fell again.

Owl admired courage. He also recognized hopelessness. He put down his load of wood and brush and gear, and scooped up the boy, robe and all.

Owl said nothing. The boy also had no words, or was too weak to say them. Owl scrambled to the lookout that was behind the falls, directly under the rock overhang. Most of it was not dry, but there was a hollow in the rock that would serve as a nest. He put O-tis down there, neither roughly nor gently. If a son was too soft, he was not worth saving.

Owl was very close to the crevices, ledges, and caverns that housed the scattered bones of *piamempits*. He could feel that terrible dry-white skull watching him through walls of rock. He said nothing of this to O-tis.

Owl ignored his aches and pains. He simply willed them out of existence. He wriggled and slipped back for the wood and brush and parfleches. He got a small fire going. He did not use his fire drill, which he kept in *naka*, his holder of buffalo horn. It worked well with dry moss, but the Mexican trade gear of flint and steel was faster.

It would soon be too dark to move on the trail. The stinking bats brushed the exhausted face of the boy. Owl could not help that. There were worse things than bats.

He made a final trip, all the way down to the gravel beach where Heart waited with infinite patience. He did not look at Heart except out of the corner of his eye. Heart was looking at him.

Owl gathered up all the venison he had. There had not been time to dry it properly or mix it with fat and winter berries. Only the cool weather had preserved it,

and it was not entirely free of white worms. He thought
wistfully of the great catfish that swam in the green pool.
He had almost no chance of getting that fish with an arrow, and his taste for catfish was very slight, but with unlimited time he might have given it a try.

He did not have unlimited time.

He filled another skin bag with water, bundled up
all the robes and pads he had, slung his bow over his
shoulder, and picked up his quiver of arrows. He carried
no gun. He always had his trade knife belted around his
waist.

He returned to the trail one last time. If he had not
known every handhold and rock hole like the back of his
hand, he could not have made it. There was no light
there. The glow of the flickering fire ahead of him was
welcome.

Owl sliced off some venison to broil. He rigged a
tripod for a bag of water. He pushed some stones into the
little fire to heat. He pitched some venison into the water. He added more wood to the fire.

"Food soon," he said.

The boy did not respond.

Owl was not concerned that the light of the fire
might be spotted. It was back far enough so that it would
take a very lucky shot to penetrate the rock hollow. In
any case, they would know about where he was. They
were not fools, those men who had trailed him for so
long and so far.

But there was one thing he had to do at once. He
did it.

The little fire had not been burning long, but already
there were coals and ashes. There was some firewood that
had charred at one end. Owl had plenty of water.

He plunged the charred stick into the water supported
by the tripod. It made a satisfactory hissing noise. Owl wet
his hands and scraped some ashy coals from the fire. He
rubbed the wet sticky stuff into the skin of his face, hard.
Then he marked his face with the charred stick. He did it
with enough force to draw a tiny bit of blood.

Black was the color of war paint. Owl was as ready as he knew how to be.

The boy watched and shivered. The first time he had ever seen Owl, the Comanche's face had been painted black.

"Not for you," Owl said.

O-tis might or might not have understood. In any case, there was no action that he could take. He was so weak that even thinking was difficult. After the stones had heated for boiling, it would still take some time for the stew to cook.

Owl squatted down, stuck a chunk of half-raw venison into his mouth, and sliced the venison in half with his knife. He shoved what was left back into the fire to broil. The meat had a peculiar taste to it, but the juices revived him. He did not try to feed the boy any of the partially cooked venison. He knew that would be a mistake. Chewing away with his soot-blackened jaws, he recognized that his own tough stomach had come close to rejecting the meat.

The small flames danced their orange dance and threw shifting shadows on the rock walls. Owl was always surprised at the size of the shadows cast by little fires. They seemed to have a life of their own.

Inevitably his thoughts were drawn to Spirit Shadow. He had asked her many questions.

The answers would come soon, or they would not come at all.

The Ancient One was still watching. Owl was sure of it. He did not look back into the darkness where it stood. He did not call its name again. That could wait a little longer.

Owl was thinking of the great white skull and the dead dry eyes that could see through stone. That skull of *piamempits* was very close.

It was partially the need to get some stew into the boy that held Owl where he was. It was also his inability to make a proper torch without the necessary grass and grease. Just a tiny flame on the end of a stick would not do the job. The skull could see and he couldn't. That was not good.

There may have been something else. There were answers that Owl did not wish to hear. There were things that Owl did not wish to see.

Sometimes a man had to search whether he wanted to or not. It was possible to delay things, but not when time was running out.

Owl had no fear of leaving O-tis. The men who were following the trail would not enter the canyon at night. This was true even if they spotted the shielded glow of the fire. It was too tricky to ride upstream over those slippery rocks in the darkness. They might know where the fire was, but they could not know where Owl was.

As for climbing down the cliff face on either side of the waterfall, that would be crazy in the daytime. At night it was suicide.

All the boy had to do for now was to stay exactly where he was. The pursuers could not get to him.

Owl himself would have to make his move at dawn, as soon as there was enough light to see. That would be the dangerous time.

Owl waited until the stone-boiling had produced something that resembled broth. It was a poor food with which to rekindle a life, but it was all he had.

He propped O-tis up in his nest. Using a small horn spoon and a hide pouch, he forced the hot liquid into the boy's mouth.

At first Owl had to hold the teeth apart with his fingers, but after O-tis made a few convulsive swallows, he got it going down in a fairly steady stream. The boy came out of his stillness enough to struggle some. He had all the broth he wanted, but Owl kept it coming.

Food was strength. If O-tis threw it up, Owl was prepared to do it all over again. It was possible that the boy knew that. He kept it down.

When Owl was satisfied, he covered O-tis with the buffalo robe again. Owl sat by the flickering fire, letting it die at its own pace.

If it was meant to be, he could always build another fire. By morning there would still be coals.

For now, there was Mother Moon. High above the stone canyon, she was splashed and blurred with silver by the hissing cascade of the waterfall.

Owl did not know what to say to her.

He did know that he would not sleep this night.

He checked the tautness of his sinew bowstring. He fingered the arrows from his quiver, going over them one by one.

When there was nothing more that he could do, Owl sat quite still by what was left of the fire and stared into a darkness that had no end.

Owl moved with the first light. It was not the time when Father Sun sent pale colors into the sky to announce his coming. It was the time before that, the time when blackness turns to gray and the worms of shadows move. There were no colors.

The boy was asleep. He may or may not have been stronger. Owl did not awaken him.

Owl climbed with the light. He needed only enough light to see his way. He did not want full daylight to splash down into the canyon before he returned. The best protection he had for his son was darkness.

Owl climbed and crawled and slithered. He knew that he would not have to follow this trail again. That thought did not displease him.

Like a lizard pressed flat against a rock, Owl moved across the never-forgotten ledge that whispered to him of too many yesterdays. There were the scattered bones of the Cannibal Owl. His heart jumped in his chest. Yes, there was a faint glow coming from the limestone-encrusted bones. He could not have seen it if the sunlight had been brighter. The glow was yellow now, not orange, but it was there.

Alive, oh yes. Dead for more seasons than Owl could count, dead when the past was young, but alive with a power that was forever.

It had been here, in this exact place, that Owl had found the grooved flint point. He could feel the medicine pouch burning against his chest. He did not touch it with his hands.

He kept going. He disturbed some furry bats, gorged from a night of feeding. They swooped against his blackened face. One of them got tangled in Owl's greasy braids. He brushed it away, hating the feel of it.

The stone cavern that he sought was above him. Owl pulled himself up and flopped inside. The chamber was not tall, but it was deep. Only the edge of the cavern was wet.

Inside, it was bone dry.

Owl managed a small smile, even at the end of his world.

Bone dry indeed. It was the lair of the giant white skull of *piamempits*. It was waiting for him.

See the empty socket holes on the sides of the flat, pulsing face? See the bulge in the top of the skull? See the great cavity where eyes had once burned? See those scars on the bone, extending all the way up above the eye shelf?

There was no lower jaw. Owl did not have to look again at that massive upper jaw to know what was there. But he had to look. There was a contest of wills here, and a chaos of questions.

At the end, a man must have some answers.

Owl crawled forward. He crawled against a huge negative force that tried to push him back. His lacerated belly left a path of blood on the stone floor of the cavern.

Owl was ready for the skull to speak. He was prepared for a gush of moist warm breath to howl from that dead-alive bone. He did not know what the thing might do. The swollen skull of the Cannibal Owl could do almost anything.

It contained much of the power in the universe.

Owl was only a man. But he kept coming. Sometimes it came down to this. Do it or die. Or both.

He sensed the growing luminosity of the light. Father Sun was not yet up to the edge of the hidden canyon world. He was getting close.

Owl had little time, even in this rock chamber that was out of time and beyond time.

It was not just Father Sun who was getting close.

The men who stalked his trail were nearing this canyon, or already in it. Spirit Shadow had said that there were two men, perhaps three. Did it matter? Owl could retreat no farther. Against one man or an army, it was here that he would make his stand.

Was this not the home of his Guardian Spirit? Had not the Ancient One said, "*You will always see me when you need me most.*"

If this was not the time and the place, then when and where might it be?

Owl dragged himself forward. He could feel some heat from that bone-giant of a skull. He did not have to touch it. That might have been too much for him. But he only had to get his head under that monstrosity of an upper jaw. He only had to see the teeth again.

It was as though *piamempits* wanted to preserve its secret. The power pushing against Owl almost blinded him. He half expected the Beast to close its mouth, even without a lower jaw.

The mouth remained open. The teeth were exposed. Yes. Row upon row of worn, ridged, grinding teeth.

Owl had known what he was going to find. He had seen the teeth before. But this time was different. This time he was going to understand. This time he *must* understand.

He held steady against the repelling force of the Ancient One. Here, in this dimly illuminated stone chamber screened by the canyon waterfall, it was not man against Beast. It was far more than that.

It was a merging.

It was a revelation.

It was all the horror and hope and mystery in the universe, shimmering and pulsing in the dawn.

Teeth! Grinding teeth!

These were not the teeth of a bird. These were not the teeth of an ancient Cannibal Owl that swooped down out of the night on the villages of The People.

He had not forgotten the cryptic words of Spirit

Shadow. She had said: "I can tell you that the Cannibal Owl has more than one shape. It is a shape-changer." Oh, she was clever, that one. She did not lie. Nor did she tell the whole truth.

Spirit Shadow had told him that there was one question he could not ask, even in his mind.

Owl did more than ask it now. He answered it.

He slipped back, sliding in his own blood. He stared at the great skull. He did not know whether he felt betrayal or the beginnings of hope.

He still did not touch the grooved point in the pouch that dangled from his neck.

Owl said it aloud. He had no time left for secrets, even the mightiest of secrets.

"You," he said. The power of his voice surprised him. It had truth in it. It might not strike a hammer blow, but all the strength was not on one side. "You cannot hide from me again. I know you now."

The silence in the stone chamber was absolute. It was the silence that precedes a storm. It was the silence of an emptiness that had to be filled.

Owl lay there in the stickiness of his blood. He was not sure what he had done, or why. He only knew that he had done it.

It was all so obvious, once you dared to look.

The flaring sockets on the sides of that huge flat face. What else could they be but the holes that held the great curving tusks? The bony scar-wrinkles above the recessed shelf of the eyes. Did that not have to be where the segmented trunk was attached? That bulge in the top of the massive skull. Had Owl not seen that dome on a Beast that moved in the shadows, a Beast with patches of red-brown hair that were infested with bugs?

Had he not smelled the dung of that Beast and heard its Voice?

They were the same. The Cannibal Owl and his Guardian Spirit were identical. The Ancient One and *piamempits* shared the same skeleton.

What did it mean to a man when his Guardian Spirit

was the most feared enemy of his people? Had the world turned over?

Unexpectedly, the Ancient One found its voice.

First the great white skull seemed to pulse. There was a yellow-orange glow that burned around it. The old, old eyes returned to their sockets. The trunk sprouted and it was spotted with bristle hairs. There was a tongue, red and wet. It flopped loosely where the lower jaw should have been.

The Ancient One did not assume its full shape. There was no room for that in the rock chamber. It would have to move out into the open space beyond the pool. It created just enough of itself to speak.

Owl could smell the wet breath. It streamed a little in the cold.

Owl was stunned when his Guardian Spirit spoke. He had convinced himself that he would never hear that voice again. Or was he truly hearing words? Was this only in his head?

The sad, ancient eyes of the Beast transfixed him.

The heavy animal smell filled the cavern.

This was real, this was real!

"It was in this canyon that I first appeared before you," the skull head said. *"It was here that I gave to you the name of Owl."*

Owl said nothing. What could he say? It was one thing to speak brave words into emptiness. It was another thing to say them directly to the Beast.

"I gave to you more than your name. I gave you a single task to perform. Most Guardian Spirits would have been more demanding."

Again Owl was stunned. Did the Ancient One have a sense of humor? Was it playing with him?

"Do you remember what that task was?"

Was this really happening? A conversation with a giant trunked skull in a rock chamber behind the waterfall?

"DO YOU REMEMBER?"

Owl shivered. Somehow, he had to answer. He could not even imagine what might happen if he did not.

"I remember," he said. His voice was not nearly as

powerful as it had been before, when the skull was only a skull. It was little more than a whisper.

The Beast lapsed into silence. Its liquid breathing was enormous and labored. It seemed to be gathering its resources. Owl did not know whether it would speak again or not.

It did. *"There is much that you do not understand. But you must understand this much. Do not let questions weaken you. Do what it is that you must do. The pathway of your shade depends upon it. My own existence in eternal time is in your hands. When we are completely forgotten, we are gone. Whatever we are, are we not worth remembering?"*

Owl had no answer for that one.

"You must go now. It is very late. They are coming. They are here, in this canyon of stone."

Owl hesitated, despite the words.

Could a skull head smile? *"Go. This has been very much talk for a Guardian Spirit."*

There were many things that Owl did not know. He did know that he would hear no more words from the Ancient One. That was over for him, forever.

He became very aware of the seeping light. There were colors now, even in this chamber where colors were few. The morning was upon him.

Hurry!

Owl crawled back and dropped down. He slipped and stumbled his way across the ledge where the giant scattered bones still glowed slightly with a living yellow.

Owl wiped the blood from his chest and scraped his hands on the rock walls to dry them. His grip must be sure and certain. It would not do to miss.

The outside light from Father Sun seemed to mix with the glow of the bones. Owl could hear the waterfall very clearly. It seemed to him that he heard every distinct white bubble as the water hissed over the rock ledge and splashed into the pool.

Owl did not know whether he was breathing or not. He only knew that he kept moving, toward the boy. He was not certain which world he was in. It may have been that he was between worlds. Could that be?

What did it mean that his Guardian Spirit and *piamempits* were one and the same? Had The People been wrong for all of their seasons about the identity of the bones? Was it all about shape-changing, or did that have nothing to do with it? If the grooved point in his medicine pouch had not killed the Cannibal Owl, what *had* it killed?

"Do not let questions weaken you. Do what it is that you must do."

And hurry!

It came to him as a kind of revelation in that strange world that had somehow run out of time. The Ancient One was what it was. Owl was what he was. They were both part of something lost, something that could never come again. It was Owl's destiny to save what he could. It was the task of the Beast to do whatever a Guardian Spirit could do.

That was all.

Owl burst out on the lookout ledge that was directly behind the waterfall. He was a wild sight, truly an apparition that had wedged from one world to another. His face was smeared with blood and charcoal black. His braids were unknotted and his dark greasy hair framed his face like a hood. His eyes burned.

The little fire still smoldered.

His son had left his nest. The buffalo robe was crumpled and empty.

Owl screamed. It was a pure animal scream. He unslung his bow. He nocked a feathered arrow into the sinew string. He was very fast.

O-tis was out on the ledge, in plain view of anyone below. He was as thin as a skeleton. He was dressed only in a breechclout. He was waving his hands and shouting. His shrill voice echoed through the canyon of stone.

Owl took it all in with a single glance. There was a dark figure descending the canyon wall. There was a glint from Father Sun reflecting off a rifle barrel. There was another *Taibo* rider down on the gravel beach where Heart was. The rider was still mounted and his face was turned upward toward the ledge. He drew his Colt so rapidly that Owl never saw his hand move.

Two of them, then. One climbing down the rock wall with a rope to guide him. He had a rifle and had contrived a kind of support loop in the rope that would allow him to fire. The other man down below, all set to open up with a revolver. Where was the third man who had followed the trail? Or had he too been part of a dream?

It did not matter now. Owl shrieked again. This was no haunting death song. This was an explosion of bitterness and frustration and loss.

His son was standing out there on that ledge. He was not even trying to help. He was *calling* to the enemies of Owl.

Owl could not wait. He launched his first arrow. His aim was very sure. He did not have to see it strike home.

The heavy animal smell of the Beast was in his nostrils. The Ancient One had come. It was not in its rock chamber any longer. It was down there in the brush that lined the gravel beach, not far from Heart. It lifted its hair-pocked trunk and trumpeted a screech that rocked the canyon walls. There was no sign that either of the Taibo men noticed it. But Heart jerked to one side and flattened his ears. For just a moment O-tis froze into immobility.

The appearance of the Ancient One brought no gladness to Owl. It was too late for that. But he felt less alone.

Owl strung a second arrow. It was just right, perfectly balanced. The feathered shaft was true. The barbed metal point was sharp.

Just as the gunfire shattered the morning silence of the stone canyon, Owl loosed his second arrow. His face contorted. It may have been that there was more blood on him.

Owl had all the strength he needed.

He dropped his bow. He launched himself forward. There was no weakness in him, no unsureness.

Owl reached out with his worn, scarred hands and seized the throat of O-tis.

16

Coffee, 14–15 March 1856

Coffee knew exactly where he was. He knew the name of the sinkhole pond that was formed by the waterfall at the head of the canyon: Hamilton Pool. He had not been there often, but he had been there. It was only a two-day ride from Austin.

He knew that Owl and Otis were somewhere in that rock-walled canyon. The trail was plain enough, as far as it went. It would have been senseless to ride that rough pathway into the canyon and then turn around and ride back out again. It would have been equally foolish to ride downstream to the Pedernales River. There was simply no point to such ventures, and Owl could have little energy left for playing games.

No. The quarry he sought was in the canyon. Once Coffee got down in there, Owl could not hide from him. Not for long.

There were problems, though. It seemed to Coffee that this chase had been nothing but problems. He was ready for action, impatient for release.

But Coffee was not stupid. He was not a man to

walk into a rattlesnake den and stick out his bare hand in the dark.

The question that concerned him most was the whereabouts of Lee. The black man had been ahead of him. The trail up here in the flat country was not clear. Dead grass did not take prints easily, and the earth was very dry. There was some prickly pear around, but that was of interest only to Pear. Coffee found it difficult to keep his horse's mouth out of the stuff. This would have been a singularly poor time to have to deal with cactus needles.

Was Lee ahead of him on the canyon trail? Had he found another way down? Had he hung back, waiting?

It was not that Coffee was afraid of Lee, or that he expected an ambush from that source. It was just that he needed to know where Lee *was*. If he did not know, he could not plan his own move.

Then what about the other rider, the one who had thrown the blue bottle of laudanum away? The man who had left a single white hair where his saddle had marked the earth? It did not really matter much who he was, although Coffee had more than a suspicion on that score.

It was *where* he was that counted. The man almost seemed to have a horse that floated down out of the sky. Was he in the canyon too?

"God damn," Coffee said. He thought it over some and amplified the sentiment. "God damn it to hell."

There was a wind up here on the flatlands above the gash of the canyon. The wind was cold again.

Pear snorted. He did not like this indecision. Coffee's lead horse was not a particularly intelligent animal. He just stood where he was, waiting. It was all the same to him.

There were shadows marching across that lonely land. Coffee could hear nothing but the moaning of the wind. He knew precisely where the waterfall was, but it was silent from this angle. A man had to get down into the canyon to hear it. Either that or ride to the top edge of the sinkhole, where the fine spray-mist hung like a lost cloud fallen among the rocks.

The longer he hesitated, the more unyielding his problems became. Of course, there were times when a man simply had to plunge into whatever was waiting and hope for the best.

This was not one of those times.

The reason was Otis.

Coffee had to assume that Owl would maintain a lookout. He had to figure that Lee was already in the canyon, or about to be. There was no way for him to guess where the other man might be.

"White Hair," he said, "you sure have a way of making things worse."

There was no answer from White Hair, if indeed he was in the area at all.

If Coffee charged into the canyon, he might as well do it whooping and hollering. As long as there was daylight, he would be seen.

Coffee did not doubt that Owl's eyes were as good as the night hunter whose name he had taken. Nor did he doubt that Lee could spot a horny toad at fifty yards.

It was a dangerous situation in that canyon. Dangerous for Otis. If Coffee went in, that might upset a lot of plans. Whether he rode in or walked in or did a belly flop into the waterfall pond, things would start to happen.

There would be shooting.

The chances of getting Otis out unscathed would be somewhere near zero.

Damn that black man! Why hadn't he stayed out of it?

It may have been the toughest decision of his life, but Coffee made it. If he could not risk entering the canyon by daylight, he had to wait until full dark. That way, whoever was down there, a fire could guide him.

He remembered the smoke-marked rock shelter at the foot of the trail. That was as good a place as any for his first move.

His best hope was for total surprise. He had to get into position and he had to know exactly where everyone was.

Then he had to move without hesitation. Fast, yes, but speed was not everything. He had to know what he was doing. He could not make a single mistake.

Coffee eased Pear into a clump of cedars. He had already decided to leave his packhorse up here on top. He could be tethered. Coffee did not plan on staying down below for a long time.

Coffee waited while the wind died and the night chill grew. The stars above him looked as big as frying pans.

Seen in shadowy silhouette, Noah Coffee seemed dead calm and as patient as a statue.

Inside, he was seething.

Coffee was ready to go.

It was called a Comanche Moon, anywhere in Texas. It was a moon full enough to light the path of night raiders. It was turning to silver, but this moon was still low enough to be tinged with gold.

A Comanche Moon for sure, Coffee thought. It favored Owl. Coffee would have preferred no moon at all. He could have used some clouds to mask the stars, if it came to that.

When he could wait no longer, there was still too much light to suit him. Coffee went anyway.

He walked Pear down the slippery trail that wound into the canyon. The click of Pear's shoes sounded like cannon shots in the silence. A less surefooted horse would never have made it in the gloom. The deeper they went, the less light there was.

The smell of the cypress trees was very strong. They were greening up early. The bubbling whisper of the stream might have concealed many noises.

There was nothing wrong with Coffee's memory. He went straight to the rock shelter and dismounted. Pear blew a little and then stopped suddenly, as though ashamed of himself.

Coffee could feel the rock walls. It was absolutely impossible to tell whether he was alone or not. They could all have been within thirty yards of him for all he knew: Owl and Otis, Lee and the stranger.

It did not seem likely.

Coffee pulled his big Colt and moved along the edges of the trail. For a man in boots, he made little sound. He had the constant sensation that he was going to walk right into something. Something squishy. Something sharp, like the blade of a knife.

Something.

There was nothing. Coffee encountered only moist air and twisted roots and slabs of rock. He could actually see the looming walls of the canyon on both sides of him. They formed the deeper blackness below the lighter hole in the sky.

When his ears told him that he was nearing the lake and the gentle hiss of the falls, Coffee dropped to his belly. He crawled through a tunnel of rock that he knew opened up into a gravel beach and a rearing series of rock ledges. His clothes were stained from moss.

Ahead of him a horse snorted. There was a shuffle of hooves.

Coffee stopped cold. He held his breath. The horse was to his left. Mounted or riderless?

Coffee figured that it made no sense for a rider to be waiting there in the moonlight. Of all the possible defensive positions, that was the worst.

Of course, the man might not have defense on his mind. He might be drawing a bead right now.

Coffee didn't think so. He bet his life on it. He crawled closer. He sensed an opening of space.

He looked up, against the slight phosphorescence of the cascading waterfall. Yes. There it was. Behind the sheet of water.

No roaring inferno, certainly. More like a faint orange glow. A light that could only be made by a dying fire.

How many times had he sat by such small fires, watching the coals shrink down and turn into ashes? Not half the nights of his life, maybe, but close.

Coffee knew what he was looking at. The only

strange thing was that he could not smell the wood smoke. That must be due to the screen of the waterfall.

Coffee had no doubt whose fire that was, perched up there under the rock overhang. He had found Owl. He had found Otis.

Now what? There was no way that Owl would be asleep. He would not have left a horse down here for no reason.

Coffee stared until his eyeballs ached. He could see no sign of another person. Not even a decent moving shadow. Coffee rolled from side to side, studying everything that he could see. It wasn't much.

Unless Lee was on the horse that had snorted, he was well hidden. As for the stranger, he could be hanging in a cave upside down like a bat and Coffee would not have known it.

Coffee rejected the idea of getting close enough to the horse to see it better. In his gut he knew that it was a riderless horse. If a man could not sense such things, he died young.

It seemed to Coffee that he had made some progress. He had located his prey. That was maybe half the battle.

What he needed now was a certainty about Lee and the stranger. He needed just enough light to know what he was doing.

And he needed his horse. There was no way to figure what that other horse was waiting for by the side of the pool beneath the stars.

Already the darkness was easing a little. This scout had taken longer than he had planned.

It was frustrating. He knew that he was close enough so that Otis would hear him if he called.

He did not dare do that. How many ears were listening in that shrouded canyon?

Coffee wormed himself around, slid back along the trail, got to his feet and walked as fast as he could toward the rock shelter that held his horse.

No matter how good you are, it takes time to move a horse quietly along a difficult trail. It does not help any when the light is tricky and changing. Coffee rode with every nerve alert, trying to see in all directions at once. He had come too long and too far to risk everything now.

There was morning light in the canyon when Coffee reached the last barrier that shielded him from the pool. He could see the clear blue-green water. He could see the fresh green of damp ferns. He could see the yellow-brown gravel of the beach.

He spotted the lone horse at once. It was riderless and unsaddled. He knew the horse the way a man knows any animal he has tracked for months. It was Owl's gelding.

Coffee had no chance to reflect on how this knowledge changed the situation. With the suddenness of a lightning bolt out of nowhere, time stopped. Coffee could only react. The man who had tried to plan so carefully found himself caught in a whirlwind.

There was a thin, high, desperate cry. Strained as it was, the voice was that of Otis Nesbitt. Coffee did not have to calculate the location of that cry. It came from up on the ledge behind the waterfall, up where he had seen the glow of the dying fire.

Then, instantly, there was the agonized scream of an adult. The screech was not in any language. It was beyond language.

Coffee kicked Pear forward into the open. His startled horse nearly bucked. Pear had been held back so long he could not adjust quickly enough. Coffee himself was confused. There was too much to take in all at once.

There was a man with his boot in a rope loop descending the canyon wall, dropping down from the top. The man had a rifle. He lost his hat as he climbed through the morning. His hair was as white as new snow.

Coffee could see Otis behind the waterfall. He was as skinny as a stick and half naked. He was waving his hands in some kind of signal.

Jesus! There was Owl, black-painted for war, moving up behind Otis. Owl was screaming again, the crazed sound of a wounded animal. He had a bow. He was letting fly with arrows. Their razored points glistened as they flashed through the thin sheet of water falling into the pool. The water did not have enough force to deflect his aim.

Coffee was not even aware that he had drawn. His Colt was in his right hand, the hammer full-cocked. Pear had steadied some. Owl's riderless horse seemed to shy at something.

There was the sound of gunfire. Coffee was not sure of its source. He was not sure of anything. Events had gotten out of control.

He saw Owl drop his bow and lunge for the throat of the calling boy.

Otis was between Coffee and Owl.

It did not matter that Coffee's shot had to be perfect. It was his only hope of saving the boy's life.

Coffee fired. The crash of his Colt stunned him in a way that had never happened before. He found himself unable to comprehend what was going on.

Just before or after he pulled the trigger, something slammed into his left shoulder. There was no pain. There was only a numbing shock and surprise.

All Coffee really knew was that he had been knocked out of his saddle by a blow that struck him like a crowbar.

He had gravel in his face and something sticky like blood, and then there was nothing.

17

Exodus, 15 March 1856

It was cool throughout the morning, and the pale afternoon sun brought little warmth. That was a good thing. Even when they were tightly wrapped in blankets and robes, corpses did not do well in the heat.

It was a strange procession that rode out of the canyon of the Cannibal Owl. There were five riders and five horses, although one horse had been left behind on the gravel beach that bordered the blue-green pool. Not every rider was on the same horse he had ridden into the canyon.

Two of the riders were dead. They were lashed crosswise to the backs of their horses, wrists tied to ankles. They flopped and gurgled as they rode. From a distance they looked remarkably like flour sacks. One of the sacks seemed half empty.

Another rider had what appeared to be a terrible arrow wound in his left shoulder. The shoulder was heavily bandaged from a medical kit taken from the packhorse, but the man had lost a lot of blood. He was still losing blood. The bandages were no longer white and there was

a stain spreading across his torn shirt. He was somewhere between alive and dead. He had trouble sitting on
his horse. He was so dazed that he hardly knew where
he was. Without a will of iron, he would have been just
another flour sack.

Of the remaining two riders, one was a boy. At any
rate, he had been a boy a few long weeks or months ago.
It was hard to say what he was now. He was very thin,
with a loss of flesh that comes from sickness and then re-
covery flab and then from being pushed almost beyond
endurance. His blue eyes glinted like ice. He wore moccasins and a breechclout. His long hair was so greasy
with animal fat and poultices that it was impossible to tell
what color it was. Despite his exposure to the winds, his
skin was very white. He had been wrapped in a robe or
dozing in a tipi most of the time. He had a shirt on now
that was much too big for him. It was one of Coffee's
spare shirts. The man-boy had it buttoned all the way up
to the throat.

The last rider was an older man. He was darker than
a man should be who had only spent much time in the
sun and the wind. His face was lined with weariness, but
the creases were not soft. They were like chisel slices in
granite. He spoke neither to the dead nor the living. On
this day he had done things he had sworn to himself that
he would never do. He had risked much and lost much.
There were deep holes of worry in his mind. He kept
changing his position in the group. He would drop back
to check on the swaying man with the bandaged shoulder. He would move over and ride beside the skinny
boy-man. He said no words but he tried to lend reassurance. He spent much time riding next to one of the dead
men. Once he even reached out his hand and touched
the mounded blanket. It was as though he hoped against
all hope that he would find some sign of life. The butt of
his Paterson Colt kept slipping up in his holster. The trigger was retracted. The dark man never looked at his
Colt. He seemed to reject it. He just reached down and
jammed it into its holster. It was as if he had no intention
of ever drawing it again.

Behind the procession, down in the cypress-lined canyon, a horse named Heart waited for nothing at all.

The water glided over the rock ledge as it had done for thousands of years.

Behind the waterfall, hidden in its chamber of rock, a Skull watched the world through dead eye sockets of bone.

18

Lee, 16 March 1856

Lee kept them moving toward Stafford. It seemed to take an eternity. He had to hold to a slow pace. The dead did not care, but the fact was that he was the only healthy one in that party of five.

Otis was far from well, but he did not complain. He had aged beyond his years. He would endure.

It was Coffee's bleeding that clawed at Lee's guts. The matter was really very simple. *Coffee could not be allowed to die.* That was all there was to it.

Lee dropped back again until he was riding directly abreast of Coffee. The booted stirrups of the two men touched.

"We can stop," Lee said. "Fix that bandage."

Coffee's eyes were glazed. He was so bewhiskered that it was hard to tell whether he had a mustache or a beard. He had no expression on his face at all.

"Don't like the bleeding," Lee said. "Arrow wounds are bad that way."

Coffee said nothing.

"I had to pull the shaft through, you know," Lee

said. It was almost as though he were offering an apology. "There was no other way." It occurred to Lee that although this was strictly a one-way conversation, it was the most words that had ever passed between them.

"We still have some alcohol," Lee said. "Clean that thing out. Even got some laudanum left. He didn't drink it all." He paused, wishing for some words to fill the silence. "If you want it. If it would help."

Coffee said nothing. Lee could not be sure whether he was listening or not. My God, did the man still resent him? Even here? Even now?

The wind was cold. It brought no answers.

Lee tried one more time. He had to get through to Coffee somehow. He had to help him. Everything depended on that. "Ranger man, we are on the same side now. Like it or don't like it, to get this boy home we've got to pull together. If you won't do it for me, and if you won't do it for yourself, how about doing it for Otis? Why the hell else are we out here?"

Amazingly, that penetrated. Something in Coffee responded. "Did I get the son of a bitch?" he croaked. His voice was harsh with disuse.

It took Lee a moment to figure what he was talking about. Then he thought back to that instant when Coffee had been hit. Of course, that was where he was in his head. What had happened since would be unknown to him.

"You got him," Lee said. "You got him good."

Coffee started to come out of it, then swayed and almost fell. That damned bleeding! It had to be stopped. "Man on a rope," Coffee muttered. "White hair. *His* laudanum. You know him. Who is in Stafford? Got to get to Stafford!"

That did it. Coffee slumped and fell forward on Pear. His slack hand dropped the reins.

Lee caught him and gestured to the boy. "Need some help here, son. Ain't all that many folks here left alive."

They got Coffee off his horse and peeled his sticky shirt down to the bloody bandage. Lee washed the entrance and exit ruptures as best he could with the alcohol. The wounds were very different.

"Makes a big difference, an arrow does," Lee said in an almost conversational tone. "Whether it's going in or coming out."

Otis did not comment on that one.

"You know, boy, we've got to save this man."

For a wonder, Otis spoke. They had all been through so much, the living and the dead, that nothing was predictable. Sometimes Lee talked to himself and sometimes he got answers. When Otis did speak, his words took peculiar twists. Even considering what Otis knew and what he had experienced, Lee could not always tell when the boy was serious and when he was just funning around like the child he used to be.

"Save him for my sister?" he asked. "Save him for you? Or just save him?"

Lee stared at him. He could not read those cold blue eyes. He played it absolutely straight. "Not for your sister," he said. "That much is for sure."

Otis retreated back into his silence. One skinny hand fumbled with the shirt at his throat.

Lee worked with Coffee, willing him to live. He wanted the wounds to dry some before he tried another bandage. He did not know whether Coffee could hear him or not. He continued to address his words to Otis.

"Mr. Noah Coffee here," he said, "he was just trying to save your hide. You know that?"

Otis was not in an answering mood. Lee decided that it did not much matter whether Coffee could hear him or not. Coffee was in no shape to understand anything, even if you hit him over the head with it.

Lee looked slowly and deliberately at the two dead, blanketed bodies lashed to the horses. He looked first at one and then at the other.

Lee went back to his conversational tone. "Not an easy thing to lose a father," he said.

Otis did not look at the mounded blankets.

"Even worse when you lose two of them," Lee said. That must have hurt, but Otis said nothing. Lee knew that he was prodding O-tis and he did not like it. It was against his nature. He understood that it might have something to do with his own father, or lack of one. The realization did not help him.

"Thing is," Lee said without emphasis, "a body's only got so many fathers in this world." It might have been a kind of an offer. It might not.

Whatever it was, Otis did not take him up on it.

Lee turned his full attention back to Coffee. It was like going from one type of wound to another. The bleeding had subsided for now. Lee wasn't sure whether that was a good sign or not, but he did know that a man had only so much blood in him. When it was gone, it was gone.

He applied a fresh bandage and tied it as tightly as he dared. Thank God for that packhorse. He even had laudanum if he needed it. All the comforts of home.

He waited as long as he could. Then he replaced Coffee's gummy shirt. It was beginning to stiffen up. Coffee groaned. It was almost like a snore. The man had no idea where he was.

The wind stayed cool and dry. That might help.

"Put his left boot in the stirrup," Lee said. The tone was still conversational, but it was an order.

Otis knew what to do. He had been assisted on and off horses a few times himself.

With Otis holding the boot just tightly enough so that it would not slip out, Lee picked up Coffee and swung him into the saddle. It looked effortless, but Lee was secretly pleased that he still had that much power. Otis got the other boot in the stirrup without prompting.

Already there was a widening crimson stain seeping through the bandage. It was not a lot of blood, but Coffee was bleeding again.

"Don't you die, damn you," Lee said. There was real anger in his voice, and there was pain. "Don't you dare die."

Lee started them off again, five riders caught somewhere between whatever had been and what might still be. Otis kept one hand at the collar of his borrowed shirt.

The two dead men were swelling up some. Coffee was just barely able to sit his saddle. If riding had not been as natural to him as breathing, he could not have done it.

Lee had a blunt awareness that, in most respects, it would be much easier for him if Coffee did not survive.

But that would leave just Lee and Otis.

And that was unthinkable.

Lee knew in his heart that whatever happened, he had to get Coffee to Stafford alive. He owed him that.

How long to Stafford? Lee knew precisely where he was, but he could not estimate the travel time. With three dead men and a boy, he could move right along. But he only had two dead men, and the aim was to prevent a third.

Coffee had to make it home. And no matter what, Coffee must never learn what had truly occurred in that morning canyon where a man named Owl had waited for them behind a waterfall that tumbled out of a dream. . . .

When Lee had first reached the canyon, he knew at once that Cole Nesbitt had gotten there ahead of him.

It was neither possible nor impossible. It simply was.

Lee had ridden many a trail with Cole Nesbitt. He lived in his house. He certainly knew the old man's favorite horse, Blaze. And he recognized the spare horse Cole Nesbitt often took with him. His name was Molasses. He had been born slow and steady.

Both horses were saddled and tethered. Lee could tell at a glance what gear was missing. Blaze had no coiled lariat, and Cole Nesbitt's rifle was not in its scabbard.

Of course, Cole Nesbitt was missing too.

"Cole Nesbitt!" Lee called softly. He did not dare yell. He just spoke a little louder than normal. "You there, Old-Timer?"

There was no answer, and Lee had not expected one. How in God's name that white-haired old bastard had crawled out of a sickbed and hauled himself to this

forsaken place, he did not know. What he did know was
that if Cole Nesbitt wanted to be seen, he would have
met up with Lee a long while back. If he didn't want
company, then Lee could never find him and neither
could any other man on this earth.

Yes, Cole Nesbitt was very probably out of his head.
He was still Cole Nesbitt. Lee had a respect for his old
trail companion that bordered on veneration. Whatever
Cole Nesbitt was fixing to do, he meant to do it on his
own. Maybe he figured he owed his only living son that
much. If he was playing a loner's game, Lee would be
taking a long chance if he interfered. He didn't even
know what the game was.

Maybe the old man could pull it off.

Maybe not.

"I'll stay out of your way," Lee said, knowing full
well that the old man was somewhere out of hearing
range. "You stay out of mine. That fair enough?"

Silence.

Lee was just stubborn enough so that he could not
meekly turn aside simply because Cole Nesbitt was here.
Cole would never have expected or asked that of him. Besides, Lee told himself, there was Otis to think about.
Good as he once had been, Cole Nesbitt must be half
dead. He might be crazy to boot. In order for Otis to have
a chance, Lee had to go in.

Then there was one other little problem. Where in
the hell was Coffee? Closing in fast, Lee figured, unless
he had already found another way into the canyon.

If Coffee came busting in here, then what chance
would Otis have? The fur might fly for sure if Coffee believed he had to head off Cole Nesbitt. How good was
Coffee's judgment, anyway?

The whole thing was ridiculous, and Lee knew it.
Here they were, three grown men, and all they were trying to do was to save a boy from an Indian. They all
wanted exactly the same thing.

So why couldn't they team up and do what they had
to do in a reasonable way?

Lee also knew the answer to that one.

People were people, and that was the long and the short of it. In Lee's experience, people seldom did the sensible thing. Lee could not change the kind of man that Coffee was. Coffee could not change Lee. And Cole Nesbitt was off in a little world of his own. In his condition, he was totally unpredictable.

God knew what Owl was thinking. Laughing his head off, probably.

Lee was ready to move, and move fast. The one question that stumped him was what to do with Blaze. There was an unwritten law between men who rode long trails together. Whatever you did, you did not change the position of your partner's horse without notifying him. If contact was impossible, you left the horse where it was.

In his whole life Lee had never violated that rule. Then again, he had never before been in a spot quite like this one.

Cole Nesbitt had made no attempt at all to conceal either Blaze or Molasses. The old man might or might not be out of his mind. But if Lee spotted Blaze, Coffee would do the same. They were following the same trail. Coffee had good eyes.

Lee did not worry about stranding Cole Nesbitt. Mr. Cole Nesbitt could find Blaze at midnight in a buffalo herd. He had forgotten more about finding horses than Lee had ever known.

Of course, it was dangerous to leave horses unprotected. But Cole had already done that, and Lee was about to do the same. That was just a chance you took.

But suppose that by moving Blaze he took away from Coffee something that Coffee had to know? What if this time around it was going to be Coffee who would reach Otis first? Was Lee exposing both Cole Nesbitt and Coffee to a danger he did not understand? Did he have any right to do that?

Lee spat. He had to bet on himself this day. If Coffee blundered into trouble, Lee would get him out of it. Hellfire, there was just one Comanche! As for Cole Nesbitt, Lee's confidence in him was total. He had chosen to ride this trail alone.

Lee moved Blaze and Molasses into a stand of scrub
oaks just distant enough so that they could not be readily
seen. He tethered them lightly and left the saddles on.
He did the same with Doc. Cole could not find one
horse without finding three, and that would tell him everything he needed to know.

Lee slipped his Hall-North .52 caliber carbine from
his saddle scabbard. He was ready.

It was getting on into the afternoon. Lee had only a
general idea of the layout of the canyon, and a long scout
of the canyon rim would be very risky. He doubted that
he could see much of anything from the top.

Lee knew two things. If he ran into Coffee before
he got himself into position, that was bad news for
both him and Otis. And he was not familiar enough with
that canyon to go charging in there on horseback. He
might as well hold up a target and invite Owl to shoot
at it.

Lee was not a good walker, and his boots were made
for riding. Just the same, he walked.

Fast.

He gripped his carbine tightly and followed the blue
paint trail down into the canyon.

Lee had his position staked out by the time darkness
descended like smoke into the canyon. He was holed up
in the cliffs to the right and downstream from the waterfall. For once, he was amused by his own blackness. Nobody was going to see *him*.

He could see Owl's riderless horse on the gravel
beach. He could see the orange glow of the fire in the
cavern behind the waterfall. He knew where Otis was.

As the stars frosted the chilled sky of night, Lee
gave serious consideration to grabbing Otis then and
there. He rejected the idea simply because it was impossible. There was no easy way into that space beyond the
waterfall. It would take time to get there, too much time.
Owl would have to be blind to miss him. This was not a
game where if you lost you got a second chance. He

would have one opportunity, and only one. He had to make it count.

Lee sat silently in the darkness. He saw Coffee when the Ranger made his stealthy late-night exploration of the trail that ran along the gliding cypress-lined creek. Coffee was making every effort at concealment, but Lee saw him real good.

He could have dropped him in his tracks with the Colt or carbine.

He could have called out.

He did neither. He now knew where Coffee was, and where his horse probably was. Lee had not missed the smoke-scarred rock shelter in his scout of the canyon. Unless he didn't know his man at all, the Ranger would have ridden his horse down. The pack animal would be up on top somewhere. Lee smiled a little. There was getting to be a pretty fair collection of horses up there on the plateau.

Watching him, Lee found himself thinking how young Coffee was. You could certainly not call the Ranger inexperienced, but the plain fact was that he was the youngest person in the canyon except for Otis.

Young folks had a way of getting impatient at exactly the wrong time. Young folks had a way of making critical mistakes.

Lee was satisfied to leave the situation where it was. He had everybody pretty well located, except that he could not be dead certain where Cole Nesbitt was. He could guess, having sided with Cole Nesbitt in similar corners before. That would have to be good enough.

Lee figured that he had the advantage. He knew more about the others than they knew about him. He did not know Owl's precise position, but that was the way the world worked. He had never gone into a fight knowing *everything* that he wanted to know.

As Lee saw it, the one key factor was that Owl had to be closer to Otis than he was. If Lee moved blindly, Owl could take care of Otis no matter what he did.

Therefore, Lee waited.

It was a very long night.

Lee was a man who sensed things. He might not know as much as Mrs. Ruth Nesbitt thought he did, but he knew some things that other men missed. He had an awareness of some ancient presence in this dark-walled canyon. He did not know what it was, but he thought that it was near Owl's riderless horse. Once, he caught a heavy animal smell in the cold air. Once, he was sure that he heard breathing strong enough to create waves on the pool at the foot of the waterfall. The thought came to him that the animal must be very large.

He put it from his mind.

The sky was lightening. Color was returning to the canyon world. This was not the time to be distracted by the beasts that prowled through dreams.

With the dawn, everything seemed to happen at once. It was as though the swelling light sent a signal that ignited every character in the drama into sudden, explosive action. Lee had believed that he was ready, as ready as any man could possibly be, but he was almost overwhelmed by the suddenness of what occurred.

He had experienced the feeling before. It was not a stranger to him, and that helped a little. When the action started, you saw everything with a sharp clarity that was unique. You heard sounds that normally you would have missed. But sequences that should have taken minutes or even hours just happened in an eye wink. Time stopped. Whatever you did, your reactions had to be faster than thought.

The first thing that penetrated his awareness was the sight of Cole Nesbitt going down the jagged canyon wall on a rope. Lee knew who he was before the old devil lost his hat and his cloud of white hair flared like spray in the fresh morning light. Lee had seen Cole Nesbitt pull that rope trick before, and he had seen damned few others who could do it. It was one thing to be lowered on a rope by a partner or two, and it was quite another to slip-slide unaided down a rope in such a way that your hands were periodically freed for action. Cole Nesbitt was carrying a carbine and he obviously intended to use it.

Lee knew how the trick was done. It required a perfectly spaced series of loops and knots in the rope. It also required a man of uncommon courage and agility. Cole Nesbitt was as exposed as a turtle sunning on a rock. The old codger was half dead. The last time Lee had seen him, it had taken a major effort for Cole Nesbitt to get out of bed. If he made it down that rope, it would take a miracle.

Of course, it may well have been that Cole Nesbitt didn't give a hoot in hell whether he made it safely to the bottom of the canyon or not. What he was after first and foremost was a shot. He had chosen his position well. He was almost behind the sinkhole waterfall. He had the perfect angle to drill the man who had stolen his son.

Cole Nesbitt, crazy or not, was an acute observer. Always had been. He knew who had been on that trail. He knew that Lee was in the canyon somewhere. If the old man fell, Otis would not be left alone.

Simultaneously with his recognition of Cole Nesbitt, Lee heard Otis screaming. He sounded very close. Otis was not a boy who screamed a lot, and Lee found the noise strange. He looked up and saw Otis through the shimmering water. The boy had spotted his father.

Otis stood there on the ledge, waving his arms like a wind-flapping scarecrow and hollering for all he was worth. He was not as naked as on the day he had come into the world, but he was hardly warmly dressed against the chill of the morning. He was thinner than Lee had ever seen him, all skin and bones.

Lee's vision was supernaturally keen, as though he could look through stone if necessary. Despite the screen of water, he saw a stooped figure emerging out of the cavern behind Otis. He saw details: wild tangled black hair and a face that was smudged with more than dirt.

Owl. Had to be.

Owl let out a shocking shriek that pierced the canyon. Even on a morning of such surprises, Lee was stunned. That was no calculated war cry, no resigned chant of death. That was an animal howl, a tortured screech of unbearable loss and pain and desolation.

Owl was coming up fast in back of Otis. He seemed to have his arms extended, but Lee thought he saw the outline of a bow. Lee froze. He had no shot.

Then—or at the same time—Lee saw Coffee. The Ranger was mounted and he did not seem to have good control of his horse. Coffee exploded out of the canyon trail into the big fat middle of things.

"Jesus Christ," Lee whispered.

There was a yellow flash and a puff of smoke from Cole Nesbitt's carbine. The crack of the rifle shot was magnified in the corridors of rock.

Instantly there was a shower of metal-pointed arrows flashing through the air. One of the shafts transfixed Cole Nesbitt. It broke in two against the stone wall behind him. The old man hung there on his rope, but not for long. He fell, leaving the rope dangling there like some leafless vine. He seemed to bounce down the sharp-edged side of the canyon forever, and then his body hit the moss-covered rock beside the green-water pool. Moss makes a good cushion, but not that good. The liquid plop when Cole Nesbitt's body struck told Lee all that he needed to know.

God, how fast could it happen? Lee was certain that Cole Nesbitt could not have survived that fall. Even without the broken arrow sprouting from his chest, the old man had taken too much.

Lee didn't even have time to feel for him.

He saw Owl lunge for Otis on the ledge. This time his arms were extended for sure, reaching out for the boy. Lee knew that Owl was trying to reach the boy's throat while Owl still had life in him.

Coffee got his horse steadied and whipped out his big Walker Colt.

"Jesus Christ!" Lee said again. There was no way on this earth that Coffee could make that shot. He didn't understand. Owl was *behind* Otis.

Lee's gut took over. He forgot a lifetime of hard-learned lessons. There could be no more rules or cautions or codes.

His own Paterson Colt was in his hand. He wasn't

sure how it got there. The carbine might have been a better choice. But Lee was not making choices. He was close enough, and he was better with a handgun. That was the whole of it.

Lee fired a split second before Coffee. It may have been the fastest shot he ever made. He saw Coffee's shot kick up a shredded mushroom of limestone rock fragments from the edge of the cavern behind the waterfall. Coffee had missed. His shot had been harmless.

Lee had not missed. He saw Coffee slammed back in his saddle by a lead fist. There were those who claimed that a .36 caliber slug was not big enough to get the job done. Coffee could have told them different. He slipped from his saddle and sprawled on the gravel beach like a stranded catfish.

Lee noted the arrow that had missed the Ranger. The arrow had sparked off a rock and skipped harmlessly in the direction of Owl's horse. Lee thought that Owl had made a pretty good shot, considering.

Lee knew exactly where his bullet had hit Coffee. It had not been a difficult shot physically. He had shot Coffee in the left shoulder, just far enough out to avoid the heart. If Coffee lived, his gun arm would not be slowed.

If he lived. There was no telling about that living thing. Some did and some didn't.

Lee was not worried about Owl. He had been among the Comanches enough to understand what Owl was attempting to do. At any rate, it hardly mattered. Lee also understood that Cole Nesbitt had not missed. That had been the most important shot the old geezer had ever made. There was no way that he would have wasted it.

Owl might keep moving around for a spell. Chickens did that when you chopped off their heads.

But Owl wasn't going anywhere.

Owl was a dead man.

Owl's riderless horse seemed to sense it. He ignored Coffee. The bouncing arrow had not alarmed him. But he knew it when Owl went down. He stopped moving. He was literally motionless. It may have been, just for a moment, that he stopped breathing.

Lee thought he caught a glimpse of some shadow creature with patches of rust-brown hair in a stand of sycamores against the rock wall of the canyon. It was a very large animal with strange curving tusks that looked like ivory. Lee blinked and the creature was gone.

Lee holstered his Colt. He came back to real time. He had no idea what to do next. He was sickened by what he had done.

He had committed the one unpardonable sin. He had not only shot a white man, he had shot a Texas Ranger.

And he had done it from ambush, or so it would seem. It was a bushwhacker's shot. Coffee had never had a chance.

Yes, that shot had saved the life of Otis Nesbitt. Who would believe that, if it came down to explaining time?

The boy had stopped screaming. Behind the waterfall, he was as motionless as Owl's horse. Talk about loss! Otis had suffered his share this morning.

Lee stepped out into the open. He steadied himself. He looked up.

"Well, boy," he said in as natural a voice as he could produce, "looks like you and me got us a small problem on our hands."

Overhead, the flaming ball of the sun was just moving across the open space above the cut of the canyon. It burned down on questions, but it provided no answers.

Otis Nesbitt came unstuck. He moved from the cavern behind the waterfall. He made no attempt to carry Owl's body down with him, not that he could have managed it alone anyhow. That could only mean that Owl was dead. Otis would not have abandoned him otherwise, no matter what had taken place between them.

The boy was not strong, and he looked about as substantial as a ghost, but he was agile. He wriggled along the spray-washed pathways and climbed through the narrow tunnels as though he were smoke. He did not pay any attention to Lee at all. He went directly to the crumpled body of his father.

Lee did not watch. He felt like an intruder. He knew that there was no life left in the body of Cole Nesbitt. Nothing could be done there. Of course, the boy would have to find that out for himself.

Lee tried to function. He still was not quite sure what he was doing, much less what he was going to do. But he did know that he had to get Coffee into some shade.

He also knew that Coffee would not remain unconscious very long, unless the bleeding was the pumping kind that could not be stopped. It was the shock of the bullet that had put Coffee out, not its power. That might be important. Maybe. Maybe not.

Lee did not have to move far.

"Easy shot," he muttered, "easy shot."

Take Cole Nesbitt, now. The slug he had put in Owl had been something of a masterpiece. Owl's arrow, which had briefly pinned the old man to the rock wall, hadn't been a bad piece of work either.

Lee picked up the arrow that had skipped past Coffee. He did not know why. He noticed that the metal head was twisted a little where it had struck the rock. But it was very sharp and it had a lot of flare to it. There were three turkey feathers attached to the notched end of the shaft. They were both threaded and glued. Lee was uncertain as to why he noticed the feathers so carefully.

Lee took Coffee by the shoulders and dragged him. He walked backward and his left hand was sticky. For some strange reason, Coffee's hat stayed on. Good hat, Lee thought. The Ranger was hard, but he was not heavy. His boot heels made straight, narrow trails in the gravel and then in the brush.

Coffee made noises, but he was not conscious yet. Lee did not have to examine him closely to know that there was too much blood. He could feel the blood dripping from his wrist.

He got Coffee into the shade. Now what? Lee took his knife and cut away part of Coffee's shirt and his wool undershirt. He wiped enough of the blood away so that he could see the wound. He rolled Coffee partially over and studied the back of his shoulder. There was an exit wound. It was bigger than Lee had expected. The bullet had flattened some, in going through.

There was no lead in the body, unless there were some tiny fragments here and there. That was the good part.

Lee blanked his mind. To the extent that he was thinking at all, he had a notion to wash out the bloody cloths in the pool and then press them against the wounds until the bleeding stopped. He shook his head. He had to do better than that.

A voice. Lee was so absorbed that the voice seemed to come out of nowhere. He knew that voice. Otis Nesbitt.

"We can't leave them where they are," the boy said.

It took Lee a moment to realize that he was talking about Owl and his father.

"Too much sun," the boy said. His voice was very matter-of-fact. He was holding a lot of things inside of him. "There will be buzzards."

"We got a live one here," Lee said. It was funny. He no longer could think of Otis as a child. "He comes first."

"That may be," Otis said. "But we have to move them."

Lee nodded. "We'll do it. Soon as we can. Some things got to be done first."

Quite unexpectedly, Otis produced a blue glass bottle with a stopper in it. "It's laudanum," he said. "I took it from my pa's coat pocket. Miracle it didn't break. I seen the stuff around the house plenty of times."

Lee managed a smile. Mrs. Ruth Nesbitt would not tolerate spirits in her house, but medicine for Cole was another matter. There was enough alcohol with that opium to drop a mule.

That laudanum explained a lot of things. Cole Nesbitt was a tough old bird, but he had been swigging some help. It may even have been that he had gotten some sense of direction out of a bottle. It wouldn't have been the first time.

Otis fingered his throat with his right hand. With his left he picked up Owl's arrow, that Lee had brought from the gravel beach. Looking at that arrow almost cost Otis his composure, but he did not crack. Half naked and skinny as he was, the boy had achieved a strange kind of dignity.

"You going to do it or am I?" Otis asked.

At first Lee did not understand him. It may have been that he did not want to understand him. He thought Otis was talking about the laudanum.

For some reason, Lee's mind jumped back to the crude sweat lodge he had encountered on the trail. He remembered the clumsy blue-paint rock drawing that Owl had left for him. The animal that had a trunk like an elephant.

And the broken arrow on the ground in front of the rock painting. A metal war point on one end, turkey feathers on the other. Broken in two, right in the middle.

Very much like the arrow that had killed Cole Nesbitt.

Very much like the arrow that Otis held now in his left hand, except that this arrow was still intact.

"You going to do it or am I?" Otis asked again.

Lee stared at him. He got the picture. His stomach threatened to heave on him.

"Got to do it fast," Otis said. "Or not do it at all."

"Don't want you to do it," Lee said. "That would be wrong."

Otis laughed. It was a weird sound. "Laudanum first," the boy-man said. "I can do that. Then we'll both be in on it, Mr. Lee."

Lee nodded. He could hardly believe this was happening. But, of course, it was the only possible way.

"The laudanum will help in cleaning things up too," Lee said. It was as though they were discussing some kind of a game down by the stable. "You pour some down if you've a mind to. Then you get your tail up on the rim top and lead those horses down here. Don't look back. That a deal?"

Otis hesitated.

"Take Coffee's horse or Owl's," Lee said. "We got to have more horses down here to get your pa and Owl and Coffee out of this damned place. There's a packhorse up there that will have some bandages on it."

"Deal," Otis said. "I'll take Coffee's horse. Ain't nobody ever going to ride Heart again, and that's for certain sure."

"I don't want you to watch," Lee said. "It's best that you not know for dead certain."

"I already know."

"That ain't the point. You listen to me now. I've come a long way after you, Otis Nesbitt. Don't you backtalk me."

Otis smiled. It was a more natural smile this time. Almost like being back home, his father alive, and never having heard the name of Owl—

"Get along with you," Lee said.

"Laudanum first," Otis said. "That was the deal."

Lee shrugged. A deal was a deal. "Don't wake him up."

Together they got Coffee's head into an upright position. The man was absolutely limp. He groaned and muttered some, but he was out cold. Incredibly, his hat stayed on.

Lee held Coffee's mouth open and Otis poured in the laudanum. It was a healthy dose. Lee held Coffee's mouth and nose closed until he swallowed.

Coffee jerked and twitched. He rolled his eyes. He tried to say something.

The blood was coming out in a steady ooze, but it was not pumping. Lee was desperately afraid that the man would wake up too soon. But he slipped instead into a deeper coma.

There was time.

"Go," Lee said.

Otis went. It never even occurred to either of them that a youngster like Otis might have difficulty leading all those horses back down the difficult trail into the canyon. Otis was a Texan, whatever else he might now be. He could handle horses.

Lee waited as long as he dared, and then he went to work. He dreaded what he had to do.

Lee picked up the arrow that had missed Coffee and broke it in two across a rock. It was not easy—the shaft was ash, and it was strong—but it only took Lee two tries. He felt a little better when it was done. At the least, he had gotten rid of the three turkey feathers.

That left the slightly twisted metal point. It had to be sharp, of course, but there was too much flare to suit Lee. He found a flat stone to use as a platform and a fist-sized round rock for a hammer. He flattened the edges of the point as much as he could without making it obvious.

He got Coffee into position on his back. He selected a larger stone for a hammer and made sure that Coffee's bleeding shoulder was not resting on an obstruction of some kind.

"Jesus," Lee said.

Then he did it, as fast as he could.

He wiped off the point with some laudanum, picked up the broken shaft, centered the point precisely on the entry wound made by his Colt bullet, and drove the shaft through Coffee's shoulder with a single blow from his hammer stone.

He lifted Coffee's shoulder, grabbed the bloody point, and pulled the shaft out. He took the feathered part of the shaft and rubbed the feathers in Coffee's blood. He washed both the entrance and exit wounds with Laudanum. He poured some into the wound.

The bleeding was worse now. Lee was afraid that he had killed the man. Again.

Coffee opened his eyes. The shock of the blow had brought him out of it momentarily. He might or might not live, but he was taking things in.

He recognized Lee. "You," he said.

Lee showed him the two parts of the bloody arrow

shaft. "Had to get the arrow out of you, Mr. Ranger," he said. "No other chance to get you home alive. Leave it in there and it will fester. Reckon you know that."

Coffee moved his right hand up and touched his shoulder. He brought the hand around and stared at the blood.

"Owl?" he asked.

"Yes," said Lee. He chose his words with care. "He was able to get off a couple of shots."

Coffee closed his eyes. What strength he had was draining out of him. "Otis?" he whispered.

"The boy is fine. Gone to get the horses. We need some bandages."

There was a long silence from Coffee. His breathing was labored.

He said one more word: "Thanks." It was a hard word for him to say. He lost consciousness again.

Lee watched the dribbling blood. He dabbed at it as best he could with the torn shirt dipped in laudanum.

This thing was going to be very close.

"Hurry, boy," he said. There was a depth of feeling in his voice that usually was associated with prayer.

By the time Otis showed up with the horses, Lee was not sure whether he had lost Coffee or not. The bleeding had slowed. That might be a good sign. Then again, dead folks didn't normally bleed a lot.

Lee forced some canteen water into Coffee's mouth and got him to swallow it. Some life there, certainly. He went to work with the bandages. Lee was very good at what he did. He had stopped more than a few bleeding wounds in his time. He had known that Coffee would bring bandages on the packhorse. Coffee thought of things like that.

"See what you can do to get your pa and Owl out of the sun," he said to Otis. "I'll be along directly. Don't try to drag Owl's body down that trail by yourself."

"Coffee?" asked the boy.

"Don't know. He came out of it for a minute."

Otis asked a question with his blue eyes.

"I showed him the arrow I took out of him," Lee said evenly.

Otis nodded. He seemed suddenly to be very tired. The excitement of action was wearing off.

Lee kept track of him out of the corner of his eye. Otis attended to his father first, tugging him into the shade. Cole Nesbitt was almost as thin as his son. Otis stumbled a few times, but he handled the old man without difficulty.

Lee waited until Otis climbed up in back of the waterfall to go after Owl. When he was certain that the boy could not see him, Lee carefully slipped Coffee's Walker Colt into his belt.

Lee knew that this was going to be the worst part for the boy. He suspected that he would not handle it very well either. This had not been a great day for Lee, and it might well get worse.

He had done what he could for Coffee. He squatted over him, holding his hand. It seemed to him a stupid thing to do, but who knew? Maybe Coffee was riding that last trail alone. Some company often helped, even a man you had disliked all your life.

"Ranger man," he said, "all you got to do is live. I'll do the rest."

He continued to watch Otis without looking directly at him. The boy struggled down from Owl's cavern and went to Coffee's packhorse. He pulled a spare checked shirt from a bundle and put it on. It was far too big for him, but Lee understood that Otis was not thinking about either his appearance or the chill in the air. He buttoned the shirt all the way up. He was trying to cover up his throat.

Lee waited until Otis came to him.

"I want you to stay here with Mr. Coffee," Lee said.

"No," said Otis. He sounded very weary. The boy was smart, wise beyond his years. He knew what Lee was going to do.

"Not much on giving orders," Lee said. "Especially to you. But you can't watch this. It will kill you, and then what's the purpose to all this anyway?"

"I can't let you do it, Mr. Lee."

Lee was in no mood to argue. He didn't even know who was right.

"You don't have to let me do it. Just don't try to *stop* me. That's not the same thing, understand? Look. We've both been through a lot today. If I have to go through you, I will. Don't make me do that, Otis Nesbitt. I got enough wounded people already."

Otis stared at him. "You'd really go through me? You want it that bad?"

Lee tried a smile. It was not a success. "I said what I said. Don't make me a liar, boy."

Otis thought it over. He was having to make choices that were totally beyond the range of his experience. No matter what he did, it would be wrong.

"Guess I'm not worth shit," the boy said. The word sounded strange coming from him. "I can't go against you, Mr. Lee. We're in this together, right?"

Lee was touched beyond his powers of expression. He knew that what he was asking of Otis was nothing less than betrayal.

"You're some shit, boy," he said. "You just set here with Mr. Coffee until you hear it. Then you come as fast as you can and we'll do what's proper. Deal?"

The boy's voice was strained with grief, but he got the word out. "Deal," he whispered, clutching Coffee's checked shirt to his throat.

Lee moved as fast as he could. In some ways, a head shot would be best. From the front. Not too close a range. That would be consistent with the positions that Coffee would remember.

The trouble with head shots was that you could not be sure whether they would come out or not. A bullet from a .44 Colt kicked up quite a commotion. Lee needed that bullet in the body.

A shoulder shot, then. Right where the big knob of the upper arm went into the socket. That should do the trick.

Stafford's Doc Patterson was not observant enough to spot where half of an arrow shaft had been jammed through a preexisting hole, but he could tell the difference between a slug from Cole Nesbitt's carbine and one from Coffee's Colt.

Lee hoped to God that his hand would not shake. He could not afford to miss this shot. He was sick to death of this whole mess.

He found Owl where Otis had dragged him. Owl was sitting with his back against a boulder. There was a kind of raw chunky strength about the man even now.

Owl was looking at him.

No. That couldn't be. The eyes had opened but they were clouded over. Owl wasn't seeing anything. Not on the outside.

Despite the gloom, Lee could see the raw wound over the heart where the bullet from Cole Nesbitt's carbine had struck home. Cole Nesbitt's last shot had been true. Only a slight angle, really. Cole Nesbitt had chosen his position well.

Lee did not know if the bullet was still in him. He was not about to probe for it. The simple fact was that no man could take a heart shot like that and live. It was why Lee had been so careful with Coffee.

Lee felt terrible. He figured he ought to say something. He forced himself to look straight into those dead eyes.

"Owl, you old son of a bitch," he said. "For what I am about to do, I ask your forgiveness." He had never been more serious in his life.

Lee pulled Coffee's Walker Colt from his belt, stepped back to avoid any remote possibility of powder burns, and fired one crashing shot. The noise was almost unbearably loud in the cavern. The Walker Colt felt heavy and awkward in his hand, but the hand was steady.

A red-meat hole cratered in Owl's right shoulder. The tough old body jerked and spasmed. There was very little blood. Owl sighed and gurgled some. That was all.

The waterfall glided on, as it had done for a large chunk of forever. For some reason, Lee found himself thinking that there should be more water at this time of the year. It had been very dry.

Suddenly Otis was there. The boy hadn't waited very long. He had left Coffee before the shot had been fired.

Otis shuddered convulsively. His eyes were wet with tears. He reached out for the stricken Comanche but his hand trembled so that he could not control it. Lee wanted to tell him that he would never encounter more horror than this in his life. The worst was over. He could not say the words.

Instead Lee said: "He didn't feel a thing." He wondered if that was true.

Otis did not and could not speak.

Lee felt a compulsion to spit out words, even the wrong words. "I owed Mr. Coffee one, you understand? Now we're kind of even. If he lives."

He did not insult the boy's intelligence by explaining what he had done. Otis was anything but stupid. He had put that arrow into Coffee to get himself off the hook. If Owl had shot Coffee, that was just the way things were. It wasn't like a black man had done it. He had fired one of Coffee's bullets into the dead Owl so Coffee could get some credit for saving Otis. He might have to share the honors with Cole Nesbitt, but Coffee could be a hero now. Another Ranger exploit to tell around the camp fires.

In any event, Otis's mind was elsewhere.

He wiped his eyes on the sleeve of Coffee's shirt and steadied his hand.

"Got to fix Mr. Owl up before we drag him down there," Otis said.

"We ain't got a lot of time."

"We got time enough for this."

Lee could not argue. What could be done for Coffee had been done. A few minutes one way or the other would not matter much.

Lee sat down on a boulder and waited. Otis seemed to know what he was doing. For now, the emerging man had again replaced the dazed boy. There was no way to tell how long this might last.

Otis closed Owl's eyes. His touch was sure. He still

had some of the blue paste left. He coated Owl's eyelids with that. Then he went to work on Owl's hair. He couldn't do much about the clothing, but a Comanche was very particular about his hair. It would be humiliating to go from one world to another with your hair a tangled mess.

Otis combed the hair out with Owl's quill brush. His braiding job was on the hasty side, but he got the part neat and straight. He knew exactly where Owl kept his cache of vermilion paint, and he applied the streak of bright red expertly. It precisely covered the part.

Otis wiped some of the black smudge off Owl's face with the tail of Coffee's big shirt. He picked up Owl's bow by its sinew string. It would go with Owl when the time came.

"About all I can do for you now, Mr. Owl," Otis said.

To Lee, he said: "You know, we need some red clay for the eyes. And when we bury him, we got to pull up the knees and bend the head forward."

"We can't do that now."

"And we'll need to take that buffalo robe to wrap him in," Otis said. His eyes looked strange. He was almost in a trance.

Lee figured he had waited long enough. It was time to move out of this damned place.

"I'll help you when the time is right," Lee said. "Now, Otis Nesbitt, you help me. Getting Owl out of here is not going to be easy. We have to drag him, understand? There is no other way. I'm still bigger than you are. I'll take the shoulders. You grab the legs and ease him along. Deal?"

Otis wavered a bit when he touched Owl's bootlike moccasins, but he held himself together. "You won't bounce his head on the rocks, will you?"

Lee was getting a shade impatient. "I'll do my best, boy. We got a deal or don't we?"

"Let's put the robe under him. That might make it simpler. I'll take the bow."

"Deal?"

"Deal, Mr. Lee."

They got after it. The series of cracks and ledges that

obstructed the cavernous canyon trail were a problem for a man slipping and sliding on his own. Carrying the dead weight of a chunky man like Owl made it really tough.

Lee was bone tired. He was determined not to show it.

He could not imagine what the boy was feeling. All he knew was that he had to get that body down there with Cole Nesbitt's. There must be no unanswered questions.

Lee did just that. Somehow, they maneuvered Owl's body into the shade next to Cole Nesbitt. The birds had not come yet, thank God. Cole Nesbitt's frail body was so thin that it looked like a skin sack over a pile of bones. Maybe there wasn't enough meat left to interest the buzzards.

Cole Nesbitt still had Owl's broken arrow protruding from his chest. The two men lay in the gravel, side by side. They were almost touching, but a space remained between them.

The boy stared down at them. The muscles in his face were twitching. He stood perfectly erect, but he rocked back and forth on the moccasins that Spirit Shadow had made for him.

"Pa?" whispered Otis Nesbitt.

It was impossible to tell which man he was addressing.

The way Lee looked at it, they were all going back to Stafford or none of them were. He was pleased to find Coffee neither better nor worse than when he had left him. It would have been hard to take if he had lost Coffee while messing with Owl's body.

Lee took one glance at Heart. He knew the name of Owl's horse now. He had known the tracks of that gelding for what seemed to be an eternity. He understood at once that Heart was not going anywhere, not even carrying Owl's body. Lee would have been the last man to pretend to know what went on in the mind of a horse, but he knew that Heart was stricken. That horse would never leave this canyon of the damned. Dead or alive, he would be there beneath the sky-smear at the side of the blue-green waterfall pool forever.

Well, they could make it without Heart. They had enough horses.

The trick was to get them all mounted and up that slippery trail. Even without the weariness that made his arms and legs ache, that was going to take some doing for Lee.

Dead men did not vault into saddles and gallop up into the windy sunshine of the flatlands.

Coffee may have believed that he was all man and a yard wide, but he could no more swing into Pear's saddle than he could sprout wings and fly.

Lee needed help and he needed rope. He also needed to get on a trail to somewhere. He had been out for a very long time. It would be nice to let go. It would have been great to say, "Well, I gave it a try."

No matter which way it went.

But he couldn't let go yet. Coffee was his responsibility. So was Otis Nesbitt, although he suspected that the boy had broken through to some strange new world of his own.

Lee figured that this was no time for explanations. He would tell Otis Nesbitt what to do and the boy would by God do it. Lee was too tired to cut much slack.

Somehow, working together or working apart, they got the thing done. Cole Nesbitt, light as a ghost already, was lashed to his own horse, Blaze. His body was covered with a tattered blanket that would have shamed Ruth Nesbitt. Owl was a much tougher problem. They got him tied to the packhorse and covered with a robe, but it was not easy. The horse did not welcome his burden. Owl kept slipping around until he was almost dragged underneath the horse.

Owl! That peerless rider, now unable to stay right side up. Lee tried to see some humor in the situation and failed.

Coffee was somewhere between conscious and unconscious when they boosted him into Pear's saddle. He would not allow himself to be tethered. He was bleeding too much. He was holding himself together with a will of iron. Lee shook his head. Whatever you thought of Coffee, that man had some sand in him.

Otis Nesbitt rode point, sitting his father's spare horse without visible effort. He had removed his leggings and was dressed in moccasins, breechclout, and the tightly buttoned, floppy checked shirt that belonged to Coffee. Lee figured that the boy knew the trail as well as anyone. He had gotten the horses into the canyon. He could get them out.

Lee brought up the rear, hoping that Doc was steady enough to bring some order out of chaos. His eyes were so bloodshot that even the stately cypress trees seemed bathed in pink. When he thought about it at all, his feeling was that Stafford was maybe a million miles away. . . .

Lee kept his head down through the fading hours of daylight. He used no more energy than he absolutely had to in order to hold a check on Coffee. He was aware that he was herding as strange a caravan as had ever crossed the rolling hills of Texas, but he missed the change in the weather.

It was profoundly unusual for Lee to be surprised by anything. There were always signs, and he had learned to be alert to them.

But Lee was not in any shape to notice shifting winds and dark-edged clouds. Lee was riding through a dream.

In his dream, Lee was crossing a river. It was a small river, little more than a trickle after the long dry spell. There was nothing spectacular about it. There was no limestone sinkhole, no cascading fan of white water falling into a pool, no cypress-lined creek that sparkled through enchanted rock cliffs. There were no mysteries.

This was just the San Gabriel.

Ahead of him was Goacher's Fort. Stafford was still beyond his vision, but he could *see* the fort. There was the wall of stone that had not yet had time to weather, there was the springhouse, and there was the wooden tower they had taken so much trouble to build.

Ah, he could more than see it.

He could hear it. The unique ringing of the welcoming bell at Goacher's Fort. He could not mistake it. The old cracked church bell they had installed in the wooden tower had a tone that was unlike any other.

And there was Ruth Nesbitt, tiny and rawhide-tough as ever, striding out to welcome her only living son.

"Mrs. Nesbitt," Lee said, calling her name as he always did, "I told you I'd bring him back."

It was the rain that jerked Lee out of his dream. The first fat warm drops brought him back to reality. He would have preferred the dream.

Stafford and Goacher's Fort were still far away.

This was no howling spring thunderstorm, not yet. It was just soft water falling from a darkened sky. It was the first rain in months. The earth swallowed it and soaked it up before it could puddle.

Lee thought of flowers. He was still very tired. The moisture would awaken long-dormant seeds. The Texas prairie would soon come to life with bluebonnets and paintbrush and Mexican hats and daisies. That might be a good sign.

He ducked back to look at Coffee. The Ranger was exactly the same. That damned hat of his was still in place. Whether Coffee went to Heaven or Hell, he would go in with his hat on.

"*Make him live,*" Lee said to no one in particular. "*Make him live.*"

Then, to himself, he whispered: "*Hang on. Hang on.*"

The rain splashed gently in his face. It seemed warmer than the air. It washed some of the grime away.

He had to make it. He had to make it for all of them. Somewhere ahead of that phantom procession Stafford waited for them. It was beyond the rain, beyond the shimmer of silver rain that was curiously like a waterfall.

Lee tightened his grip on Doc's reins until his knuckles ached.

Tomorrow.

It would have to be tomorrow.

Part Three

THE DREAM

19

Spirit Shadow, 17 March 1856

Spirit Shadow sensed it when Father Sun dropped behind the western hills. She could not have seen it, even if she had been outside. The rain was just enough, dripping out of a sullen gray sky, to obscure the sun. What she sensed was a deeper darkness and an absence of stars.

She reminded herself that the lack of stars was not total. The vermilion circles and squares on her great painted tipi were symbols of the stars. They were always there. No wind could blow them away and no rain could smear them.

Only time, only time.

Spirit Shadow seldom left her painted lodge. It may have been the good smells of sweet grass and wild onion and sage. It may have been the aroma from the stone-boiled soups and pastes and stews and syrup medicines. It may have been simply that Spirit Shadow had grown so large that it was hard for her to move. It was far easier for her to sit by her small inside sweat house and let other people come to her.

If need be, Spirit Shadow had her own ways of seeing

the world beyond her tipi. For her, there were many worlds. She just happened to be stuck in one of them.

It was exactly when the great darkness descended that Spirit Shadow felt the earth turn over.

The sensation was very strong. Broths and thick liquids in the old hide bags sloshed and almost spilled. Her medallion ropes clicked across the considerable expanse of her great skin blouse. She had to clutch one of the four stout foundation poles of the tipi to hold her balance.

Spirit Shadow was not frightened. She knew that the earth would right itself, and it did. She understood what was happening.

When spirit messages were very powerful, they could move her world. They could move any world. It was a marvel to her that other people did not know that.

She could see most of them as clearly as though they were still in her tent. All but one of them had been in this place, some of them for many sleeps.

She looked at Owl first. She had known him the longest. She knew that Owl was shielded by a buffalo robe and tied across a horse, but she saw him erect and unprotected.

She was pleased that someone had taken the trouble to fix his hair and paint the strip. Someone! It could only have been one person.

Owl had always been so proud. Swaggering, even, and sure of himself. But she had known Owl when he was as helpless as any other man. That son thing had hurt him. He had not been too proud to seek help.

She did not like the bullet holes in his body, even though she knew that the shoulder shot had been fired after he was dead.

It made little difference to Spirit Shadow whether she was seeing the real man Owl or his shade. She did not think in those terms. Owl was Owl. He always had been and always would be.

She did not speak to Owl, although she could have reached out and touched him. The words between them had all been said.

She looked next at O-tis. Strange *Taibo* boy, perhaps as much her son, *tua*, as Owl's. The thought pleased her.

There had been a closeness between them. It was not just the relationship between *puhakut*, doctor, and patient. It was about healing, but it was about much more than that. She felt an emotion greater than pride when she saw that O-tis was well. He was not strong yet, but he would live. He would live long. She examined closely the checked shirt that O-tis wore. She looked under it. She was satisfied.

"Hnhh," she said. She might have been speaking to O-tis. She might not.

Of the others, she was most interested in the *Taibo* man who had never visited her tent. He had Owl's broken arrow in him. He was so frail and thin that the arrow seemed half his weight. Spirit Shadow felt a professional urge to pour soup and stew into that man, but of course the time for that was past. She was amazed at the cloudlike texture of his white hair. She understood that in one sense this whisper of a man was the father of O-tis. That was unimportant to her. What counted was the wonder of what this shattered man had done. How had he followed that trail alone? How had he found the canyon of the waterfall? How had he bested a man like Owl?

How, in fact, had he even left his house in the *Taibo* village of Stafford and lived?

Spirit Shadow was no stranger to what some people would call miracles. But this! An old man who could hardly walk, half out of his head from the liquid in the blue bottle, and he had beaten them all to the home of the Cannibal Owl!

She wished that she could have known him. It was plain to her that there was deep kindred here. He probably would not have realized that.

He was what he was, and she was of The People.

In some other world, perhaps.

The other two men were not ordinary, and she had spoken at length with both of them. But they had not really entered her life. The black man, who was neither Indian nor white but something of them all, was like other men she had known. Harder, perhaps. Smarter, perhaps. More determined, maybe.

But still one of those men on the edge, a man not

completely sure of who he was. There were many such. She wished them all well, unless they gave her cause to feel otherwise, but they could not be central to her being. That was what it meant to be on the edge.

The last man was a Texan, and that more or less said it all. He was also a Ranger, and that was no cause for affection to swell within her. It was the opinion of Spirit Shadow that it would have been better if the Texans had never come to Comanchería. There was much bitter trouble ahead. She did not know how it might end.

But there was nothing personal in her feelings about the Ranger. He too was just what he was. She was more intrigued by the nature of his wounds. That trick of driving the foreshaft of an arrow into the hole made by a bullet was truly puzzling. It was beyond the range of her knowledge. *Taibos* did peculiar things sometimes, things that no human being could comprehend.

It was her expert opinion that the man would live. That gave her neither pleasure nor pain.

The rain drummed on the painted hide walls of the great tipi. Spirit Shadow poked up the fire a little, although it was not really cold. She chilled easily when the nights grew long.

She saw the riders, the living and the dead, moving into Stafford. She heard the cracked notes of the old church bell. She could feel the excitement as the villagers swarmed out to welcome O-tis home.

Home?

Or just from one place to another?

Spirit Shadow closed her eyes and rocked on her knees. The firelight pushed back the darkness some. Her jade bracelet gleamed.

She tried to see more.

She tried to see farther, both for herself and for The People.

There was a barrier. She could see nothing.

She did not try very hard.

"Hnhh," said Spirit Shadow. She was content.

Sometimes it was better not to see the trail ahead in too much detail. Sometimes it was better not to see it at all.

20

Lee, Spring

It was the first day of spring.

The bodies had been in Stafford for two full days. It was really too soon for a funeral. There had not been enough time to get all the kinfolk together.

Lee could see the humor in that, but he kept it to himself. The trail grime had been washed from him. He had shaved the iron spikes from his face. His clothes were clean. He had rested, but there was a tiredness in him that would not go away. Get all the kinfolk together! As far as the town of Stafford was concerned, there was just one real funeral, and that was Cole Nesbitt's. Lee knew better than that. Whatever his feelings for his old friend, he had not forgotten about Owl. What would happen if they tried to get all *his* relatives together?

What if they just came anyway?

The problem, of course, was that the bodies would not wait. There was plenty of sawdust in Stafford, but precious little ice. That had a tendency to speed things up.

Lee was something of a forgotten man, and that

suited him just fine. It wasn't that he was avoided, and indeed the folks of Stafford had gone out of their way to praise him for what he had done. Nevertheless, the bullets that had brought Owl down had come from the guns of Cole Nesbitt and Noah Coffee. Cole was being planted with honors. Noah Coffee rested in what had been Lisa Nesbitt's bed, his upper body wrapped in clean white bandages. He said he was going to make it to the funeral standing up, and Lee took that the same way everyone else did.

If Coffee said it, you could hang your hat on it.

After all, Lee hadn't actually *done* much of anything. He had just sort of been along for the ride, difficult as that may have been.

Otis Nesbitt kept his mouth shut. He was much quieter than he had been before the abduction. People figured that was only natural. The boy had been through a lot.

The lady Otis called Mizruth knew nothing and she knew everything. Ruth Nesbitt had not heard the details, and maybe never would, but she had known Lee too long and too well to believe that he had been a spectator and nothing more. That was not the Lee she knew. All that had to wait. Mrs. Ruth Nesbitt had lost her man, and it hurt. At the same time, she had her only remaining son back home again.

And she had more than that. No matter how tough you are, or how caring, it sometimes saps your respect for a man to have to baby him. You have to keep reminding yourself of how things used to be. Mrs. Nesbitt had lost her man, but she had found him too. That had been no invalid who had somehow left this house and ridden into a Texas he knew as well as anybody.

That, by God, had been a man.

Lee agreed with that judgment. Black or white, what did it matter? His old partner had been one of a kind. He had always been there when it counted, and he had checked out the same way.

How in the hell he had done it, Lee did not have the faintest idea. But that had been Cole Nesbitt for you.

He had always gotten the job done. He had never bothered himself with questions about what was possible and what was not.

The first day of spring! Lee snorted. This was no time for a funeral, much less two of them. Lee suspected that both Cole Nesbitt and Owl would have taken this as a joke. In different ways, of course.

Sure enough, the first flowers of spring colorsplashed the prairie. They were amazingly fast. It did not take much rain. It was as though the flowers knew that they had little time and whatever they were going to do they had to get on with it.

This was the one time of the year that Central Texas might truly be called beautiful.

Lee sat in his hard-backed rocker and puffed on his pipe. He considered reading his Bible and decided against it. There was no hostility in him toward the book that Ruth Nesbitt valued so highly. It was just that it was hard for him to read, and he figured he would hear more than enough Bible words on this day.

His padlocked trunk was lighter now. He had traded much of what he had for information. Some of it had been useful.

Lee had no mirror. He had no need of one. He knew that he looked as good as he was going to look, and that would have to do.

There was a knock on his door. It struck Lee as fitting somehow that there were two people left in the world who could walk into his room without knocking, and they were the ones who always knocked.

"Come on in, Otis," Lee said.

The boy opened the door without haste and stood there, twirling a foolish-looking brown town hat in his hands. He was dressed in a hot wool suit with knickers. He looked miserable. Lee noticed that the big knot in the tie that Ruth Nesbitt had choked him with concealed his throat very well.

"It's time, Mister Lee," he said. His voice was emotionless. How many times could a boy say good-bye to his father?

"Guess we better do it, then," Lee said. He knocked out his pipe on a saucer that rested on his wobbly table. He pulled on his polished boots.

Lee stood up and strapped on his Paterson Colt. There were those who felt that it was wrong for him to wear a gun in church.

"Reckon they'll let me in?" Lee asked.

Otis Nesbitt did not smile, because he was dead serious. "You don't go," Otis said, "then neither do I."

Lee played with him a little. He was having some trouble with his own feelings. "We'll just stash old Owl in a tree somewhere," he said.

"He'd like that. He never wanted no hole in the ground. He wouldn't like it your saying his name out loud that way neither. He's dead."

"You teaching me about Comanche ways, boy?"

"I was closer to him than you were. Maybe closer than anybody."

Both of them realized that they were stalling. It was Cole Nesbitt they had to send on his way first. Owl was a private thing between them, and he would come later.

Lee took a deep breath and squared his shoulders. He marched out of his quarters into the main house.

He literally marched. He felt like he was on some damned parade. Otis shuffled along behind him. Lee appreciated that, although he could not have said why. For once, it was important to him to be out front.

Ruth Nesbitt was waiting, all in black. She had a square felt hat with a veil on it. Lee could not see her face. He didn't have to.

And there was Lisa. She had been crying and her face was puffy. She looked beautiful anyway.

And there, Jesus Christ, was Coffee. He was standing and he was fully dressed. He even had that fancy hat of his in his hand. It had been cleaned up some, and so had Coffee. He was very pale, and Lee figured he would just about make it through the ceremony and collapse.

He wouldn't collapse until it was over, though.

Coffee wasn't wearing his Walker Colt. Too heavy for him maybe, Lee thought sourly.

"Howdy, Lee," the Ranger said. His voice was weak but there was no mistaking the words. Lee felt it like a hammer blow. The man had actually spoken to him!

"Mr. Coffee," Lee acknowledged.

Lee took one of Mrs. Ruth Nesbitt's hard, tiny hands and pressed it. There was nothing he could say.

He gave Lisa a quick hug. Coffee didn't even react.

Lee looked around. It was like they were all waiting for him to do something.

"Well, by God, this was Family!

Lee said the only thing he could manage to get out.

"Let's go," he said.

There was a Methodist church in Stafford. It wasn't quite finished when it came to details, and it had a raw look to it. Just the same, it was there.

There was no resident minister, but there was a stagecoach preacher who made the rounds nearly every Sunday. He always dressed in black and he was forever brushing trail dust from his suit. He carried a worn Bible that could be stuffed into a saddlebag.

The parson was reliable. He did not drink, and one of his most popular sermons involved hellfire and alcohol, which in his view were directly related. He could be counted on to show up on important occasions.

He was there and he was ready. He had a mouthful of solemn words that could hardly wait to be poured out upon the faithful.

There was only one coffin. It was plain and it was made out of unpainted wood. It had some wildflowers on it. There were no other flowers available.

Lee liked the wildflowers. He didn't get all choked up about them, but the fact was that Cole Nesbitt had admired the flowers. Once he had even turned to Lee and said, "Kinda nice, aren't they?"

Lee felt like an actor who had no lines. He just sat there on the hard bench and let the service flow over him. To an outsider, it would have looked strange. There he was, a black man sitting with a white family in the middle of Texas.

No matter. There were no outsiders here.

With half his mind, Lee listened to some of the words that drifted around the church. He sang when he was required to sing. At the point where it seemed to be appropriate, he said, "Amen."

It seemed to him that there was much talk about pioneers and a hard new land and how the trailblazers would be remembered down through the years.

Lee thought some about Cole Nesbitt stretched out in that fresh-cut box. The man he had known would never have referred to himself as a pioneer. He had a gift for fun in him before life kicked him in the teeth, but he was a hard and practical man. He just did what he had to do.

He had not been gifted with a world of patience.

Lee knew exactly what he would say if he could sit up and talk. Cole Nesbitt would say, "That's enough of the horseshit. If you're going to plant me, plant me and be done with it."

Eventually they did. The preacher took up a rather large portion of the eternity that he said Cole Nesbitt was going to grace, but there was still some cosmic time left when the wagon pulled into the graveyard.

The cemetery was between Stafford and Goacher's Fort. The graves were few and huddled close together, as though for comfort and support. There had not yet been time for the dead to outnumber the living in Stafford.

They didn't have a headstone for Cole Nesbitt yet. After they put him in his hole and shoveled the earth back in, they stuck up a temporary wooden cross.

The last words were said: "Ashes to ashes and dust to dust . . ."

Nobody cried. The eyes of the friends of Cole Nesbitt were as dry as flint. They all understood that what had happened to Cole Nesbitt was long ago and far away. This was just something the family had to endure. Cole Nesbitt was probably just glad the damned thing was over.

That was when Noah Coffee fainted. There was some blood seeping through his bandages and soaking the front of his shirt.

They hauled Coffee back to Stafford in the same wagon that had carried Cole Nesbitt out to the bleak little cemetery. Lisa Nesbitt rode with him.

Lee waited until they got back to the house and the widow set up the receiving line. He knew that she would not break. She was not the breaking kind. He also recognized that the neighbors were truly friends. They had taken turns guarding this house and the Nesbitt women after all the men had gone.

But he could delay no longer. His absence would be noted and there would be talk about Otis Nesbitt. That could not be helped.

"Mrs. Nesbitt," he said firmly, "you know what we got to do."

"Get along," she said. "I understand."

Lee thought that her response was extraordinary. But then, this tiny woman was remarkable beyond her time or her years. She did have a way of understanding things, even the hardest things.

After all, she had no cause to love Comanches or even to consider them human. They had killed one of her boys and stolen another. A Comanche arrow had splintered in the body of the man they had just buried.

His Comanche arrow.

"We'll be back," Lee said.

He collected Otis Nesbitt, who had already shucked his suit, and they left the back way.

Owl was waiting.

There was no coffin for Owl.

He was still wrapped in his robe, the ends tied with rope. Doc Patterson had examined the body enough to check out the gunshot wounds, but that was all he had done before binding the body up in the buffalo robe.

The robe was cold and greasy and flecked with sawdust. What was in it smelled exactly like what it was.

"Guess we're going to have to skip the red clay over the eyes," Otis said. "I ain't going in there."

"That makes two of us," Lee said. "I got another idea anyway. I brought some stuff."

"Can we flex him? That would be more important than the clay."

"We'll bend him some. Don't you fret about that."

It was getting dark, and that was good. It would have been unthinkable to bury Owl in the Stafford cemetery, of course. There were lines they could not cross. But wherever they put him, they did not want witnesses. They were not concerned about someone digging Owl up. Comanches were not the only ones with ghost fear. It was just that this was a private thing.

They had rigged a pole travois behind one of the horses. That seemed more suitable for Owl than a wagon. They hauled the wrapped body out to a bluff overlooking the San Gabriel. It was high enough so that it would not wash out in a flood. It was, in fact, not far from where Owl had tethered Heart when he had gone into Stafford after Otis.

Digging a hole was not easy, even with a pick and shovel. The earth was hard here, mostly rock and caliche, and the recent rain had only affected it down for an inch or so.

A scaffold burial was out of the question. The odor was too strong and there was no way the two of them could get Owl high enough in a tree to protect him from carrion eaters. Where there were buffalo there were wolves, and even the hounds of Stafford were notorious for rooting out dead meat.

Lee and Otis were sweating pretty good before they got the hole deep enough.

"Not real sure why we're doing this," Lee said. "I don't dig holes for just anybody."

Lee said it as much to lighten the mood as anything, but Otis felt that he had to respond to it.

"He done the best he could, by his lights," Otis said. "All he wanted was a son."

"I know that, boy. Here. You want to flex him?"

"Got to. Either that or dig a deeper hole. We could stand him up in it then."

"We'll flex him, I think. You take that end. It's the feet. I'll take the other end. That ought to be the head, unless this world is even crazier than I think it is."

They each got a good hold and shoved. Nothing much happened except that Otis was pushed backward. The body was stout and it was stiff.

"Again," Lee said.

The legs bent up a little. The head went down toward the chest.

"Once more," Lee said. "Either that or we grab ourselves a club and ram him into that scrub oak yonder."

"He wouldn't like that."

"No, he wouldn't. So shove, boy. Shove!"

This time they more or less got it. They could at least get the wrapped body into the hole in the correct position. It had to face east, toward the rising sun.

"He should have a horse to ride," Otis said.

"I hope to God you're kidding."

"I am."

Neither of them was in any condition to dig a horse-sized hole. They were tired. Emotionally, the hard part was yet to come.

They filled up the hole without any ceremony at all. They piled the biggest rocks they could find on top of the grave.

"You said you had an idea," Otis said. "You said you brought some stuff."

Lee nodded. In truth, he would just as soon have forgotten about it.

"We'll need some words too," Otis said.

"I got the words. Not many, but I think they're right."

"It ain't the number that counts." Otis was clearly remembering his own father's funeral. Had that really been this very same day? Lots of words. All wrong.

"We'll need us a flat rock," Lee said. "Not too big. Not too little."

Otis understood at once. He had never been slow. He was a lot faster now.

"Ain't got an arrow," he said.

"Don't need one. I got some blue paint and a brush. That will have to do."

Otis found a suitable flat stone. He was wearing Coffee's checked shirt again, buttoned at the throat. He used the tail of the shirt to wipe the rock clean.

"I can't really draw," Otis said.

"Me neither," admitted Lee.

"What'll we do?"

Lee shrugged. "Owl was no artist. He got the job done. If he could do it, we can do it."

Otis didn't argue. He just said: "*You* do it."

Lee was willing. He opened the tin of blue paint and dipped in the brush. His fingers felt as clumsy as fat sausages.

"It's the idea that counts, Otis encouraged.

"Sure," Lee said. He agreed with the principle, but it didn't help his drawing any. It was grotesque.

Lee stuck with it. To the best of his ability, he drew what Owl had drawn back there by the sweat lodge on the trail to the canyon of the waterfall. It was little more than an outline.

Lee thought of the figure as an elephant, but an elephant that was deformed or monstrous. He had never seen an elephant in the flesh, of course. But what else had a trunk like that, snaking up above the dripping mouth?

The tusks were a problem. He remembered them very well. They were huge and twisted in such a way that the animal could not use them for impaling. In Lee's view, they were useless. So was the bulge in the top of the head. So was the small tufted tail that would hardly disturb a persistent fly.

Still, this was the Beast that Owl had drawn. It must have had some sort of significance for him.

"Best I can do," Lee said. "We'll prop it up on two sticks, just like he did."

Otis was more than impressed. He was awed. He recognized the animal.

"It is the Ancient One," he said. "It is the Spirit Creature."

Lee stared at him. "Reckon you were with those folks a mite too long," he said. His tone of voice was not accusing. He was not being sarcastic. He was simply stating a fact.

"Maybe so," Otis said. He did not smile.

They sharpened two sticks and used them to prop up the rock painting. Lee doubted that the marker would stay in place very long. Some kid would steal it, just for the hell of it. Or the preacher might come and smash it to bits.

Then again, The People might come. They would know Owl's sign. They would know what to do.

Lee supposed that it didn't really matter much. The point was to avoid sticking Owl in a hole with no more ceremony than they would give a dead dog. Lee was not certain why he cared, but that seemed wrong to him.

"We'll need some words now," Otis said.

"Fine. You say 'em. I've done my share of this burying business."

"I don't know what words to say."

Lee knew. He had a gut feeling for such things. "You remember that song your father used to sing?"

Otis frowned. "His trail song?"

"That would be the one. It fits."

"I can't sing."

"Count our blessings. Just say the words, boy. Just say the words. It's time we got out of here."

It was getting on toward full dark now. Mother Moon would be rising in her bed of stars.

"Feel like a fool," Otis said.

Lee shrugged. The night was full of sounds. It might be that more than the moon was coming. "You wanted words. Say the words."

Otis said them, slowly and distinctly.

> *"Oh, it takes a medicine man*
> *To ride a medicine horse*
> *Way in the middle of the world.*
> *And it takes a medicine wind*
> *To move a medicine heart*
> *Way in the middle of the world—"*

Otis broke off suddenly. "That's all I know," he said.

"That's enough," Lee assured him. "And then some."

They mounted their horses and headed back toward Stafford. There were still lights visible at that other funeral.

They rode in silence, rushing a little.

Lee thought: Always trying to get to Stafford. I guess this is my life.

And he thought: When my time comes around, where will they bury me?

21

Ruth Nesbitt, Spring

Mrs. Ruth Nesbitt had learned long ago that it was not wise to show all that she felt. A small woman in a rough world, she had even cultivated a hard exterior that suggested she felt very little.

Her manner convinced doubters that Ruth Nesbitt could cope with anything. It was stupid to cross her, and it could be dangerous. She never forgot and she never forgave.

To the extent that anyone ran Stafford, that person was Ruth Nesbitt.

Of course, she was harder on herself than on others. She was never rude. She was capable of great kindness. Her strength was real.

The fact remained that she had lived a long time and she had lost her husband. She had lost a son in that nightmare raid on Webster. Her second son had been stolen by the Comanches, and he was not quite the same boy he had been before. Ruth Nesbitt was anything but obtuse, and no mother in the world could have missed the fact that Lisa would be going off with Coffee soon.

It would not happen right away. Coffee was still a very sick man, and there were arrangements that had to be made.

But it would happen.

Ruth Nesbitt was used to taking the long view. She did not think in terms of tomorrow or the day after that. She thought in terms of a lifetime. She had to. In the secret places of her heart, she knew that if she failed to provide for herself, there would be no magic hero to rescue her.

She did not relish the idea of being alone. Even if Otis came out of the muddle he was in, even if he turned out to be half the man his father had been before Webster, he was still only a boy.

That left Lee. Everything depended on him.

He *had* to stay.

She told herself that her motives were not purely selfish. The fact was that she admired Lee. She liked him. She trusted him. If they had lived in another world, she would have married Lee and done her level best to make him a happy man.

She regretted more than anything in her life the moment when she had lost control of herself and struck Lee. Ruth Nesbitt understood a lot of things. The significance of that blow haunted her.

Those were some of the reasons why she had deeply resented the departure of Lee and Otis from the reception following the burial of her husband. She had been gracious about it and had covered for them as well as she could. It was her belief that not a soul in her house that afternoon and evening had sensed her displeasure.

Just the same, she had been deserted.

She did not appreciate it.

She would never show it by word or deed, but there was a shaft of betrayal in her heart. Since she could not focus her anger on Otis or Lee, she turned it elsewhere.

A lady could not live as Ruth Nesbitt lived in Stafford without having eyes and ears all over the town. She ran her small empire on information, and when she wanted to know something, she found it out.

It was no secret to her what her men had done.

She knew where they had done it too.

Ruth Nesbitt got her buggy hitched up and headed for the San Gabriel. She carried no weapons and she went alone. She was utterly fearless. She did wear a flaring bonnet against the sun. Summer was not here yet, but it was just around the corner.

She admired the sturdy little wildflowers, especially the evening primroses. Despite their name, the pale pink primroses bloomed all day for a few short weeks. There was not much beauty in Ruth Nesbitt's life, and she accepted it when it showed up.

She did not have to ford the San Gabriel, which would have been a minor problem in any case. There just had not been enough rain to put a real rise on the river.

She located the bluff, got out of the buggy, and tethered the horse. She climbed the bluff in her high-topped shoes as casually as though she were strolling along Congress Avenue in Austin. She didn't know whether anyone was watching or not. She did not care.

There it was, just as it had been reported to her.

"Well, I never," said Mrs. Ruth Nesbitt.

She recognized the blue paint on the flat white rock. That paint had come from her own barn. That annoyed her considerably.

She could not tell for sure whether Lee or Otis had drawn the picture on the stone. Lee, probably. Her son had no artistic talent whatsoever. Lee didn't have much more.

She stood there, rather enjoying the waves of hate that washed over her. Her skirts were weighted, of course, but the wind blew them around some. It was spring, after all. The still, hot calm of summer would come later.

What was that accursed thing?

She had seen pictures of elephants. They were mentioned in the Bible. But that blue apparition was no elephant. Then again, when folks could not draw, it was difficult to tell what they had intended.

The exact nature of the Beast did not concern her unduly. The thing was a heathen sign of some kind, and that was all she needed to know. It did bother her that either Lee or Otis had painted the thing.

It bothered her even more that they would want to. Well, men were funny sometimes. A person had to make some allowances.

There were, however, limits.

She located the stones that marked the grave quite easily. She was not blind. There had been no attempt to hide the burial. It had not been disturbed.

Ruth Nesbitt had been told the name of the Indian who was buried there. Otis had not been very forthcoming about the savage, but he had not hidden his name.

Owl.

What a stupid name!

Ruth Nesbitt knew many things that she was not supposed to know. She knew, for instance, that it was an insult to say aloud the name of a dead Comanche warrior.

"Owl," she said into the wind.

She said it louder: "Owl! Owl! Owl!"

She hoped that it hurt him.

There were people who had fanciful notions about Indians. Her own husband had told her some admiring stories. She knew that Lee was no stranger to Comanche camps.

God only knew what Otis thought after all those months.

Well, Mrs. Ruth Nesbitt had no crazy ideas about savages. That was what they were.

Heathen savages.

She thought often about what her life might have been without the Indians. This was a hard land. It was also a good land. It was not bountiful, but it gave you back what you put into it. There could be rewards if you were willing to take the risks and put in the hours.

It was the Indians who had twisted everything. It was the Indians who had made a mockery of what civilized people had tried to do here.

She did not bother to distinguish between them.

Comanches, Apaches, Tonks, Cherokees—they were all the same to her.

They were trouble.

They were death.

They were the difference between the life she might have had and the one she had actually lived. She told herself that there was no room for sentimentality in her soul. She saw life the way it was.

Take away the Indians, and she would have her old husband back. The real one, the one before Webster. She was proud of what he had done, but that did not bring him back.

Take away the Indians, and her other son would be growing into manhood. Take away the Indians, and Otis would not be going through whatever it was he was enduring.

Those were the specific things. How could you count the others? How many nights had she spent staring into the shadows that lurked beyond the firelight? What phantoms had she seen there?

How did you measure that?

She understood that the Indians had preceded her into this land. Some of them, anyway. She was willing to make an effort to feel what they must be feeling. That was the Christian thing to do, wasn't it?

Making an effort did not always produce success. Try as she might, deep in her soul Mrs. Ruth Nesbitt found no sympathy for the Indians. None. If that was a failing in her, then so be it.

If she could have waved her arm and made them all disappear from the earth, she would have done so. She was pleased that her daughter might know a time when there were no more blood-chilling drums throbbing beneath the Texas moon.

"Owl," she said again. She said it softly this time, but she said it precisely as she would have said the word "Satan."

Mrs. Ruth Nesbitt was confronted by a problem. She had not climbed all the way up here just to see a grave. She had a statement she needed to make, and she was not sure what it was.

She thought of taking the painted marker stone and hurling it from the bluff. Tiny as she was, she was quite capable of the act. Nobody had ever accused her of weakness.

The stone might shatter or at least break, and that would be the end of it. She did not do it, finally, because Lee and her son had gone to so much trouble to place the stone where it was. However misguided their efforts may have been, she was reluctant to do anything to nullify their work. Sometimes you just had to take men for what they were. In her view, they were not entirely rational.

The same logic dictated that she not destroy the grave. Besides, that was not only more effort than it was worth, but also more effort than she had to give. Strong as she was, she was no longer young and she did not possess the muscles of a full-grown man. She could not move those big rocks alone in anything short of a life-or-death situation. The idea of bringing some kind of Christian posse up here struck her as just plain silly.

Therefore, she did what was left to her.

Mrs. Ruth Nesbitt took a stance before the painted stone. She did not have to check which way the wind was blowing. That knowledge was as much a part of her as the blood that flowed through her veins.

She took her time, working up a good wad. Then she spat. She hit the elephant-thing right in the circle of one blue eye.

Rather daintily, without looking back, she scrambled down the bluff, brushed off her dress, untied her horse, and clattered off in her buggy.

She was reasonably well pleased with herself.

Beneath the Texas sky, above the hole where Owl rested, the dry wind blew against the stone marker where the Ancient One stood.

The saliva from Mrs. Nesbitt dripped down, touched the earth, and was gone.

It took very little time to disappear in that wind that swept down from Father Sun.

22

Otis Nesbitt, Spring

Otis Nesbitt had lost all fear of the night.

He lay on his bed with his eyes wide open and his feet bare. He had not bothered to pull the sheet up over him. His long musket was on the floor by the bed.

It was warm enough to have the shutters open. Otis had swung them wide without a second thought.

Of course, Owl had come through that open window. It had not been funny then, and it was still nothing to laugh about. Nevertheless, Otis had to smile a little when he remembered.

Owl had not *come* through that window. He had hurtled through it like a thunderbolt.

How long ago had that been? Had it happened to another boy in another lifetime?

Otis did not reason it all out. That was not the way his mind worked. In any case, Otis was only ten years old.

Going on eleven, as Mizruth would say.

The sandy-haired boy could not have put it into words, but down deep inside he did understand a few things. For one, if your worst nightmare came true and you came through it in one piece, that particular nightmare could never be as terrible again.

For another, that black-painted intruder who had nearly killed him with a blow to the head had not been some faceless devil from a ghost story. Otis had not forgotten a later blow to the head, but there was just no way that the intruder that night could be thought of as a fiend, or even a bloodthirsty savage.

He had been Owl, after all. No crazier than most, once you got to know him. Not a man you would care to introduce around Stafford, particularly as your father. A man capable of casual cruelty if he was provoked.

Still, Owl had his soft side. He would not have been pleased to hear that judgment, but the plain fact was that the man was nearly human.

It was not that Otis admired him to the point where he wanted to be exactly what Owl had been. It was not even that Otis wanted to turn his back on his own life and be a Comanche warrior. He was quite aware that he knew enough now to go out through the window on his own and rejoin The People.

The idea never crossed his mind.

It was nothing like that at all.

It was simply that Otis Nesbitt had discovered a world far bigger than Stafford. It made no difference whether he had discovered it voluntarily or not. There was no room in that larger world for hatred of Owl.

There was one other thing.

Otis Nesbitt reached up to the throat of his nightshirt and touched it. He was careful to keep the rough cloth between the object and his hand, but he touched it.

He felt the slight pulsing heat.

And he remembered. His memory jolted back to that last morning moment before Owl's universe had shattered forever.

Otis knew what it must have looked like. God knows, Coffee had told him often enough. Lee had described it in sufficient detail so that Otis could understand why Cole Nesbitt had fired that final impossible shot.

Otis had been on the ledge behind the waterfall, yelling and waving his arms. Looking back on it now, he was somewhat ashamed of himself, but that was how it had been.

Coffee was down below, pushing Pear across the gravel beach. Cole Nesbitt, his hair as white as a cloud of snow, was climbing down a rope loop. He had a carbine at the ready and the first rays from Father Sun were glinting off the barrel.

Owl had come back from the dark cavern, his face contorted and his voice pouring out screeching noises of agony that Otis had never heard before.

Owl knew then that he had lost everything.

Or was it almost everything?

It had all happened so fast. There was gunfire and Owl was hit. The old devil was giving as good as he got, loosing jagged-headed arrows with incredible speed.

Owl didn't have a chance and he knew it. The last faint hope he might have had would have been to abandon O-tis and fade back into the limestone cracks and tunnels behind the waterfall. Even that hope was probably an illusion. Otis figured that the first shot that hit him had finished Owl, whether he was still moving or not.

It would never have occurred to Owl to quit. He was not made that way. Instead of retreating from O-tis, he had lunged toward him. He had reached out for the throat of the boy.

To any observer, it would have looked like an attack. If Owl could not live, he was going to take his captive with him into death.

That was not what had happened.

Otis knew. After all, he was the one who was there.

What Owl had in his worn, leathery hands was his deerskin medicine pouch. He had slipped it, thong and all, over O-tis's head when he realized that his death was near.

Had not Owl himself told O-tis of his first encounter with the giant Spirit Creature? Had he not explained in the flickering light of the painted medicine lodge how the Ancient One had given Owl his name? Had he not been instructed concerning the one thing he was to carry in his medicine pouch? Had he not been told of the strange grooved lance point that had killed the Cannibal Owl?

And had not the Ancient One in his last words to Owl described the very situation that was now taking place?

The words had been: *"When you have a son and before you die, pass the medicine pouch to him in exactly the proper place. In that way, the Spirit Creature will not fade into nothing. In that way, the shade of Owl will know the trail."*

In his final moments of life, Owl was doing neither more nor less than his Guardian Spirit had described. He was transferring the deerskin medicine pouch to the only son he had. There was no other way to do it than to reach out for the neck of O-tis.

There were many things that Otis Nesbitt did not know, but he understood this one perfectly. He helped all he could.

He wanted desperately to say something to Owl, anything that would make him feel better, anything to ease that final passage into darkness. But Otis was only a boy. He had no such words. His last insult to Owl was silence.

It may have been that Owl too had words he wished to say. But it was too late. There could be no more words from Owl, ever.

That was how it had truly been.

That was what Otis Nesbitt remembered, lying there in his bed, staring at the moonlit shutters through which Owl had come.

He felt the deerskin pouch suspended around his neck. He touched the outline of the grooved flint. His fingers traced the edges of the lance point.

This was the time.

There had been no visible signal, but this was the time.

He had waited long enough.

* * *

With a calm that he knew was unnatural, Otis Nesbitt slipped out of bed and walked on bare feet across the wooden floor and out through the open shutters.

It never even crossed his mind that he might take his musket with him.

Mother Moon blazed down on the boy. She was not full, but she was astonishingly brilliant in her quilt of stars.

Once he was outside, feeling the dampness of the night air against his skin, Otis stood very still. His tousled hair glowed in the silver light. It seemed very much like the hair of his father.

He did not remove the deerskin pouch from around his neck. He simply stood there, nightshirt billowing slightly in the cool breeze, and reached inside the pouch to touch the grooved flint point.

There was no protective layer now. He could feel the pulsing heat of the point, just a little.

He took the flint point out of the pouch. He held it in his hand. He had never done that before. He felt a quick surge of warmth. It subsided. He could not tell whether the flint lance point was glowing or not.

Mother Moon drowned out any lesser radiance.

Otis Nesbitt was not sure what he should do next. He did not even know exactly what was going to happen, if anything.

Certainly, he had no words. If he had, he would have been too embarrassed to speak them. After all, this was no remote cypress-lined canyon with brooding cliffs and a magic waterfall. This was the dirt yard of his own house in Stafford.

But something *was* going to happen. He knew it as surely as he knew his own name.

He extended his hand, palm up, with the point exposed to the moonlight. There was nothing ghostlike about the point. It was about the same on both sides. It was as solid as what it was, a chipped chunk of rock.

He waited.

He did not have to wait long.

It could not be said that the Ancient One arrived. The Beast did not stroll into the yard like an ordinary animal, twitching its tufted tail.

It was just suddenly there.

Its identity was so plain to Otis that he did not bother to question it. This was the Beast that had come to Owl in the enchanted canyon. This was the Guardian Spirit that had given Owl his name.

The smell of the immense, rumbling animal was very strong. The strangely curved ivory tusks shot back the moonlight. The old, old eyes in that domed skull gazed directly at Otis.

Otis saw that the Ancient One was shedding. It was preparing for the summer heat. There were many bare patches on its wrinkled skin. There were shreds and tufts of red-brown hair under it in the dirt.

Small nervous night birds swooped and pecked, feeding on the gift of bugs. The birds were like flies on a mountain. The Spirit Creature ignored them. Perhaps it even welcomed them.

Otis felt with all his being that he should say something. He had no words.

It seemed to Otis that the Ancient One had a need for reassurance. Could that be? The Beast had a lost and uncertain quality to it. It was a little fuzzy, not quite there all the way. This was an alien world to the Spirit Beast.

Gigantic as it was, the Ancient One wavered.

Some words came. "Don't go," Otis whispered. "Don't go."

The Ancient One steadied. It may have been that it attempted to speak, as it had done with Owl. But it was having trouble. Bigness was not everything. Age was not everything. The Spirit Creature was confused. Its snake-like segmented trunk thrashed the night air.

Otis sensed something in his head. Not words. Something older than words. Feelings, convictions, assurances . . .

Warm. Not altogether clear and concentrated, but strong. Not threatening. Seeking, perhaps. Otis leaned forward, almost dropping the grooved point, trying to understand.

The Ancient One either could not or would not speak. Otis did not know what to do.

Otis found himself remembering what he had heard of *piamempits*, the Cannibal Owl. Many of Owl's questions were now his questions.

Almost as sudden as the coming of the Ancient One, Lee stepped out from behind the house. He had no shirt on. He had often joked that his dark skin made him invisible in the night, but he glistened in the rays of Mother Moon. His Paterson Colt was strapped to his hip. His tough-heeled boots crunched the earth.

"Do you see it?" Otis said. He kept his voice very low.

"I smell it," Lee said. "I feel it." He moved toward the Spirit Beast, almost walked *through* it. He bent down. He picked up a tuft of matted hair. In the moonlight the hair was simply lighter than black. It had no true color. Otis could have told him that the hair was reddish-brown.

"It's here," Lee said. "Right here."

There was a large, wet plopping sound. A steaming dung pie as big as a boulder splashed into the dirt.

"Oh, it's definitely here," Lee said, and backed off.

Otis stared at the enormous spirit animal that filled the side yard. Weary eyes that seemed too small for that mighty head peered back at him. The eyes were glowing some. The drooping, hairless old-man's ears of the Ancient One seemed to signal resignation, if not defeat.

"Can you hear it?" Lee asked. "What is it saying?"

"Nothing," Otis said. "Nothing in words. Nothing I can catch."

There was a terrible silence while the Beast smothered the night.

"You'll have to talk to it, then," Lee said. "Don't lose it, boy."

Otis considered as best he could. This was not how it was supposed to be with a Guardian Spirit. He knew that much.

He gripped the flint point so tightly he almost cut his skin. He could feel Lee's tenseness. In some mysterious way that none of them fully grasped, this was for Lee too.

The Beast snuffled. It seemed to waver again, fade.

Otis was not aware that he was holding his breath. He wondered what would happen if the Beast trumpeted. Would it wake the town? Would there be no sound except for him? What would Lee hear?

Otis breathed again. It was difficult now to tell dream from reality. He sensed that Owl was somewhere near, waiting.

Was he good enough to be Owl's son?

Otis found words. "Ancient One," he said. He spoke in English. With the wisdom of a child who is more than a child, he understood that the Beast must have heard many languages in its time. That time had been long. This was about saying words, not the words themselves.

"I honor your coming," Otis said, searching for the speech rhythms he had heard in the painted lodge of Spirit Shadow. "I have a name. I ask only for a sign."

The great creature steadied, solidified. The trunk reached out. It had bristle hairs in it. It was less agitated. It did not actually touch Otis.

For a beat of eternity, nothing.

Then: *I will be with you always. You have more than a name. You are already a man. You will see me again when you need me most.*

The message did not come in words. It just filled the head of Otis, like light from Mother Moon. It staggered him.

Weirdly, he thought of his mother. Mizruth was saying, in words, "Mind your manners, boy."

"Thank you," Otis managed to say. Not the right words, of course, but then there were no right words. It was better than nothing.

He knew what to do next. All uncertainty was gone. It was as though he had always known. He was exposing the Ancient One to a danger he could not comprehend. That must end.

Otis slipped the grooved flint back in its deerskin pouch. He removed his hand from the throat of his nightshirt.

Instantly the Ancient One was gone. It did not move away. It disappeared.

The heavy smell lingered in the air. There was a breeze from an older world stirring beneath the stars. The little night birds swooped in confusion for a few moments, and then they flew away.

There was only the swollen mound of still-steaming excrement to show that the Spirit Creature had ever been there. That and a few tufts of hair.

"I'll go fetch a shovel," Lee said. There was satisfaction in his voice. He did not know all that had happened, but he could guess most of it. Lee had lived much among The People and knew their ways.

Otis nodded. He was too shaken to speak again.

Moving very quietly, Lee got a shovel and pitched the dung out of the yard. It took some doing.

"Otis?" he said.

Otis looked at him.

"Next time," Lee said. "Let's don't bring it into the yard. Plenty of room out on the prairie."

Otis recognized that Lee was trying to ease him, but he was unable to respond. He sensed the weight of two worlds on his slim shoulders.

"Get along back to bed," Lee said. "You can't sort it out all at once."

Otis could see the sense in that. He stumbled back in through the open shutters and fell upon his bed.

Mother Moon got herself into position and flooded the room with silver.

Otis Nesbitt slept.

Gradually his taut body relaxed. What might have been a smile lightened his face.

He must have been dreaming.

He heard the song drifting in from far away:

> *"Oh, it takes a medicine man*
> *To ride a medicine horse*
> *Way in the middle of the world.*
> *And it takes a medicine wind*
> *To move a medicine heart*
> *Way in the middle of the world . . ."*

Yes. That was right.

Was it not a song of his father, words said for Owl, a song shared with Lee?

Hear it, singing in the wind?

Feel it, pulsing in the blood?

Otis stirred in his sleep. The outside smile faded. It had gone inside.

Man or boy, asleep or awake, Otis Nesbitt had discovered some things beyond his years.

He was hearing a distant dream-song that told of hope and of strange things yet to be.

A life without dreams was no life at all.

This way was better.

Author's Note

There are a few things in this novel that I would like to say something about.

Suppose that we begin with the Stone Walker. I was older than Otis, but still very young, when I first was shown the dinosaur tracks in the stream bed of the Guadalupe River. There is an early photograph of me standing in those tracks and holding down a cowboy hat to show how big they were. Such ancient tracks are not uncommon in Texas, and these are precisely as described in the book. Even the tail impressions are there. These particular tracks are located not far from Hunt, which is near Kerrville. I will not be more specific than that. The last time I looked, the tracks were still intact.

The grooved, bifacial flint point carried by Owl in his medicine pouch is what archaeologists call a Clovis point. Scientists refer to such points as fluted points, because of the channels taken out on each side of the base of the point. It seemed to me highly unlikely that any of the people in this story would use a term such as fluted point, and so I avoided it as an anachronism. Clovis points have been dated back to around twelve thousand years ago, and are usually associated with mammoth hunting sites. Some of them are a bit older than the more famous Folsom fluted points. Folsom points, which are smaller, tend to be linked to an extinct type of bison. (The historic bison, which happily seems to have been saved from oblivion, is the animal Americans refer to as the buffalo.)

The Cannibal Owl was a being of some importance in both Comanche mythology and Comanche medicine. I am here using the word "medicine" in several senses. Although it could assume other forms, the general idea was that the Cannibal Owl was a gigantic bird that could swoop into a Comanche camp and devour those who had defied the rules of Comanche society. Comanche parents used the story in a familiar way, telling their children: "Better behave in the proper way, or the Cannibal Owl may come and eat you!" When Comanches found the skeletal remains of mammoths, they identified the bones as parts of Cannibal Owls. The bones were used for medicinal purposes, particularly for drawing poison out of infections and treating sprains. It may seem fantastic that people as observant as the Comanches would mistake a mammoth skeleton for that of a huge owl, but supernatural thinking follows its own logic. It must also be remembered that no Comanche had ever seen *either* a living mammoth or a real Cannibal Owl. The mammoths had vanished forever from this earth long before the Comanches arrived on the scene. Given these circumstances, I do not find it at all surprising that many of the characters in this novel are confused about the nature of the relationship between the mammoth bones and the dreaded Cannibal Owl. How could it be otherwise?

I will add, on a purely personal note, that when I look at the skull of a mammoth, I have no difficulty at all in seeing the face of a prodigious prehistoric owl. Part of this, of course, is simply an effort to see things as others once saw them. However, it is a fact that trunks do not fossilize and tusks frequently have come out of the sockets in fossil skulls. The great eye shelf tends to dominate the skull, and in the days before paleontology, I can understand why these skeletons might have wound up in the wrong taxonomic bin. In any event, I am grateful to my friends at the Texas Memorial Museum in Austin for allowing me to stare at mammoth bones and perhaps to see what other visitors were missing.

This is not the place to cite all of the familiar sources dealing with the Comanche, the history of Texas, and the Texas Rangers. I will only mention the names of Wallace and Hoebel, Fehrenbach, and Webb. We stand on their shoulders. Nevertheless, I feel obligated to refer to several less obvious works that helped me a great deal. The first is *Sanapia: Comanche Medicine Woman*, by David E. Jones. The second is *Texas Indian Troubles*, by Hilory G. Bedford. First published in 1905, this book contains the best account of the Josiah Wilbarger story that I have read. Finally, there is *Austin: A Historical Portrait*, by Larry Willoughby. This work draws heavily on the rich resources of the Travis County Collection of the Austin Public Library, and the Barker Texas History Center at the University of Texas at Austin.

While hardly claiming to be an authority on the subject, I thought I knew all I needed to know about the Walker Colt. As frequently happens when you are in a remote area on a fly-fishing quest for trout, I discovered that I still had a few things to learn. I want to thank Richard Steinberg, who called the Texas Ranger Hall of Fame in Waco for me. Needless to say, I am also grateful to the Hall of Fame, which promptly faxed me the complete photographs and specifications of every part of a Walker Colt.

The enchanted waterfall canyon where so much of this story takes place is now called Hamilton Pool Park, and it is administered by Travis County. (The city of Austin is located in Travis County.) Somehow, writers are blessed by finding people who are willing to help them. I knew Hamilton Pool from my days as an undergraduate at the University of Texas, but I decided that I needed to check out what I remembered. My wife Beje and I drove out there one rainy December day and looked and crawled over all the places described in the novel. I want to express my deep appreciation to Colleen Buckley, Park

Technician I, Southwest District, Travis County. She had the thankless job of answering all my questions and volunteering to look up what she did not already know. She did it all in the rain too!

That brings us at last to Strickling.

You will not find the name of Strickling in this novel, but in a sense that is where it all began. The ashes of my oldest friend are scattered along the San Gabriel River, very close to where Strickling used to be, but that is another story.

In this novel, I have changed the name of Strickling to Stafford. Stafford is not a literal re-creation of what is known about Strickling, but it is an imaginative reflection of it. In short, Strickling is fact and Stafford is fiction.

Strickling was founded in 1853, largely by survivors of Indian attacks in other communities. By the turn of the century it ceased to exist. Strickling was in Burnet County, Texas, and the nearest modern town to it is Bertram. If you should go there today, you will find that almost nothing has survived. There is an informative historical marker (on Farm to Market Road 1174) which tells most of what is known about Strickling. The old cemetery is still in place, though hard to find. Indeed, it is still in use; there were fresh graves there the last time I visited. The "fort" referred to in the novel as Goacher's Fort is modeled after Black's Fort, outside of Strickling. A good deal of Black's Fort is still standing. It is on private property but is plainly visible from the road (Burnet County Road 210).

Why did it all begin with Strickling? Let us simply say that there are special places in this world, and the land there along the San Gabriel River is one of them. The ghosts of Strickling are very strong. If you cannot see Comanche warriors and stubborn settlers and undaunted Rangers there, you cannot see them anywhere.

My thanks go to Howard Waldrop. Along with my wife, Beje, he endured much that went into the writing of this book. My appreciation, as always, goes to Carole Smith, who was invariably there when I needed her. My debt to Mariah Wade is expressed in the dedication, and to Jean Walls—thanks for the music.

A final question remains.

When I went out to Hamilton Pool and walked that cypress-lined stream that leads to the gravel beach and the waterfall, did I look around for Heart?

Yes, I did.

Did I see him?

Yes.

If you go there, with a little luck and the right kind of vision, it may be that you will see him too.

ABOUT THE AUTHOR

CHAD OLIVER was born Symmes Chadwick Oliver in Cincinnati in 1928. At the ripe old age of fourteen he decided to become a writer with a capital W. He acquired a secondhand typewriter, taught himself to type, and commenced. When he was twenty-one years old, a student at the University of Texas, he sold his first story to Anthony Boucher of *The Magazine of Fantasy and Science Fiction*. In 1952 his first novel, *Mists of Dawn*, was published.

Chad Oliver wrote for nearly all of the science fiction magazines and also wrote western fiction for such magazines as *Argosy* and *The Saturday Evening Post*. In addition to having his work chosen for many anthologies, he contributed to such diverse collections as Harlan Ellison's *Again, Dangerous Visions*, and Joe Lansdale's *Best of the West*. Some of his novels of science fiction, such as *Shadows in the Sun*, *Unearthly Neighbors*, and *The Shores of Another Sea*, have achieved classic status. His western novel, *The Wolf Is My Brother*, won a Golden Spur Award in 1967. In 1989 his second western novel, *Broken Eagle*, was awarded a Western Heritage Award from the National Cowboy Hall of Fame.

Chad Oliver received his doctorate in anthropology from UCLA. He was Professor of Anthropology at the University of Texas at Austin, where he served for eleven years as Department Chairman. The Plains Indians were one of his major research and teaching interests, and he also worked in East Africa.

He was everything from a disc jockey on a show called *American Jazz* in the 1950's to a toastmaster at the North American Science Fiction Convention in 1985, but hoped that if he was remembered at all, it would be for his writing. He lived with his wife, Beje, on an Arabian horse farm just outside of Austin, Texas, with his children and grandchildren nearby.

Chad Oliver died in August of 1993.